C000093938

About the author

Jamie Smith was born and raised in Birmingham, and studied history and journalism at the University of Wales, Bangor, before working as a journalist in Wales, Australia and Warwickshire. He then bounced around London and Brighton for several years and qualified as a therapeutic counsellor. Now living in Oxfordshire with wife, Anne, and daughter, Órla, when not working or parenting, he can be found playing and watching too much sport, pottering around at his allotment, travelling and cooking (with mixed results!).

THE SOVIET COMEBACK

Jamie Smith

THE SOVIET COMEBACK

Vanguard Press

VANGUARD PAPERBACK

© Copyright 2021
Jamie Smith

The right of Jamie Smith to be identified as author of
this work has been asserted by him in accordance with the
Copyright, Designs and Patents Act 1988.

All Rights Reserved

No reproduction, copy or transmission of this publication
may be made without written permission.
No paragraph of this publication may be reproduced,
copied or transmitted save with the written permission of the publisher, or in
accordance with the provisions
of the Copyright Act 1956 (as amended).

Any person who commits any unauthorised act in relation to
this publication may be liable to criminal
prosecution and civil claims for damages.

A CIP catalogue record for this title is
available from the British Library.

ISBN 978-1-80016-049-1

Vanguard Press is an imprint of
Pegasus Elliot MacKenzie Publishers Ltd.
www.pegasuspublishers.com

First Published in 2021

Vanguard Press
Sheraton House Castle Park
Cambridge England

Printed & Bound in Great Britain

Dedication

For Anne

Acknowledgements

This book took a decade to complete, and I am indebted to a lot of people who have helped me get to this point along the way. Not least the book has lived with me in Australia, Leamington Spa, Brockley, Brixton, Brighton, Islington, Bounds Green and Thame along with various solo writing trips at home and abroad, so it has been both a physical and emotional journey!

From its very humble beginnings as an idea while living in Brisbane, I thank Ariane Cohin for putting a roof over my head and encouraging me while I began to draw the concept together. Over the years a lot of people have been given eyes on various iterations as the story began to take shape, and I particularly thank Kirsty Smith for providing the hugely positive feedback just when I most needed it, and Ben Williams and Alex McDonald for their great insights.

I consulted hundreds of books, articles and websites while preparing this manuscript, far too many to cite here, but I would be remiss if I didn't cite a couple of places that gave me extra help. I'm grateful to the staff at the Civil Rights Room in the Nashville Public Library for sharing their experience and wisdom, the owner of the KGB Museum in Prague for the incredible depth of knowledge, and the excellent feedback of Will Piovano. I'd also have been completely lost without the Greek translations of Harry Papadopoulos (s' efharistó!) and the Russian translations of Vitaliy Drohomyretskyy, (spasibo!).

I thank everyone I have spoken to who has been able to give me, a white man, even the faintest understanding of what life was like as a black person in the 1980s. Some of it sits uncomfortably, but I am continually trying to educate myself and further my understanding. I felt it was a story I wanted to try and tell and have tried to write it as sensitively as possible, albeit in the vein of a spy thriller! Getting it completely right was impossible, and I can only hope I'm in the right ballpark and have told a good story.

My love of writing is a direct result of my parents, Baden Smith and Deborah Williams, who always encouraged creativity. Their editing and feedback, has been invaluable.

And finally, to my amazing wife, Anne, I am forever grateful to you for never doubting me, even when I doubted myself, and for all of the proof reading and positivity in the final few months, despite being heavily pregnant with our wonderful daughter. Simply put, I love you.

Author's Note

The Soviet Comeback and the story of Nikita is a work of fiction from beginning to end. That said, it is set in a real period of history and works around some real events. However, it is essentially a rewriting of history, and real events have been moved around for the story.

Nikita's family and his story, are a complete fiction, but the KGB was a real and ruthless organisation that existed until the fall of the Soviet Union in 1991. They invented and used a number of creative and gruesome weapons, including the Spetsnaz ballistic knife used in this story, and it is also fact that the nerve agent novichok, which has unfortunately reappeared in the news in recent years, was invented in the Soviet Union in the 1970s and '80s. They really did manage to weed out almost all of the US spies on Soviet soil, and it is generally accepted they had their own spies embedded in various organisations in the US, including the CIA.

The Cold War took its toll on the Soviet Union, which by the 1980s was beginning to struggle. The USSR had been engaged in a long and expensive war in Afghanistan, in which hundreds of thousands of innocent Afghan civilians were massacred. In turn, the Soviets suffered significant casualties themselves at the hands of the mujahideen who fought a guerrilla war in rugged mountain terrain, where battles were fought for control of the mountain caves.

The Intermediate-Range Nuclear Forces Treaty (INF Treaty) which underpins much of The Soviet Comeback was a real treaty signed, in a watershed moment of the Cold War, between the US and the USSR. It signified an important thawing in relations between the two superpowers. In 2019 the USA suspended its compliance with the treaty... how quickly the world forgets the mistakes of the past.

It's important to note that there is no evidence whatsoever to suggest that the police in Skyros are, or ever were, in the pay of the KGB. It's just a very lovely place, that is situated in a convenient location for the story.

Pamyat is a real neo-Nazi group that came to prominence in the late 1980s in the Soviet Union, at a time when unrest was growing throughout the constituent republics and throughout Russia itself.

There have been many reports of extreme Russian racism stretching back to the days of the Soviet Union, and in 2006 Amnesty International described racism in Russia as 'out of control' following a wave of hate crimes. Much of it is rooted in the ethnic cleansing and state-enforced policies of discrimination particularly notable throughout the reign of Josef Stalin. Of course, not all Russians are racist — far from it, but Nikita Allochka is the hero, and as such he needed to encounter some of the villains.

If the story seems too damning of Russia or the US, that is not my intention. Both are fantastic countries of which I would love to see a lot more, full of wonderful people I would love to meet, but there is no denying that both have severe intrinsic issues with racism — although it often takes different forms in both countries, just as it does in my own country, the UK. It felt important not to overlook or ignore these difficult, and often avoided, subjects.

PART 1

CHAPTER 1

KAMENKA, SIX HUNDRED KILOMETRES SOUTH EAST OF MOSCOW, USSR, 1981

His piercing blue eyes were the brightest thing on the otherwise colourless landscape, but Colonel Andrei Klitchkov was not there to admire the view. The plain grey suit did little to disguise his military bearing, from the close-cropped grey hair to his stiff, straight posture and highly polished shoes.

He made his way out of the picturesque and sparsely populated small town, and into the run-down scrublands beyond. He was flanked by two black-suited bodyguards the size of small houses and picked his way over the rubble from dilapidated buildings and garbage towards an isolated shack. As he approached the building standing alone on a bleak, grey stretch of land, he could see that it had been pieced together from sheets of graffiti-covered corrugated iron. The grass around it was sparse and ill-looking, like a stagnant swamp starved of sunlight for years. Soviet winter was on its way.

He stopped outside the building to read the graffiti. Tilting his head, he read, in large black letters, 'Иди домой. Мать Россия = belaya.' *Go home. Mother Russia = white.*

He smiled a crooked smile, and raised a hand cloaked in black leather to knock on the door, but it opened before he could touch it.

Staring up at him was a small black girl, dressed in rags which had been scrubbed clean and crisp. If this surprised the colonel, no trace of it reached his face.

Crouching down, he gave a cold smile that did not extend to his icy blue eyes. "Hello Milena, are Mummy or Daddy home? Or… perhaps Nikita?" he asked in a liquid voice.

Suddenly there was some movement behind Milena and the colonel looked up into the face of her father. Milena hugged her father's leg, trying to hide behind it.

The colonel extended his hand. "Ah, Mr Gabriel Allochka... or should I say Solomon Wadike?" he asked conspiratorially. "I am Colonel Klitchkov and I was wondering if I might impose myself upon you and your wife for a moment or two?"

Gabriel Allochka was a big man with gentle, sad eyes. He stiffened at the mention of his real name, and ignored the outstretched hand. Instead, he looked to see if anyone was watching, eyeing the bodyguards with alarm, and stepped aside to allow the colonel in. The colonel raised a hand to his companions once more, instructing them to stay outside, a hulking menace to any who would try to enter... or leave.

As he entered the shack, the abject poverty instantly struck the colonel. It was just one room with a bed, some rags on the floor in the rough shape of a second bed, two chairs and several patched pots and pans which were lined against one wall. A woman with a kindly face sat on the bed, looking frightened. The room was very bare. Pushing past the colonel, Gabriel sat down on the bed, putting an arm around his wife, and sat Milena upon one knee. He signalled to the chair for the colonel to sit down.

"What is it you want, Mr Klitchkov?" Gabriel asked, in African-accented English. "I'm afraid my English is still better than my Russian, after all this time."

"It is Colonel Klitchkov, and English is no problem," he responded buoyantly, waving his hand and smiling, looking a little crazed. He leant back in his chair and crossed his legs. "I see that you, like myself, are not one for idle chitchat so I shall get straight to business matters. Now, my organisation—"

"Which organisation is that?" asked Gabriel.

"Is well aware of your family," continued the colonel, acting as if he had not heard Gabriel. "Indeed, I am afraid that you do rather stand out in this country, as I am sure you have noticed." He waved his hand in the direction of the graffiti outside. "We know that you are here illegally," he finished without a pause.

Hanging his head, Gabriel sighed in defeat. "You must understand, Colonel, I had no choice."

"You would be amazed at how poorly that argument holds up in a Soviet court," Klitchkov replied.

"Does the murder of all five of my brothers and both of my parents in the Nigerian civil war hold up?"

"Not when it doesn't explain how they all died but you and your family survived."

"I don't have to explain myself to you. You cannot imagine what it was like."

"I do not have to use my imagination; I fought in the Battle of Stalingrad."

Gabriel shrugged. "Seeing one horror does not mean understanding another, and I will not force my wife to relive what happened. When you have a family, nothing else matters, not me or you or this country. I did what I must to get them away from the atrocities, and I bear the scars; they are mine alone now," he said, lifting his shirt to show an ugly, puckered scar running from his right armpit right down his side.

"And you chose Russia? You chose here?" Klitchkov asked incredulously.

Gabriel dropped his shirt and laughed bitterly. "What I paid the captain of the cargo ship for and what he delivered were two very different things, sir. He told us he would sail to Greece, but the ship never docked there and he kicked us out on the eastern bank of the Black Sea. We had no money and nowhere to go, and were shunned by many towns until we found ourselves here. I have done the best I could. I intended to get enough money to move us to Europe, but nobody will give me proper work. But both of our children are Russians; they were born here; they are your own," Gabriel finished.

The colonel raised his eyebrows and opened his mouth to speak, before stopping.

"Ah… It is a touching story, of course." It did not look like it had touched him at all. If anything, it seemed to Gabriel, it looked to have amused him. "However, it doesn't escape the fact that you and your wife have no more right to be here, than that capitalism nonsense." He chuckled at his own joke.

"But there is a way to overlook this, indeed a way to greatly improve the quality of your lives," he continued, enjoying the control he had over the room. "As you may be aware, the Soviet Union is in the midst of a situation that the Americans," he spat the word out as if it was dirty, "have called the Cold War. If they really want to know about cold, they should spend a couple of days in our Siberia! Right?" He said, laughing again at his own joke, before stopping abruptly, his face suddenly serious.

"To go straight to the point, we know that your son," he paused to flick through a notepad, "ah, Nikita? Yes? I do enjoy how you have given your children such thoroughly Russian names!" He grinned. "Yes, Nikita is fifteen years old, and in a position to be of much assistance to this great nation. In return for his services, we could relocate you to somewhere where your neighbours may be... warmer."

Gabriel gave a feeble smile and fixed his strong gaze on the colonel. "Mr... Colonel Klitchkov, I don't have much, anything, in this world. I don't have any argument with anyone. All I have is my family. I will never give up my son."

"That's a very admirable sentiment Mr Allochka, but ask yourself — what sort of life are you giving your family? You live in poverty, outcast by everyone in this town and subjected to daily abuse, with no prospects for the future. You would give your children no hope?"

"I would let them make their own choices, a chance to choose a better life than this."

"Then it seems like we want the same thing for your family, Mr Allochka."

"I do not think so, sir. You would take my child away from me."

"Yes, and make a man of him."

"But what kind of man?"

"A Russian! The best kind of man!"

Gabriel sighed and closed his eyes. His wife, Sophie, was silently shaking her head.

"I have to say no, Colonel. I will never give up my son," he repeated.

The colonel let out an exasperated noise, but before he could say anything, a small but firm voice interrupted from the doorway. "I will go with you."

They all turned to see the teenage boy standing almost silhouetted in the doorway. He had a short Afro, and an honest, determined face. Blood was trickling down his cheek from a fresh cut at his temple.

"Whatever it is you want, sir, I will do it," he added defiantly.

Gabriel stood up hastily, putting Milena gently on the bed. "No, Nikita, you will not."

Nikita pointed at his temple. "Father, look at this. A stone thrown by an old woman in the town hit me, just for trying to find some firewood in the woods. These people hate us! What happens when they turn on Milena too? I will do this to protect our family."

"You are a fifteen-year-old child; it is us who should protect you. You know nothing of the world, and even less what they are asking of you."

Ignoring his father, Nikita turned to the colonel. "What protection will you offer to my family?" he asked.

The colonel had been watching the proceedings with a slightly amused expression. He enjoyed that this filth thought they had any choice.

"My, my, you are a determined boy, Nikita. The Soviet Union rewards determination. This is excellent news. Of course, for the service you will do to your country we will reward you and your family most handsomely. A proper home away from angry eyes, and food all your bellies!" He bent down to Milena. "Would you like to have some nice cake in your belly, Milena?" he asked, showing all of his tobacco-stained teeth.

Sophie Allochka quickly pulled Milena to her. "Please do not try to bribe my children, Colonel," she said haughtily.

"Of course not, Mrs Allochka! I only want to help your family. Da, Nikita, not only will we give your family a home, but even Russian citizenship. Mother Russia always looks after those who seek to protect her. But, like any deal, we can only give you all of this in return for something. You will not see your family, perhaps for years."

Sophie began to sob into Gabriel's shoulder, who himself was muttering something about 'madness'.

"Mother, please. I will do what I must for our family; you know that it makes sense for us," Nikita said with forced calmness.

The silence was broken as Klitchkov clapped his hands. "Excellent! I shall give you five minutes to pack your things and say your goodbyes. Your boy will return to you a man, Mrs Allochka." He rose smoothly, and with a nod to Nikita, walked out of the hovel and lit a Belomorkanal cigarette.

The two bodyguards stood waiting, looking tense. "At ease, gentlemen," Klitchkov ordered. "There will be no trouble here."

"What a beautiful day," he then said to no one in particular as he gazed off across the grey landscape and exhaled a cloud of smoke through pursed lips, a smirk curling one corner of his mouth.

Minutes later, Nikita walked out of the shack, pulling the door closed, muffling the sound of his mother's anguished cries.

He walked forwards without looking back and joined Colonel Klitchkov with a look of quiet anger and determination on his face.

"What is the organisation I am joining, Colonel?" he asked.

Klitchkov smiled. "Why, the KGB of course."

CHAPTER 2

GENERAL SECRETARY MISHO PETRENKO'S OFFICE, THE KREMLIN, 1986.

General Secretary Petrenko was known for his humour, but today he was in a foul mood. Sitting at his ornate wooden desk, alone in his office, he pored over a report. It was titled 'The Budapest Problem'.

"It certainly is a problem," he muttered to himself. "They are all a problem." He balled the report and then threw it at the bin, missing horribly, and the ball landed amidst the others he had already angrily tossed.

He rubbed his temples and closed his eyes. He felt tired. Beyond tired.

The speaker on his desk buzzed. He smoothed the hair around his bald pate and sighed heavily before bracing himself. He pressed the button on the intercom.

"Da?"

The tinny sound of his receptionist's voice crackled through. "General secretary, Comrade Yerin, the chairman of the KGB, is here to see you."

"Yes, I know who Yerin is, thank you, Anna!" he snapped. "Let him in."

Outside, Anna raised her eyebrows, giving the granite-faced visitor, all the information he needed on the general secretary's current mood.

The door to the office opened and Viktor Yerin strode in purposefully, without hesitation, brushing snow from his heavy coat. He had thick wire-rimmed glasses and a tightly drawn, humourless face with squashed cheeks. Heaving his bulk out of his chair, Petrenko walked round to the front of his desk, extending his hand.

"Viktor! Thank you for coming. You are well?"

Taking the general secretary's hand, Yerin, who towered over the rotund figure in front of him, said, "Surviving general secretary, surviving."

"That is no mean feat in these dark times, Viktor," the general secretary responded, signalling to a seat as he walked back behind his desk where he sat, opened a drawer and pulled out a bottle of vodka. Yerin observed that it was a fluid motion, and one with which the general secretary was clearly familiar. Opening another drawer, he extracted two glasses and filled them both, pushing one to Viktor.

"Indeed, sir," Viktor responded.

The general secretary raised his glass and they both threw back the clear liquid with practiced ease, neither gasping at the burning alcohol.

"You are always so formal, Viktor! But then I suppose that is to be expected from a man of your position."

"With respect, sir, it is not a position I ever asked for."

"Ah yes, but a masterstroke of my predecessor Brezhnev's to put you in the position nonetheless. About the only masterstroke he ever had actually. Thanks to you, the CIA operatives infiltrating our country are being well weeded out. But now I think it is time for the hunted to become the hunter. I need a man in America."

"We already have many men in America, sir; this is how we have taken care of the CIA operatives on Soviet soil."

"But we need something more; I feel that we are getting only scraps," said Petrenko, then looked pointedly at the KGB head. "Unless of course you are keeping things from me, Viktor? Are you still Brezhnev's man?"

Viktor looked coldly at the general secretary, visibly bristling at the accusation. "I have never withheld information from you. I serve the Soviet Union dutifully and faithfully, as I always have done."

"Calm down, Viktor, I meant no offence" said the general secretary, holding a weary hand up. "As you are well aware, there is growing discontent throughout our great nation. The economy is dying; the Baltic satellite nations are pulling ever away; I have been forced to withdraw from the arms race with the US as our nation grows weaker by the day. And to make things worse, there are these goddam neo-Nazis running around Moscow, flaunting their swastika tattoos and killing anyone with the slightest tan. The iron curtain is a little rusty at present! My own are turning against me. I have to be careful in whom I put my trust. As Winston Churchill once said, 'Behind me are my enemies, opposite me is my opposition'."

"Then, sir, how can I prove my loyalty... again?" Yerin asked, his face unreadable.

Leaning back in his chair, the general secretary looked Viktor directly in the eye.

"I need a man in the US." He held up his hand. "I know, I know, you have your man who gave us the American spies. But now I need someone to help us go on the offensive on American soil, not on our own. Not some low-level CIA mole. I need a man of action, a man to get me the information I need. A man who can blend, a man who can do what is necessary. I want to know what the smug son of a bitch President Callahan, is thinking before he thinks it. I want him to fear us once more. If we are to go down, then we shall go down fighting."

Viktor smiled broadly, the cracks in his face betraying his face's unfamiliarity with the expression.

"It seems I may have misjudged you, sir. I believe Colonel Klitchkov has been training just the man for your problem."

"A novice?" the general secretary exclaimed. "You can do better than that, comrade."

"Ah but, sir, this is no ordinary novice. They call this one the Black Russian."

Petrenko's eyes widened in surprise, and he swallowed heavily. "The rumours are true then? It's an impressive name, but he'll need more than that for the mission to be successful."

Nodding, Viktor replied, "He has been in training for five years solid. At Leningrad and Kiev."

The general secretary exhaled deeply, his eyes widening slightly. "Jesus. Five years with Denisov, and at that Leningrad hellhole to boot? He must be tough."

"Denisov says he's the best he has ever seen, and quite lethal. As I understand it, he has already endured more than most of our men do in their entire careers, and he is still little more than a boy."

"How do we know that he can be trusted?"

"Well, sir, I believe that Klitchkov has taken certain... ah... measures, regarding the young man's family."

"That wily old fox Klitchkov. A lunatic bastard, but a cunning one."

"Indeed, sir. I understand he is field ready."

"I would hope so after five years of our finest training. Very good. See it done."

He poured himself another vodka and threw it down. "Who'd have thought, old friend. Blacks, fighting for the motherland. Stalin would turn in his grave."

Viktor's face was impassive. "Just as long as he stays there."

Petrenko laughed and filled their glasses once again.

CHAPTER 3

KGB MILITARY SCHOOL, NEAR KIEV, UKRAINE, USSR.

Nikita opened his eyes. It was still dark outside but he had learned to wake before anyone else; it avoided any unpleasant surprises. Despite being instantly alert, he struggled to throw off the dark thoughts of his dreams. Memories of the past five years blended into one another: the underwater knife fights, the firearms training in the northern forest, the naked ice-water swimming, hunting bears in Kamchatka. Hunting western sympathisers in Leningrad. A nightmare for some, adolescence for Nikita Allochka.

He shook his head to clear it of thoughts of the past. He filled the chipped enamel basin in his room with ice-cold water and then plunged his head in. His senses screamed, and the adrenaline emptied his mind of memories.

He began an intense routine of press-ups, lunges and pull-ups — four sets of twenty reps without pause. He was stripped totally naked and his finely-honed muscles visibly strained, accentuating the scars across his body. The knife wounds on his arms, a coarse bullet wound on his thigh — reminders of the brutal world he had chosen to enter five years ago, and the brutal colleagues he must now call brothers. Tovarishches. Comrades. With every press-up, sit-up, pull-up or lunge, he recited American accents and phrasing. Sit-ups saw him speaking a monologue in a southern drawl, pull-ups practising verb tenses while getting his mouth around the relaxed Californian SoCal accent, while the more neutral American tones of Virginia with a slight southern bent came while doing core planks. Barely uttering a gasp from his exertions, he moved seamlessly from one accent to the next, as he had trained himself to be able to do through his gruelling years with the KGB - after repeatedly failing the language tests early in his time as a trainee. He intended to survive, and that meant perfecting every area demanded of him and more.

After giving himself a cold-water shower and dressing in his standard issue uniform, he heard footsteps coming down the corridor. He stood facing the door and readied himself. He was prepared. It opened and the summons arrived.

***

Nikita's face told the story of one much older than his twenty-one years, and betrayed the pain he had endured. Sitting at a table in the whitewashed box room with leads connected to his temples, a woman dressed in a nurse's outfit busied herself around him, wiring him up to the lie detector before him. He looked down and noticed that his hands trembled silently. Deep breath, Nikita, you have trained for this, he repeated to himself in the confines of his mind.

Lean and muscular with a shaven head, Nikita sat opposite a man he didn't recognise. As he stared at him, unblinking, with dead eyes, Nikita's hands became completely still, like a tightly wound tiger, bunched and ready to pounce.

"I will be your instructor in this exercise. Answer my questions truthfully and briefly," said the stranger. He had blond hair combed into a fierce side parting, a thin moustache and thick glasses that enlarged already bulbous eyes.

"Is your name Nikita Allochka?"

"Niet," Nikita replied.

The signals on the lie detector remained absolutely still.

"Then what is your name?"

"Nathan Martins."

Again, the needle barely flickered on the detector.

"Where are you from, Nathan?"

"Daytona Beach, Florida."

The signal remained flat.

"And what do you do in your spare time?"

"You mean aside from killing enemies of the state?" Nikita asked with a faintly raised eyebrow.

"This is not a game, Allochka!"

"You mean Martins?" Nikita said, smiling coldly. He sig.
to surf, eat quarter pounders with extra cheese, and have a beer v
guys," he added in a flawless Floridian accent.

The needle remained still.

Behind the one-way glass, Colonel Klitchkov and other officials watched Nikita's test. Klitchkov was smiling.

A middle-aged man in a lab coat was almost trembling with excitement. "I've never seen anything like it. He is totally emotionless," he spouted.

"He is finally ready," Klitchkov replied.

"But he is so young, colonel. He will make mistakes if you put him in the field," replied the man in the lab coat.

"Of course. But that does not mean he is not ready. He is our most magnificent creation," Klitchkov answered, with a satisfied expression.

The interrogator looked up at Nikita from his notes. "Where is your family?" he asked.

A tiny flicker was visible on the lie detector's reading as Nikita turned and looked directly at the mirror, directly at Klitchkov. Despite being unable to see him, he fixed him with a piercing stare through the glass.

He paused for a moment. "Somewhere safe," he answered, with no small amount of accusation.

ed. "I like
ith the

CHAPTER 4

The valley lay beneath him, with a snow laden hill sloping smoothly down from his vantage point on the road. Nikita's breath rose before him as he looked out across the crisp, white landscape to a stone izba, nestled in the valley, smoke snaking its way out of a chimney to the dark, cloudless sky. The flickering glow of candlelight in the window screamed of warmth to Nikita, his body temperature ever dropping in the freezing twilight. His dark eyes burned in the moonlight with suppressed rage.

It looked so idyllic, like a postcard sent from the Swiss Alps. But the reality was a far cry from a luxury chalet. This reality was a cold stone cottage nestled in the far northern reaches of Siberia.

He made his way down the road, more closely resembling an icy track, and his eyes fell upon a snowman. Clearly built some time ago, the snow had iced over and the carrot nose lay half buried in the ground.

He bent down and attempted to screw the carrot back into place, but it was now so frozen that the carrot no longer fitted. Bending over, he hitched up a trouser leg, and pulled from his sock a glistening six-inch dagger. His large hands worked deftly as he fashioned a small cleft to slide the carrot into. Eventually satisfied, he smiled gently to himself before moving towards the small homestead.

As he drew closer, he began to pick up the sound of laughter, a sound unfamiliar to him now, with a sense of humour not high on the list of priorities for Soviet operatives. But then neither are nerves, yet Nikita could not deny a sense of trepidation squirming in his stomach as he approached the black door.

He looked up and noticed that the window frames were also painted black, along with the awnings. So unnecessary and so out of place in the surroundings, he thought to himself. "Perhaps the KGB do have a sense of humour after all," he muttered wryly.

He raised his hand and knocked on the door. The sounds from within stopped instantly.

After a long pause, he heard the voice of his father shouting through the door in poorly-accented Russian, "Who is it and what do you want?"

"It's a memory trying to find its way home," said Nikita, responding in English.

There was a scrabbling at the door as the chain was pulled off and several locks clicked into place. The door was yanked open and Nikita looked up at the huge silhouette of Gabriel Allochka. Even in the shadows, Nikita could see that his hair was now lightly dusted with grey.

Wide-eyed, he appeared almost scared. A silence sat between them that felt like an eternity to Nikita. "Father…" he said tentatively, feeling confused, almost like the boy he thought he'd left behind five years ago.

Gabriel's eyes crinkled sadly, and he reached out and tentatively stroked Nikita's cheek. "My boy, is it really you?" he said softly.

"Father it is me, your Niki," Nikita replied, feeling his eyes stinging, fighting back the tears he had been trained not to show.

Gabriel pulled him into a rough embrace and began to laugh, a deep sound that came all the way from his toes and transported Nikita to a different time and place.

"My son! I feared we had lost you forever. Quick, come in out of this freezing cold."

Nikita forced the thick wooden door shut quickly and the warmth of the cottage then hit him, giving his hands chilblains.

Before he had time to take in his surroundings, a small figure flew across the room with arms wide open, and shouted "Niki!" before stopping suddenly a few yards from him. His little sister Milena's eyes were wide and she appeared suddenly cautious. She had grown a great deal and now approached the slight awkwardness of being ten years old.

"Milena," Nikita said softly and moved towards her, opening his arms. But she stepped back before turning and running back upstairs, fear on her face. "Milena," he whispered again as his stomach dropped and his heart ached.

"Do not worry about Milena," Gabriel said from behind him. "You look… different now; it is hard for her to understand."

Nikita nodded silently.

A voice thick with emotion suddenly rolled down the stairs. "I know that voice…" Appearing down the staircase, Sophie Allochka had tears streaming down her face. She almost fell into his arms, and grabbed him so tightly that it hurt. "My baby, come here. I love you, praise be to God!" she gasped, hugging him even tighter as if afraid he might escape again if she let go. She pulled back and held his face in her hands. Again, a flash of something that almost looked like fear crossed her face, but as quickly as it appeared it was gone and she kissed him on the forehead. Over her shoulder, Nikita could see Milena peering from behind the bannister of the stairs, slowly moving down the steps.

"You are years late," she squeaked to him from the safety of the stairs.

Nikita bowed his head. "I know. I am sorry, little sister. Will you forgive me?" She said nothing.

From his pocket he pulled a small teddy bear and held it out. She didn't move, fear still on her face. He laid it on the floor between them and then backed away. She moved tentatively out from the stairs and grabbed the teddy bear, but said nothing.

"Milena, it is your brother, say thank you," said Sophie, despite also looking at Nikita with some concern as he sat down beside the fire.

"Thank you," she squeaked. Nikita looked unhappily at them all for the first time in five years, feeling a leper among his own family.

***

Later that night, as Nikita sat by the fire, letting the warmth wash over him, his father walked into the room to join him. "They are both sound asleep; it's been an emotional day for them. For us all," he added, passing Nikita a whiskey, keeping another for himself. Nodding in agreement, Nikita held the whiskey up to the firelight to inspect it.

"They've put you in the arsehole of the world, but I see they are at least keeping you well, Father." He put his drink down to one side. "But it is not for me just yet."

Gabriel nodded acceptingly. "They kept their promise; we are well taken care of. Although, we hadn't imagined we would be quite so far from civilisation. It must be harder than they thought to hide a black family in Russia." They both laughed bitterly. "I do worry what it will do to Milena to never have other children to play with. She never complains but sometimes she looks so lonely, it is not fair for her. Every child should have other children to play with. Maybe one day we will be able to return to Nigeria; you never know."

"I am hopeful that Colonel Klitchkov will release me from my duties once I have returned from the US…"

"If you return from the US," replied Gabriel. "Do not trust the word of the colonel, Niki. He would as soon throw you to the dogs as go out of his way to help you."

"When I return from the US," said Nikita pointedly, "then I will try to take us all home to Nigeria."

"Truly?"

"Truly, Father, and we can be a family once more."

"This is not the life I wanted for you. Your eyes have lost their light."

"I have become who I must to survive."

"It is not too late for you to turn your back on this life son; we can all run."

Nikita felt the pull of tears taking him over, before resolving himself. KGB agents do not cry, he reminded himself. "There is nowhere we can go that they would not find us. This is the only way. Whatever they ask of me I will do, without hesitation, because I do it for us," he said flatly.

CHAPTER 5

The snow was falling as Nikita walked up the track towards where he had left his car on the distance road the next morning. He could still hear his mother's sobs following the latest goodbye, but he already felt cold to it. His focus had shifted to his next mission, and his heart was steeled against the things he knew he must do.

He spotted small footsteps leading up to the snowman, but did a mock jump when Milena leapt from behind it, giggling. She wore Gabriel's ushanka; it fell over her round face, forcing her to keep pushing it up.

Suddenly she stopped giggling and looked up at him, her big brown eyes a pool of sorrow at his going.

"Come back, Niki; I love you."

His steely defenses nearly shattered at her words, and he bent down to kiss her on the forehead.

"I will always come back, Milena, always."

Without another word, he turned and walked away. Milena watched him until he disappeared into the swirling snow.

***

The KGB safe house was in the Yakimenka District on the west bank of the Moskva River in south central Moscow.

There was no need for stealth — they knew he was coming. He had seen the watchers on the roofs and streets clumsily trying to hide in the shadows. If the spies had not relayed messages of his arrival, the sneering gang of teenage boys following him with exaggerated monkey noises would have.

Must stay calm, thought Nikita, reminding himself that without breaking sweat he could disable them all. He could, and maybe one day he would. But not today — he must stay focused. He suppressed the uncomfortable thoughts and moved towards the concrete block, climbing the wrought-iron stairs. The door opened as he approached, and he moved inside without breaking stride.

He knew better than to expect this secret hideout to be full of high-tech gadgets, but even he was surprised by the sparsity of the room. Peeling wallpaper looked out on a room with only a deeply sagging sofa, an old paint-smudged table and two frail-looking wooden chairs. A gently buzzing electric fire was the only sign of indulgence in the dour, grey room.

Sitting in one of chairs was Colonel Klitchkov, smiling that slightly crazed look he usually sported.

"It's not the Ritz, but it's a step up from a shack in Kamenka; am I right, Agent Allochka?"

"It's functional," shrugged Nikita, selecting a solid looking arm of the sofa to perch on.

"Is life merely about functionality for you?"

"It is about my family. As long as everything else functions correctly, then I will know that my family is safe."

"And what of Mother Russia?"

"So long as Mother Russia functions correctly and keeps its promises to me, then I will keep my promises to it. My love and respect for it has yet to be fully earned."

"Is there no love in your heart? Love of the mountains? The lakes? A woman, perhaps? Love of vodka even?" Klitchkov chuckled.

"Every Russian has a love of vodka. But no Russian has any love for a black Russian," Nikita replied blandly. "I am under no illusions that I am where I am only because I am useful to you, nothing more than that."

Klitchkov's eyes widened and he smiled brightly. "Au contraire, my boy, au contraire! I think you magnificent, and after all these years watching you grow, I hope you will forgive my admitting a certain fondness for you."

He leant back in his seat, surveying Nikita. "Win us this war, Allochka, and the Black Russian might mean more to the Soviet Union than just a vodka cocktail."

Nikita looked at Klitchkov with the detached eyes he had been trained to have. The words were of a politician, one trying to manoeuvre his way into the trust of an asset. But the warmth of the words was not matched by those eyes, which retained a slightly maddened twist in their pale blue depths. The scars on his body were a reminder of the cruelty of the man. He knew there would be a time when his usefulness to Klitchkov would run out, and he would need to be prepared.

Nodding, Nikita replied, "Perhaps. But what is it I'm here for, Colonel? I am fully operational and ready to do my time in the field."

"You do seem ready, but you are not quite fully operational."

"Colonel?"

"There is one more test to pass before we send you to America. Your red test."

"I thought…"

"You thought yourself too special? Above ordinary KGB agents?" The colonel's tone had quickly changed, and his face was cold. "You are little older than a child and already you overestimate yourself. You have not yet done a thing."

"I am eager to serve…" The atmosphere was suddenly tense, and Nikita felt alert. Something didn't feel right and his finely honed senses tingled. He felt a single bead of sweat snake its way from the pit of his arm and down his side.

"You serve only your sentence for the rehoming of your family. You forget them now!" barked Klitchkov, leaning forward. "You serve me. You serve Mother Russia."

Rising, Nikita put his hand on his heart and recited, "I, a citizen of the Union of Soviet Socialist Republics, joining the ranks of the Komitet Gosudarstvennoy Bezopasnosti, do hereby take the oath of allegiance and do solemnly vow to be an honest, brave, disciplined and vigilant fighter, to guard strictly all military and state secrets, to obey implicitly all KGB regulations and orders of my commanders, commissars and superiors.

"I vow to study the duties of a soldier conscientiously, to safeguard army and national property in every way possible and to be true to my people, my Soviet motherland, and the Workers' and Peasants' Government to my last breath.

"I am always prepared at the order of the Workers' and Peasants' Government to come to the defense of my motherland — Russian Union of Socialist Republics — and, as an agent of the Komitet Gosudarstvennoy Bezopasnosti, I vow to defend her courageously, skilfully, creditably and honourably, without sparing my blood and my very life to achieve complete victory over the enemy.

"And if through evil intent I break this solemn oath, then let the stern punishment of the Soviet law, and the universal hatred and contempt of the working people, fall upon me."

"Well recited, boy. Prove you mean it; show what we do to enemies of the state and become a man." Klitchkov pulled from his heavy overcoat a revolver, silencer and spare magazine, and passed them to Nikita. He pointed to a closed door on the far side of the room, before lighting a cigarette and sitting down. "Double taps. To the head," he added, as he unfolded an old newspaper and then began to flick through it.

Of course. The KGB trained to always take two shots or more, always to the head where possible. To leave no doubt.

Nikita took the gun, flicked off the safety catch as he had been trained to do, and moved swiftly towards the door, his nerves tingling. He had known this day must come, but had hoped it never would.

He opened the door onto a dark corridor, and after quickly checking the magazine was full, held the gun ahead of him as he screwed the silencer into place. He could hear his heart hammering in his chest and worked to keep his breathing calm. He could almost feel the burning adrenaline coursing through his veins, but his hand stayed steady. His training had taught him to be the best and to feel no fear.

The door closed behind him, leaving him in pitch darkness, and he could see nothing. He felt a light switch on the wall but chose to ignore it, preferring to run on sound and touch than to announce his approach to whatever lay ahead. He began to move slowly forwards, keeping both his ears and the gun cocked. He trusted his instincts.

The air was dusty and tasted of the past, and swirled around him as he moved along the corridor. He could see the outline of a door ahead with a dim glow emanating from the cracks around it. Approaching it, he flattened himself against the wall and listened carefully. He could hear whimpering and heavy breathing, but no loud noises. He didn't like it —

he was going in blind to a situation that was probably ready for him and the odds were not stacked in his favour.

But he was KGB. Pushing the door open, he immediately absorbed all the information that the room threw at him, and knew he was in no immediate danger, but didn't relax.

Entering from the back left side of the room, directly ahead of him was a man in military uniform who had a gun pointed at him. To his left, against the far-left wall were four figures on their knees, with old potato sacks over their heads. The room was dimly lit from a failing lamp, casting long, sporadically flickering shadows across the room, which was even barer than the room he had come from. The walls were heavily peeling, with furry black mould stretching from one corner of the room above the blacked-out window down to the floor, and damp stains streaked across the ceiling.

Nikita's dark eyes snapped back to the man aiming a gun at him. He was not much older than him, but his skin was sickly white and his hair was closely cropped. He was well built, and despite the raised gun he didn't look tense. Nikita knew the man was not ready to use it and had been expecting him.

"You the black spy?" He spat the words between yellow, nicotine-stained teeth.

"No, I'm the white postman," Nikita replied, his weapon aimed at the soldier. "At ease, soldier, I know you are expecting me."

"I am no soldier; I am Agent Vagin, KGB." Then seeing Nikita's eyes scanning the uniform, he added. "There must always be someone to take the fall," pulling at the soldier's outfit he had donned.

A loud whimper from one of the figures turned the man's attention.

"Shut up!" the agent shouted at the person, and he fired a warning shot into the wall above them. Plaster crumbled down, scattering over the sack-covered head of a figure Nikita could tell was a woman. The whimpering stopped, but the figures on bended knee began to shake uncontrollably. A wet, dark circle spreading out on the floor and around the crotch what looked to be a teenage boy betrayed his fear.

"Animals from Tajikistan," Agent Vagin said, looking towards the cowering group with no hint of shame. "Filth contaminating mother—"

his words were cut off as he turned back to Nikita to find the gun pointed at his face.

He paused and cocked his head to one side, smiling disdainfully. "Unfortunately for you, I am not the mission."

"What is the mission? Who are they?"

"That is on a need-to-know basis. You do not need to know. You follow orders, and your order is to eliminate these enemies of the state."

"And if I refuse?"

"Then you too will be dealt with as an enemy of the state. Personally, I hope you do not do it; one less chernozhopiy poisoning our country is only a good thing." He laughed, his challenge hanging in the murky air between them.

"Maybe I kill you and take my chances. These people have done nothing to me."

The woman on the floor suddenly spoke. "Please, kill me but let my family go free."

Suddenly there was the click of a safety catch, followed by the snap of a silenced bullet and the woman fell to the floor. Blood and debris oozed from a bullet hole on the wall.

"I told the bitch to shut up," said Vagin. "See, I've done a quarter of your job for you." He pointed with his gun and grinned at Nikita. "Now get on with the rest."

The world stood still for Nikita; the bullet had been silenced but the sound of it somehow still echoed around his head. The oddly bent figure on the floor with a pool of sticky blood blossoming around it, the frantically shuddering figures either side of her, the grinning murderer before him, his hand dropped with the gun at his side. The world had gone into slow motion; he could see the dust in the air, almost feel it whirling around his face, and his sight seemed somehow more acute than ever in the dimly lit room.

"I knew it," exclaimed Agent Vagin. "Chernozhopiys don't have what it takes to become KGB…"

There was another dampened whoosh of a silenced bullet, but this time it was Nikita's. Vagin fell, crying out in alarm, shock and pain as the bullet passed through his kneecap. His gun skittered across the floor as he thrust out with his hand to break his fall.

Nikita could smell the burning cordite from his gun, smell the blood he had spilled, but his arm remained raised.

"Are you crazy?" screamed Vagin. "You will be dead before you leave the building; we are comrades."

"It is interesting to hear you say that we are now comrades. I thought I was a chernozhopiy? A *black ass*? Not good enough for the KGB?" Nikita said, seething with fury at the cold-blooded murder he had witnessed.

"You cannot kill me," Vagin gasped.

"Maybe not. Or maybe no one will miss a scumbag foot soldier who kills women for sport," said Nikita. "Everyone can die."

"I told you, the uniform is to redirect the blame... I am KGB!" Vagin protested, his top lip wet with sweat and his face contorted in pain.

"The KGB would seek to put blame for an assassination on the very army that we fight alongside? Does that not sound a little strange to you, agent?"

"I do not question my orders."

"And where do those orders come from, I wonder? You see, there is something I noticed when you murdered this young woman..." He walked over and pulled the sack from her head. It revealed a woman with bright red hair. Her face was unblemished. "Putting aside the fact that this woman's hair shows that she is clearly an Udmurt, quite some way from the Tajikistan you claimed, about three thousand miles in fact, let us focus on something else. You see how the bullet has passed through the back of her head and out of the top, only two inches above? Really, she very nearly survived; this bullet literally grazed her brain just enough to kill her; it is a terrible shot."

"I was never the best marksman."

"That is very clear, agent. But there is something that every KGB agent knows; it is tattooed into our brains. When shooting to kill, you never shoot once. Denisov drilled that into us every day, every night. Empty your magazine, leave nothing to chance. This is even ignoring the fact that KGB never put the safety catch on our weapons. When we draw our gun, it is to use it and you had to flick the safety to murder the Udmurt woman. You are not screaming 'seasoned KGB operative' to me, soldier."

There was no trace of the arrogant smirk left on the now clammy face of Vagin.

"I know your story, Allochka. You would not sacrifice little Milena by killing me."

One shot. Two shots. Three, four, five. Nikita, arm out straight in front of him, closed on Vagin as he emptied the magazine and quickly replaced it with the spare, with a lightning quick motion.

Agent Vagin fell backwards, dead.

"Nobody should know my story," Nikita whispered.

The door behind him suddenly opened and he wheeled around. Klitchkov entered the room and surveyed the carnage in front of him. Nikita began to lower his gun but heard a movement behind him and saw that the three-remaining people on the floor had removed the sacks and now had guns trained on him.

Klitchkov smiled and walked over to Vagin, pulling his head up by the hair.

"This is an interesting take on a double tap, Agent Allochka, but I cannot deny that I appreciate the symmetry," he said conversationally. The ruined face of the fallen soldier stared up blankly, with a bullet through both eyes, one through both cheeks and one that had gone through the mouth and out the back of the head.

"What is going on? Why did he know about my family? Who are these people?" Nikita demanded.

"You forget yourself Allochka; remember who you are speaking to."

"My apologies, Colonel," Nikita said, attempting to get his racing heartbeat under control while trying to understand the situation he found himself in. He dimly noticed that his hands were shaking uncontrollably.

"Quite OK, old boy, understandable in the circumstances. But do try to remember your training — you do not question orders. The Udmurt girl — congratulations on matching her hair colour with the region — was an enemy of the state, and Vagin was an incompetent army private who had been leaking low level secrets to help feed his drug habit. He had to be eliminated, and discreetly. That is more than you need to know." He held out his hand. "You passed the red test; welcome to the KGB, Agent Allochka."

Shaking the colonel's hand, Nikita felt dirty and contaminated, and also felt certain there was more to the story. The agents in the corner were all resolutely looking away from the body of the Udmurt woman, and they looked shaken as they lowered their weapons upon a signal from Klitchkov. Remembering his family, he inclined his head politely and embraced his acceptance into the Soviet Secret Service.

Klitchkov and the agents left the room and walked down the corridor, Nikita following behind. As they marched purposefully towards the front door of the apartment and out of the door, he dropped back. Making to follow, he stepped back into the apartment and with a huge exhale released a stifled sob as he collapsed onto the decrepit old sofa which groaned under him. He crossed his arms around him at the horror he had just committed, the blood he had spilled in just the room next door. Fighting to keep the tears back in his eyes, he dug his fingernails into the flesh of his arm, drawing blood.

Droplets of blood trickled down his forearm and onto the sofa as he clenched his jaw, to force away the feelings he knew he must not have.

"We do what we must, and we must continue," he whispered to himself. Pulling himself towards the door, he punched the doorframe and yanked it open, driven by the purpose to which he had committed. As he stepped out, he turned and saw Klitchkov leaning against the metal railing, looking out across the concrete estate.

"Out of your system?" he asked without looking at Nikita.

When Nikita said nothing, Klitchkov turned and faced him, leaning backwards on his elbows against the metal handrail. His face was unreadable. He looked into Nikita's eyes.

Suddenly he leapt forward, pushing Nikita back against the wall, his hand around his throat. He was grinning, the same crazed look in his eyes that Nikita had seen before.

Spitting the words out, he said, "Did. You. Get. It. Out. Of. Your. System? Your disgusting display of weakness?"

"Yes, sir," Nikita gasped, his eyes full of hatred.

"If it happens again, I will kill you myself," Klitchkov said, releasing Nikita. Then, sneering, he added, "Comrade."

CHAPTER 6

Warm wind whipped at his face as he disembarked the Czechoslovak State Airlines flight at José Martí Airport, Havana in the way wind seems to at airports the world over. The climate in the Republic of Cuba was hot and humid, and after growing up in the Soviet Union, Nikita was unfamiliar with the heat in which he found himself, and the contrast to the USSR was not lost on him.

As he made his way down the metal steps, he stretched his legs and arms, working a kink out of the bunched muscles in his left shoulder. It had been a long flight, in which he had first been sent to Helsinki in a military plane from Moscow, then travelled overland by train to Prague before the final journey across the Atlantic — all to evade the keen eyes of those scrupulously watching anyone brave enough to step from behind the iron curtain, especially those that did so to head to Russia's communist cousin. It had given him too much time to think about what he had done, what he knew he now was, and dark circles shadowed his eyes.

The large plastic red letters 'Jose Marti — La Habana' were looking out from the oddly winged concrete structure that made up Cuba's international airport, hazy in the beating sun. He breathed in deeply. The air was warm and dusty and filled him with a surge of excitement at the journey ahead. "Perhaps my training brainwashed me more than I thought," Nikita muttered to himself, grimly reminding him of what it was he would have to do.

***

As he stepped out of the front doors of the airport, a black Lada with darkened windows pulled up, its brakes screeching horribly, drawing the stares of everyone nearby.

The USSR had reliability and brutality in large doses, but subtlety was not an area in which it flourished.

The sweating red-faced driver rolled down the passenger window. His blond hair showed beneath his wide brimmed black hat, and wire rimmed sunglasses covered his eyes. "Allochka?"

Nikita gave no response but narrowed his eyes. He opened the passenger door and got in, but couldn't help smiling bitterly. The elaborate and gruelling journey to get to Cuba for the sake of a subterfuge which had been immediately dispelled by the driver's blunt approach.

As soon as the door closed, the wheels screamed once more as the driver ground the stick into gear and pulled away.

Rather than give the driver, who had left the windows rolled down, the opportunity to give away any more of his identity to a casual passer-by, Nikita elected to hold his tongue until they arrived at the embassy. The drive took about forty-five minutes, and he marvelled at the relative emptiness of the roads compared to the relentlessly busy Moscow he had journeyed from.

As they entered the Miramar district of the city, he could immediately see the Soviet embassy rising above the surrounding buildings, for all the world looking like a giant concrete syringe. He cringed as he recalled reading in the news the cost to the Russian taxpayer that the building, which had taken nine years to construct, had totalled. As they made their way through the brightly coloured but shabby streets, filled with smiling faces and loud music, he couldn't help but feel the building was lording a wealth and authority over a people who simply didn't care. Looking around, he saw smiling black people, Latin American people, white people all mixing, laughing and smiling and he realised that for the first time in his life, he was not the minority.

***

As Nikita was shown into the ambassador's office, he was confronted with two men in dark suits, standing talking in front of a large desk. As he closed the door behind him, they halted their conversation mid-sentence and looked up. One of the men was unremarkable-looking, with a weak chin, heavily veined nose and thinning hair, but a warm, genuine smile and bags under his eyes. The other immediately looked dangerous to Nikita. Lean, yet solid-looking, he appeared totally in shape. His handsome high, cheek-boned face was framed by short blond hair and split by an angry scar running from the outer corner of his pale right eye and going across to his ear.

Saluting, Nikita stated, "Ambassador Yitski, I am Special Agent Nikita Allochka reporting for duty."

The man with the veined nose smiled and moved forward. "At ease, agent." He held out his hand. "Do come in; it is a pleasure to finally meet you."

"Sir?"

"You are already a legend in the KGB; nobody believes that there is really a black Soviet agent!"

"Perhaps that is a good thing, sir; I just want to do the job that is required of me."

"Of course, of course. Please do sit down." He gestured to one of the seats in front of his desk. "And where are my manners! Agent Allochka, this is Agent Brishnov, one of our finest."

"An honour to meet you, comrade," said Nikita, extending his hand.

Brishnov looked disdainfully at Nikita's dark hand, and with clear reluctance extended his own, with a forced smile. "Good of you to join us out here," Brishnov said, almost mockingly, as his cold, clammy hand shook Nikita's hand weakly, as if afraid to properly touch him.

"Do sit down, both of you," said Yitski, pulling a bottle of vodka from his heavy wooden desk drawer, along with three glasses. Out of the corner of his eye, Nikita could see Brishnov wiping his hand on the back of his trousers.

"Ah, none for me sir, but thank you," said Allochka.

"A Russian who doesn't drink vodka? You won't drink with us, comrade?" said Brishnov, outwardly sneering.

"Come, Allochka! You will need something to settle your nerves for what lies ahead," added Ambassador Yitski.

"Forgive me, but I think I will need my wits to be as sharp as possible for what lies ahead. I mean no offence."

"Nonsense, my boy, vodka is good for the heart, wits and whatever else you need it for! But I shall not force you." Filling two glasses, Yitski pushed one to Brishnov, raised his own and said, "To the Black Russian!"

"Rodina," responded Brishnov. *The homeland.*

Coughing a little as he slammed the glass back on the table, the ambassador wiped his red nose and withdrew a document from his desk. Suddenly his demeanour took on a nervous edge and he looked quickly at the door to check that it was closed.

The document had a photo on the front, and the hairs on the back of Nikita's neck began to tingle.

"And so, to business Allochka. Here is your assignment. One of our agents, Josef Zurga, has crossed. He had high level clearance and the information he has could prove catastrophic if it falls into the wrong hands. We do not believe he has told them everything yet; he is trying to play both sides and needs to be terminated immediately. He was seen recently in New York when he had no business being there. He had travelled there using a false passport, but by chance we had an agent at the airport who recognised him."

"How do you know he has crossed, sir?"

Bristling, Brishnov said, "You do not need to know."

"Ignore Taras, he has been doing this for too long and has forgotten how to talk pleasantly," said Yitski.

"There is nothing pleasant about what we do. Let me take out Zurga, why have this n—"

"Enough, Agent Brishnov!" snapped the ambassador. "It is not for you to decide who carries out what mission. You follow orders, agent, and you would do well to remember that."

Nikita was staring coldly at Brishnov. "Any special requirements?" he asked the ambassador, without taking his eyes off his fellow agent.

Before Yitksi had a chance to reply, Brishnov spoke. "Make it messy. This svoloch has betrayed Mother Russia; we need to send a message to anyone else who might think about betraying my country."

"Calm down, comrades," said ambassador Yitksi. "But Agent Brishnov is right; we need to send a message, also to the Americans."

Nikita looked into the eyes of Ambassador Yitski. "It will be done."

Brishnov rose and walked quickly from the office. Nikita followed behind, and as he stepped over the threshold into the secretary's office, Brishnov whispered into his ear, "I will be watching you. Slaves cannot be trusted."

With the eyes of the secretary on them both, Nikita clenched his fists and fought the urge to respond, instead smiling passively at the secretary as he received his documents for the mission ahead. When he turned to look behind him, Brishnov was gone.

"Agent Allochka, are you listening?" the business-like secretary demanded, noticing him looking at the doorway. The elderly lady peered at him over her half-moon spectacles, her face looking all the more severe for her hair which was fiercely pulled back into a bun.

"Ah yes, of course, Mrs Shapova."

Her eyes softened slightly. "You are not the first new agent to come through here you know, all puffed up with their own belief in how invincible they are. So often it is the last time I ever see them; do not be one of them. Stay vigilant, young man."

Nikita was stunned; Mrs Shapova was the first Russian to ever show even the slightest interest in his wellbeing.

Losing his cool demeanour for a moment, he stuttered, "Ah, oh, OK, yes, I shall hope that this isn't the last time you see me, ma'am."

She smiled benignly, handing him his documentation. "Your flight to Athens—"

"Athens? I thought I was going New York."

"Our sources tell us that your target is currently on the Greek island of Skyros. Your flight leav—"

"I do not speak Greek; I have learned an American accent."

"You had better learn fast then, comrade," said Ambassador Yitski from the door.

Mrs Shapova handed him a Greek-Russian phrasebook.

"A phrasebook?" he exclaimed disbelievingly.

"We all have to start somewhere, dear," she responded. "Your flight leaves in two hours."

Yitski chuckled from the door, "You do not want to start disagreeing with Mrs Shapova here. Think of it as a working holiday! Good luck, agent, we are relying on you."

CHAPTER 7

Nikita sat on the balcony of his room at the San Marco Hotel in Houlakia Bay on the North West coast of Skyros. The tiny island, only eighty-one square miles in size, sat at the foot of the Sporades Archipelago, lost somewhere between Greece and Turkey, somewhere between the east and the west. He allowed himself a moment to absorb the view before him of whitewashed walls overlooking the deep blue Aegean Sea, with islands dotted on the horizon and a warm breeze gently playing across his face. He had never seen anywhere so beautiful.

I'm a long way from Kamenka, he thought to himself, sipping a glass of cold water. He bit into his chicken souvlaki and spread the contents of the envelope Mrs Shapova had provided across the table in front of him.

The face of Josef Zurga looked up at him. He had an ill-favoured look, although Nikita suspected it had been doctored to look that way. He was grateful; he needed to dislike the man. Zurga was almost snarling at the camera, his balding, coarse black hair giving way to the oily-looking face of one who has been corrupted by politics.

"So this is what a double agent looks like..." he muttered to himself.

He cast his eyes across Zurga's vital statistics, and saw nothing to strike fear into him in the forty-year-old man standing at only five feet ten inches. But he knew that what Zurga lacked in brawn, he made up for in brains, which is how he had managed to stay alive this long.

More intimidating would be getting into the fortress where he was staying, atop a hill overlooking the old port of the island. A sniper shot from across the valley would be ideal, but would not be nearly messy enough for the men at head office, and more significantly for Brishnov, who, Nikita suspected, might be a problem he would have to deal with at some point. In a strange way Nikita could see why Zurga would have been drawn to hiding away on this tiny, barely inhabited island. With its history in the Greek civil war, which pitched communists against the US-backed capitalist government, and its location between Europe and Asia,

Zurga had found a place that reflected his own politics — caught in two minds.

Gazing out across the pink oleanders to the green-blue sea, a plan began to take shape in his mind. As he began ruminating on it, he suddenly heard the slightest sound coming from inside the apartment, like the slow exhalation of one trained in being silent. Fighting the instinct to tense up, Nikita channelled the calm from his years of training, and looked casually around for what was at his immediate disposal.

On the balcony with him was just a table, chair, and collection of papers and photographs. He propped up one of the photographs, and with the slant of the light was able to see the blurry outline of the apartment behind him. He rocked slightly on his chair, noticing that the front right leg was slightly loose. Keeping his eyes fixed on the photograph for any sign of movement, his right hand reached down and began to swiftly, but silently, unscrew the rusty old bolt holding the leg in place. He fought to keep his posture relaxed, but through straining his ears heard the feather-soft footsteps of an intruder inside. Quickening his unscrewing, he began to work out a plan, but froze as he saw the reflection of what he was certain was the cold metal barrel of a handgun.

As the gun moved closer, he could see that it was extended due to a silencer being screwed on. A silencer meant someone who was here to do only one thing.

He heard the whisper of a faintly quickened breath as the feather-light steps moved towards him, and as the hammer was pulled back, he pushed off with his right foot, launching himself at the intruder, chair leg in hand, the balcony furniture crashing around him. The face was barely visible in the shadows, but the gun was all too clear, and he swung the leg up, knocking it to the side. He vaguely noticed that the trespasser had not attempted to pull the trigger before he fell on him.

His victim was older than he would have guessed, perhaps mid-fifties, which explained the slightly heavier footsteps than those of a younger assassin, but he was agile. He somersaulted backwards as Nikita rolled forwards, jabbing the chair leg in a move towards the throat that would have been fatal had the intruder not leapt out of the way with a movement that defied his years.

"Enough!" shouted the man, dressed in black and sporting a grey, almost white, beard, as he raised a hand and rose to his feet.

Nikita stood up, light on his feet, assessing the situation. Something didn't feel right. The man was also standing, but his pose was not one of readiness for combat. He was dabbing at his lip, which had been split when he and Nikita had collided.

"Who are you? Who sent you?" Nikita demanded, not relinquishing his hold on his makeshift weapon. He was aware that the gun lay on the floor between them, and began to move slowly and subtly towards it.

The man cocked his head, squinting slightly as the sun shone through the balcony doors into his eyes. "I am your contact, Agent Allochka. I am Sabirow Kemran, the Soviets' man here in Greece. They told me you were the best the academy had ever seen, but I wanted to make sure for myself. I can see now that the rumours were not exaggerated."

Nikita recognised the Turkmeni name, and saw now that his assailant had the darkened skin and delicately slanted eyes of someone from Turkmenistan in the south of the USSR. They had one of the loudest voices calling for devolution, and were looked down on by many Russians — a feeling Nikita could identify with.

"A Turkmen working with the KGB? You will need a stronger argument than that to stop me eliminating you."

"This is what I like about you KGB agents, you are so warm and friendly," Kemran said. "Even Turkmen can have their uses to our delightful nation, something I would have thought you might be able to empathise with, Allochka. Plus, my skin colour enables me to pass for Greek when I need to."

"Can you tell me where the market is?" Nikita recited the code phrase, with great suspicion.

"The market is closed, but never in Moscow," replied Kemran calmly.

Nikita slowly lowered the chair leg. "OK, I will listen to what you have to say, but I don't trust you. Contacts do not usually break in and point loaded guns at agents. One twitch and I will kill you."

"Not so much as a cough, comrade! Come, let us sit; I have important information for your mission." Kemran glanced at the open balcony doors. "It is of course not for me to tell an agent how to do his job, but you might want to close the doors from eavesdroppers, agent."

Nikita strode over and closed the doors, picking up the gun from the floor as he did. It felt light, and he checked the barrel, noticing that there were no bullets in the chamber. He looked up and Kemran was holding a box of ammunition.

"Beginning to trust me yet, Allochka?"

"I trust nobody. What is the information you have for me?"

"Zurga, as you know, is here on this island. His home is almost visible from this room, atop the hill to the north of here. He may be stupid to oppose the USSR, but he is no fool and it is heavily secured. He knows that he is not safe, that the wealth he now has from selling secrets makes him a target. Rather than try to hide, he has been quite overt with his fortune since coming here a few weeks ago."

"Sounds like a fool to me," mused Nikita. "Why would he believe himself infallible? Surely he must know that we would come for him once he revealed his treachery?"

"He believes himself to be under the protection of the US. But he is really of very little use to them at this point; he has most likely given them everything he knows by now but that is enough to do significant damage. I understand it is important that you break into the fortress," Kemran said with artful avoidance. "The US have at least provided him with security guards. They work in shifts of five hours, and all are armed. The perimeter of the land is marked by barbed wire," he handed Nikita some wire cutters, "and trenches which I cannot help you with. There will be dogs, and again you will have to circumnavigate them through your own ingenuity. I cannot tell you how to conduct your mission; you are the expert, but you tell me what you need and I can provide you with it."

"It will be loud. Stealth will get me only so far, and I will need there to be a delay to any emergency services."

"This is easily taken care of; the island has only limited services, and the chief of both police and fire brigades are in our pay. It is not difficult to bend people to your will in an island so remote. Everyone has a price, and in Skyros it does not cost the Kremlin a great deal."

"I will need grenades, flash grenades, tranquillizer darts, a tactical sniper and handguns. Perhaps a Stechkin." He paused, thinking. "No, make that a Stechkin Avtomaticheskij Pistolet Besshumnyj. Also, plenty of ammunition."

"You sure you want an APB for this mission?" asked Kemran disbelievingly.

Nikita paused. The APB, a silenced version of the Stechkin sub-machine pistol, was KGB to the core. Perfect for a mission making a statement.

"Yes, I am sure. And also, I need a knife."

"Flick-knife? Two-inch blade?" Kemran suggested, indicating small and easy to carry weapons.

"No. An eight-inch serrated hunting knife," responded Nikita coldly, trying not to think of what it was he must do.

Kemran looked into Nikita's eyes, any hint of humour gone from his baleful face. Nikita returned his gaze, setting his jaw.

"There is no doubting you are KGB, but don't let your eyes betray you, comrade. You have a heart but you can ill afford mercy in this coldest of wars." He stood, "Very well. The Kremlin have us very well stocked and funded in Greece due to our interesting political location, so I should be able to get you everything you require." He turned back as he reached the door to leave. "You must not leave any survivors; the secrecy of your identity is more important than the mission."

Nikita looked up and nodded. As the door closed, he exhaled deeply and his body sagged. He held his head in his hands, rubbing his eyes, trying to rub away thoughts of what he must do. His heart was screaming against the horror awaiting him. He tried to remind himself of what he was there for. He focused his mind on Milena, on his father, his mother, on the life he wanted to give them. "Do not think about it, just do it," he muttered to himself.

He returned to the balcony windows and gazed down the track to the deep azure of the sea. He made an instant decision. He quickly hid any evidence of his work, and grabbing a towel from the bathroom, left the apartment and headed down the track. It was lined by pink oleanders, stunningly beautiful flowers that Nikita knew were some of the most poisonous to humans in the Mediterranean.

The path led across the sunburnt road and down towards the sea. To the left he could see craggy brown rocks and made his way to them, climbing atop the sea-worn outcrop. From the vantage point he could see that they led down to a small and deserted cove, invisible to passers-by on the road. He clambered down to the cove, which was lined by smooth, white stones a foot across, piling down into the clear water. He stripped off his clothes until he was wearing nothing but his briefs. His dark muscles were glistening in the sunshine, which was beating down on him from a cloudless sky, giving his skin an almost blue translucent sheen, punctuated by the tiny scars across the top of his arms and back. Making his way across the cobbles, seemingly impervious to the small stones digging into the soles of his feet, he walked into the water. A slight gasp uttered from his lips as the bracingly cold water struck his legs, but his steps didn't falter, though his mind was suddenly far away.

***

SHELEKHIVSKE LAKE, SUMSKA OBLAST, NORTHERN UKRAINE, JANUARY 1983

"On my whistle, you will dive in. Anybody resurfacing in under ninety seconds will receive five lashes. First blood wins each pairing," screamed Captain Denisov, spittle flying everywhere, mixing with the spray from the wind-whipped water.

The boat rocked slightly as the bitter January wind swept across the iron-grey water. The nine young men tried to disguise their fierce shivers as they pulled their thick clothing off. Nine young men and one seventeen-year-old boy. Nikita was wild-eyed and his teeth chattered uncontrollably as he stripped down to his underwear and fitted the weighted belt around him. He was squatted at one end of the dinghy, slightly away from the others, who didn't seem to want to be too close to him. That was how it had been since Klitchkov had left him at the training base. Always separate, only spoken to in taunts and barbed comments. What was he doing here in the middle of an icy lake in some godforsaken forest in the far reaches of Ukraine? The hairs on his arms were almost rigidly on end, adrenaline coursing through his veins. Denisov thrust a short dagger into his hands without looking at him, and distributed similar knives to all the other recruits, noticeably less forcefully.

"Fear nothing, prepare for everything. You know your pairings. Three, two, one…" shouted Denisov, then the whistle sounded, shrill as it echoed across the deserted lake, muffled from the world by the woods surrounding its shores.

"Don't think about it, just do it," Nikita muttered to himself, before throwing himself backwards over the side of the dinghy and into the frigid waters. The world turned upside down as he saw the mountains shimmering in the mist, and momentarily imagined how beautiful it must be in the summertime. Then the water tore at his skin like a thousand tiny knives, his whole body protesting violently against the sub-zero temperatures. The belt pulled him down to the lake bed, some three metres below. He was aware of shapes around him and as his feet hit the bottom, he descended straight into a crouch, his knife held out in front of him in his right hand as he had been trained. His heart was beating frenetically, trying to pump blood around his freezing body to keep his core temperature up, but Nikita knew he would not have long. Dimly aware of shapes in front of him, he cast around in the dark but crystal-clear water for his sparring partner. Suddenly there was a searing pain in the triceps of his right arm and he let out a silent scream as his knife fell to the murky lake bed. A small cloud of red burst from his arm and as his head snapped around, he could just see a dark shape disappearing into the gloom. As he did, he felt another stab in his left arm and more blood. He was becoming dizzy in the sub-zero temperatures and the confusion as to what was going on began to overwhelm him. Suddenly in front of him he saw the grinning face of the oldest of his fellow trainees, Vladimir Neski, knife held at the ready. Nikita made to find his knife but suddenly there were knives at his back, pinching, nicking, darting. He screamed, but it was lost in a burst of bubbles and he fell forwards, blood streaming from his skinny frame. So much pain and so many cuts. The butchering had stopped as quickly as it had begun, the freezing temperatures forcing them hastily back to the surface now ninety seconds had passed. Moving was becoming hard for him as his muscles stiffened from the wounds, and pain wracked through his back and arms. He knew the cuts were not fatal on their own but also knew that he did not have the strength to make it back to the surface. His lungs were screaming but his mind was fading. So cold, so very cold.

Then Milena. Gabriel, his father. Sophie, his mother. Their faces hovered before him in the dark reed-strewn depths of the unforgiving Ukrainian lake. He couldn't save himself for him, but he sure as hell would never give up on them. He was almost face down on the bottom but his feet found a rock and with every last bit of his strength, now underwater for nearly two minutes though it felt like a lifetime, he propelled himself forwards and upwards. Blood had begun streaming from his nose as blood vessels ruptured and his organs began to slow towards a stop. He would not die today, not like this. He would not let his family die because of his failures, because of the cruelty of Mother Russia, which had been no mother to him. He would only go on his terms. With a last shove despite his searing lungs, his bleeding limbs, his body so numb with the horrendously low conditions, he broke the surface and screamed, "Not like this!" His head was spinning and he began to lose focus as his body began to freeze and his eyes closed. He was vaguely aware of being roughly grabbed by the arm and he gave in to the darkness.

***

Nikita's mind snapped back to the present and realised he was now at waist height in these infinitely warmer Greek waters. He shook his head, trying to shake off the gruesome memories, but his hand absently stroked across his right triceps, feeling the scars that would forever be there. He pitched himself forwards, driving his lean body under the water and feeling the cool saltwater flow over him and press at his lungs. Several powerful strokes took him further underwater, challenging the protests of his lungs and enjoying the absence of any other thoughts. Above water, his mind was full of unwelcome memories and reflections, but here beneath the surface, now safe and alone, his mind was clear, as if the water were washing away the sins, he knew he would commit. Eventually giving in, he broke the surface and turned back to look at the shore, now some thirty metres away. Above his private cove, set back from the road, he could see a small chapel, a whitewashed cross silhouetted in the sunshine. Holy water indeed, he ruminated.

Enjoying the therapy of the physical exertion, he swam for perhaps half an hour, heading against the waves and out to sea, his powerful arms scooping the water and propelling him forwards. Some way out he stopped, and treading water, he gazed back at the shore, taking in the dry rolling hills spotted with short, tough, green bushes and dusty terrain. He looked down and saw some fish swirling around beneath him and for a moment wanted nothing more than to just stay there, floating, away from the violence of his life on land. He sighed and began making his way back to shore. As he climbed out of the sea, he picked his way over the sharp pebbles and stared out across the Aegean. The gentle breeze made him shiver, but he was already beginning to disassociate himself from his own feelings, in preparation for the night ahead.

Once dry and dressed, he climbed back up the rocky wall to the rear of the cove, scaling the sea-beaten stones and testing his strength. As he pulled himself over the ledge and onto the roadside, he caught his index finger on a shard of stone, puncturing the skin. Blood swelled from the small cut and trickled down his finger.

Still human, then, he thought, as he sucked on the wound. He began walking and tried to push the images of Vagin from his mind, and the Udmurt woman whose true story he might never know.

He strode along the dusty road, admiring the skill of the occasional passing drivers in navigating their ageing vehicles around the huge potholes in the sporadic stretches of tarmacked road. As he stood aside to let an old truck pass, avoiding going through a particularly severe pothole, it slowed to a stop next to him. He noticed that the bumper was held on by duct tape and there was a significant dent in the driver's door. A man, perhaps in his sixties, with crooked teeth, a patched hat and a leathery brown face that could only belong to one who spent most of his time outdoors, peered out at him, a smile on his face.

"Éla tha se páo egò?" the man asked.

Nikita's Greek was very limited, but after his intense studying of the phrasebook Mrs Shapova had given him, he vaguely understood the offer of a lift.

"Entáxei," he replied in acceptance, relieved to get out of the beating sun and cautiously climbing into the passenger side of the cab.

The islander nodded benignly to him, before throwing the truck into gear and pulling away with a screech of the engine. The road ahead was barely visible through the thick dust on the windows but the driver navigated his way confidently, like a man who had a lifelong affinity with the roads of this small speck of land on the eastern edge of the Mediterranean.

The truck's cab was sparse and well worn, the seatbelt long since disintegrated. Groaning its way to the top of a hill, the truck reached the peak and treated them to a stunning view of the old port town of Skyros and the blazing azure of the bay glinting in the rising heat.

The driver caught Nikita's wide eyes admiring the view, and he laughed. He pinched his thumb and index finger and kissed them like a French chef celebrating a fine meal, before opening his hand to the view.

Nikita smiled in spite of himself. "It's a beautiful island," Nikita said loudly in an effort to be heard over the indignant engine and the grinding of the suspension taking on the bumpy track.

"Yes, very beautiful," responded the man in heavily accented and stunted English, clearly delighted to see Nikita sharing his love of the view. He offered Nikita a cigarette, which was refused, before lighting one of his own, the pungent smell filling the cab. Nikita would have suspected they were strong Turkish cigarettes if he didn't know better than to think any Greek man would be seen smoking a Turkish product.

Ten minutes later they had bumped their way down to the harbour and the truck ground to a halt in another screech of unhappy brakes. Nikita, spluttering slightly at the heavy smoke in the vehicle, cranked down the window a crack to let in some fresh air before turning to thank the driver, who was offering his hand. He shook it, feeling the smooth, beaten leatheriness of his hand.

"Welcome to Skyros; I am Giorgos," he said, again trying to get his old Greek mouth around the English words, but seeming to Nikita to have more familiarity with them than he let on.

"Thank you for the ride," replied Nikita. "Martins, Nathan Martins."

Giorgos' crinkled eyes twinkled, and he nodded at Nikita. "Adío, Nathan."

"Adío."

Nikita climbed out of the truck, and watched as it pulled away, thick smoke still snaking out through a crack in the window. He took a deep breath, feeling relaxed from his interaction with a normal person. Aside from his brief visit to his family, he could not remember the last time he had spent any time with someone who was neither KGB nor politician. He realised he missed it, although it was such a long time ago now, he could scarcely remember exactly what it was that he missed. The more he considered it, the more he realised he was missing something he had never had. It was more the missing of an innate human need than any real personal experience.

He strode down a ramp to the seafront, past the first of many seafood restaurants, making his way towards the town centre and its smattering of gaudy shops hocking tourist tat, before making his way into the heart of the port town.

The narrow, paved streets were all bordered by the same whitewashed buildings with blue shutters, creating a feeling of sunshine, space and beauty.

Finding his feet taking him down Serakonta Street, he paused outside a small shop in a narrow road heading inland. The shop window was full of small wooden carvings, with everything from masks to bowls and earrings, mainly carved from pale brown olive wood.

But it was none of those that had caught his eye. Almost obscured by a particularly ugly attempt at a giraffe was a small carving of a dog. However, it was carved in an unusual black wood, and was not just any dog; it was unmistakably a Black Russian Terrier.

Nikita was stunned by the piece, not only to see a carving in a wood that was unvarnished but somehow as black as him, but also of the Russian military dog, a dog he had come to know well during his training with Denisov. He stood there transfixed by the piece, and became momentarily oblivious to his surroundings.

He pushed open the small door, and stooped to enter. The shop was empty except for a young woman behind the counter, idly flicking through a magazine.

She did not so much as look up as he entered, and he suddenly felt awkward about announcing his presence. He couldn't see her face as it was obscured by the book, but he could see a tumbling mass of brown curls exploding out from behind the words Vogue Magazine.

He began wandering about the shop, inspecting the various carvings largely hewn from olive wood. He was avoiding the Black Russian dog; for some reason he felt awkward about going straight to it, although he could almost feel its presence and was slowly working his way towards it. He was very nearly there when the woman's voice behind him said, "What is it you are looking for?" in an accent he struggled to place.

Taken aback by her directness, Nikita looked up at her, and now that the magazine was down on the counter, he could see her more clearly.

Big, liquid brown eyes peered at him out of a high-cheeked, golden-brown face, with freckles dappling her nose, and her curls now looking more golden than brown as sunlight landed on her face. She was the most beautiful woman he had ever seen.

Her thin eyebrows were raised in a question.

"I'm, ah, I'm just browsing, thank you," he stammered, for the first time in his life.

"Not true, because you were staring at something in the window for nearly five minutes before you came in."

Nikita flushed, angry for losing himself so quickly on his first full mission.

He looked closer at her, and she gazed back at him defiantly. Time to put some other aspects of his training into practice.

"Maybe it's not your stock that I found entrancing, maybe it was something else," he said, lowering his voice and fixing his eyes firmly on hers.

The girl laughed. "You really think a line like that would work?" She asked, lighting up a cigarette, the smoke circling up towards a gently rotating ceiling fan. Her voice had a curiously American twang to it that was throwing him off guard. In a world that had always made it crystal clear that where you were from was vitally important, he felt unnerved by his inability to place her, on an island where it should be obvious.

He grinned. "Epitrèpste mou na sas keràso èna potò." *Let me buy you a drink.*

She smiled. "Is that a question or a statement?"

"That depends which will get me what I want."

"And what is it you want?" She responded, tipping her head to the side as she exhaled the smoke. "Aside from a lesson to improve your truly awful Greek?"

"Right now, all I want is your name, a drink, and…" he picked up the dog carving, "this."

She looked at him and smiled playfully, "OK, strange man who speaks Greek badly, I'll let you buy me a drink. But the carving will cost you; it's from a rare wood only found on the nearby Cyclades islands, called Cyclades ebony. And the sculptor gets to work with it very rarely."

"The cost is unimportant. Who is the sculptor?" He asked quickly.

"Does it matter? I would guess that you don't know all of the sculptors in the Sporades."

Nikita paused, feeling wrong-footed and not knowing what to say.

She laughed at him, a rich throaty sound that came up through the body and closed her eyes.

He giggled sheepishly, immediately feeling idiotic for being sheepish. This was not in his training and it felt uncomfortable and oddly pleasant at the same time.

"You make a good point. But what of my third request? Your name?" he pressed, as she picked up a scarf, and walked with him to the door. They exited the shop as she turned the sign to say closed.

"You tell me yours and I'll tell you mine."

"I'm Nathan," he seamlessly lied, conscious of his American accent. "And you?"

She fixed her dark eyes on his, and they glinted in the bright sunshine. "Elysia."

***

Elysia led him up the narrow street next to her shop which went up a slope and away from the touristy shops lining the streets closer to the seafront. The homes were still pretty and whitewashed, but the paintwork slightly more chipped and the buildings increasingly in need of some love and care.

"Where are we going?" he asked her.

"You said you wanted to go for a drink, so I'm taking you to the sort of place that the islanders go for drinks," she responded in that direct tone that singled her out as a strong Greek woman. Again, though, he was struck by the hard-to-place accent she used when speaking English.

"Then I shall be led by you," he said, doing a mock bow.

She smiled but said nothing, and stopped as they came to what appeared to be a house like any other on the street. The door was covered by strings of beads hanging down over it, rattling in the breeze. The door behind them was only half closed and nothing but darkness was visible through the beads. Elysia parted the beads and pushed open the door. Nikita paused, his KGB senses tingling as they always did when entering an unknown property, especially as in this case he was with an unknown person and there was no clear secondary exit. How could he have been so stupid as to be led into such an obvious ruse?

Elysia smiled at him and beckoned him to follow her down what he could now see were dark stairs. Despite his apprehension and the bead of sweat he could feel at his temple, he stepped through the beads and onto the staircase. The stairs curved round to the right as they went down in a half spiral, but he could see a warm glow emanating up from the foot of them past the silhouetted form of Elysia. He could hear some music playing gently and as he reached the foot of the stairs, his eyes quickly drank up his surroundings. He was in a small bar, and his eyes immediately sought out all the available exits, which were not plentiful. The small bar was painted terracotta, with a couple of wooden tables and chairs in the corner and high wooden stools at the bar.

To the right of the bar was a pair of French windows, wide open, with pale translucent curtains pulled aside, swaying in the gentle breeze. Sunlight streamed through the windows, and beyond it Nikita could see there was a terrace looking out over the harbour.

Spotting that he had again stopped in the doorway, Elysia grabbed his hand and pulled him to the bar, which an elderly man was sat behind, smiling broadly at Elysia. His face was heavily aged, with deep creases scored across his forehead. Nikita could see a lifetime of laughter there, and great hardship too in the callused old hands.

As Elysia approached the bar and saw the old man's smile she cried, "Pappoús!" before throwing her arms around him across the bar. He pulled back and held her face in his hands and landed two firm kisses on her cheeks.

Nikita stood there awkwardly, trying to look confident without feeling it at all. He knew enough of Greek from his phrasebook to know that 'pappoús' meant grandfather. Elysia turned and introduced the old man to Nikita in Greek. He smiled at Nikita and shook his hand, but there was a twinkle of cynicism there too. Nikita wondered if a black man had ever set foot in this back-street Skyros bar before. He suspected not.

"This is my grandpa, Theo. He doesn't speak much English, but this is his bar. Anything there is to know about wine, he knows it." She gestured behind the bar to the rows of wine bottles in racks.

If nothing else, Theo clearly knew the English word for wine, as his eyes lit up and he turned to pull a bottle of red wine out of the rack.

"Greek wine is best," he said in a powerful and rich voice at odds with his small and wrinkled body, which made Elysia laugh. Theo spoke with her, pointing at the bottle before turning.

"Grandpa says that this is a special wine because it is made from only Agiorgitiko grapes which can be found nowhere but Greece."

"That sounds great to me, but I can't pretend to be a wine connoisseur," replied Nikita, feeling totally out of his depth.

"Well then you're in the perfect place to learn; Greek wine has more history than any other," Elysia said with a tinkling laugh, as she again grabbed his hand and pulled him outside through the French doors. He looked at Theo, who nodded his head to him before turning his back to begin wiping down the bar.

Outside, the sun was searing despite it now being around five p.m. and Elysia led them to a table shaded under a grapevine. It was fairly busy with men dotted around, sitting on their own reading newspapers and sipping wine, and a group of women of all ages gathered around a table, sipping a bright red drink that Nikita couldn't place. They were talking very loudly and animatedly, about what Nikita could only guess. Looking around the terrace, he could see it had been created in a traditional Greek style, with grapevines overshadowing half of the terrace, and in the other half small olive trees grew in large terracotta pots, with some of the scrubbed wooden tables shaded by rusting parasols. The terrace wasn't large, but looked out to the harbour and the surrounding mountains. The sea was glistening and shifting gently, a vivid blue under clear sunlit skies.

As they sat, she placed down the bottle on the table. "I forgot glasses!" she exclaimed, rolling her eyes. "I'll be back in just a moment." As she left to wind her way back to the bar, Nikita noticed that all conversation had stopped and everyone was staring at him. He sat up straight and stared boldly back at them. What it must be like to be white and not always be the only black man in every room, he thought to himself. Nikita reprimanded himself for losing focus on the reason he had come to Skyros. It wasn't to enjoy himself, but to carry out the assassination of a Russian double agent. He slipped into musing about the task he was here for, forcing himself to think of the gruesome murder he must commit. Not murder, he told himself. Not murder, but political assassination. He had to hold on to the difference.

As Elysia approached the table, she saw that everyone was still looking with judging eyes at the pair of them. Some of them looked positively livid.

"Ti?" she asked them all defiantly. A couple of them muttered to themselves but most of them turned back to what they were doing. "Ignore these people. They aren't too used to black men in this part of Skyros."

"Trust me when I say I'm used to it," Nikita replied with a wry grin.

"I don't doubt it. I don't care though, and that's all that matters," she said matter-of-factly, with her chin raised and a half smile playing across her full lips.

Nikita couldn't help but laugh. It was a strange feeling to him.

"Your face doesn't look like it's used to laughing; what's your story?" she said, hitting rather too close to the bone.

"You're not wrong, Elysia. But what I'm really interested in is your accent; I can't place it. I can hear the Greek, but when you speak English it sounds pretty American, but not quite." He picked up the bottle and began pouring it into both glasses. The dark red liquid was almost translucent in the bright sunlight.

She smiled. "Well, that would be because I am American actually."

"You are?"

"Sort of."

61

"You're infuriatingly vague, you know."

"This coming from the man who avoids questions about himself, only telling me his name and that he has a weird thing for statuettes of small black dogs."

He said nothing, but smiled at her, staring intently into her eyes.

"OK Mr Intense, I'll bite. My grandparents are all from Skyros, but in the forties my mom's parents moved to Baltimore. There's a big Greek community there; it's even now called Greektown. My mom grew up as an American, but despite marrying my father, also from Skyros, she felt out of touch with her roots and wanted me to grow up Greek, not American. So she sent me to an international school in Athens where I got my weird Greek-come-American-come-vague-European-type accent."

"That would explain it. So do you feel more Greek than American, as your mother wished?"

"Instead of making me Greek, it made me feel like I don't quite belong anywhere. At least in Baltimore I can feel comfortable with others who don't know whether they're American or Greek, but at the same time nowhere has ever been as comfortable for me as Skyros. My pappoús rented the shop for me because he wants to keep family close, as family is the most important thing for Greeks, but I may try moving back to the US for a while soon I think."

"Maybe instead of needing to just be one thing, you will come to love being many different things," Nikita said.

She looked intently at him, and for the first time her face softened. "I like that way of looking at it," she replied. "And you? Are you many different things?"

"I think that's a very good way of putting it. But like you, I haven't yet found the joy in it. For the moment I can content myself with the American bits of me, as I grew up in Daytona Beach, Florida."

He felt like a fraud, responding to her openness with KGB lies. He couldn't help but feel totally captivated by Elysia, who seemed to wear her heart on her sleeve and hide nothing. He took a long drink of his wine and was struck by how rich and complex it was, barely considering his personal pledge to stay teetotal throughout his mission.

At that moment in walked Giorgos, his lift from Houlakia Bay earlier that day, and upon seeing Nikita he opened his arms in a broad smile. "Nathan!" he called out, accidentally knocking over the bottle of wine of a man in a wide-brimmed straw hat who had just sat down at a nearby table. The man swore at Giorgos, who waved him away jovially. Nikita stood, and Giorgos embraced him like an old friend. Again, unsure how to react to kindness, Nikita tried to seem as though he was comfortable with it.

He turned to Elysia. "This is Giorgos, a recent acquaintance of mine."

"Well, there is certainly more to you than I expected, Nathan," she said, looking amused, then kissed Giorgos, who embraced Elysia fiercely and again planted the two kisses firmly on her cheek and spoke to her in rapid Greek too fast for Nikita to follow. "So my uncle tells me he brought you into town earlier," she said with a twinkle in her eye.

"Your uncle?"

Giorgos and Elysia chuckled, and Giorgos put his arm around her, planting a big kiss on her cheek.

Nikita smiled begrudgingly, again feeling wrong-footed. He briefly noticed the man in the straw hat trying to shake the last drops from his bottle of wine, still muttering to himself, before standing and heading into the bar for another bottle. The uncle and niece sat down opposite him. "So how are you finding Skyros, Nathan?" Giorgos asked.

Nikita smiled insincerely. "I had a feeling you knew English," he said, his senses prickling.

"It pays to know things on this island," Gorgios said with a wink.

"It's always useful to know the people who know useful things," Nikita replied, his shoulders bunching.

"This is one of the vaguest conversations I've ever heard," Elysia said, breaking the tension.

Nikita laughed, but didn't take his eyes off Giorgos. Giorgos was staring right back, his deeply lined face showing a mixture of concern and humour.

Nikita topped both his and Elysia's glasses up. "Will you join us for a glass, Giorgos?"

"Of course. There is always time for wine on Skyros."

At that moment, Elysia's grandfather called her name from inside the bar.

Elysia rolled her eyes. "He probably needs help reaching something at the bar. I'll bring a glass for you on my way back, Uncle. Be gentle with him!"

She got up and wound her way back through the tables, but Nikita wasn't watching, his eyes still fixed on Giorgos. He leant back in his chair. Something didn't feel right.

"You like my niece, yes?"

Nikita said nothing.

"Men like you are no good for girls like her."

Nikita's eyes flashed, and his jaw clenched. So this was what it was all really about.

"Men like me?"

Giorgos laughed. "You think I mean because you're black! This isn't what I mean. Although yes, that would be hard for the family and the island to understand. It would provide entertaining gossip for years! But no, my friend, I mean because of what you do."

Nikita said nothing, but slowly put a hand round to the small of his back where his revolver was tucked into the waist of his jeans.

"You say very little, my friend," said Giorgos.

"I have little to say. Stop speaking in riddles and tell me what you are working towards."

"So, I deliver wine for a living in Skyros."

"Good for you. Why are you telling me?"

"I make deliveries to some very wealthy people around the island."

The smile disappeared from Giorgos's face as he stood and put his hands on the wooden table and leant forward until his head was next to Nikita's ear. "Tonight, I deliver wine to a fortress on a hill," he said breathily.

Then he said loudly in Greek, "Where is my niece with that wine glass? Whom God wishes to destroy first he makes mad!" he said, reciting an old Greek proverb with a look of comic tragedy on his face that caused people around the bar to laugh. As he turned to walk to the bar he winked and whispered one word: "Kemran."

Nikita leant back on the legs of his chair and exhaled. This island was full of unlikely surprises. His mind was now clear and back focused on the mission ahead. He needed to get out of this bar and speak to Kemran about Giorgos and check in with Ambassador Yitski to confirm the trustworthiness of these sources. If Giorgos was telling the truth, then his job of getting into the fortress just became an awful lot easier.

Elysia returned to the table and Nikita noticed she wasn't carrying an extra glass. She smiled at him as she sat down and Nikita was knocked out all over again. Now he was more prepared for it, however, and steeled his heart and mind to keep him in mission mode.

"Where's your uncle?" he asked.

"He got called on to do a delivery," she replied. "Before he left, he said to tell you that he would be driving back past your hotel tonight at eleven p.m. if you wanted to hitch another ride with him."

"That's very good of him; I may just take him up on that offer," Nikita said, smiling.

Noticing the pensive look on his face, Elysia said, "Don't mind my uncle. We struggle to understand him as much as you."

He smiled but said nothing.

She poured him a glass of wine and raised her own to him. "In wine there is truth," she said.

"So that's where the truth has been hiding," Nikita replied as they clinked glasses, and she laughed.

"You like your secrets, don't you?"

"I like you more," he said, taking another deep drink of the wine. It really was delicious. So much fuller of fruit and flavour than any he had tasted before. He rarely experienced alcohol other than vodka in Russia, but that was sharp and strong and designed to keep you warm. His experiences of wine had been limited to training in being able to pass off a working knowledge of wines should he ever need to mix with that crowd. None of his training had given him Greek wine, however.

"That's delicious," he said to her, nodding to his glass.

"As my grandpa said, Greek wine is the best."

"He's clearly a very wise man! Why have I never had it before?"

"As with everything else, Greece doesn't get the respect it deserves around the world. We have fallen behind and there doesn't seem to be the motivation to catch up and let the world enjoy what we do here. Also, I must admit that we are over-inclined to keep it all for ourselves."

"I'm happy to be sharing in the secret with you, Elysia."

During his second glass of the wine, as he took a sip, he deliberately put his glass down so that his hand would touch hers. He left his hand there so their little fingers were just faintly touching.

Nikita was no longer even aware of what she was talking about, and tried to refocus.

He noticed she had fallen silent and was looking at him and her finger shifted slightly so that it was on top of his own.

He was aware of his heartbeat quickening, as he felt awkward and excited simultaneously.

The sun was lower in the sky now, casting long shadows across the bar, and the cicadas were in full voice. Nikita gazed out at the view, which he'd taken little notice of until now. The sun hovered on the horizon, giving everything a golden glow. With the boats visible, bobbing gently on the water, and the mountains diving down into a long outcropping peppered with small red flowers, it was as if traced from a postcard.

"Thank you for bringing me here, Elysia. It's unlike anywhere I've ever seen."

He could think of nothing but their touching hands, and he gently wrapped his little finger around hers.

"Thank you for walking into my shop today; I think it was just about worth losing out on any customers this afternoon," she chided. She moved her second finger under his.

Looking fixedly at the view, he swept his hand across hers, and squeezed it. She turned hers upside down so that the palms were facing, and laced her fingers into his.

He brought his gaze back round to her and they both looked at their hands and laughed awkwardly.

At that moment her grandfather appeared through the French doors, making his way towards them. Nikita quickly withdrew his hand. Elysia looked momentarily hurt before he nodded behind her towards the old man, who was tottering slowly towards them carrying a bottle of wine and a plate piled high with food. Nikita sighed to himself. So much time building towards holding hands only for it to be immediately taken away.

Theo laid the food and wine down and kissed Elysia on the head, before looking disparagingly at Nikita. They both thanked him as he muttered something in Greek and headed back in to the bar, teetering slightly as he made his way past the tables and chairs.

Looking at the food Nikita saw olives, flatbread, hummus, tomatoes and stuffed vine leaves.

"Well don't just stare at it; we Greeks believe food is there to be enjoyed," she said as she scooped up some hummus with a stuffed vine leaf. Nikita was fairly sure that was not how they were meant to be eaten but 'when in Rome', he thought and dived in.

Elysia went to open the second bottle of wine, but Nikita raised his hand. "I'd better not have any more to drink; I need a clear head for the evening ahead."

"You presume a great deal, Nathan," she said, arching an eyebrow.

"No, no you misunderstand," he replied hastily. "I have to meet a business acquaintance this evening so I need a clear mind."

"Oh… OK."

"But by all means you enjoy some more wine. I'll be sorry to have to leave," he said, picking up some flatbread. It was warm and powdery in his hands.

She smiled unconvincingly, and he sensed a sudden tension between them but knew he needed to go.

"I don't know what you're used to, but I'm a bit different to other men."

She laughed. "I don't doubt it, Nathan."

Finishing his glass of wine, he stood up.

"You're leaving already?"

"I must," he answered, his head already moving back to his mission.

She pouted slightly, looking even more beautiful for it. He leant down and kissed her on both cheeks, very slowly. Their cheeks rubbed softly against one another and he breathed deeply, taking in the smell that can only come from sun-warmed hair. Like warm bread, honeysuckle and fresh cut grass rolled into one.

He paused above her and she gazed up at him. He became keenly aware of the other patrons in the bar looking surreptitiously at him out of the corner of their eyes. Some were more obvious. He reluctantly moved away, and asked, "Can I see you again?"

"You want more wooden statuettes?" she asked archly.

"I meant can I see you again... like this."

"Why?" She asked, again using that direct approach that he found so disarming.

He groaned inwardly. "Ah, because I... ah. Because some things in life feel worth pursuing."

She looked at him impassively and he grimaced at his choice of words — unrecognisable from any version of himself he'd ever encountered to date.

"I can't decide if you're really this sweet and awkward, or just very, very smooth."

"I'd like to think I'm pretty smooth."

"I think it's probably the former."

"I see," he said, not sure how to take it but aware that it wasn't a dismissal. "So perhaps I could call into the shop again?"

"I can't stop you."

"Would you want to?" he asked.

"Come to the shop and find out would be my advice," she said, smirking openly at him now.

"Do all Greek women make things this difficult for someone asking them out, or is it just you?"

She laughed that rich throaty laugh again that seemed to tickle the very air in front of her. "You have a safe journey home, Nathan."

"Is to epanidìn," he said, touching her on the shoulder gently as he walked past. *See you soon.*

The man in the straw hat was snoring gently with his head on the table, revealing a curious mark on his neck, and two empty bottles in front of him. Stepping past him, Nikita noticed the judging eyes from the local patrons were back on him again, although some of the eyes were now also resting on Elysia. But already his heart was cold and steeled to any sense of feelings as he began to play the night ahead through in his mind.

He had a plan, but it would not be easy.

CHAPTER 8

It had not been a good day for Maria Demopoulos. As maid to Josef Zurga, she'd already seen more than would be enough to turn her to God, had she not already been a devout member of the Greek Orthodox Church for all of her seventy-five years. But today he was in a foul mood. He had run out of wine which never meant a peaceful day at work for the members of his household at the lighthouse fort on the east coast of Skyros. The members of his household consisted of Maria, the butler Cato, and whichever whore he had flown in that week. Them, and the huge array of security guards and Alsatians that constantly rotated watch, surrounding the small complex. She shuffled down the corridor, with the note that had just been delivered clutched in her hand which looked more like a claw these days, the arthritis making the unfurling of her fingers ever harder.

As she reached the door to his bedroom, she heard a crash and saw Cato hurriedly leaving the room, an empty tray in his long-fingered hand and what looked like tzatziki dripping down his left shoulder.

"The old goat didn't want lunch today, it seems," he said calmly to Maria, his face fairly impassive. He was a tall man and extremely thin, with his black hair fluffed into a rakish side parting and a thick black beard, giving him the look of an upside-down broomstick. "Good luck," he said, winking, forcing a scowl from Maria, before loping away down the corridor, looking all the while like he might tip over.

She breathed in and pushed open the door.

"What is it you want now? Can I not be left in some peace?" said Zurga in a heavy Russian accent as she entered his bedroom. A sallow faced man was sitting on the bed in underpants and an unbuttoned shirt, revealing a distended paunch. A thick rug of chest hair nearly connected at the neck with the hair of his unshaven face. Far from obese, he rather had the look of a fit and vital man gone slightly to seed, with soft edges and crumbly skin from too long spent overindulging and not enough time outside.

He pushed himself up, an empty bottle of wine rolling off the bed and clattering onto the floor, its fall broken by an array of debris surrounding the tiles around his bed.

Maria looked witheringly at him, paying his tone little heed. Her eyes scanned his bedside table which showed empty sachets of white powder. No wonder he was in a foul mood, out of both cocaine and wine.

"A letter delivered for you, Josef."

"I told you to call me Mr Zurga. Give it to me."

She tossed the note to him negligently and he snatched it up from the bed sheets and ripped open the manila envelope as she turned to leave the room.

His eyes quickly scanned the crumpled paper within, and then widened in fear.

"Tonight? TONIGHT?" he muttered to himself.

Maria turned back, her interest piqued.

"Who sent this? Talk fast, woman."

Maria shrugged. "He didn't give a name. I couldn't even see his face because he was wearing a large straw hat."

Josef leapt out of bed and rushed past her, his unbuttoned shirt flowing behind him.

"What is happening tonight? What did it say?" Maria called after him, but he ignored her.

She stooped down to pick up the note from the floor where it had fallen in Josef's haste, to see what had caused his panic.

It said simply:

Tonight, with the wine comes the enemy. Get out

As he dashed up the corridor, he began shouting, "Guards! Guards!"

Cato appeared around the corner, his legs visible before his stringy body followed.

"What is it, Josef?"

"Why do none of my servants call me Mr Zurga!" Josef exclaimed, spittle flying slightly from his lips. "Where is my head of security?"

"I imagine he's in the security tower... Mr Zurga," he said. "What is it? What has happened?"

But again, Josef was off through the house in search of his head of security.

CHAPTER 9

Nikita's head was attempting to play out every scenario. Denisov's voice screaming, "Fear nothing, prepare for everything," over the biting Russian winds rattling around his head like a mosquito he couldn't swat away. Today he must turn the mosquito into his weapon.

He sat cross-legged on the floor of his hotel room, palms face down on his knees and his eyes closed, as he slowed his breathing and meditated on the plan for the night ahead. The Havana embassy had confirmed Kemran was their man in Skyros, and also confirmed that Giorgos was on Kemran's payroll, while Klitchkov had confirmed the mission was a go. Nikita did not like so many people being involved. People were liabilities. Trust nobody but yourself, he thought to himself. He repeated it out loud, forcing the reminder to be vigilant into his head, wrapping itself around everything else.

He opened his eyes and surveyed the floor before him. Directly in front of him was Zurga's file — blueprints of the fortress along with satellite images of the complex and an ordnance survey map of the surrounding hills. Either side of that were the weapons which Kemran had already left in his room by the time he returned to the apartment. It looked enough to start a small war.

He glanced at his watch. Twenty-one hundred hours. That gave him ninety minutes before the arrival of Giorgos for the wine delivery.

On the bed was an array of garments, all black, which he began to pull on. Kemran had left a Kevlar vest for him and he picked it up, weighing it in his hands. It was heavy and would limit his movement. He laid it back on the bed and stretched. He would need to be as mobile as possible for his plan to work. Without a vest, mobility became even more important.

Pulling on a heavy belt with a thick leather sheath at the hip, he picked up the hunting knife. A crueller looking weapon he had never seen. The eight-inch blade was serrated on both sides, leading to an evil curved hook at the tip. It looked akin to shark teeth, and was capable of similar levels of damage. He slid it into the sheath and moved onto the other weapons.

He picked up two KGB standard-issue Makarov semi-automatic pistols and smiled grimly to himself. Kemran had risen admirably to the challenge of making sure everything pointed to the KGB. The pistols were old and battered, but they would do. He put one in a shoulder holster and the other he tucked into the belt at the small of his back. Not his favourite place to keep a weapon, and Denisov certainly would not approve, but it was always good to have something extra up your sleeve. He clipped the grenades to a strap across his chest, the tranquillizer gun into a holster at his hip and slung the sniper over his back by the strap. He stretched and darted around the room, testing his flexibility and versatility while carrying his one-man army.

The Stechkin APB remained on the floor. He knew exactly the weight of that, and knew the destruction it would carry out. An old fabric army holdall sat next to it, laden with ammunition. He leant down and unloaded it, leaving only what he would need in there and no more.

At eleven p.m. he saw the lights of Giorgos's truck come bouncing down the track. Little chance of catching anyone off guard in that dilapidated old thing. He would have to make do regardless. The lights shut off as the truck pulled to a stop at the bottom of the driveway to the hotel.

He sloped out of his room and walked slowly down the track, his right hand held out and stroking the pink flowers as he passed. He tore off a small handful as he walked, feeling the cool petals against his skin.

"A very bad choice if they are for luck," Giorgos said, looking at the flowers still in Nikita's hand.

Nikita's face remained impassive as he stared down at the oleander petals that were bright pink, flecked with red.

Giorgos grunted and started the engine, the lights throwing shadows across the dusty track. "Let us deliver some wine," he said grimly.

They clattered along the track that went through the valley before it wound up a hill. At the top they could see across a small valley to the hill ahead. The fortress was perched at the top, bathed in spotlights which lit up the boundary fences clearly.

"Time for you to get into the back," Giorgos said to Nikita. "There are a lot of boxes to hide behind, and the guards do not look hard if I give them wine. Only the cheap wine though. Zurga refuses Greek wine, demanding only French piss."

They stepped out of the truck, and walked round to the back, Giorgos opening the doors out. Nikita heard dogs barking across the valley and sighed. He did not look forward to the dogs.

"Careful with this piss; it is for the vlàka," he swore, motioning to the boxes packed in near the door. Nikita climbed up and into the midst of the boxes.

"Do not wait for me afterwards Giorgos."

The old Greek man nodded soberly, and went to close the doors. He paused and then said, "I meant what I said. Leave Elysia, she is not for this life. And good luck." He shut the door before Nikita had a chance to reply.

Nikita sat down next to Zurga's wine and braced himself for what was now nearly upon him. The engine started up again and the truck began rocking and swaying over the potholed track.

***

Giorgos was glad of the bone-shaking bumps and lack of suspension as they disguised the shaking of his hands. He could not stop thinking about the mass of weaponry adorning the strange dark-skinned man in the back. He had never expected anything like this when Kemran had first approached him; it just seemed like some easy money to paper over the cracks of his failing wine delivery service, to keep his eyes and ears open any time he entered the complex.

As he trundled up the hill, he heard the bang of a box of wine in the back. The shit better not be breaking my wine, he thought. As the trees and shrubs cleared, he rounded a corner and the road was bathed in spotlights. Barbed wire fencing two metres high surrounded the site, and visible about a hundred metres back from it was the stone building where Zurga resided.

As he slowly approached the gates, a huge guard approached the vehicle, leading an Alsatian the size of a small bear.

Giorgos swallowed nervously, and kept his hands firmly fixed on the steering wheel to avoid giving his nerves away. He tried not to think about the Jericho 941 pistol in his coat pocket, which he had no idea how to use. He wasn't even sure if it was loaded.

The guard tapped on the window and he rolled it down. "What is your business?" the guard asked in heavily accented English.

Giorgos rolled his eyes. "The same as it is every time, Johann, to give your boss his piss."

Johann was so tall that he had to stoop slightly to see into the truck, and his broad shoulders stretched wider than the width of the window. He looked like a mythological Viking, with high cheekbones, bearded face and blond hair. His face was expressionless as his pale blue eyes scanned Giorgos, taking in his white-knuckled hands on the wheel.

Giorgos could hear the dog panting. It did not help his nerves.

"Open it up," said Johann, tapping his gun on the door frame and stepping back.

Giorgos climbed out and walked to the back of the truck, wondering what on earth Nathan had planned and wanting absolutely no part of it. The dog was uncomfortably close as he slowly opened the double doors, the saliva dripping over its huge teeth and onto his sandalled foot.

"You seem nervous, Giorgos," said Johann, noticing a sheen of sweat across his brow.

"You try driving this piece of shit along these roads without sweating."

Johann charged the cocking handle on his weapon and turned to face the door. A weapon even Giorgos recognised — an AK-47. The ultimate Russian assault rifle, used by mercenaries as much as the Soviets.

Opening the door, Giorgos was careful to keep to one side and moved backwards with the door to allow Nathan to pounce.

Nothing happened; there was only darkness.

Johann shone a torch around the cabin, showing only boxes, and then led his hound inside. Giorgos felt like his heart had stopped.

Again, nothing.

Now Giorgos felt on the verge of cardiac arrest. Where was he? A box of the Merlot on its side was the only sign to him that anyone had been there.

Johann climbed out, his face still unreadable, and led the dog around the vehicle, checking the underside.

"Let's move this along, Giorgos," he barked, seemingly satisfied.

"A pleasure as always, Johann," Giorgos rasped as he climbed back into the truck. "Where is he?" he breathed, his brain racing and wondering how and when Nathan had got out. He fired up the reluctant machine and rolled through the gates to the next check point.

This is new, he thought to himself, and noticed that the place seemed to have at least treble the number of guards normally there. Not good news for his rookie assassin, wherever he was.

"He's alone. Just the old man and his wine," he heard Johann shout.

He slowed to a stop. Up ahead he saw Zurga standing near the front door. He was holding a gun.

Something wasn't right. He saw a movement to his right and saw two guards standing about ten feet away. He looked to the left and saw the same on that side.

All four raised their weapons.

"Skatá." *Shit.*

They turned out to be his last words.

All four opened fire simultaneously. Giorgos's old leathery skin was no match for white hot metal and his body was thrown from side to side as he was riddled with bullets.

The clicking of empty chambers signalled the end of the shooting. A guard approached slowly and after poking Giorgos with the barrel of his Kalashnikov, signalled to the group that he was dead.

Zurga, who had watched the proceedings from the doorway, walked purposefully towards the truck, which had died along with its owner. He was wearing a bullet proof vest and holding a Glock 17 pistol, a present from the Americans for his recent services.

"Open the door," he spat to the guard, who obeyed immediately.

Giorgos's broken body slumped sideways, his head stopping him from falling out and leaving his body contorted.

Zurga opened fire and emptied the entire magazine from the gun.

The body fell to the ground. Blood quickly pooled around Giorgos and the Jericho 941 tumbled from his overcoat pocket in the fall. Zurga felt some of the tension leave his shoulders.

"Search the vehicle," he ordered the guards as he approached the corpse. *This is who they send to kill me?* he thought. *And there was me thinking I was a high-profile target, how humbling.*

"All clear, boss," said a guard. "There's nothing in the back except for crates of wine."

Zurga smiled and walked to the back. Wine was running freely from the doors, with many of the bottles destroyed in the gunfire. "What a waste!" he groaned. "Even if it is Greek muck."

A box near the door was on its side and seemed to have escaped the attentions of the bullets. He pulled out a bottle and lifted it up. "Merlot!" he exclaimed. "This night just keeps getting better." The top had come loose in the fall but the wine was still good and he swigged straight from the bottle. "Bring the rest inside," he commanded as he ambled back towards the house.

***

On the hill across the small valley, Nikita lowered the scope on the sniper rifle. There was nothing about his cold expression to suggest he felt anything at the death of Giorgos. Nothing but a single tear snaking its way down his dusty cheek.

Losing a man was not a part of the plan.

CHAPTER 10

Nikita picked up the sniper again and raised the scope to his eye. He was lying flat on the ground, obscured by the low, coarse shrubs that covered the hills hereabouts. With his dark skin and black clothing, he was totally lost in the shadows, stretched out on the hard earth. The sniper pointed out in front of him looked like an extension of his body, making him appear like a black dart waiting to pounce.

He surveyed the scene across the valley. The guards were back patrolling the grounds but were noticeably less vigilant. Two of the guards were at the body, one picking up the Jericho and placing it into his belt, while the other laughed.

Nikita gritted his teeth. They would be first.

Panning the scope around the complex, he focused his attentions on the building windows. Little could be seen other than an elderly woman in a small, ground floor bedroom, packing a bag.

In a large, upstairs bedroom he could see an outline of what he thought was Zurga. He was drinking wine straight from the bottle. Time to move, thought Nikita, as he pushed himself up, before slinging the sniper over his shoulder and making off through the underbrush at high speed, making barely a sound on the dry ground.

***

"Going somewhere?" Cato asked, ducking under the doorframe as he entered Maria's small room.

She barely glanced up from the suitcase laid out on the bed which she was filling with her meagre possessions.

"Fifty years I serve this house, but I never see such thing as this. Josef is a bad, bad man."

"You think you can just flee?"

"You intend to stop me?" Maria said, pausing and looking up at her colleague.

Cato smirked at her. "To the contrary, Maria." He reached back into the corridor and pulled his own suitcase into the room with his rangy arms.

She grinned a crooked smile and snapped her suitcase shut.

"I suggest we leave now, while the fool is distracted by his wine," said Cato, picking up Maria's suitcase as well.

As they made their way down the corridor towards the front door, they heard the drunken calls from Josef upstairs. "Maria! Maria! Come here, you old crone!" He screeched to the house, no doubt wanting her to clean his room for the next batch of whores, or some such thing.

The pair quickened their step. Reaching the front door, Cato then pulled it open and they moved out, heading along the track towards the steel gate.

"You look like you're leaving us," said the guard as they got to the gate.

"We are," said Cato, lifting his chin and attempting to leave no room for doubt.

"You see, that might be a problem," said the guard. "If word gets out of what happened here tonight there would be a lot of problems. I prefer to make problems go away, and right now you two are a problem. I'm going to have to make you go away." He reached for a gun at his waist.

"Please, no," Maria sobbed. Cato moved in front of her as the guard raised the weapon. Embossed on the side of it was the word Jericho. The guard smiled as he began to squeeze the trigger.

BANG.

Cato and Maria fell to the ground. They couldn't see, couldn't hear, and everything hurt. There was just a blinding white light.

Cato began to realise he wasn't dead, and he heard the groaning of Maria next to him. His hearing returned and he heard a dull thud close to his feet as his sight slowly returned.

Through the smoke from the flash grenade appeared a figure cloaked in black with a gun raised in one hand and a khaki green sack in the other. Cato realised that the thud at his feet was of the guard hitting the ground;

a double gunshot to the head had left him dead, still with the stupid grin on his face.

His senses returning, he saw that Maria had broken her arm; it was sticking out at a strange angle and she looked up at him, and for the first time he saw something other than irritation or apathy in her eyes. Now he saw fear.

There were two cracks in quick succession and another guard fell, another double tap to the head.

Guards were now appearing from everywhere, as the man in black holstered his gun, dropped to the ground, tossed a sniper to the ground next to him and opened the bag. In less than two seconds he was back propped up on one knee and holding an enormous gun with a long feed of bullets trailing from it.

He took a deep breath and squeezed the trigger, wreaking destruction across the entire site. Starting from one side of the vast lawn he mowed down guard after guard. As the weapon began to move round in Cato and Maria's direction, Cato threw himself down on top of the old woman, who moaned loudly, and the bullets passed above him. He could feel the back of his shirt move from the wind of the closely passing bullets. His senses still slightly askew, he viewed it all as if from far away, the screams of the security guards feeling like an abstract backing track.

Suddenly the bullets stopped, and daring to look up, he saw the gunman grappling with the feed of bullets.

Maria pushed at him with her good arm and he rolled off. "Help me up," she croaked, the old cantankerous energy feeding her again. He pulled her up and she staggered over to the gunman who widened his eyes in surprise, and reached for the gun at his waist.

"No need for any of that." She swatted at him. "Now move over." She stood beside him and lifted the ammunition belt with her good arm.

"Cato, don't just stand there ogling; don't pretend you don't know how these work. I know all about your old activities against the Turkish swine."

He loped over, aware of gunfire now beginning to return in their direction. He put his hand under the long shaft of the APB, which was still balanced on the knee of the black garbed man. He felt the skin on his hand sizzle from the intense heat of the weapon, but gritted his teeth and with the butt of his left hand, threw his force behind it and hit the opposite site of the loading belt. With his burned hand he pulled at the belt until he felt the familiar click of the jammed bullet dropping into place. He stepped back and the shooter nodded at him with cold eyes. He was a lot younger than Cato had first imagined; he couldn't be more than twenty years old, the butler realised with a jolt.

He squeezed the trigger and began the awful slaughter once more. Some of the remaining guards had got closer and now the trio could see with dreadful closeness the damage the automatic weapon did to the victims, ripping through muscle and bone like knives through butter. The many Alsatians were fleeing from the bullets, their owners all now lying dead or dying, and the gunman passed over them, a fact not unnoticed by the butler.

Maria had a ferocious look in her eyes, her grey hair loose and her right arm hanging limp and crooked at her side. She looked more like a battle-hardened old warrior than a septuagenarian maid.

Suddenly the shooter stopped and surveyed the scene. The windows were broken, the walls pitted and around twenty bodies littered the field and track within the barbed wire fencing.

There was no sign of Zurga.

Maria cackled. "It reminds me of beating the Turks in seventy-four, and what a glorious day that was."

Cato smiled in spite of himself, but the dark shooter eyed them suspiciously. The butler turned his attentions to the old woman's arm, despite her trying to bat him away. He looked at her. "Where did you learn to do that?"

"The same place as you, you think I don't know of your time in Limassol for the Cypriot Guard, Cato? You're a Greek hero. I was there to nurse the wounded."

He smiled fondly at her. "Then it sounds like you were far more the hero than I."

Her eyes crinkled as he touched her forehead on his and she kissed him on both cheeks.

As she pulled away to lie down, suddenly she was thrown backwards as a bullet went straight through her heart. Her look changed from a gentle smile to one of mild surprise as she clutched the crucifix at her neck.

"Theé mou," she muttered. *My god*, and breathed her last breath.

Outrage and pain ripped through Cato's whole bean-like body. He snatched the sniper from the ground and spun, spotting the guard on the roof and in one swift movement took aim, exhaled and fired. A distant cry was heard as he hit his mark and the guard fell forward from the roof and toppled the two storeys to the ground to land in a crumpled heap.

He tossed the sniper to the ground and knelt back next to Maria. He brushed his fingertips across her brow and gently closed her eyes.

"Wait here," Nikita said to Cato, as he crouched and softly but quickly made his way towards the fortress.

The accent of the strange gunman was not placeable to Cato, who sat back on the grass and wrapped his arms around his long legs.

Nikita glided across the grass, moving past the litter of corpses lying in his wake and towards the door. Now for Zurga. He pulled the Makarov from his shoulder holster, nudged the front door open with it and made his way cautiously inside. He padded confidently through the house, the blueprints tattooed into his mind from his studies and meditation earlier, and moved up the stairs towards Zurga's room.

He heard him before he saw him.

A gurgling and sputtering sound was emanating from the bedroom and Nikita kicked open the door, gun raised. Zurga was on his bed, again shirt open and bottle of wine beside him. The most obvious difference from the scene Maria had earlier seen was that this time Zurga had soiled himself.

Zurga's eyes were half closed, but narrowed further as he saw Nikita enter the room.

"The wine?" he asked, before breaking into coughs and sputters again.

Nikita nodded, and pulled the hooked, serrated knife from the sheath at his waist.

If Zurga was shocked or afraid of the knife he did not show it. "They said that wine would be my undoing. That, but never… one of *you*."

Nikita could see the effects of the massive dose of pink oleander flowers he had inserted into the bottles of Merlot were in the advanced stage. One of the most toxic plants in the world, the mottled red rash spreading across Zurga's face and the diarrhoea were some of the more visible symptoms. Inside, Nikita knew, his organs were failing and quickly. A fact illustrated as Zurga lurched to the side and vomited. It was heavily laced with blood.

Nikita moved towards him, knife in hand. "Save me," Zurga pleaded, wheezing heavily as foam bubbled at the corner of his mouth.

"This is the only salvation I can give you now," Nikita replied, and thrust the knife into his heart.

Zurga's eyes widened in pain and shock and he grabbed Nikita's arms, pulling him closer. "Who are you?"

"I am the Black Russian," whispered Nikita coldly, remembering Giorgos and Maria, and pulled out the knife, the hook pulling chunks of heart muscle and sinew with it. He forced himself to watch as the light in Zurga's eyes faded.

Once Nikita was sure he was dead, he began his gruesome work with the cruel knife on the former double agent, to ensure it looked as grisly as possible as per his instructions from the ambassador. Wiping his hands on one of the only remaining blood and excrement-free patches of bed sheet, he turned away from the horrific scenes in front of him and headed down the stairs and out onto the lawn.

When he got outside, he saw Cato and Maria faced by a pair of angry, and apparently hungry, Alsatians. Cato was cowering, with Maria over one shoulder, and was trying to back away. Nikita briefly thought how leaving him to the dogs could make his life easier, but immediately thought against it. That's an ending I wouldn't wish on many, he thought to himself and drew his tranquillizer gun, quickly unloading two darts on the dogs who staggered briefly before collapsing and falling still.

Cato looked at him gratefully before he realised that Nikita had a gun raised at him.

"You have seen me; I cannot let you live. It is a matter of national security," Nikita said softly.

Cato nodded knowingly. "I suspected as much, though which nation's security, I wonder?" Then, tilting his long sloping head, he added, "You do not have the eyes of a killer."

"Neither do you."

"My killing was done to protect my family and the people I love," he replied, looking sadly down at Maria.

"Mine also."

Cato nodded gently. "Then be careful it does not claim your soul. It claimed mine."

"I think you are wrong; I see a lot of soul in you. I am truly sorry about your friend," he said, nodding at Maria.

Tears welled in Cato's eyes. Then, smiling benignly, he closed his eyes for the bullet.

Nikita raised the gun and knew what he must do. As he looked down his arm at the old man looking so serene and accepting of his fate, he lowered his arm.

I'm an assassin, not a murderer, he thought to himself.

Cato's eyes opened slowly.

Nikita was gone.

CHAPTER 11

Nikita strode back down the track, taking a brief diversion to collect the wire cutters he had buried in the undergrowth after cutting his way into the compound only thirty minutes earlier. So much had happened so quickly. It did not take long to kill.

He was in a daze. So much killing he had carried out, and the deaths of two good islanders were on his hands now too. He thought suddenly of Elysia and felt sick.

It all felt at a distance, like the work of someone else. He didn't like it, but didn't feel overly burdened by it. Becoming colder than a Siberian winter, he thought to himself.

He brushed it all from his mind as he pulled a huge mobile phone from his ammo sack and carefully dialled Kemran. "It is done; the site will need to be cleared."

"First a photographer is needed to help spread the word."

"That is your concern; my assignment is completed."

"Do you require extraction?"

"No, I will find my own way."

Nikita ended the call, turned to face the track and began his journey home. Ordinarily he would work to remain hidden after such a mission, to keep his identity secret and leave no connection to the scene of the crime. But in such dark and rural territory he would be able to see and hear any vehicle or person approaching long before they were able to see him.

In the warm night, Nikita prowled the dusty road, hearing the buzzing of the cicadas, noticing the feather-light fluttering of bat wings overhead. Now a true assassin, he was tightly wound and saw everything.

Sometime later he arrived back at the turn off to his hotel. The moon was cloaked by clouds, rendering the hotel complex almost invisible, with only a couple of lights dotted around the site.

He circled around to the back of the hotel, making his way through rough, hard soil and tough tufts of grass, and entered slowly, keeping to the dark shadows. His skin prickled; something didn't feel right. Nothing visible, only a feeling. He approached his apartment cautiously, eyes alert for tripwires or traps. After satisfying himself there were none, he padded silently to the door. He turned the key soundlessly and drew his handgun from the hip, easing the safety off with a tell-tale click before moving sharply through the doorway, gun aloft and covering the whole room as rapidly as he could. It was clear.

It was only after he had checked all of the remaining rooms that he was able to release a long breath.

On the living room table was a thick envelope, and next to it were two bottles — one of vodka, the other of Kahlua: the ingredients for a Black Russian. Kemran's joke was not lost on Nikita, but he did not smile. Next to the bottles was a note: *Everyone needs an escape — Russians drink. SK.*

Nikita felt a tightness in his chest, like a clock that had been wound too tight. His hands shook from the adrenaline still coursing through his veins. He felt elated, horrified, powerful and disgusting.

If I am a Russian then I must escape like one, he thought to himself, and grabbed the vodka by the neck, ignoring the Kahlua. He unscrewed the cap, took a swig straight from the bottle and felt the burn as the alcohol hit the back of his throat. He gasped, and then felt the heat as it moved into his stomach, working into his bloodstream. He needed to feel warm.

He took the bottle with him and headed to the bathroom to wash the blood from his skin. He left the clothes on the floor of the shower, letting the blood and dirt seep out of them, creating a dark brown pool trickling down the drain like something from a horror movie. He scrubbed at himself, periodically picking up the vodka to swig from it. Numbly noticing a wound on his calf, he poured vodka on it, almost to feel something. Even the sting felt subdued.

He closed his eyes and allowed himself to feel the darkness, and encouraged the steaming water to wash away his sins.

***

The thudding on his door entered his dream before it roused him. His head felt heavy, his mouth thick and dry.

Nikita forced himself up off the bed where he had collapsed the night before. The towel he had wrapped around his waist had long since fallen off, leaving him naked and shivering slightly.

The banging on the door was louder now.

As he stood up, he swayed on his feet. The half-drunk bottle of vodka was lying on the floor next to his bed. He looked at it and retched.

The banging on the door got louder and he quickly grabbed the towel, wrapped it around his waist, and staggered his way through, finding his coordination to be unfamiliarly poor.

Nikita grabbed his handgun off the table as he passed, and approached the door cautiously, albeit slightly heavier-footed than normal.

A glance through the spyhole quickly woke him up. Elysia was standing there, her tear-streaked face clearly visible. She was in a battered blue pinafore, stained and plain. Somehow, she looked even more lovely for it.

He quickly looked around the room, taking in the array of weaponry scattered haphazardly. If Denisov could see him now, he would be kicked out of the KGB without a second chance.

Darting around the room, he called out. "Who is it?"

"It's Elysia, please let me in," she pleaded, sounding distressed.

Immediately he felt a heaviness in his heart, and he glanced at the vodka bottle.

"One minute," he replied, "I'll be right there."

He gathered all of the remaining equipment he had returned with the night before and stuffed it into his khaki sack, before dashing into the bedroom and throwing it into a wardrobe, before heading into the bathroom, balling up his bloody clothes and wrapping them in a plastic bag. Nikita returned to the bedroom and put the bag into the wardrobe on top of the khaki bag before slamming it shut and returning to the front door. He glanced again over his shoulder. The room was a mess, but it wouldn't give him away.

Opening the door, Elysia fell through it and threw herself into his arms. "Oh, Nathan!"

Catching her, he pulled her up into his arms. "Elysia! What's up?" he said, seamlessly switching back into character as Nathan Martins. She clutched at his arms and buried her face in his chest, sobbing.

He held her close to him, sensing the perfume of her dark hair in his nostrils as she shook from the sobs wracking through her. His mind felt heavy and sluggish. There was something else too, an unfamiliar feeling.

He pried her away from him and led her into the apartment, closing the door behind her after quickly glancing around the deserted pathways surrounding his building.

He took her hand and led her over to the sofa, and then strode to the kitchen and got her a glass of water.

She took it from his hands and put it straight down on the table before looking up at him as he lowered himself onto the couch beside her.

"Giorgos is dead, Nathan."

"What?" he replied sharply, looking completely dumbfounded.

"My uncle, Giorgos, who you met at the bar yesterday, he is dead," she said, struggling to control the wobbling in her voice.

"I'm so sorry, Elysia; he looked so well and full of life yesterday. What happened?"

"He... he didn't die from sickness," Elysia said. "He was in a car crash."

"A car crash?" Nikita exclaimed, genuinely surprised this time.

"Yes, that useless truck of his finally betrayed him. They think the brakes failed and took him over the edge of the mountain road inland from Houlakia. They won't even let us see the body because it is so ruined."

Kemran is earning his money, thought Nikita.

"Oh man, that's a damned waste of a life. I know I hardly knew him, but he seemed a good man."

"He was a fool," said Elysia, anger flashing in her dark eyes. Then as the anger quickly seemed to deflate from her, she added, "But a fool with a good heart."

Nikita smiled warmly at her, finding it harder and harder to deny that feeling growing in his breast. "Can I fix you a drink? Tea?"

"Perhaps something stronger?" She said, nodding towards the vodka and Kahlua.

"Of course. I've recently been introduced to Black Russians…"

"That sounds good."

Carrying two of the cocktails over to the sofa, he looked into her puffy eyes and raised a glass. "Stin igià Giorgos".

She touched her glass to his. "To Giorgos."

More tears snaked their way down her cheek and she tried to sip the drink. "I can barely believe he is gone. So many times, we told him to get a new truck, but he loved that thing nearly as much as the wine he carried around. Pappoús is inconsolable."

"Something like this… must be hard to accept. For everyone," he said, grabbing and squeezing one of her hands as her eyes filled again with tears.

Feeling instantly awkward, he made to move his hand away, but then she clutched it.

"It makes me realise that maybe Giorgos was right all these years. The moment to be lived in is the present one. He would always recite this Groucho Marx quote to me: 'I, not events, have the power to make me happy or unhappy today. I can choose which it shall be. Yesterday is dead, tomorrow hasn't arrived yet. I have just one day, today, and I'm going to be happy in it'. He made me memorise it when I was small, because he said too many people now, even on this island, get caught up worrying."

"He's a wise man. He didn't strike me as a worrier."

"He wasn't. At least the last time I saw him, he was happy."

The image of the bullet-riddled truck flashed through Nikita's mind.

Elysia held his hand and looked into his eyes. "Giorgos would want me to find joy in everything," she said and kissed him fully on the lips. She smelt warm, like old summers.

Nikita pulled away, and saw her eyes fill with pain and confusion. Those eyes, liquid brown like those of a doe. A strand of her dark hair fell across her face, and he couldn't help but push it back behind her ear, eager to keep drinking in her beautiful, sorrow-filled face. He leant forward and kissed Elysia deeply, allowing himself to give in to another kind of escape.

He woke suddenly feeling a warm hand on his bare shoulder. "Nathan... kalimera ómorfe."

He jerked upwards quickly, disorientated. Elysia was there sitting on the bed, looking over at him, her hair falling across her face.

"It's OK, ómorfos," she smiled at him. He could smell coffee, and noticed a cup on the bed stand beside her.

"Ómorfos?" he asked.

She laughed, a tinkling sound full of joy in sharp contrast to the deep sadness she had shown earlier that morning. "Your Greek needs some practice. It means handsome, or beautiful man."

"Then it's you that is the ómorfos one," he said, looking up at her, causing her to roll her eyes. He wrapped her in his arms and pulled her down onto the bed. She felt light in his muscular arms but he kissed her only gently.

She laughed again, but stopped when she saw his pained expression. His insides raged with a cyclone of emotions. "What is it? What's wrong?" she asked.

"It's you I'm worried for. We shouldn't have done what we did; you're grieving."

"We did what we did because I wanted to, and I don't regret it."

"I just... don't want to hurt you."

"Then don't," she replied, pulling away slightly to better look at him.

He steeled his heart, and reminded himself that Nathan was a character he was playing, not the person he was.

"OK then." he smiled at her and kissed her again.

"Good. Now, I have to go; my family need me and will be worried about where I am," she said to him.

He nodded at her and watched as she gathered her things and arranged her mussed-up hair. He was entranced by her, and hated himself for letting it happen so easily. He felt dirty and corrupted by the vast amounts of blood already on his hands. But every time he felt himself indulging in these feelings, his training would kick in and force him to suppress it, leaving him with an internal see-saw of emotion to no emotion and back again.

He walked her to the door, which she pulled open, her eyes filling with tears again as the real world flooded in with the sunlight.

"Thank you for this morning," she said, and pecked him on the cheek before turning and walking purposefully away.

***

LENINGRAD, 1985

"You want to cry, Allochka?" Major Koryan leered, his face inches from the pitiful specimen in front of him. His skeletal face looked like the skin had been pulled back, leaving it pale and translucent. His brown eyes held no warmth, only disdain at the trembling boy before him. "This is the best you have, Maxim?" he said, turning from his crouched position to look at the impassive face of Denisov behind him. "You must be losing your touch."

"Mastering emotion is the biggest remaining obstacle," replied the steady voice of Denisov, everything about him a masterclass in controlled emotion. "That and a discomfort with heights which will be conquered eventually."

"Is that right," muttered Koryan, crouching back down in front of Nikita. "Your weakness disgusts me," he whispered into his ear.

It happened in a flash. Nikita's teeth latched onto the ear of the major and tore at the lobe, ripping skin and sinew. The major screamed and leapt back, the bottom of his ear half dangling off. A look of deepest loathing and fury crossed his face and he drew his weapon and aimed it at Nikita. Denisov, spotting the danger, moved quickly and wrestled the firearm from Major Koryan.

"If you had let me finish, Igor, I would have said that the emotion we have to contain is his rage, not his tears."

"That mudak has ruined my ear; I will have blood!"

"Igor, let me deal with this. Go and visit the doctor; he will sew it back together. I will make sure he is punished."

Koryan's eyes burned as he looked at the newly named Lieutenant-Colonel Denisov, and held his tongue. Barely. He spat at Nikita as he walked to the door. Nikita smiled back through his blood-smeared mouth.

"Be careful with that ear, comrade."

Koryan turned to strike him, but Denisov caught his hand and forced him to the door. Closing the door behind Koryan, Denisov locked the door and paused, with his back to Nikita, taking a deep breath before turning and walking back across the room. He picked up a chair and turned it so that the back faced Nikita, straddled the chair and leant his arms on the frame.

He said nothing.

Nikita held his gaze for as long as he could but eventually his will broke. "I am sorry, Lieutenant-Colonel, I failed you."

"You failed your comrades and you failed your country. The Soviet Union does not tolerate failure," Denisov said, the contempt oozing out of him. "You are an important asset to us, boy, but not indispensable."

"I have done my best."

Denisov spat at the floor in front of him. "You want my pity? The KGB accepts no weakness."

"I will do better."

"This I know. First, you must pay for your crimes to Koryan."

Nikita hung his head; he knew what that meant.

"How long, Lieutenant-Colonel?"

"Two weeks in the cold box."

"Two weeks? Nobody can survive that!"

"Nobody can survive that, SIR."

"Yes, sir."

"Consider yourself lucky; Koryan would have had you die by firing squad. I am lenient because frankly, I've wanted to do the same thing to Koryan myself." He threw Nikita a small smile. "Survive this, and you can survive anything."

"Please, sir, please, I will do anything. Please not the cold box. For that long. I will die."

The lieutenant-colonel stood up. "You will be brought food occasionally. Good luck, comrade," he said, then walked from the room. As he left, two soldiers came in. Nikita began to sob.

"Please, sir, I beg you!"

Despite being chained in a snow-covered stone shed, some way from the compound, his yelling could still be heard from inside the warm building. But they quickly faded as the temperature dropped. Inside the hut, he could hear his comrades' laughter over the sounds of the rats at his feet. He began sluggishly jogging on the spot, all he could do to keep warm as the chains limited his movement. It was all he could do to stay alive.

Two weeks later, the two young trainees were sent to let Nikita out. They found a man barely conscious. As they unfastened him, he fell to the ground, and they caught him before he landed. He tried to shrug them off but did not have the strength. They dragged him across the snow and inside to the first warmth he'd felt in two long weeks. He made not a sound throughout and his eyes barely opened.

They tossed him on the floor inside, at the feet of Denisov. Nikita looked up from the ground, forcing his sunken eyes open. Looking down, Denisov saw cold rage emanating up at him. The eyes, now, of a killer.

***

Nikita watched Elysia as she disappeared around the corner. Then, exhaling, he leant against the door frame and closed his eyes.

He banged a hand against the door before pulling it shut, blocking the emotions of the real world and cursing himself. The Soviet Union did not tolerate weakness, and would not forgive it. He must be tougher. He must remember the cold box.

Walking back in, he picked up what was left of the bottles of alcohol and emptied them down the sink. Time to become the KGB agent.

No sooner had he emptied the bottle of Kahlua than there was a knock on the door. Putting the bottle down gently, he strode over soundlessly with one hand on the gun tucked into his belt at the small of his back, easing back the safety with a gentle click, and put an eye to the spyhole. He saw Kemran standing there. His handler smiled at the spyhole and gave a small wave.

He opened the door and stepped aside as the Turkmen agent walked in.

"Must feel strange, waiting for me to let you in to my apartment," Nikita said wryly.

Kemran chuckled. "Good to see you still have your sense of humour after yesterday." He sat down on the sofa and looked at Nikita. "That was quite a mess we had to clean up."

"Those were my orders."

"And by God did you follow them. A statement was certainly made. But remember, one successful mission does not make a successful spy. You are very young, beware of getting cocky because you *will* make mistakes."

Kemran looked at the kitchen counter and saw the empty bottle of vodka lying on its side by the sink. "I see the shop girl isn't your only vice." He winked. "Or perhaps you can't have one without the oth—" His words were cut off as Nikita put a hand to his throat and pushed him back onto the sofa.

"Utter one more word and I'll slit your throat where you sit. You've seen Zurga; you know it's not a problem for me."

Kemran lifted his hands in surrender, and Nikita relinquished his hold and took a small step back.

Kemran winced and rubbed his throat. "Interesting you say that, because when I looked at it him, he had all the symptoms of a man who had been poisoned." When Nikita said nothing, he smiled and said, "Don't worry, Agent Allochka, both of your secrets — the girl and how you killed Zurga — are safe with me. I actually think it was an ingenious tactic you employed; you may yet be as good as they hope." Seeing Nikita's suspicious look, he added, "You may not believe it of me, considering our line of work, but I really do deplore violence. It's unfortunate that life has taken me to a job so mired in it. I want you to succeed, Allochka, so we can get this whole thing over with as soon as possible and I can go back to Turkmenistan and live a life completely unembroiled in politics and espionage."

"Does such a world exist for a man like you?"

Kemran shrugged. "Only God knows the answer to that."

"You should be careful talking of God, comrade. That could be considered treason by those in the Kremlin."

Kemran laughed. "Ah yes, religion is the enemy of the proletariat, and bolshevism a friend to us all. As long as Soviet Russia remains, my God remains whoever is in charge of my pay check."

Nikita remained impassive. "That almost sounds like capitalism."

Kemran shrugged again. "Even our beloved communism cannot deny human nature, my friend. But come, we are not here to discuss theology and politics. I wish no ill upon you or the girl, although I know you do not need me to tell you that you can never see her again, yes?"

Only a barely noticeable slump of the shoulders gave away any indication of his true feelings, but Nikita's voice was strong and emotionless. "I know. She is just a girl, of no consequence to me."

Raising his eyebrows, Kemran said nothing more. "I have your orders," he said, leaning back and interlocking his fingers.

"Yes?"

"You are a changed man."

"My orders, Kemran."

The older man pushed his mane of salt and pepper hair back and from the inside pocket of his jacket produced a manila envelope, which he tossed onto the coffee table. "Very well. These were sent through from Brishnov this morning. You, comrade, are going to America. Your tickets are inside."

"Agent Brishnov? Is that normal?"

Kemran shrugged. "I don't question where the orders come from. You will be surprised to hear that most people outrank the Soviets' Greek attaché. I presume he was merely an intermediary."

Nikita chewed on the information. He leant forward to pick it up, but made no move to open it. "There is one more thing. An enemy remains on the island."

Kemran sat up straight, eyes alert. "Go on."

"Zurga knew I was coming."

In an instant they both had drawn their weapons and the revolvers were focused directly at each other, hovering just inches apart.

"Tell me," said Nikita, "have you always sold your soul to the highest bidder, or is it just since you were posted to Greece? Perhaps you feel more aligned with nearby Turkey than with Mother Russia?"

"I have sold my soul to no one. Are your accusations based on nothing other than the colour of my skin?"

"Come now, think who you are talking to. Do you think I did not notice the man in the straw hat in the bar? Your knowledge of the girl incriminated you if nothing else."

Kemran laughed and lowered his gun. "My boy, on an island the size of Skyros, everyone knows about your little fling. It is the best gossip the people here have had in months. The local girl and the black man? It will be the talk here for some time. What benefit would there be to me in betraying you to Zurga?"

Doubt began to creep into Nikita's thoughts. The old man held his gaze solidly and unflinchingly.

"And who is this man in a straw hat? Hardly a strong point of identification on a Greek island," Kemran continued.

"We'll come to that. Giorgos was your source?" He lowered the gun slightly.

"Of course. The man was a mine of local information, and I would have appreciated it if you had not used him as bait."

Nikita raised the gun again. "His death was not my intention."

"But an inevitable consequence of your plan nonetheless."

Nikita lowered the gun and pinched his tired eyes. "Probably."

"A rather sick twist in the tale of your love affair with the girl, wouldn't you say?"

"She will never know."

"Let's pray you're right. You will make sure Georgios's family is well renumerated for his service?"

"I will," Kemran replied with sincerity. "Now enough of this nonsense; tell me of this straw-hatted man and please tell me you have more for me to go on than that."

Sitting back down, Nikita said, "He was an older man. His hat was wide-brimmed which cast much of his face into shadow. He dressed to fit in, but it looked as if he had tried too hard. His shirt and trousers were the right style but were brand new."

"I need more than an old man in clean clothes, comrade."

"There was one more thing. On his neck was a tattoo. Much of it was obscured, but it almost looked like it could be a swastika. But unlike one I've seen before."

"Now that I can work with. Was it three-pronged?"

"I think so, but I could not be sure. Why?"

"That is the Russian neo-Nazi symbol; they are proliferating back home. But why would Russian Nazis be in Skyros? Zurga was a traitorous son of a bitch, but he only operated with people who would be to his advantage. I do not see how the Nazis would fit into that."

"He is the one who alerted Zurga. But if he is not your man, whose is he?"

"This is impossible to hide for long on Skyros. But do not let this concern you; you have done the job you came here for and must focus on your next assignment."

"I will expect to hear an update on the Nazi, Kemran."

"You think to give me orders, you little shit?"

Nikita smirked. "You know how we need to operate. No loose ends. The Kremlin does not forgive."

Kemran stood. "You do not need to tell me that, Agent Allochka. Go with God."

"Or whoever pays the bills," replied Nikita. Kemran winked and left the apartment, leaving Nikita alone with a tsunami of thoughts and the manila envelope on the tray table in front of him.

CHAPTER 12

Elysia sat behind the counter of the shop, legs crossed and eyes focused on a carving. The shop was empty; it always was. So many hours spent perfecting pieces from Greek woods, only for them to be dismissed as tourist tat and overlooked by islanders and visitors alike. Not by everyone though, she mused.

The piece was taking shape, but the Cyclades ebony was a very hard wood that took patience to fashion into a figure like the dog he had requested. She wondered how he would feel about her making him a second one to keep the first company. "Why would anyone want a carving of a black dog?" she muttered to herself. Even despite the tears in her eyes that had rarely left since the news of her uncle's death had reached her, she couldn't help but smile weakly. There was little about Nathan that made sense. He said so little and was so impassive, but somehow, she felt a deep well of emotion within him, disguised by the mystery and enigma in which he cloaked himself. She wanted to know more; she wanted to see him again. She flushed at the thought of the morning, and how unlike her it was to do anything like that. She found she didn't regret it at all, which made her flush all the more. She wondered if he would come to the funeral with her; the support would make the thought of facing it somehow less daunting, but perhaps it was too much to ask so soon.

She put him from her mind and her thoughts drifted again to her uncle Giorgos. It just felt so wrong that he wasn't around any more. Everyone had known that truck was on the brink of dying, but no one had seriously thought it would take him with it. Of all the things to take him, he who claimed to know every pothole, bump and track better than any other on the island.

She realised she had drifted to gazing absently out of the window, lost in thought and turned back to the carving of a dog, unaware it bore an eerily close resemblance to a Black Russian Terrier, the type of dog being trained, thousands of miles away to work in a world she was unknowingly teetering on the edge of.

***

Nikita gazed through the shop window, this time careful to avoid being seen. He stood well back in the shadows, with stray tourists ambling past. Leaning against a faded blue wall, he could see directly through the open door to where Elysia was sitting, her bare feet just visible poking out from behind the wooden counter and her hair shielding her face as she worked intently on something in her lap that he couldn't see.

A part of him ached to enter the shop, ached to feel that warmth, but already that part of him had been packed away so deep that he was barely aware of the longing.

He saw now why he'd been sent to Skyros first. Not because of Zurga or the island's strategic importance between East and West. It was because here mistakes could be made and learnt from without the repercussions being felt far and wide.

A dark car stopped down the street. The driver got out, his face obscured by mirrored sunglasses, and beckoned to Nikita. Choosing to overlook the fact that Kemran had clearly known he would return here, he took one last look at Elysia, soaking up every detail of her beautiful golden face, before walking to the car and not looking back.

Inside the shop, suddenly sensing eyes on her, Elysia's head snapped up from the carving to the open doorway. Nothing could be seen other than a dusty street, a couple strolling past and a blank faded blue wall. In the distance she heard a car fire up and pull away.

***

As the small propeller jet ferrying him and a smattering of other tourists lurched away from the island, taking them back to Athens on the Greek mainland, he gazed down from the window at Skyros, with its clear blue seas, golden beaches, villages and mountains all packed into just a few short miles. Somehow his fear of heights never bothered him on planes. The island was so small, yet so much had happened in only a few days there. A part of his soul would be forever lost on the island, lying with all the blood that had soaked into the earth at his hand. That, and the murder of Giorgos and the old woman would remain forever on his conscience. His training meant he felt detached, but he nonetheless knew that there was no going back from the point he was at now. He was a killer, and he could no longer convince himself otherwise. Not only was he a killer, but he was good at it.

But I will never enjoy it, he said to himself. Blood would be paid for with blood, and he knew not if he would get out of it alive and cared even less. But his family, they were different.

Reminding himself, as he had so many times before, of the reason he was here, and the reason he had become what he had, he sat back, closed his eyes and prepared himself for what lay ahead. Prepared himself for the United States of America.

On his lap, clenched firmly in his fist was a manila envelope, the contents of which laid out the challenge that, if successful, would alter the history of the entire world.

CHAPTER 13

US Secretary of Defense Simon Conlan leant on the wooden post and cracked open a beer as he looked out across his sprawling ranch, basking in the knowledge that everything visible right to the horizon belonged to him.

The dusts of Texas were being whipped up in the November winds blowing across the arid plains west of Odessa. In his grandaddy's time the soil had been black with oil but now much of the land lay barren. Some cattle roamed, living off the tough Texan grass that seemed to endure anything.

The Cherokees who had once roamed freely across these plains had believed the oil seeps to be gifts from the heavens, using it for medicine. His grandaddy, Terry Conlan, had seen it more as a gift to him and had set about creating an empire with a bloody singlemindedness that had made the Conlans one of the wealthiest families in Texas. The Cherokees had lost their land and heritage, but as Terry had always said, "When the dust settles, money and power are the only things that really matter."

Simon breathed deeply, soaking up the clean, dry air. This was a rare treat. He could count on his hands how many times he'd got back to the ranch since Callahan appointed him secretary of defense back in '81. Away from the whining politicians, high security, and not even any wife and kids this time; they'd had a last-minute call to visit her mother in Arkansas this weekend, and praise God he hadn't been asked to go. He pulled the sleeves up on his old blue and red chequered shirt, over the arms that had once been strong and muscled, gained through a childhood of working the cattle. They had got him through a hard war in the Pacific too. Now they looked every inch like the pen-pushing, hand-shaking arms of the seventy-year-old he'd become. A formerly handsome man, he still exuded a natural authority, with broad shoulders and a full head of steely grey hair. Broken veins on his nose and the absence of any laughter lines gave away both his indulgences and his lack of humour.

He sighed. Life had been so much simpler fighting the Japs. See one, shoot one. So straightforward. Now life had become so goddam complicated and consumed by the Russian commies. Sometimes he wondered if politics had been the right career choice.

"Take the weekend; think it over, Simon, and I know you'll make the right decision on the INF Treaty. The world needs this to happen," the president had said.

Negotiations for the Intermediate Nuclear Forces Treaty had dominated his entire term as secretary of defense, and he was starting to grow tired of fighting it. But fight it he would. The only way to beat communism was to destroy it, and he wasn't about to let more than eight hundred of his nuclear warheads be destroyed because that snake Petrenko said he'd do the same. However, many the Russkis had, Simon wanted more.

"We do not negotiate with communists," he'd told Congress again and again, but he was fast being overruled and was ready to play dirty to undermine the agreement. Even making his position clear in the press hadn't generated the level of public support he'd hoped for.

He downed the rest of his beer, tossed it to the ground and walked towards the stables. He looked over his shoulder and shouted, "Is nobody going to pick that up?"

A young black woman appeared silently from the side of the house and ran quickly to pick up the bottle, her wide eyes avoiding the haughty glare of Secretary Conlan.

This is why I love politics, he thought to himself. So much power over so many. He made efforts to make the staff black. Politically it helped him look good in the eyes of the northern states. Privately he'd never forgiven the Confederacy for losing to the anti-slave north. For him there was an order to things, and the blacks were firmly rooted at the bottom with the Cherokees.

He ambled over to the stables as the girl scampered away with the bottle. The massive wooden construction had been redeveloped by his father who was horse mad. Simon had never fully shared the enthusiasm, but horses were in his blood as a family of Irish descent, his great grandfather racing horses back in County Donegal before making the move over to the US in the famine. Jane and the kids got a lot more out of it than he did, but he liked to keep a stable and an eye on it as his father had before him.

He walked over to a chestnut stallion in its pen and stroked its head as it bowed slightly to him and pawed the ground. There was straw in his mane.

"Nat! Where the hell are you?" he yelled.

Appearing from another pen, a young black man appeared. "Here, sir. How can I help, sir?"

"What the hell are you doing with these horses? This one looks like he's not been cleaned in weeks!"

"He was sleeping in the straw. I clean him every day, sir."

Nat ducked quickly as an old horse shoe came flying at his head. "You going to tell me I'm wrong, boy? Don't make me throw you back to the dirt you were born in with the rest of you bootlickers."

Nat looked terrified. He was eighteen and yet to fill out his wiry frame, appearing gangly. "Please, sir, sorry, sir."

"Don't let it happen again. I'm docking your pay for a week."

"Sir, please! I have to pay for my momma's medicines." The boy had tears in his eyes.

"You should've thought of that before you let him get all strawed up. Now get out of my sight."

The young man fled, all legs and arms. The stallion whinnied as he saw the stable boy leave, and pawed the ground again. Simon smiled. It was good to be home.

He left the stables and as he returned to the house, he heard the phone ring. "I suppose it's asking too much for anyone to answer the goddam phone?" he yelled. He heard footsteps running. "Whatever happened to slaves being neither seen nor heard? No, no, it's fine, don't let me interrupt all y'all's rest."

He picked up the phone in the broad living room, its wide French windows thrown open onto the plains beyond, casting light across the pale blue and white room.

"Secretary Conlan speaking."

"Good afternoon, Mr Secretary, sir, I'm patching through Secretary of State Schultz."

"Very well. Tell him to hold one moment."

"Yes, sir," replied the secretary. Conlan pushed the phone to his chest to cover the receiver. "Nat! Come here," he yelled to the house.

The young man hurried into the room, eyes fixed on the floor.

"Come here," Conlan ordered, and Nat duly complied. When he reached the secretary, the old man reached out and rubbed his head.

"Rubbing a nigger's head has always brought me luck," Conlan said matter-of-factly. "Now run along," he added and lifted the receiver to his ear. "Secretary Conlan speaking."

"Simon? Surprised to hear you answering the phone yourself, isn't that what you pay your army of slaves for?"

"The key word there is that I pay them. This better be good, Harry, it's the first weekend off I've had in years."

"Are you safe to talk?"

"I'm in my own home."

"This is a matter of national security."

"It's fine, Harry, I'm alone; spit it out."

"I need to know where you stand on the INF Treaty; things are moving fast and we need you on board."

"You know where I stand, Harry, and I made that clear to the president just yesterday."

"For Christ's sake, Simon, Petrenko is giving us exactly what we've wanted for the past seven years. Why are you still fighting it?"

"Exactly what y'all want, Harry. I've fought this the whole way. Why would he just suddenly want to give in to your requests? Giving up all the things he said were non-negotiable before? The man's a crook."

"Come on man, you know his new slogan, Glasnost — Russian Government transparency. The world is changing; you need to keep up and keep on board."

"Glasnost! That's horseshit and you know it. Just like their ailing campaign in Afghanistan, none of it means that the Soviets have given up their long-term aggressive designs. Communism can't be contained or appeased; it needs to be crushed."

"You're becoming a relic, Simon. The chief of staff is clear on this; you need to play for the team.

"Chief of Staff Baker is going to be out the door as quickly as he's just entered it."

There was a long pause.

"I know about the Iran Contra dealing, Simon. And so does the chief of staff."

Simon froze where he stood. He stood in silence for some time.

"Simon, are you there?"

"Yes, I'm here," he replied icily.

"I'm on your side with this, buddy; we've been together on the cabinet since eighty-two…"

"You mean since you hijacked my move for secretary of state."

"Since the president appointed you secretary of defense, not exactly a bad gig. None of this needs to come out. I just need to know that you'll at least stay away from the press and let us get this thing through?"

"No," said Simon and slammed down the phone.

His usually bronzed face had turned red with anger as he grabbed the whole phone set and threw it across the room. So consumed was he by his rage that he didn't notice the red dot hovering over his heart.

***

Precisely eight hundred and fifty metres away, Nikita lay flat against the hard, cracked ground amidst the wispy yellow grass in full camouflage gear, his Dragunov sniper rifle firmly pressed into the crook of his shoulder and his eye pressed to the scope. In his ear he had heard it all. He didn't know who their source was, but a KGB agent had at some point turned someone in the Conlan household. Bugs throughout the ranch had meant Soviet espionage had been able to follow his stance over the past seven years. Listening in to the conversion, Nikita could not imagine it had been a challenge to turn any one of the people in his household.

He sighed. It didn't seem to matter where he was in the world, his race was either seen as a threat or inferior. Never as people.

Nikita dragged his thoughts back to the target. It was amazing, really, how arrogant Conlan was to think that he could speak so publicly and critically of the Soviets and think there would be no consequences. He watched him through the scope, standing there openly in his living room with the French doors thrown open to the world. He really didn't need the bugging equipment; it would be so easy to get into the house and listen in person, especially with the secretary of defense not qualifying for secret service protection.

It would not be hard to kill a man such as this but Nikita was aware of a part of him silently praying for Conlan to reverse his stance. Just let the INF Treaty happen and nobody needs to die. One week into being a full KGB agent, he had enough blood on his hands.

He had shuffled on the ground to get more comfortable and the gun shifted slightly so that the laser sighting suddenly slipped over onto the wall, the tell-tale red dot vivid against the pale blue walls. Mercifully, at that moment Conlan had turned to look out the window, leaving the dot behind him and Nikita had carefully adjusted it to move back onto his chest without passing his eyes — no mean feat from eight hundred and fifty metres away where even the slightest nudge would move it several yards.

After more than a minute he had guided it back onto Conlan and was satisfied he had full control again.

As he heard the conversation rise to a crescendo, he prepared to take the shot, giving a last sweep to his surroundings, the gentle breeze rolling across the plains. He was calm and confident. Top of the academy for sniping, it was one place where he couldn't be attacked or undermined by his fellow students or commanding officers.

Conlan slammed down the phone, and Nikita began to exhale and gently squeeze the trigger as he'd been taught over and over. At eight hundred and fifty metres it was at the very top end of the Dragunov's range, but he knew the Russian weapon intimately and had every faith in the gun to push past its limits, and every faith in his own ability to make such a shot. If he could make the hit at the same range in a Russian winter storm, he could do it on a calm prairie in Texas.

As his finger began coaxing the trigger, out of the corner of his eye his attention was taken by the young woman who had been forced to pick up the beer bottle for the politician earlier, and his trigger finger relaxed slightly. She was loitering in the hallway just through the doorway to the right of Conlan.

'Slaves should be neither seen nor heard.' The words of Conlan still echoed in Nikita's head. The poor girl just had to constantly hide close by, ready to jump but never be seen, valued, thanked or cared for. Nikita felt the familiar rage burning up in his chest and again focused on Conlan, now throwing the phone and storming about in a fury.

Again, he started to squeeze the trigger, this time to make the shot. But again, something stopped him. Something just didn't feel right; it didn't add up. Conlan walked to the French doors and stood looking out across the land. Nikita could even just about see him with his naked eye.

He took his eye off the scope for a moment and reflected on the situation. If he shot Conlan from this range, it would initially be blamed on his servants, which didn't sit right with him at all. But then once the police ran their ballistics tests, they'd quickly realise that he'd been picked off by a sniper, which would immediately make headlines everywhere. If that happened, the Americans would instantly point to the Soviets for carrying out the assassination of the one person opposed to the INF Treaty, and would smell a rat. The whole deal would collapse in on itself.

It just didn't make sense.

What to do, what to do, Allochka. Think.

He held in his hands the decision over world war or a move to world peace, and the whole thing stank.

His instructions had been to take out the target by sniper, with the goal of removing the obstacle to the INF Treaty. But a sniper kill made it clear it was an assassination, and surely that was the last thing Petrenko or Klitchkov would have ordered.

It didn't make sense.

He made his decision. Staying flat to the ground, he began to dismantle the sniper in front of him and packed it away in its case, keeping the scope to hand. He put it to his eye and watched as Conlan took a deep breath and turned back into the house, disappearing from view. Doing a quick scan of the rest of the property, he made sure nobody was watching, then keeping low to the ground, retreated to his car, hidden in a small copse of trees half a mile away, and prayed to God that he was making the right decision.

***

The dusty expanse glowed almost luminous in the moonlight as he stepped out of his car and looked over from the copse of trees to the ranch in the distance. A blanket of stars glittered overhead, and nothing could be heard but the crickets chattering in the night air as the temperature began to drop.

Leaning against a tree he paused, pensive. The vast plain was illuminated by the near-full moon, rendering any chance of a covert approach near impossible. He saw a large bank of cumulus cloud drifting across the moon-drenched night sky, in the direction of the silver orb. It was a long, thin cloud, and there was little breeze. Again, raising the scope to his eye, he scanned the ranch and saw only the glow of lamplight creeping around closed curtains.

He weighed the odds in his mind. It was around a mile to the ranch, and at the pace the cloud was moving he'd have no more than four or five minutes to cover the distance.

There was nothing for it; the ranch was surrounded by flat land and minimal tree cover, rendering any other kind of approach impossible.

The cloud was about thirty seconds away from cloaking the moon. He took a deep breath, and burst out of the trees and began his charge across the hard, cracked ground, hoping that distance would buy him the extra seconds before the land was cast into shadow.

Starting low, he slowly rose into a fully upright position, his back straight and his legs and arms pumping simultaneously. Had he looked back, he would have seen a low trail of dust in his wake, but his eyes were fully focused on his destination as darkness fell.

His pace didn't falter, and his confidence was supreme. Speed and stamina were not areas in which he had failed yet, but then, he thought to himself, he had never raced against a cloud before.

As he hurtled towards the house, with around two hundred metres remaining, he chanced a glance up at the sky and saw that the cloud had twisted and mutated slightly, clumping together and buying him some extra time. But as he fixed his gaze firmly forwards, he saw movement in one of the upstairs rooms as the curtain shifted. He threw himself forwards onto the ground, sliding forwards and skinning the front of his body. He grimaced slightly but kept his head flat as the curtains opened and the face of the girl he had seen earlier looked out.

He lay unmoving, hoping the unavoidable eddies of dust he'd left in his wake weren't visible in the gloom. Dressed in camouflage clothing and black leather gloves he was confident he would be hard to spot, but the clouds of dust might lead her gaze in his direction.

His right cheek flat against the ground, he had nowhere to look other than the sky and saw the cloud moving determinedly. He had only about thirty seconds at the most. Easing his head slowly around to look towards the house, he saw the face still staring out and realised what he would have to do. Moving his hand under his body to his chest, he withdrew his nine-millimetre CZ-75 pistol and began commando-crawling forwards at pace, covering the distance expertly and rapidly. He kept his eyes firmly on the face in the window, as it continued to gaze absently into the distance. At a hundred yards, the moon began to peer through the thinning cloud and he had no choice but to stop and raise his weapon.

The shot was near impossible but he had no choice but to try and make it; his whole mission relied upon nobody knowing he had ever been there. Easier to hide the murder of a black servant than the US secretary of defense. Propping his elbow up, he aimed the pistol in his right hand and wrapped his left hand around his right wrist and the butt of the gun. He exhaled and as he began to pull the trigger, the curtains suddenly closed and the face vanished.

At that moment the entire expanse was again bathed in moonlight and his location clearly visible to anyone who should look. In one swift movement he leapt to his feet and began running powerfully towards the stables at the side of the house, careful to land gently and not alert anyone to his approach. This time he ran with the gun in his hand, ready to take a shot should anyone spot him. He lowered it briefly as he vaulted the low wooden fence, set up, Nikita imagined, to prevent cattle from straying too close to the home.

He felt his muscles bunching as he propelled himself forwards, but although his breathing was heavy as he reached the shadows at the side of the stables, he had scarcely broken a sweat.

He squatted down, and breathed deeply, taking a moment to gather his thoughts and prepare himself for the next move. He could feel a temptation to just walk away, and knew if he paused too long, he would give in to it.

Keeping low and to the shadows, Nikita made his way past the stables, keeping to the numerous blind spots of the security cameras, where he heard a horse whinny gently, but he didn't stop and continued around to the front of the house. Due to the isolation of the ranch, he'd been unable to scope it out as completely as he would normally have preferred, forcing him to use his imagination to gain an entrance. But the isolation, and the rarity of the secretary's presence there, had meant that security was minimal. Behind the stables a path led between a grassy verge and an elaborate flowerbed that had been carefully trimmed to keep back from the path. It felt oddly out of keeping with the barren landscape behind him.

All of his senses felt highly tuned, noticing the slightest buzz from a cricket or throaty croak from a toad. But he didn't hear a sound from indoors. He checked his watch. It was eleven p.m. and from the dark windows, and the occasional glow from a room on the first and second floors, it looked like most of the Conlan ranch had headed to bed. No doubt he had his staff up early to prepare breakfast for him. How hard is it for a man to fix his own breakfast, Nikita thought, as he rounded the front of the huge house?

Huge sloping grass lawns and a curved driveway bordered by ornate hedges and statues led down to a road which snaked away through the desert towards the twinkling lights of Odessa in the distance.

So strange, Nikita thought, to put so much effort into the front of the house, and to leave the back of the house so open to the plains with little more than wooden fences to separate them.

He stepped behind the hedgerow set back from the white stone driveway, separated by a few metres of lawn. Eyes everywhere, he crouched next to a marble bird bath set in an alcove of the hedgerow, noticing as he did that the side hidden from the road was covered in moss and grime. Conlan seemed to only care about what the world could see of him and gave little care to what they couldn't.

He gazed up at the front of the ranch, and realised that the word mansion would fit it better. Three floors up and ten rooms across, it was everything you would expect and more from a billionaire politician. Security cameras were mounted on either side of the building, but pointing inwards at a forty-five-degree angle, to cover the approach to the main entrance. He picked up a medium-sized stone from the ground next to him, and after moving further behind the hedge he tossed the stone onto the lawn in between the two sides of the driveway. He waited to see if the cameras were motion-sensored. Neither moved.

Always make sure. He groped around and found a thin tree branch, about three yards long. Again, he tossed it onto the lawn, this time a little closer to the front door. Again, there was no motion sensor.

Things felt a little too easy to be true, which made Nikita feel very nervous and he doubled his focus. Conlan was without doubt an arrogant man, but you could rarely make secretary of defense if you were stupid.

Casting his eyes over the mansion's façade, he weighed up his entry options. The rear of the home would provide the easier access, but he assumed that the stairs to the first floor were at the front of the house. This would require him to make his way through the entire house just to get upstairs, where he would still have to find a way to identify Conlan's quarters.

On the far side of the house, he could see what looked like a garage bolted onto the side of the building. That would be where he would find his way in.

To avoid the gaze of the cameras, he crept his way back to the rear of the house, and circled round to the other side, approaching the garage from the back. No lights were on anywhere on the ground floor now and he moved with more confidence as he drew towards the low building.

The side of the garage was met by a hedge which would be very difficult to get through without generating a significant amount of noise. Allowing himself to stand up to his full height and briefly stretching his cramped back muscles, he looked at the building. There was a wooden door at the back of the garage which he approached softly, and held his ear against. He could hear nothing, but while leaning his head against the door he noticed he was directly facing a wrought iron drainpipe leading up the side of the house.

He followed the line of the drain upwards and saw that it carried right up to the rim of the roof. He could easily climb it, drop onto the flat roof of the garage and enter through the window of the house visible above it.

He swiftly dismissed the idea, knowing that it would likely create more noise and difficulty than was necessary for the operation, but logged it as an escape route should he need one.

From his pocket he withdrew two long pins and went to work on the garage door, careful to make no sound. In under a minute, he heard the welcome click of the lock.

Without prompt, the old door opened slightly, the wood clearly slightly shrunken and only held in place when forced closed and locked. He was grateful that it made little sound as he pushed it further open, and moved swiftly inside, on high alert, with his weapon drawn and, as always, the safety off.

Once inside, he dropped into a crouched position, his back to the wall and his ear cocked, while he let his eyes adapt to the gloom. He breathed deeply and slowly through his mouth, knowing that nasal breathing was always louder and more recognisable.

As his vision became accustomed to the darkness, he could see four cars in the large garage; inside it looked even bigger than he had anticipated. A battered jeep sat next to a gleaming station wagon, which was itself alongside a Silver Spirit Rolls Royce and cream Porsche 911 Carrera 3.2. Nikita gave a low whistle; these were some serious cars. The jeep, with a thick layer of dust on it, looked like it hadn't been touched in years. Conlan was clearly not a hands-on ranch owner and every inch the wealthy Southern politician, a fact reinforced by the absence of tools, old paint tins or any of the other clutter you would normally expect to find in a farm garage. The place was pristine. Aside from the muddy old jeep, the only things to suggest he was in rural America were the ornate shotguns on racks on the wall, over a long, low apothecary cabinet. Nikita crossed to it and checked the drawers, finding old boxes of shotgun cartridges in one of them. He closed the drawer gently, and again noted their location should he need them.

He turned now to the door on the right of the garage, connecting it to the rest of the house — a far newer door than the others. He ran his fingers gently around the edge, checking for sensors and ready to make his escape if an alarm was triggered. He paused. Nothing happened.

The door was made of a heavy wood — Nikita guessed oak — and fitted the frame perfectly, with two locks.

He peered at them and put his ear to it, listening for any sound. He was grateful, but surprised, not to have not seen or heard any dogs on the ranch. But then Secretary Conlan seemed to have little interest in having a ranch in anything other than name.

Going to work on the first lock, Nikita again made quick work of it, feeling the tell-tale turn of the bolt, but the second lock proved to be more stubborn. No hint of frustration showed on his face, his training having kept him calm and patient through far more than a difficult door lock.

Eventually it began to turn, and his fingers strained to hold and turn the heavy latch, which clicked over with a sound that felt loud in the night-time silence of the ranch.

He pushed down the handle, which squeaked painfully before the door opened. The handle again complained noisily as it was eased back into position. Gun first, Nikita entered what he could immediately see was the kitchen — a large room with an island in the middle, and polished wooden surfaces surrounding.

Once he had ensured the room was clear, he moved swiftly through it, clear where he needed to get to. He left the kitchen and entered the adjoining dining room, and saw what he was looking for in the corner. The drinks cabinet. It was a huge globe of the world that, when smoothly swivelled round, retracted and revealed the array of beverages within. Taking in the offerings, his eyes lingered on the familiar vodka, but moved past it to an unopened bottle of amber liquid. Picking it up in his black leather-clad hands, he examined the label. *Very Old Fitzgerald, for connoisseurs of fine bourbon, bottled in 1958.*

"Perfect," he mouthed to himself, as he eased the lid off. It smelt potent. He paused briefly, then raised it to his mouth, and careful to not touch his mouth to the bottle, poured it directly in.

It hit his tongue like sugar, the back of his throat like fire and settled in his stomach like hot coals, burning through his entire body. This was nothing like the potato vodka he'd had thrust upon him in the USSR. This was good.

He raised the bottle again for another slug, but paused, and then lowered the bottle. What was he doing? This was a live operation and this bourbon had other, more important uses. He eased the cork back into place.

He left the dining room by a different exit, bourbon in one hand and raised gun in the other and moved out into the entrance hall. He could see the corridor leading to the rear of the house which he'd seen through his scope earlier, but he knew what he was looking for wasn't back there. Still not a sound to be heard, he moved towards the wide staircase leading upstairs from the hall. Keeping to the edges to avoid creaking floorboards, he put much of his weight on his hands. He pushed down heavily on the handrail, to ensure minimal pressure was put on the old wooden stairs hidden beneath the deep, plush, cream carpet.

At the top of the staircase, he reached a T-junction as the landing corridor ran down to the left and down to the right. From here he was entering the realms of guesswork, and his brain was working furiously to calculate just how high the chance of the operation failing was, and the deadly action he would have to take if any of the house staff intervened.

He had no choice. To keep his family safe, he could not afford to fail on a mission of such gravitas.

Remembering the woman in the window earlier, he made an educated guess that Conlan would room the staff in a different part of the house to him and his family, and opted to go right, the opposite way from the woman's room and back in the direction of the garage.

The corridor was pitch black, but looking up and down it he could see a glow filtering through from under doors of some rooms.

Walking down to the right, he again kept close to the walls to avoid creaking floorboards. Putting his ear to each door as he passed, he was desperately looking for any sound or signal that the room could be the one housing the secretary. He couldn't afford to pick the wrong one, but the door to every room stood white and plain, with no indication at all.

He passed one door that was slightly ajar, but with no light shining from it. He nudged it open soundlessly and saw that it was a bathroom. He stepped inside and looked around swiftly, his eyes resting on the medicine cabinet above the sink. Opening it, he cast his eyes over the array of bandages, paracetamols, sleeping pills and other basic medical paraphernalia. He stuffed some of the pills into his pockets and moved back into the hallway.

He reached the room at the end of the corridor and again put his ear to the door. The glow from this one was different, giving a bluish flicker from a television rather than from lamplight. Pressing his ear gently to the door, he could hear the sounds coming from the television and concentrated to work out the nature of the programme.

It didn't take long to work it out, with the sounds of the CNN newsreaders describing the tensions surrounding the INF Treaty and President Callahan's determination to see it through.

Bingo. Nikita reached into his pocket and pulled out a silencer, which he screwed into the CZ-75. If all went to plan, nobody would get shot tonight.

He stuffed the upturned neck of the *Very Old Fitzgerald* into his belt and, with the gun held firmly in his right hand, reached down, turned the handle and threw open the door into the bedroom of the US secretary of defense.

CHAPTER 14

Conlan was lying on the bed half clothed. Nikita was reminded strongly of Zurga, which already felt like a lifetime ago. But not long enough to forget, he thought, and felt a momentary urge to take another slug of the bourbon.

The room reeked of wealth and luxury. The satin sheets shone on the bed, illuminated by the light of the huge television screen facing it on the wall, next to the door through which Nikita had just entered.

With no lights on other than the TV, Conlan was cast in a flickering blue light, but unlike Zurga, he was very much alert and awake.

"What the — who the hell are you?" he exclaimed before seeing the gun in Nikita's hand and falling silent. His eyes widened, and he pushed himself up against the headboard, fear showing in every part of his body.

Nikita sighed. This was going to be such a tedious way of killing someone. He grabbed a chair from a dresser under the television, dragged it near to the bed and sat down.

"Drink?" he said, unveiling the Old Fitzgerald and pulling out the cork with his teeth, which he spat on the ground and handed over the bottle.

Conlan took it but said nothing.

"Look, Secretary, just tell me you're not going to run away or anything so I can lower this weapon. Nobody likes having a gun pointed at them, and to be perfectly honest I don't much like pointing it."

Conlan nodded, and relaxed just a fraction as Nikita put the gun in its holster.

"Who are you?" Conlan asked again. He had a sheen of sweat on his head, but otherwise had recovered his composure remarkably well.

"I can see why you rose to become secretary of defense. Look how quickly you've adapted to having a man with a gun in your bedroom. Did you serve?"

"I imagine you already know that," he replied curtly.

"Very sharp. I know your résumé says you served in Korea, but I'd be interested to hear from you the ins and outs of that experience. Please, take a drink of that lovely bourbon."

Conlan looked sceptical.

"I give you my word I haven't tampered with it, other than to give it a taste. Can you believe I had never before tasted bourbon?"

"You picked a good one for your first taste. It might ruin any others for you. Are you here to kill me?"

"That's entirely up to you. But I certainly won't warm to you if you don't drink with me."

"Either way, I guess I'll need a drink then," said Conlan and took a slug of the amber liquid and closed his eyes in pleasure. "I've had this bottle for years."

"I bet you never imagined sharing it with someone from the slave race?" said Nikita, looking him in the eye.

"I think you have me misunderstood; I'm a friend of black people."

"Is that right, Secretary? Your house of slaves doesn't stack up in your favour on that front."

"I pay every one of them!"

Nikita laughed. "It seems more like it's them that pays, but that's not why I'm here."

"Why are you here?"

"All good things come to those who wait, Secretary. You didn't get to where you are by being an impatient man."

"Is your plan to irritate me to death?" Conlan said as he took another swig of whiskey.

Nikita noticed him attempt to ease himself over towards the other side of the bed while trying to appear to just shuffle uncomfortably about. He decided not to comment on it just yet, allowing the politician to continue drinking, but keeping a close eye on his movements. This was the Deep South; chances were there was a handgun in that bedside cabinet.

"I must say, Secretary, despite your military history, you seem oddly calm at my appearance in your room."

"It doesn't take a goddam genius to know that the Russkis would be sending someone after me. I never expected someone…"

"Someone like me, you mean?"

Conlan grunted and took another drink from the bottle.

Nikita sat back slightly, beginning to have grave doubts about his already flimsy plan. This was taking too long.

Conlan slumped slightly in bed, the alcohol clearly beginning to affect him. Looking at the bottle, Nikita could see that nearly half was gone. People drink quickly when they're nervous, Nikita noticed, mentally taking a note to never drink on the job again. Who knew how dulled his senses had been from his swig of the whiskey earlier?

Conlan pushed himself up against the headboard again. Nikita again blamed it on the effect of the whiskey. It was to his peril.

Quick as a flash, Conlan whipped a gun out from beneath the pillow where his hand had slipped while pushing himself up, and pointed it at Nikita.

"No one in their right mind would want to remember the horrors of the Korean War, but they let us keep our handguns. Most of the fellas threw theirs away, or packed them away in boxes to hand down as heirlooms to their kids, because they wanted to forget about it. But here's the thing about the Korean War. I loved it. I loved shooting commies, and I sleep with this beauty every night just hoping I'll get another chance to put it to use. But shooting a black commie? And doing it in self-defence for breaking and entering into my own home, well sweet Jesus, that really is the Texan dream."

"Wait—" started Nikita but got no further as the secretary fired the pistol.

A flash at the end of the muzzle was all he saw, and then white-hot pain coursed through his body.

***

KLYUCHEVKSAYA SOPKA VOLCANO, KAMCHATKA PENINSULA, EASTERN USSR, 1984

The game trail led up the side of a lush green hill in the shadow of the volcano, affectionately known as Klyuchevskoi by the people of this remote peninsula in the far-flung corner of the Soviet empire, closer to

Tokyo than Moscow. For five days Nikita had trekked inland from his drop site near Ust-Kamchatsk, bordering the Kamchatka River and the Pacific Ocean, to his final location on the far side of Klyuchevskoi, the highest active volcano in Eurasia.

Never had he seen so many different landscapes in one journey, all unbelievable in their beauty, and never had he been so challenged, or exhausted. Initially he tried to keep to the salmon-rich Kamchatka River. He had learned quickly how to fish and had eaten well. But he had equally quickly come face to face with the reality of an area that had the highest density of brown bears in the world, none of whom took kindly to competing with him for the fish. He had only narrowly avoided a mauling, and been forced to turn inland and cross the undulating land towards his destination. Throughout the journey, the conical volcano had loomed in the distance, standing ominously above the surrounding land and he had carried with him the whole time a sense of foreboding.

As he climbed higher up the track, the grass began to thin and be replaced by snow, with the temperature suddenly dropping noticeably. As he reached the summit of the hill, he looked down over the snow-dusted valley. Across the way saw a clearing in the dense evergreen trees, with an isolated wooden hut which marked his destination. He sighed with relief, and not for the first time tried to suppress the hunger in his belly. Since leaving the river four days ago the unforgiving land had provided little in the way of nourishment. Yesterday he had managed to kill a hare with the rifle, but there had been little in the way of meat on the creature once skinned and roasted over a small fire. With no cooking utensils he had been forced to fashion a spit from an old branch he had found, and it had snapped and burned through the meat, leaving much of it inedible and full of splinters.

He knelt, swung his rifle down and placed it on the ground before shrugging off his rucksack. He opened it to pull out his poncho to keep him warm from the chill that was getting into his bones. As he did, he thought he heard a sound that didn't belong to any of the creatures native to the area. He froze, his ears pricked for the slightest follow-up sound. Weighing it up between rifle and pistol, he eased the Makarov from his holster and held it low in front of him, remaining in a squat.

Had he imagined it? Not a sound could be heard other than the distant rumblings of the volcano which he had felt in his feet for the last fifty miles, and the chirruping of birds.

After two minutes he released a breath. He must have imagined it, but remained on high alert. He closed his bag, deciding against the poncho in case he needed the easier movement, and slung his rifle over his shoulder, ensuring it was easy to swing forward and fire should he need to.

As he stood, he saw a flash and heard the bang, and felt himself thrown backwards onto the track.

Momentarily stunned and unaware of what had happened, he leapt to his feet before his leg immediately gave way beneath him and he saw the blood flowing freely from his thigh. Then the pain caught up with him. Somewhere between furnace hot and ice cold, he tried to push it from his mind and be alert for his attacker.

He reached for his Makarov PM which he had dropped in the attack and lay on his back with the gun raised and pointed at the place in the trees some twenty yards away from where the flash had come. His eyes were screwed up and watering furiously from the pain, and he wiped the tears away with a grubby hand to see clearer but there was no sign of anyone. Were it not for the pool of blood forming around his leg, he could have nearly convinced himself he had imagined it.

After several minutes and no sign of his attacker, he cautiously turned his attentions to his wound. Using his hunting knife, he tore open his trousers around the hole that the bullet had created, all the while throwing frequent glances around him. It was hard to see anything with so much blood. He reached into his bag again and tore off a strip of cloth from the poncho, and poured some water on it from his canteen. He wiped gently at the wound and could not help but let out a yell of agony as he touched upon the sensitive bullet wound. Biting his lip he looked up again at the trees but again saw nothing.

Despite the wiping at his leg, the blood continued to flow and he remained unclear as to the severity of his injuries. He tore off another strip of poncho, this one much longer, and tied it around his upper thigh to act as a tourniquet and stem the bleeding. Then he pulled from his pack the military issue small bottle of Russian vodka, unopened. He stuffed some of his poncho into his mouth and unscrewed the bottle. Taking a deep breath, he poured the spirit onto the wound and bit down hard on the mouthful of poncho, screaming soundlessly as the searing liquid burned into the wound and cleared it of any bacteria. Much of the blood cleared and he saw that it was a deep graze rather than a full bullet entry and he breathed a small sigh of relief.

The pain was no less, but he knew now that no arteries were in danger. Now he had to focus on making it to the pick-up point on the other side of the valley. He dragged himself to the side of the path and searched around with his eyes for a hefty stick to use as a staff. The only one he could find that would support him was slightly too small. It would have to do. Using the stick and the bare trunk of an evergreen he pulled himself upright and grimaced at the pain. He made his way slowly over to the area where the shooter had been, keeping one hand on his staff and one on his Makarov. He saw a glint on the ground and cautiously made his way over to it, and saw that it was a gun lying discarded on the forest floor. He picked it up and inspected it. A Colt 1911, an all-American weapon that had no place being in the forests of the Kamchatka Peninsula. But then, neither did an illegal Nigerian immigrant, thought a mocking voice in his head.

His teeth began to chatter from the shock racing through his body as he hopped back to his pack. To lighten his load for the next few miles he quickly discarded anything he would not need to carry and began the journey that would feel like a marathon.

Along the way he stayed alert and thought intensely about his attacker. Either someone thought they hit him with a fatal shot or they had only intended to injure him, not kill. It had to be KGB, but who? And how did they get an American weapon out here? If it was an officer they would surely never have missed, but a fellow trainee might have been trying to kill him and got spooked. Whoever it was, they were still out there.

Dark thoughts began to consume him as his head got lighter and began to spin. He looked down at his leg, bare below the tourniquet at his groin with blood dripping down. The sun was beginning to go down and he knew that the wolves that roamed this part of Russia would begin to circle in on him. Already the howls he had consistently heard in the distance now sounded closer.

The lower the sun got, the closer the howls and yelps began to sound and he clenched his gun tightly. He was glad now that he had opted to keep his rifle with him, despite the awkwardness of it swinging across his back while he walked with the stick.

It was pitch black by the time he reached the clearing; his breathing was harsh and rasping and his leg was numb. It looked unhealthily pallid in the moonlight. He stumbled unsteadily over to the hut, and after banging on the door, collapsed to the ground, his fingers grasping handfuls of the cold green grass as he breathed in the smell of the hard earth.

The door opened and light flooded out over him. He heard a man laugh and then felt himself being roughly dragged inside and fought to keep the darkness from overtaking his vision.

He was thrown onto a canvas camp bed but was only semi-conscious. Suddenly, ice cold liquid was poured onto the wound and his eyes burst open. He roared and saw Colonel Klitchkov pouring vodka onto what he could now clearly see was a gash that had taken a deep groove of flesh away from his powerful thigh.

"Lie still, it needs to be cleaned."

"It hurts, Colonel."

Klitchkov grabbed Nikita by the collar and pulled him up, rage in his eyes.

"Listen boy, to be KGB is to conquer pain. Today you failed. You missed your helicopter; a flesh wound is no excuse to be late. You are weak. I will not accept another failure; you would do well to remember your family's safety is in your hands."

Nikita said nothing but turned on his side and lifted his leg. He bit down so hard that he drew blood from his lip as Klitchkov worked on fixing the gash, and salty tears poured down his adolescent face.

Through the tears, he saw on the floor just behind Klitchkov an unfamiliar-looking bullet which had fallen down from a half open, unmarked ammunition box on a table by the wall. He reached for it under the guise of reaching out in pain and grasped it tightly in his hand.

Later as he lay back on the bed in the darkness, he inspected the bullet in the moonlight streaming through the window behind him. Along the side it said .45 ACP. A bullet made for the Colt 1911 pistol. He looked over to Klitchkov's sleeping form, his body rising and falling gently, and hatred burned through Nikita such as he had never known. He pocketed the bullet. One day he would have his revenge.

***

Nikita snapped back to the present, but the memories continued to course through him as he knelt on the floor of the secretary's bedroom, breathing deeply as he worked to conquer the pain.

"Down on the floor, you Russki scum," said the voice of Conlan above him. He laughed loudly. "I've not felt this alive in years. I can't believe they sent such a young amateur, to not even guess I'd have a gun under my pillow."

Nikita inwardly berated himself for his lapse and looked up at the man standing above him laughing, a gun pointed at him and he remembered the sound of Klitchkov's laughter as he pulled him into that Kamtchatkan hut, remembered the bullet on the floor and remembered the Colt, just the same as the one above him.

He closed his eyes and focused. The pain was in his shoulder but he had endured worse. He could endure more.

There was a knock on the door and a voice said, "Sir, is everything OK, sir? I thought I heard a gunshot or some such."

"Everything is fine; leave me alone, Amancia."

"Yes, sir, sorry to bother you, sir."

Looking back to Nikita he said, "See. Why couldn't you have just known your rightful place in the world like Amancia? Bottom feeders, not spies."

"OK, OK, I'll do whatever you ask, just stop talking," Nikita said, putting a hand to his injured shoulder, feeling the bullet grind against the bone.

"You goddam Russkis are all the same, spineless to the core. Now lie down, I won't ask again," he said and took another swig from the bottle of whiskey, which was now two thirds empty, before slamming it down on his bedside table.

Nikita nodded, and hand on his left shoulder, moved sideways to ease himself onto his right shoulder then onto his back. Suddenly he fell sideways and swept his leg up, kicking the gun from Conlan's grasp and rolling backwards and propelling himself back onto his feet. His shoulder protested loudly and he physically felt a pump of blood splurge from his shoulder, as a dark stain worked its way across his black top.

Conlan threw himself forwards to grab the gun from the floor, displaying impressive athleticism for a man in his seventies, but he was no match for a KGB agent honed to optimum physicality, even one with a bullet wedged in his shoulder. Nikita stood on the old man's hands as he stretched for the gun. With his good arm, he reached down and picked up the gun and aimed it back at its owner.

"You see, Secretary, I'd really wanted to do this the easy way, but you've just made life a lot harder for yourself." He awkwardly shoved the politician and threw him back onto the bed with his working arm, and grunted heavily at the exertion. "How will it feel, I wonder, to be killed by someone you think so far beneath you?"

"I'll die a patriot."

"You'll die a racist, pathetic, old man."

Conlan slumped and suddenly looked every inch the old man as he lay back, jowls around his neck engorging his face. Just another rich, white landowner living off his power. Never had Nikita wanted to shoot someone so much, but he knew he couldn't. Out of his pocket he pulled a tub of sleeping pills that he had swiped from the bathroom along the corridor.

"Now, how about you wash a few of these down with that lovely bourbon?"

Conlan looked up at him pleadingly. "Please, please, I'll do whatever you say." He moved his hand towards his pocket and Nikita took aim again, but Conlan pulled out his wallet. "I have money, much more than this and you can have it all."

"You goddam politicians are all the same, spineless to the core," snarled Nikita, mimicking the secretary's southern drawl. "I'm afraid you've found yourself up against someone who can't be bullied, bought or overwhelmed by power. Now, either you take the sleeping pills, or I make you. Your choice."

"You planning to let me sleep it off?"

"You could say that."

Conlan's hands shook as he took two pills and put them in his mouth, and washed them down with the bourbon.

"I think you can manage rather more than two; it's been a long day and you'll want to make sure you sleep well, Secretary."

Tears now formed in the old man's eyes as he took two more pills and washed it down with the last of the alcohol.

"Any regrets?" asked Nikita.

"Not having a better aim," he replied, without an ounce of humour as he turned his face to the barrel of the gun. "I'm guessing the sleeping pills weren't to soften the blow of a bullet, so what's the plan? Four pills won't kill me."

"True, but enough to find them in your system, enough that you won't throw up everywhere."

"So this is all what, part of the grand Soviet plan?"

"This isn't the movies, Secretary; I'm not going to reveal the whole dastardly plan," said Nikita, and then he pounced.

Using his good arm, he pushed Conlan down on the chest and grabbed a pillow with the other one and pulled it over the secretary's face, before putting his whole weight on it. He could see droplets of blood running down his arm onto his leather clad hands and his face was scrunched tight in the agony of the pressure on his shoulder. He wanted to keep the blood from getting onto the pillow but it was unavoidable. Better the pillow than the bedspread.

Conlan's yells were muffled and his legs kicked but in his drunken state he was uncoordinated and lacked the strength to overcome the young KGB agent. Nikita felt as if he were looking down on himself committing the murder and felt a chill in his core. Then he thought of the stable boy, of the house staff, of the condescending disdain with which Conlan had looked at him and put aside his reservations. He pushed down with renewed vigour.

Nikita knew the slightest reduction in downward pressure would allow a pocket of air to get in, buying Conlan another minute or two.

Conlan was a military veteran and a rancher who had kept himself in good condition, and he didn't give up without a fight.

It took almost four minutes for him to die.

Nikita leant back and internalised a yell of agony as he again felt the still-hot metal of the bullet grinding and grating against his shoulder joint. He withdrew the pillow and checked Conlan's pulse. The United States secretary of defense and billionaire oil tycoon was dead, his eyes wide open in a look that was far from peaceful.

The pillow was soaked in blood, and some had gone onto the bedside table also, but mercifully none had gone onto the bed covers or Conlan himself. Nikita used the pillow to wipe the small pool of blood on the table and carried it to the en suite bathroom through a door just behind him.

Over the sink was a large wall mirror and he was shocked as he looked at himself. He looked pale and gaunt, his eyes hangdog and deadened. The face of a forty-year-old on the body of a twenty-one-year-old. He put the pillow in the sink and pulled his shirt down to reveal the wound in his shoulder. It was a small bullet hole leaking dark red blood. He ripped off a clean strip of the pillowcase, ran it under some water and held it to the wound. It hurt like hell but would do some sort of job temporarily. Ripping another strip of cloth, he wrapped it around his shoulder and under his arm to hold it in place. Enough to not drop blood through the house on his escape. There must be no sign he was ever here.

He pulled his t-shirt back over the wound, wiped down his gloves thoroughly, returned to the bedroom and inspected the dead politician.

His feet were lying over the side of the bed so he picked them up and swivelled him around to lie on the bed properly, before gently closing his eyelids. He checked him over quickly for any sign of a struggle and seeing none, placed the bottle of *Very Old Fitzgerald* next to one of his hands. Then he prized open the dead man's mouth and pushed his tongue back as far as he could to cover the throat.

He stepped back and surveyed his work, before inspecting the rest of the room. He emptied a dribble of the whiskey onto the bedside table and again wiped it down before returning the bottle to Conlan's side. He returned to grab the pillow, wiped down the sink and made his way to the door. He opened it a crack, holding the gun to the pillow and made his way down the darkened corridor and down the stairs.

He returned to the dining room and grabbed a bottle of whiskey, an *Old Forester*. Nikita didn't have to be an expert to know this was not of an Old Fitzgerald vintage.

He went back through the kitchen and out through the garage, thankful that he would not have to escape down the drainpipe.

The blood was beginning to pump harder out of the hole in his shoulder as his heart beat double time to keep his blood pressure up. He made his way across the prairie towards his car, much slower than his earlier sprinted approach had been. His legs felt weak and he could taste bile, sour and burning at the back of his throat, whether from blood loss or from his latest assassination, he was not sure. His mind was clear of everything other than making it back to his car as quickly as possible. He put his hand under his shirt and tenderly felt the hole where the bullet had entered. It was slick with blood, which was spilling out in pumps. Grimacing, he put a finger gently into the hole to try and plug the stem of blood.

Clouds now covered the sky like inky silhouettes and there was little risk of moonlight revealing his presence. It was nearly half an hour later that he arrived back at the copse of trees where his rental car was hidden.

He clambered behind the wheel and sped off across the prairie due south. The interstate lay some three miles away which would allow him to enter Odessa from the south. Time he could ill afford to waste, but it was essential to him to maintain what the KGB always referred to as 'plausible deniability'. As Nikita reached Interstate 20, he saw a sign pointing south to Toyah and his eyes flashed. The town was famous for only one thing — the brutal lynching of J. I. Pitts. The whole town had turned out, late at night, to drag Pitts from his bed through the streets as he begged for his life, before stringing him up to the sound of cheers. All for the crime of being in love with a white woman.

The pain brought Nikita back to the present and he veered onto the interstate, ploughing in the opposite direction to Toyah. As he approached the edge of Odessa, the pain became unbearable. He pulled over to the side of the road and leant his head on the steering wheel, breathing deeply, drenched with sweat.

"Focus, Nikita," he said to himself loudly, again inhaling deeply and exhaling slowly. He felt his heart rate slow slightly and the pumping of blood sensation in his shoulder ease just slightly. He looked around him, and saw that he was on what could only just be described as a high street, in a downtrodden area on the outskirts of Odessa. In the dark night the street was deserted but he could see a flickering neon sign about fifty yards away.

He quickly checked himself in the rear-view mirror, and using some tissues from the glovebox, wiped away any visible blood as best he could. He would have to trust to darkness to disguise the rest of it. He knew he needed to call in the completed mission to his superiors, who would be anxiously waiting, but he had to make sure he survived first.

With a groan, he climbed out of the car and made his way towards the bar, reminding himself that he was Nathan from Daytona Beach, and adjusted his gait to a relaxed swagger, trying to block the pain from his mind.

As he approached the bar, he saw the buzzing sign saying Paddy's Irish Bar, with a green shamrock flickering next to it. He pushed open the door and entered the gloom beyond.

The room was long and narrow, with a bar stretching out on his right with stools beside it and tables beyond. It looked like St Patrick had thrown up, with green paint splashed over every door, and pictures of Guinness, bric-a-brac and hurling sticks inauthentically plastered over the walls. Nikita doubted an Irishman had ever set foot on the premises, and as he looked around the bar he wondered if a black man had ever entered either.

Conversation had stopped as he entered, as a sea of white faces all turned to look at him with a mixture of rage and disbelief plastered across their faces.

He walked cautiously towards the bar and conversation seemed to gradually begin again. As he reached the bar, the bartender walked over.

"You lost, boy?" he asked gruffly, a bear of a man with a greying beard and tattoos on his forearms.

"No sir, I'm here to drink."

"Look around you, boy, you're on the wrong side of Odessa," said the barman again in a slow Texan drawl.

Nikita glanced around, aware of a fat man with a thick black beard sitting on a stool just to his right, glaring coldly at him, a cigarette hanging loosely from his lower lip. Further up the bar another man, who looked similar but slightly younger, with a grey-flecked red beard and squinty eyes, bared a toothless grin at him.

"I can see you serve whiskey so I can guarantee I am in the right place," replied Nikita, trying not to grimace at the icy agony now coursing through his shoulder as he signalled to the line of bourbons on the wall behind the bartender.

"I don't want no trouble here, son," the barman said.

"Unless that's the name of a whiskey, I don't want none either."

The barman grunted and turned to pick up a bottle of *Wild Turkey*. He slammed down a grimy glass on the bar and poured Nikita a whiskey, which he drank whole immediately, feeling the burn run through his body and numb his senses.

The barman turned away, but Nikita grabbed his arm and said, "Leave the bottle."

The barman looked down at his hand with disgust, pulled his arm away and held the bottle away from him.

Nikita cocked his head sideways, "How about the bottle to go?"

The barman grunted again and relaxed slightly, slamming the bottle down and taking the twenty dollars Nikita held out to him.

"Thank you kindly, it's been a pleasure visiting the asshole of Ireland," Nikita said. He pushed himself up, a slight groan escaping from his lips but fully aware of the rage in the barman's eyes, and the continued glare of the man sat at the bar, his face now mostly lost in a cloud of reeking smoke.

Nikita walked from the bar unconcerned; a room full of white people hating him was nothing new. He knew going to a bar had been reckless, but he needed to clean the wound and a bar was his only option at this time of night.

He swaggered out but as soon as the door closed behind him, he fell to one knee, the pain coursing through his veins. He felt dizzy and lightheaded from the blood loss. He vomited straight onto the sidewalk outside the bar.

He pushed himself up, wiped his mouth roughly, and started to stagger towards the car, but spotting an alleyway half shrouded in darkness, the other half luminous in the moonlight, to his left, he veered down it and allowed himself to fall to the ground. He produced his smaller knife from its black sheath on his calf and ripped open his shirt. He took another swig of the whiskey and then poured some over the bullet wound, letting out a low cry as the alcohol seared the wound.

He glanced skywards briefly, looking to the gods he was not sure he believed in, and plunged the knife into the hole.

Initially he felt the point of the blade push the bullet hard against the bone and stuffed a piece of his shirt into his mouth to stop himself screaming. Moving the knife around he managed to get underneath the bullet and began to ease it out, feeling the razor-sharp knife slicing into the skin and sinew, widening the wound. He slowly eased the blade out, bringing with it the bullet, which mercifully had stayed whole and not fragmented.

He spat on the ground in pain. How can something so small cause so much pain, he thought through the throbbing.

Returning to inspect the wound, he saw that it looked like the profile of an aeroplane, with the hole in the middle and thin slits either side from the knife cut. It needed stitching but he had no needle or thread, or any way of getting any until the morning. He knew what he had to do.

He again poured whiskey on the wound before wiping clean the knife and pulling from his inside pocket a lighter which he held underneath the blade of the knife until it glowed red hot.

He looked again to the skies. "Lord, if you're there, please give me strength." He thrust the flat of the knife against the wound.

Pain such as he had never felt overtook him. White hot, searing agony burned through him. He struggled to hold onto consciousness, but held the knife in place as long as he could before releasing and falling back to the ground, tears of pain falling down his cheek as the knife clattered over to the wall.

He was dimly aware of a shadow falling over him as he lay back, something blocking the moonlight which had been bathing the alleyway.

He didn't have to look up to know what was coming. Training with the KGB instilled a sixth sense in recruits, not through the training itself but through some other means that Nikita was unclear about, but not a single recruit came through without knowing exactly when danger loomed.

He ran the calculations quickly in his head and cursed that he had let his knife fall away. The barman, while insulted, would not leave the bar behind, but Black Beard and Red Beard would allow themselves to be separated from their Budweisers for a couple of minutes to beat down a black man who insulted their favourite watering hole. He doubted they would be the only ones wanting to get involved; this was west Texas after all. He reckoned four in total, but kept his eyes half closed and his hand clutching the Wild Turkey as he weighed his options and waited to decide his move.

The men approached quietly, not speaking, but not silent enough that Nikita couldn't identify the shuffling footsteps and see that he was correct in there being four.

His body almost quivered with the adrenaline coursing through it, numbing any pain from the burnt flesh at his shoulder, for which he was grateful.

The shuffling stopped.

"Looks like this crow can't handle his whiskey," said one of the voices, to a chorus of gruff laughs, "Let's give him a hangover he won't forget."

A single set of footsteps rapidly approached Nikita and he heard the rush of air as the man aimed a kick at his stomach.

Nikita lifted his legs and swung his body round, before leaping onto his feet. He swivelled and reverse kicked the man hard in his soft stomach, his foot sinking into the fat belly, propelling him backwards into the wall.

Nikita stood above him. He took up the Sambo fighting stance, the brutal martial art created and honed by the KGB. Entering his pose, he found a place of mindfulness and heightened awareness. He realised he could feel something other than adrenaline racing through his veins. Red hot rage.

The incorrect orders, the killing, the bullet wound and the constant, never-ending racism. He battled to control it, the words of Denisov echoing around his head — "mastering emotion is his biggest obstacle."

Then he remembered those two weeks in the cold box, and felt the ice return to his veins.

The three men in front of him looked nervous as their leader groaned and pushed himself up. The fat man bared his teeth and spat blood onto the ground at the feet of Nikita.

"You're gonna pay all sorts of hell for that, you black piece of shit," he spat, hatred in his eyes. Nikita was looking beyond him to the other three, one of whom looked in better shape than the rest, with a jarhead haircut, trimmed beard and a military bearing.

"Is it a prerequisite of being a racist American that you have to have beards?" said Nikita with a grin. He lowered his fists and took a swig of his whiskey. Running it around his mouth before swallowing, he took a moment to savour the cool drink. This was not a place for Sambo; nothing must connect him or the Soviet Union to the murder of the secretary. This was a place for street rules.

He offered the bottle to Black Beard.

"You mustn't be from around here, boy. Your kind don't come to this side of town, and we don't share a drink with slaves. It's been too long since we hung one of y'all; I think it's high time we had another, don't you, fellas?" he said, turning to his friends. Nikita took his opportunity, and swung forwards with the bottle, smashing it into the temple of the man, who crumpled to the ground.

Rather than being unnerved, the other three ran forwards, but the narrowness of the alleyway meant that one had to stand back while the other two ran forwards. Jarhead might cause him some problems, but the other was fat and soft, with beer dripping in his thick, pale brown beard.

***

KAMENKA, USSR, 1975

The pre-dawn pallor was beginning to rise above the forest next to the shack that Gabriel Allochka called home as he trudged wearily towards it.

It had been a long night of street sweeping, the only work the small town of Kamenka ever afforded him, and that was only sporadic.

Dirt was caked over his hands and cheeks from the labour, and he knelt next to an old plastic bucket filled with water, methodically cleaning away the grime. As the dirt cleared from his skin, the callouses and scars became visible across his large hands.

His eyes were stung as the tip of the sun broached the top of the forest, bathing everything in a stunning golden-green glow. He shielded them, grimaced and turned back to the shack.

He eased open the door, careful not to wake anyone, but to no avail. The small figure of his nine-year-old son Nikita shouted, "Father's home!" He then charged towards Gabriel and wrapped his arms around his waist. Gabriel could not help but chuckle.

On the makeshift bed on the floor lay Sophie Allochka and their toddler Milena, who was sound asleep. Sophie smiled sleepily up at her husband. "Welcome home, dear."

Gabriel picked up Nikita in one arm and leant down to kiss his wife. Nikita screamed with delight as he was turned upside down in the process. Incredibly, Milena dozed on through it all.

"How was work?" Sophie asked softly, as she stood and placed the blankets over Milena with great care.

Gabriel rubbed his stinging eyes. "Not good — they came at me again," he said enigmatically.

Sophie's eyes widened with fear. "Are you OK? Did they hurt you?"

"I was able to keep them at bay once more." He looked down at his son, who was gazing up at him with big brown eyes full of adoration and concern.

"Who hurt you, Papa?"

Gabriel sat down heavily in the room's only chair. "I suppose it is time we had a talk, Niki," he said with a sigh, and picked the boy up and placed him on his knee. "Son, out there in the world you will find that many of the white people do not like us."

"Why not?"

"Because they are afraid of what is different. They have been poisoned by hate. But we must never lower ourselves to their level. We can live, with God's grace, free of hate and let them be the ones held back by fear. Whatever they take, they can never take the freedom in our minds."

"I don't understand, Father," said Nikita in a small voice.

"Ok, let me put it this way. When you go out there into Russia, you are going to get beaten up. The white boys are going to come at you in a group — for some reason they always come in a group — and they are going to try and hurt you. Sometimes you will get hurt."

"Gabriel, what are you saying? You're scaring him," Sophie said sharply, and tried to lift Nikita from her husband's knee.

Gabriel held Niki down. "No Sophie, it is important for him to hear this. Niki, just because they want to hurt you, does not mean you have to let them! If they come at you, you pick out the leader, usually the biggest one, and while you are getting beaten up, you beat the leader up. If you do that, they will leave you alone. They fear us, but never ever fear them. By doing that, you can earn their respect. I want a better life for you than the one I have given us."

***

Gabriel's words echoed through Nikita's mind as he readied himself in the Texas alleyway. The leader was already down, but Jarhead represented the biggest threat. A plan was already in his head — to swing the fat man round and drive him into Jarhead, incapacitating them both.

But then came a horrible realisation.

The only sure way to avoid identifying himself with any possible connection to Secretary Conlan's murder was to take the beating.

A group of white men beaten unconscious by one black man was sure to draw attention and risk the rest of his mission in the US.

He groaned inwardly. This was not going to be fun.

He made a show of attempting to throw what felt like a painfully slow punch at Jarhead, who was able to easily fend it off, and smash a giant fist, right into the middle of Nikita's face. He felt his nose explode with the impact. He worked to remain upright to limit the damage they would be able to do, and started to make as much noise as he could, hopeful that a passer-by would interrupt, but the fat man caught him with a blow to his injured shoulder. He fell backwards against the wall and couldn't keep his balance, slumping down to the floor.

The three of them surrounded him, kicking him ferociously. He clawed his way out from the wall, but they showed no mercy with their ruthless attack. He was vaguely aware of them shouting at him. The words they used were nothing new, and nothing that could hurt him.

His arms covering his head, he retreated into his mind, face screwed up in a bloody grimace. His mind sifted through long-forgotten memories of being with his family. The faces of his father, mother and Milena drifted around, smiling benignly at him, calming him and soothing him from the ordeal his body was enduring.

His body was tensed, feeling few of the kicks, but the pain was beginning to grow and he knew that soon bones would begin to break. He tried to continue to focus on his family once more and then suddenly he felt overwhelmed by loneliness. He might die and no one here would care or notice. A tear leaked out of his eye, whether from pain or sadness he was not sure. He thought of his family and his heart suddenly ached more than his body, and another tear fell. He must survive, if only for them. "It is all for you," he whispered to them silently, willing the message to reach them across the world.

His eyes creaked open and he saw Red Beard bring a foot up to stamp down on his ankle in a move that would surely break it.

He held up a pleading hand. "Please, no."

Red Beard paused, lowering his foot, then grinned.

"There's only one thing I hates more than a crow, and that's one who forgets his place," he said then brought his foot back up.

But it never reached the ground, or Nikita's leg.

There was the crack of a gunshot which ripped through the quiet night, and stopped the men in their tracks. They all turned to look at the silhouette of a tall, slender man standing in the alleyway, with a smoking gun pointed at the sky.

"Step aside, fellas, this one is mine," said a cold, clipped, southern voice, unlike any of the men standing around their victim. More refined.

For the first time that night, Nikita felt truly afraid. This was no redneck, nor a former low-level soldier. This was a trained assassin; even as a dark silhouette, Nikita could tell just from his stance.

"Who the hell are you?" said the fat man, who was dripping with sweat from the exertion and smelt badly.

The newcomer stepped forward and pointed the gun at the fat man's face. "I'm your worst nightmare if you get in between me and this... stain on our town. Now fuck off, or I start shootin'."

Jarhead looked as if he was about to protest, but the gunman fired at the floor, the bullet ricocheting off the wall next to Nikita and disappearing down the dark alleyway.

"Now I've done you the courtesy of two more warning shots than I've ever given before. There won't be a third. Leave and live, or stay and die, it's up to you."

All three of them turned tail and passed the gunman. Red Beard leant into him and whispered, "Make him suffer."

The gunman smirked but said nothing, and as the last of the attackers sprinted back to the sanctity of the bar, he stepped into the light.

Nikita tried in vain to push himself onto his feet but was only barely holding onto consciousness. He looked up at the face of his killer, and drew a sharp intake of breath.

A scar glowed from the ear to the eye of the man looming above him, pointing the gun at his face.

"Brishnov?" gasped Nikita.

"Da... comrade," sneered the Russian assassin.

CHAPTER 15

Nikita noticed that the gun had not lowered following the departure of his attackers, but was instead pointed directly at him.

"Help me, comrade," Nikita croaked, reverting to his native Russian.

Nikita could see the lust for the kill in the eyes of Brishnov, could see the temptation.

Brishnov walked closer, the gun still hovering in front of him, and Nikita now believed the Soviet agent would kill him. The silent menace was written in the hard lines of his face and Nikita was powerless to stop him, only clinging onto consciousness by a thread.

Brishnov walked behind him and squatted down. Nikita could feel his breath on his neck; it reeked. He suddenly thrust something in front of Nikita's face.

"Do not forget this, comrade, you know better than to leave any trace." Nikita's bleary eyes focused on the bloody, scorched knife he had dropped, before it was thrust into its sheath by his fellow KGB agent.

He heard the sound of Brishnov pocketing his gun, before arms hooked under his own and lifted him up. He had no strength to fight the assassin, and consciousness finally deserted him as he felt himself being dragged away and he allowed the darkness in.

***

Brishnov dragged his body back to the car and deposited him on the back seat. Grabbing the keys which were still in the ignition, he locked the doors to make sure Nikita could not escape if he regained consciousness, and then walked purposefully down the street towards the bar.

Reaching the bar, he looked around and saw a building two doors ahead boarded up, went over to it and broke off a sturdy piece of the wooden boarding. He returned to the entrance to the bar and put the wood through the door handles, preventing anyone leaving.

He then slunk back down the alleyway in which he had discovered the men beating his fellow agent and smiled at the thought. It had been so tempting to allow them to continue and rid the Soviet Union of its black stain. But orders were orders, and now loose ends needed to be tied.

Marching down the alleyway, he reached the delivery driveway behind the bar and approached it with little caution, but with one hand on the gun at his hip. The door was not even shut; this was too easy.

Walking through it, he surveyed the surroundings. Crates of alcohol and kegs of beer were pushed against the walls in the dingy back room lit by a flickering fluorescent light above. There was a buzzing from an electric fly trap on the wall which looked like it hadn't been cleaned in years, covered with the gluey corpses of hundreds of cremated flies.

Casting his eyes around, he saw what he was looking for — the mains gas pipe running up the wall and towards the bar. Approaching it, he could see that it was painted over, and the pipes were old cast iron which would make his job that bit harder.

He pouted, and with an exaggerated sigh, picked up a heavy keg tap from the floor and began to bang at the pipe where it met the meter.

He heard footsteps approaching and the bar man walked in, his belly visible before the rest of him.

"Hey what the hell are you—" he began, but was cut off as Brishnov pulled his handgun and shot the barman in the stomach. With the close proximity the bullet passed straight through him, as intended, and ricocheted off the wall and into a case of vodka. Brishnov couldn't have the authorities finding a corpse with a bullet in at the scene of the crime.

The man screamed as blood started flowing out of the hole, both at the front and the back, and looked at Brishnov in horror. Brishnov had already pocketed his gun, and after retrieving the bullet from the vodka, didn't give his victim a second look. He picked up a bottle and unscrewed the cap, taking a sip.

"Americans make shit vodka," he said to no-one in particular. He picked up another two bottles and walked over to the wounded man on the floor, and ripped a long strip from his apron.

"Please, help me," said the barman from the floor.

"Be silent; I do not wish to have to shoot you again. Die quietly, old man."

He picked up the keg tap once more and began pounding on the pipe, which suddenly with a scrape of metal ripped from the meter. The hiss of gas was palpable. Then he ripped the rag of cloth in two, dousing both pieces in the vodka, roughly shoving them halfway into the bottles, and then he walked out of the room.

There was a narrow, short corridor ending in a door opening out into the bar. Brishnov walked into it confidently, noting that there were thirteen patrons scattered around the dingy room. Lynyrd Skynyrd's *Freebird* was playing loudly from a battered jukebox and few noticed his entrance until he passed the bar and walked towards the door.

Red Beard was laughing at the bar with Jarhead and Fatty, and the collection of empty glasses next to them suggested they had wasted no time in celebrating their victory over Nikita. By the time they noticed him it was too late. He opened the bottle without the cloth in and began emptying it near the door, forming a slick trail back towards the bar. Taking a zippo lighter from his pocket, he lit one of the rags. As he marched back through the bar, he tossed the bomb firmly over his shoulder so it smashed against the door, blocking the rear exit. A Molotov cocktail felt a poetic way of destroying a bar, he thought to himself while whistling softly.

He felt the heat on his back but didn't look round, and noticed the screams from around the bar with cold disinterest.

The trio at the bar stepped sluggishly in his way. "What the hell are you doing?" Red Beard demanded angrily, slurring. It was Jarhead who recognised him first.

"That's the dude from the alleyway!" he exclaimed, and recognition dawned on the faces of the others.

Brishnov sighed; he didn't have time for this. He could see people beginning to move away from the door and towards the rear exit.

He swiftly punched Red Beard to the temple, making him crumple, before smashing Jarhead and Fatty's faces into each other. They both fell to the floor, clutching their broken noses.

Brishnov ran to the rear, furious at being forced to speed up. He lit the other cloth, and holding it in front of him, counted the numbers. Only twelve. These guys were not separated from their bar easily, even in the face of Molotov-cocktail-wielding assassins, but one had clearly led a charge. He backed out of the door and threw the bomb in front of him, swiftly closing the door to prevent the firebomb from hurtling down the corridor.

Over the sound of *Freebird* he heard more scream from the victims who were now trapped between two rapidly expanding infernos. He was already moving quickly. He saw the missing number thirteen crouched over the barman. He was younger than the others he had seen in the bar. A handsome man, Brishnov reckoned around twenty-five, with dark stubble and a strong jaw.

As he looked up, his eyes filled with terror. He raised his fists, but was on the ground before he knew it, clutching his throat where Brishnov had spun and slit it with his combat knife. Blood blossomed from his throat and he gurgled as he tried to hold the two slippery flaps of skin together.

The barman began to scream. This would not do, thought Brishnov. It might alert neighbours and if nothing else it was quite irritating. He clubbed the barman over the head with the keg tap and the screaming stopped.

He could hear people in the bar trying to make their way through the door at the rear and sighed. Why would they not accept their fate? If only they knew that the door was the key to their death.

If he could hear them coming through then he needed to get out. Now.

The smell of gas was strong as he walked swiftly out of the door, with a glance behind him at the bodies on the floor. One was still writhing in his own blood. He closed the door behind him, grateful that it opened outwards. He rolled a heavy wheelie bin over to block the door, and dragged some boxes to further lock them in. He thought he heard the sound of voices which meant they had broken through from the bar and into the back room.

His eyes widened and he broke into a sprint as the flames of the bar met the open gas pipe. The explosion ripped through wood, iron and stone, bursting the building outwards. Brishnov flung himself forwards and began to commando crawl towards the alleyway as bricks, tiles and other detritus from the building landed around him. As he reached the safety of the alleyway, he took a deep breath and smiled. Murdering Americans was beyond satisfying. It was arousing. His hand moved down to his crotch and he closed his eyes.

The ringing of the explosion in his ears was interrupted by the sound of sirens in the distance. He cursed. There would be time for relief later, but God forbid if anyone discovered the precious Black Russian.

He stood and made his way back to the car, disappearing into the night, unseen amidst the chaos of people screaming on the street as the inferno gathered pace.

***

Nikita's eyes flickered open as he felt light fall on his face, and they quickly flickered shut again. He wanted to return to the dream; it had been a good one. Back in Russia, he was playing with Milena, laughing with his parents, nobody else around, no scent of judgement or contempt. As he awoke, he could no longer discern if it was memory or fantasy.

It was wiped from his mind as the pain caught up with him and his eyes shot back open again. His body screamed from head to toe. He tried to lift his head but it hurt too much. His shoulder was full of fire, whether from the bullet wound or his DIY attempt at cauterising he was not sure.

As he tried to push himself up, he silently screamed and was barely able to prop himself up on one arm. The injured shoulder was unable to take any weight. He had never felt so weak.

He was on a threadbare bed as hard as a table, with light streaming onto it from a window above him to the left, casting the rest of the room into semi-gloom. A rough blanket was half drawn over him, and his clothes were in bits on the floor beside the bed, as if they had been torn from him. He looked around the room for any indication of where he might be, but there was little in the way of clues.

A bedside table stood next to him and an imposing dark wood chest of drawers was on the opposite side of the room, with a wood-panelled television on top of it, complete with a portable aerial balanced on top.

He lay back so as to use his right arm, and fumbled with the bedside table, pulling open the small drawer within it. He felt around for the contents, pulling out in turn a carton of Belomorkanal cigarettes, a litre bottle of vodka and a gun.

Soviet smokes, vodka and a gun meant that Brishnov had brought him to a Soviet safe house. But where was Brishnov?

As if in answer to his silent question, the door opened and in walked the slender Russian spy. He looked at Nikita and smirked.

"Water," said Nikita, but Brishnov just smirked at him and pulled over a chair to sit next to him.

They sat in silence staring at each other for a minute.

"What of the men that attacked me? They will identify us; you should have let them finish beating me."

"Tempting as that was, you do not need to worry about them." There was no trace of the southern accent Brishnov had so smoothly adopted as the Russian rolled from his tongue.

"You killed them?"

"Such a crude question, but I suppose crudity is to be expected from one such as yourself," he replied, leaning back and inspecting his nails. "You nearly died, comrade," he added without concern. It was a matter of fact. "Klitchkov would have been inconsolable if his favourite protégé had fallen."

Nikita could think of no response and silence again invaded the room.

"You saved my life" he said, breaking the silence.

Brishnov's eyes widened in mock surprise. "And why would that ever be in doubt?"

"I know that you doctored my orders."

"Little thieves are hanged but great ones, escape," he replied with a wink.

Nikita grunted. "I am in no mood to play games, agent; talk to me plain and simple."

The smile fell from Brishnov's face. "Well naturally you would want things explained to you in simple terms," he said, glaring in Nikita's eyes, daring him. "But of course, you are badly wounded and speaking without thinking. Too much of that American whiskey shit has turned your manners rotten." He picked up the bottle from the drawer next to the bed and unscrewed the cap, taking a long drink of the vodka.

"Ah, it is not good vodka but this is still finer than water. Come, let us drink to the success of your mission, comrade," he said and held some to Nikita's lips. Nikita tried to push it away but Brishnov pulled it out of reach and poured the contents onto his face from a height, soaking his bed

Nikita sputtered and held up a hand as Brishnov took a final swig to empty the bottle before throwing it against the wall to the other side of the bed, smashing it.

Nikita thought longingly of the gun in the drawer, but knew that an agent as experienced as Brishnov would not have left it loaded for him.

Brishnov giggled. "How refreshing, no?"

Nikita lay back, controlled. "We're on the same side, remember… comrade?" he whispered.

"Ah, maybe the same side, but pointing in different directions. To represent the Komitet Godudarstvennoy Bezopasnosti is a great honour; we are the secret soldiers of Mother Russia, of the world's biggest and most powerful empire. There is no greater prestige, but you, you do not choose this. We only have you as long as we can contain you. There is no honour."

"Flaying a man only teaches him to watch his back. I have done everything asked of me and more, despite the hatred that follows me. I nonetheless serve the Soviet Union faithfully."

"You expect my pity?"

"I expect and want nothing from you. But modify my orders again and I will kill you, comrade."

Brishnov leant back in his chair and smiled at him. "Perhaps if you managed that, you would have my respect."

At that moment the door opened again. Brishnov didn't turn, instead keeping his gaze fixed on Nikita, whose eyes were distracted by the new arrival.

The highly polished black shoes clicked and gleamed on the tiled floor but it was the face that drew Nikita's gaze, the cold blue eyes piercing the gloom before the pale skin and grey hair did.

Nikita attempted to push himself up and salute. "Colonel Klitchkov, sir." But he could not sustain the pose and fell back while continuing to try and maintain a salute.

Klitchkov chuckled. "At ease, soldier, let your body rest." His eyes wandered over the broken glass and Nikita's wet face, and raised an eyebrow at Brishnov.

Nikita was full of questions, but held his tongue, waiting to be addressed.

The colonel stood with his hands behind his back and looked down at Brishnov in the chair. "Leave us."

Brishnov looked up at him petulantly. "I'd rather stay."

Without taking a breath, Klitchkov kicked Brishnov off the chair.

Brishnov looked outraged and leapt up catlike from the floor.

"You wish to say something, Agent Brishnov? To your commanding officer?"

Brishnov's face flushed red, but he controlled himself with what appeared a superhuman effort. "No, sir. Sorry, sir." He appeared to be chewing on the words as if they were sour milk.

"Then get the out of the room, now," Klitchkov said softly, with a menace more powerful than if he had screamed it.

The international assassin stalked from the room like a wounded dog, but left the door slightly open.

Klitchkov turned and pushed it gently shut until the latch clicked into place, before walking back to the chair and sitting down. He leant back and crossed one leg over the other and surveyed Nikita.

"You were very stupid."

"I had no other choice, sir."

"You may be young, but you have received the world's finest training for five years and the only choice was to be beaten to death by three stupid American brutes? You were trained precisely to employ alternative choices to that one."

Nikita said nothing.

"But you did an excellent job on your primary mission. It broke on the news this morning."

"And?"

Klitchkov raised his eyebrows.

"Sorry, sir. What are they saying on the news, sir?"

"That the death isn't being treated as suspicious, which is as much as we could hope for at the moment. I am sure they will reveal more in time, but I trust that nothing will be revealed that could suggest foul play?"

"No, sir."

"Very good. We found the Dragunov Sniper in our car. Why would you have needed that for this mission?"

Nikita paused. It would be easy to destroy Brishnov with one revelation. But I want to owe him nothing, to be even, Nikita thought to himself.

"Well, agent?"

"It, ah, it was a routine backup plan, sir, just in case something went wrong and had to be tidied up."

"You are trained so that things do not go wrong," snapped Klitchkov, uncrossing his legs and leaning forward. "A sniper shot would have ruined the entire operation and tilted the balance of power around the world. And from a Dragunov rifle, no less! This is the last mistake I will attribute to your youth." It was the first time Nikita had ever seen anger in the colonel, or any emotion at all.

"Yes, sir. I had no intentions of using it, and planned my mission meticulously," he lied.

"You know me better than to take me for a fool, Allochka."

"Yes, sir."

"Your next mission will demand scrupulous planning and detail."

"My next mission, sir?"

Klitchkov leant back again and resumed his previous relaxed pose. He briefly turned and checked the door. He stood and walked over to the television, turning it on and turning the volume up.

The news flickered onto the screen. The picture was fuzzy, with the aerial needing to be moved, but Nikita could see images of Secretary Conlan's house with a reporter speaking about the sudden death of 'one of America's most respected politicians'.

Klitchkov walked back and returned to his seat.

"You are to enter the United States Central Intelligence Agency. The importance of the International Nuclear Treaty cannot be understated for the survival of our Soviet Union. You are in a unique position to prevent the Americans from seeing all of our movements and intentions."

Nikita's head was buzzing. The pain was overwhelming and the noise from the television distracting. The CIA was the largest intelligence agency in the world, bigger than the KGB, MI6 or Mossad.

"How will we do that?"

"You will join their Soviet Counter-intelligence Branch. As a black man, it will be hard to secure you a senior position, but it should make their checks on your background and intentions a little less resilient than someone looking like a Russian."

Nikita went to speak, but Klitchkov held up a hand, silencing him. "I know you will have questions, agent, but first we need you to heal as quickly as possible. Being battered so thoroughly has robbed the operation of precious days. Your body is pitiful. You will be transferred from here as soon as arrangements can be made, most likely tonight, and you will have the luxury of every treatment we possess. You will start your new job in two weeks."

"Two weeks! But, sir—"

"You refuse your assignment? You have not forgotten your family so swiftly surely, Allochka?"

Nikita dropped his gaze. "No, sir."

Klitchkov's face registered no emotion. He nodded slightly, then rose from his chair and left the room without a backward glance. Once more Nikita looked at him with contempt, his fingers tracing the scar on his thigh, a reminder of the treachery of Colonel Klitchkov.

***

Two days later, Nikita lay in a room a world away from the hard bed in the Texas safe house. He lay on a soft bedsheet of Egyptian cotton, gazing out at the Gulf of Mexico through bay windows. The curtains were swaying gently in the warm breeze.

The journey in the middle of the night across the border into Mexico, and the helicopter ride from there back to the Soviet Embassy in Havana, were hazy. He had vague memories of drifting in and out of consciousness as the pain medication took hold and dimmed his awareness. He recalled being stretchered into the embassy under cover of darkness through a hidden entrance, masked to prevent any wondering eyes from seeing him. He was now the most important resource in the KGB's clandestine arsenal, and every precaution was being taken. And every luxury. He nestled comfortably in the new surroundings, usually reserved for only the most senior of dignitaries.

He pushed himself up into a sitting position on the bed with a low groan and inspected his wounded body. The index and middle finger of his left hand were in cast after being broken by the boots of Red Beard and his cronies, and dark bruises could be seen all over his legs, arms and stomach. But they paled in comparison to the deep purple bruising spread across his shoulder and torso. His cauterised wound had left an ugly puckering in a strip from the ball of his shoulder down towards his pectoral in the clear, curved shape of a knife blade. The skin was sunken and inflamed, and had been the source of much discontent for the embassy's resident doctor.

Nikita glanced at the clock on the wall and saw that he was due for his next dressing. Doctor Zhikov liked to let it 'have some air to breathe away your stupidity', but Nikita wished he didn't have to look at the scar he would bear for life. He felt now that he better understood people's desire to tattoo themselves; at least that was a scar you chose, not a scar forced upon you. The KGB forbade tattoos as they provided an easy way to identify you, but perhaps one day, if he ever escaped their clutches, he would consider something to cover some of his scars.

He could not see his back but it hurt almost as much as his shoulder, having borne the brunt of most of the kicks. He could feel scabs pulling every time he moved but preferred not to know the extent of the damage. He only cared about when he would be fit and ready for active duty once more.

On the bed next to him was a newspaper, the headline giving tribute to the secretary of defense who had died of an apparent accidental overdose of whiskey and sleeping pills. The president talked of a patriot, a soldier and a man of firm principle. Nikita looked at it with distaste. To be a man of firm principle was only a cause for praise if the principles were not toxic and outdated.

The door opened without a knock and Doctor Zhikov entered along with Mrs Shapova, the ambassador's secretary who had taken it upon herself to visit him each day.

The short, plump woman bustled in, and after putting down a pile of papers on the bed, immediately started fussing over him and trying to force him to lie back down. "You need your rest, Nikita; you must allow yourself to recover," she said, the first person he could recall calling him by his first name outside his family. He found he rather liked it, though he was sure it was a breach of protocol.

"Leave him alone, Mrs Shapova! And move those papers!" snapped the doctor, a short, thin Belarusian man with a large round head, topped by lank brown hair combed over a bald head. He waved the secretary away.

Nikita smiled at her with a look of gratitude. She perched herself on the end of the bed, looking like an overgrown hawk, as Zhikov inspected the shoulder wound.

"How does it feel, agent?"

"It is fine," replied Nikita.

"Oh wonderful, so it is not a problem for you to stretch your arms above your head then," said the doctor in a voice dripping with incredulity.

"None at all," said Nikita, with a congenial smile.

"Perhaps you will give us a demonstration, Allochka. I look forward to witnessing a medical miracle unfold."

Nikita closed his eyes, breathed deeply and centred himself as he brought his arms up at the sides slowly, blocking out the stretch of the scabs across his back as his muscles expanded. As he reached level with his shoulder, the screaming in his left shoulder began. He imagined he could feel the gristle rubbing against ligament and bone and paused.

To the onlookers, his face remained calm and passive, but behind the eyelids his pupils were wide with pain.

"There is no shame in not being able to do it yet, Nikita; it is only two days since you were shot," said Mrs Shapova crisply.

Nikita's eyes remained closed and he began to force his arm upwards once more. He managed about ten more degrees before hitting a wall and having to let his arm drop.

"OK, now we have that little charade out of the way, perhaps we can get on with your treatment and recovery, Allochka," said the doctor swiftly, taking hold of Nikita's arm and pressing around the joint and wound. "Much as we may wish otherwise, this cannot be healed overnight and requires patience."

"There is no room for patience in my line of work, doctor."

"It is amazing how many of my patients seem to think that there is no room in their lives for patience. All of them seem to be a hundred per cent the most important people in the world, whether they are diplomats, spies or waiters."

Nikita grunted but said nothing. He wanted to begin the mission immediately, wanted to enter the CIA and bring down the USA. The sooner he did, the sooner he could return to his family. He would pick being in Siberia with them rather than in his present Cuban luxury without them.

"How long before I can use my arm fully again, doctor?"

"Far more time than we have. I will do what I can, and with intensive physiotherapy and great care you should be able to manage your next mission. I understand it will be less physically demanding than previous ones," replied Zhikov as he injected Nikita's daily dose of painkillers into his thigh.

"What else do you know about my next mission?"

"Only that it will not be so physically demanding. I do not wish to know any more than what I need to, as your doctor, so do not reveal anything to me! Roll over onto your stomach."

The doctor proceeded to dress the wound and was in the midst of inspecting a particularly painful scab crossing the spine in the middle of Nikita's back, when there was a knock on the door. Ambassador Yitski entered without waiting for a response.

Doctor Zhikov started at the intrusion, accidentally prodding the scar deeply, causing Nikita to let out a moan of pain.

The ambassador stopped. "And there was me thinking you were meant to be the toughest agent we possessed," he said with a wink.

He had grown a short beard since Nikita had seen him last, which covered his weak chin, making him look more distinguished and giving him a certain gravitas. Nikita could see more clearly now how he had landed a position of such key significance.

"Ambassador Yitski," said Nikita, turning his head sideways, as Zhikov continued his survey of his back.

"Please leave us, doctor," said the ambassador and waited as the doctor packed up and reminded Nikita that he would return again tomorrow.

"Mrs Shapova has presented you with your mission documents I trust?" asked Yitski.

"Ah, yes of course," said Nikita, pushing himself round onto his back and up in to a sitting position. Mrs Shapova gave him a subtle nod of gratitude. "But due to Dr Zhikov's visit I have not had a chance to look at them yet."

"Very well. If your pain is manageable then we must begin preparations for your next assignment."

"I am ready to prepare, thank you."

The ambassador pulled up a chair next to the bed, asking Mrs Shapova to pass him the sheaf of papers she had earlier deposited on the bed, then asked her also to leave the room.

She did so swiftly, giving no sign of her earlier affection for Nikita other than a brief glance back at him as she left the room.

"So, Agent Allochka, you know the top line of what you will be doing on your next mission. Ordinarily Colonel Klitchkov or someone from the KGB would prepare you for this mission. However, following the death of the US Secretary of Defense, movements in and out of Cuba are being watched even more closely at present, and so I have been given special clearance to brief you on what will be expected." He paused for a moment. "You know that you will be joining the CIA's Soviet Counter-intelligence Branch, and it has taken an extraordinary amount of work to make this opportunity possible. It is absolutely vital for the balance of world power that at no point is your cover blown. Understood?"

"Understood. Will I still be under the alias of Nathan Martins?"

"No. That alias did not have a background that would be suited to a job such as this. A new alias has been created, and only through agents embedded in various other locations have we been able to assure the robustness of your background and reference checks. No KGB agent currently has a more important or more precarious mission. Mother Russia is relying on you, comrade."

"That explains why it has shown me such unceasing kindness," said Nikita, the faintest hint of a smirk upon the corner of his lips.

Yitski frowned. "Is there a problem, Allochka?"

"Not at all, ambassador."

"You make a lot of people nervous; do not give me reason to become another."

"Why do you think it is I make people nervous, ambassador? After all, I finished top in every category throughout my five years of training and have successfully completed all of my missions so far, as ordered. So I'm curious, what is it about me that would make Mother Russia nervous?" Nikita asked pleasantly, but with a warning in his voice.

Ambassador Yitski faltered under the gaze of the young man in front of him, whose cold eyes burned with intensity, daring him. He wished he had brought his vodka with him.

"Curiosity can get you killed, agent. You are little older than a child, and as such more liable to make foolish errors of judgement. I suggest you focus on continuing to be the best agent you can be."

Nikita smiled coldly, but maintained his intense stare.

Yitski chuckled nervously. "Let us not get distracted from the mission at hand!" he said as he started shuffling through the papers before him. "An apartment has been rented for you in Langley, Virginia where you will be based in your new role." He passed Nikita a detail sheet of his new home. "You will now be going under the name Jacob Marshall. We have had to age you to give you a chance to fit the role. You will be twenty-eight, but luckily the job you have has a habit of making people look old before their time and it should not be difficult for you to pull it off."

"How have you got me a job in the Soviet Counter-intelligence Branch without me ever having met them? Surely they are stringent about who they hire?"

"Correct. We have got you through the door, and we understand that the job is yours providing you pass a series of tests. Curiously for a country with a history of such racial prejudice, the colour of your skin has actually helped you a great deal in this position as they seem less concerned with some of the precautions we expected. I cannot emphasise how impressive your CV is so you have an intense period of study ahead of you."

"What sort of tests?"

"I know there will be a standard lie detector examination given to all agents, which I understand you are most adept at circumventing, da?"

Nikita nodded.

"Beyond that, I am unsure, but I should imagine that they are designed to ensure you are who you say you are, and that you are fully capable of carrying out the job to the level they require. They pick only the best for this division."

"What do I need to study? I already know quite a bit about Soviet intelligence."

"This is an analyst role; there should not be any active field duty. You should be able to adapt fairly quickly, but it is very much a position of information collection and analysing, rather than one of overt action."

"I understand."

"Colonel Klitchkov would never admit it, and General Secretary Petrenko certainly would not, but our glorious Soviet empire is on the brink of collapse; it is not difficult to see. The INF Treaty represents a unique opportunity to level the playing field with the United States and turn around our fortunes. Your new role is fundamental to that, and the fortunes of our nation are resting firmly on your shoulders. The treaty should be signed very soon following Secretary Conlan's demise and we along with the US will be expected to start visibly disarming our nuclear arsenal. They need to believe, as does the rest of the world, that we truly are disarming. Only if we deceive them can we regain a place of strength and revive our fortunes. This will then silence the Czechoslovakians and Hungarians, and avoid the crumbling of an empire."

"No pressure then," said Nikita with a faintly arched eyebrow.

"A great pressure, but the rewards will be even greater if you succeed."

"And if I fail?"

"Failure cannot and must not be an option, agent."

"A burnable asset."

"Every asset can be burned if they fail, you know how espionage works, agent. Do not feign naivety."

He hefted the documents together and passed them to Nikita. "You have a great deal of work ahead of you. You must memorise everything in these files to prepare yourself," he said as he stood up and moved his chair back to where it had been by the dresser. He gave a stiff nod to Nikita and left the room.

As the door closed, Nikita let out a gasp from the pain he had been containing during their interaction. He allowed his body to sink back down onto the bed and massaged his shoulder which was complaining loudly at the attempt to lift it.

He closed his eyes and let his body settle into a position in which he was semi-comfortable, the best he could hope for in his current condition. The visits had wearied him greatly and he was content just to rest. Reaching for the phone next to his bed, he ordered some food to be sent to his room. He had become partial to Ropa Vieja, a Cuban shredded-beef recipe, and convinced himself it was the food to help him recover.

He flicked through the documents briefly, and a small blank envelope dropped out. Curiously, he opened it and inside was a piece of paper torn from a notebook that said simply *'Straw hat = Pamyat. Yours, Kemran'*. Nikita stared at Kemran's note. What was Pamyat? The word felt familiar but he could not place it.

The documents felt heavy in his hand, and after stifling a sigh, he put them down to pick up the newspaper and continued to peruse it. As he reached page seven his body stiffened, causing a shockwave of pain to again run through his body, but he ignored it and pushed himself back to a sitting position.

The headline to the lead article read 'Fourteen die in Texas bar fire', above a picture of what Nikita recognised as the building that had once been Paddy's bar in Odessa, now little more than a burnt-out husk. The article said it looked to be a gas leak. Apparently one man, a former US marine, had managed to force his way out of the front door but had died in hospital due to the severity of the burns he had suffered. Nobody else had made it any further.

Nikita felt cold. This is what Brishnov meant by 'dealing with it'. This wasn't dealing with it; this was a massacre of innocent civilians. He was not so foolish as not to understand that the trio who had attacked him needed to be 'disappeared', but to take out another eleven innocent bystanders felt evil. This was not an assassination, it was cold blooded murder and he felt sick.

"How great the consequences of our choices can be," he said to himself, wishing he had avoided the bar and found another way to treat his wounds. Clearly Brishnov had been sent to spy on him, so he would not have been allowed to die either way.

He pulled himself from bed and rolled into the wheelchair kept beside it. He wheeled himself over to the French windows and out onto the balcony, enjoying the reduced pain levels as the painkillers kicked in. He looked out over the Gulf of Mexico and breathed in the warm early evening air. This business was evil, but he would not let his heart blacken like Brishnov's.

It was three weeks later that Nikita departed the Russian Embassy in Cuba, looking like a renewed man, albeit one with cold eyes and stiff movements. The helicopter waiting to transport him on the first leg of his roundabout journey to Langley was stirring up dust, leaves and debris from the dry asphalt and made the world look momentarily brown and chaotic. Nikita put on a pair of sunglasses, set his shoulders and walked into the swirling maelstrom and into the CIA.

PART 2

CHAPTER 16

ONE YEAR LATER

The highly polished black shoes barely made a sound on the plush carpet of the White House corridor. They belonged to the slow but steady legs of Secretary of State Harry Bernstein, who was moving deliberately towards a room at the end of the hall. Dressed in a black suit with a royal blue tie, he was well groomed, with his now firmly white hair combed back carefully in an effort to cover as much of his thinning scalp as possible.

As he reached the door, he nodded to the two Secret Service agents standing either side with hands held behind their back, and knocked firmly.

"Come on in," said a deep voice from the other side. Bernstein turned the ornate brass handle and opened the door onto the Oval Office.

Behind a desk by the window sat the president of the United States, Ernest Callahan. He was writing intently in a notebook, but on glancing up, he put the pen down and rubbed his tired and puffy eyes.

"Ah, Harry, I got your message," he said in a voice that oozed authority, as he stood up and shook the secretary of state's hand. He signalled to the two sofas on the other side of the room, as Secretary Bernstein replied, "Thank you for seeing me on such short notice, Mr President."

Sitting, the president groaned as he eased himself down. "What have you got for me?"

Shuffling slightly, Bernstein straightened his suit jacket. "Ah, sir, things are getting a little out of hand out there."

"Jesus, Harry, this is not what I want to hear. My approval rating is at the lowest it's ever been. I need good news. What is it now?"

"So this is highly classified, sir, but there has been another murder."

"Goddam it, I promised to be the tough-on-crime president. I appointed you because you were going to stop spiralling murder figures."

"With respect, sir, this is not a regular murder. We believe it is one in a chain of political assassinations."

"Then why the hell are you reporting this to me? Where's Bob McMahon?"

"Mr President, I'm deeply saddened to be the one to tell you that your assistant for national security affairs is the one who has been assassinated."

"What?" said the president, standing and putting his hand to his face. "Dear God, who killed him? Tell me you got the son of a bitch. McMahon is... was a good man."

"I wish I could, but the one we believe is responsible is proving to be incredibly elusive."

"Who is he, Harry? Stop talking in circles and talk to me plainly."

"The code name he has been given is the Black Russian."

The president snorted. "There are no blacks in Russia, Harry; they lynch them more than they did in the Mississippi Delta." He paused. "Well... maybe not quite that much."

"Quite so, Mr President, they hate them even more than they hate the homos. But the code name is not a reference to his skin colour, more to the shadows in which he operates. We have absolutely no proof that he actually exists, or even that he is Russian."

"Then why come and tell me about this fantasy? I swear to God I'm going to throttle you in a minute, Harry!"

"I apologise, sir, but I'm secretary of state and not accustomed to dealing in these clandestine matters. The director of the CIA is currently abroad for reasons I'm sure you know more about than I, and with the deputy director of the FBI position not yet filled, the FBI director is unavailable. He briefed me fully ahead of this meeting. There has been a string of deaths over the past six months, and all are of people connected to our intelligence- gathering agencies or holding some form of government office."

"How has this not been brought to my attention until now?"

"Every death has been of relatively low-ranking officials and has been treated as unsuspicious on its own merits. However, the analysts at the FBI have begun to connect dots, and believe that all the deaths were in fact murders. But it goes deeper; they believe they can trace it all the way back to the signing of the INF Treaty, and…"

"Go on," urged the president, pacing back and forth.

"And right back to the death of Secretary of Defense Conlan."

The president stopped pacing and stared at his secretary of state, utterly aghast.

"You're telling me that Simon was murdered by the Russians?"

"I'm telling you that the FBI believes it a possibility."

Callahan sat back down on the sofa and shook his head. "This is ridiculous."

Harry Bernstein said nothing, instead looking at his hands nervously. He would have his payback to the FBI director for forcing him to deliver this to the president.

"So what you are telling me is that Petrenko has somehow not only got KGB agents onto US soil, but that one is drifting around the country killing our own agents and even our secretary of defense. All while the Russians are signing the disarmament treaty with me. But you're telling me this without any evidence whatsoever. What the hell do you want me to do with this? I'm far too busy to deal with the hunches of low-level FBI analysts. I can't confront the commies with mere hearsay. I imagine they're busy enough trying to come up with a way of getting out of Afghanistan at the moment, which incidentally is an update I hope to God I'm going to get a more detailed report on."

"I understand completely, sir. I should add that every single person whose death is being investigated on this FBI list had been working on Soviet projects."

The president gazed coldly at Bernstein. "How about leading with that one next time, instead of leading me around the houses with conjecture."

"I appreciate it isn't a firm lead, but it was felt that there was enough confidence enough that there may be some foul play at work to bring it to your attention, ahead of your next meeting with Mr Petrenko. You may need to tread carefully. If he does indeed have agents working to destabilise our intelligence agencies and government it could be that he isn't as willing to move beyond the Cold War as it has seemed."

"It's no surprise that he has KGB agents in the US. We haven't been as effective in weeding out theirs as they have ours, but I can't see any reason for him to be so brash as to begin assassinations."

"Be that as it may, Mr President, I would suggest being vigilant until such time as we are able to furnish you with more concrete evidence."

"You find me that concrete evidence and we'll have our revenge on them for Conlan and McMahon, but don't come back to me on this until you have anything worth telling me. This feels like one of the more pointless conversations of my time in the White House." The president stood and walked back to his desk where he sat down. "That will be all, Harry. Transfer the investigation to the CIA; if there's any merit in this it has connotations for foreign policy. Bring me more."

"Yes, sir," said the secretary, himself standing and walking back to the door.

"Oh and, Harry," said the president.

"Mr President?"

"Would it not make more sense to code name him the White Russian?"

Bernstein smiled. "Of course, sir, I'll see to it," he said and closed the door.

Once the door was closed, the president put down his pen and sighed. Rubbing his eyes again, he pressed the intercom on his desk. "Peggy?"

"Yes, Mr President?" responded the New York accent of his personal assistant.

"Could you have them send me in a White Russian? I have a sudden craving for a cocktail."

"It is only eleven a.m., sir."

"Yes, but it's nine p.m. in Moscow," he responded and put down the phone.

***

Nine miles away in Langley, Nikita stood by the water cooler in his office at the Central Intelligence Agency's headquarters and surveyed the scene in front of him. The open plan office spread out before him, yellow in the glow of fluorescent lights. There were few windows and the cloudy midwinter provided little lighting for the room anyway.

Small Atari computer screens flickered at desks across the room, with analysts tapping away with a furious intensity. The walls were plastered with papers, post-its, maps and photographs in an organised chaos of investigations, suspects and persons of interest.

A giant map of the Soviet Union was pinned to a wall on his right next to a television which showed the news on a loop at all times.

Nikita sighed. He felt so far away from the Kamenka shanty from which he'd been plucked all those years ago, but no more satisfied for it. He couldn't deny that the last six months had been the best of his life. Being part of a team that accepted him, living an ordinary life, aside from the occasional mission at weekends or evenings, had felt fantastic. The reality that he was living a lie to all of his co-workers and also actively working against them did not sit entirely comfortably, but rarely consciously fazed him.

He walked back to his desk, lost deep in thought. Sitting down in his swivel chair, he then leant back and turned to his desk mate.

"Hey Blaine, bar tonight?"

The blond New Yorker Blaine Lahart looked up from the notepad he was scribbling in. He had the sort of face that only suited a smile. "Jeez, isn't that your third night running, Jake?"

"What can I say; this job makes me drink."

Blaine laughed. "More than my old man who was every inch the Irish stereotype. Sure, it is nearly Friday after all. Let's get the rest of the gang together."

"Cool." Nikita nodded at Blaine's notes. "Any progress?"

"Not much. Trying to get Russians to play ball on nuclear site visits is hard work."

Nikita laughed now. "You thought the commies would make it easy?"

"They're too busy trying to make the war in Afghanistan look like a success."

"How's that going for them?"

"About as smoothly as us in Vietnam."

Nikita grimaced. "You'd think these people would learn by this point."

"Well let's hope they don't learn too quick otherwise we'll be out of a job," Blaine replied with a chuckle. "How're you getting on with the KGB?"

"Slowly. Yerin's movements are almost too routine. I just need to figure out what he's covering up."

"Maybe this Black Russian holds the key."

Nikita laughed. "To the chairman of the KGB's movements? And maybe Yerin is hanging out with him and Peter Pan in Never Never Land."

At that moment the department chief Gordon Sykes walked in and clapped his hands. "Listen in everyone. I've just had a directive from the president himself that will change the face of the investigation into the Black Russian completely."

Nikita showed no outward sign of interest, but did notice his heart rate increase slightly.

"Lahart, note this down," Sykes said to Blaine, "because this is going to blow it wide open."

"Yes, sir!"

"Now, the president has requested that investigations be fully turned over to us on this. He has also asked that the code name for the FBI's phantom assassin be changed from the Black Russian to... you guessed it. The White Russian."

There was a smattering of half-hearted laughs from people at Sykes' joke, but they stopped when they saw that his face was serious.

"You're not serious!" exclaimed a woman sitting a few desks back from Nikita, with a mixture of mirth and incredulity on her face.

The rest of the office laughed, even Sykes allowing himself a rare smile. It made the laughter lines crinkle around his eyes beneath his bushy eyebrows, giving him a much softer look than the strained one he usually sported. "I'm afraid I am, Chang. Direct orders," he said as he pulled out a pack of Marlboros from the pocket of his shirt, tapped out a cigarette and lit it up, closing his eyes momentarily. Nikita had noticed that when the chief was smoking was the only time the vein in his temple stopped throbbing.

"But… but… sir… you… they… can't name the world's most secret agent after a cocktail," she stuttered, her slender eyebrows lifted in an arch of what was now purely incredulity.

"A Black Russian is a cocktail too, Chang, you moron," shouted Rodney, an overweight man with pale brown hair and a patchy beard, sitting near the front of the room.

"Since when?"

"Since always!"

Chang flushed and crossed her arms.

"The Black Russian does sound cooler though," Nikita said kindly, winking at Chang.

She smiled at him, and he felt the blood rush to his face making him grateful for one of the first times in his life that he had dark skin.

"Well of course you're going to say that," said Rodney, smiling. A shocked silence descended upon the room, as everyone stared at the obese man with his shirt half untucked.

Suddenly he widened his eyes. "No, that isn't what I meant! Honestly," he looked pleadingly around. "I meant because it's Jake… and Chang…" he floundered, as Nikita and Chang hastily looked down at the floor, a low blush perceptible on her honey-coloured skin. Rodney tried to sit up and leant too heavily on the arm of his chair which gave way under his considerable weight and the chair toppled over sideways.

Everybody laughed, and Sykes said, "Looks like Steinberg just volunteered to buy everyone cocktails tonight; I'll leave it to you to decide if you want White Russians or Black Russians, whatever the hell one of those is."

"Sorry, Jake, man," said Rodney, red and sweaty in the face. His face full of apology; it was easy to see why he had never been made a field agent. No emotion could be hidden from his round face.

"No problem, man. I'll see you at the bar for that drink you're buying me," he replied with a wink.

Sykes took another draw on his cigarette, and while exhaling signalled to Nikita and Blaine. "Sarah, Jacob, Blaine, in my office now."

Blaine and Nikita looked at each other perplexed. Nikita and Chang avoided each other's gaze as the trio made their way to the office. "This cannot be good," said Blaine.

"Why not?" said Chang.

"Dude, he never uses our first names. And nobody calls you Sarah."

"Good point."

They entered the glass-fronted office. "Close the blinds, Lahart," said Sykes as he closed the door behind them.

Blaine and Chang took the two seats in front of his desk and Nikita stood just behind them.

Sykes stubbed out his cigarette in a marble ashtray on his desk, and immediately pulled out the Marlboros again. "Smoke, anyone?"

"Thank you, sir," said Sarah Chang, pulling one delicately from the squashed red and white packet. Nikita and Blaine held up their hands in refusal.

As the two smokers lit up, the room filled with gentle clouds of smoke snaking their way towards the ceiling. It had taken some time for Nikita to adjust to being in smoky rooms all the time; it had been strictly prohibited during his training. Although many of his fellow agents had found ways to sneak them through Denisov's routine security checks, he had never felt any urge to partake, and felt even less now. The smell of cigarettes clung to clothes, and could give targets a heads up of his approach if the wind was moving against him. Already he had to clean thoroughly before any mission to ensure the stench of tobacco had been washed away.

Sykes leant back in his chair. "Where are we at?" he asked.

The trio looks nonplussed. "With what?" said Chang in her usual direct fashion.

"With making a connection between your three cases."

"You never said nothing about a connection between our three cases, Gordon," said Blaine nonchalantly.

"Call me Gordon again and see what happens, Lahart," said Sykes coldly. "You're all working in the goddam Soviet Counter-intelligence Branch; there's a fairly obvious connection right there. For Chrissake you're meant to be the best of the best."

There was silence.

"Lahart, you're looking into whether the Russians are meeting their disarmament requirements. Marshall, you're investigating Yerin and the KGB's movements, and Chang you are trying to find out if this White

Russian exists, and now have the full weight of the CIA behind you. The connection between the last two should be plainly obvious at the least. You have to all start working together if we are ever going to get anywhere."

"Sorry, Gor... Chief, but I don't see how the INF Treaty has anything to do with other two," said Blaine. "The treaty was signed months ago and there's no indication at this point that they're not doing everything they are supposed to. My eyes on the ground there tell me they've been following the protocol outlined in the treaty so far."

"Take a step back from it for a minute. After years of back and forth, the Intermediate Nuclear Forces Treaty finally gets signed just weeks after Secretary Conlan, the one key vocal opponent to it, dies. No matter how natural it seems to be, that alone should have set our alarm bells ringing and it didn't at the time because we all wanted the treaty signed so badly."

"I do see what you're saying but I've looked into it and there was no hint of foul play in the coroner's report," said Chang. "I've found absolutely nothing so far to suggest that the Bl— the White Russian even exists," she said with an arched eyebrow.

"The same on my front with the KGB," added Nikita. "No unusual activity to report from any of my investigations on the movements of all key officials."

Sykes slammed his liver-spotted hand down on the table. "Come on, guys! Are we the CIA or some two-bit private investigator? Tell me that you can't see how what you're all working on is connected? If there is even a hint that the Soviet Union is not keeping to the disarming requirements of the treaty then it's a major and direct threat to our national security. For some reason, the FBI wanted to tell the president about this at a point when we have no proof, and now the pressure is on all of us. If we don't get answers it'll be all of our asses on the line."

"What do you want us to do, boss?" asked Nikita.

"Go and do your goddam jobs!" said Sykes, the vein now bulging again at his temple, and his neck corded. He opened the door and beckoned them out. "Get me some sort of a lead by the end of the week."

The other two walked back to their desks but Nikita excused himself and went to the bathroom. Locking the cubicle door behind him, he pushed the toilet seat lid down and sat down on it. He put his head in his hands and rubbed his weary eyes. It was what he had feared. They were asking for too many assassinations, and no matter how natural he made them look, it no longer took a genius to make the connection.

He got up, left the bathroom, headed back to his desk and spent the remainder of the afternoon deep in thought for how to salvage the situation while it was still based on suspicions and nothing more concrete.

He was still distracted and gazing blindly at his computer screen when home time loomed and Blaine gave him a nudge. "Jake! Anybody home?"

Nikita started slightly. "Hey, what's up?"

"Home time man, are we bound for the bar? Rodney's buying, remember!"

"Yeah, sure. I'm gonna have to catch you up though, just got a couple of things I need to wrap up here."

"Well don't take too long, it's hard enough getting Rodney to prize his wallet open at the best of times. I'm not even sure he *has* a wallet," said Blaine with a grin.

"No chance I'm missing that, buddy, be right behind you."

He waited as they all filtered out before gathering up his belongings, slinging his bag over his back and heading out through security. He walked swiftly through the car park to his grey Ford Sierra. It was in gear before the door had even closed. He drove into town and stopped at the first payphone he saw. He put a nickel into the slot and began dialling the number he had memorised. Just before he hit the final number he hesitated, and then put down the receiver.

Never deviate from procedure.

He took a deep breath. He was allowing himself to get spooked and that was not something he could afford to do. That is when mistakes were made, like calling his handler from the first payphone available on the route into town from the CIA headquarters.

"Yoptel-mopsel," he cursed himself in Russian under his breath, and went back to the car. He drove further into town before turning down a side street and pulling over. Feeling under the driver seat, he pulled out a short stick of chalk. He left the car and walked back to the main road, and bent down next to a low blue mailbox at a busy crossroads to tie his shoelace. On his way back up he drew his hand across the side of the mailbox and left a wide chalk stripe diagonally across it above the USPS logo. Sometimes the old ways were the safest. Now he must be patient.

Leaving his car where it was, he walked the three blocks to the bar where his colleagues awaited him. A sign outside read 'Happy Hour', which explained why the bar was so crowded when he entered. He spotted his friends packed into a booth at the rear of the bar, but avoided catching their eye and aimed instead for the bar. He needed a drink before he spoke to anyone this evening.

He pushed his way through the throng at the bar until he found a small space at the front.

He caught the eye of a mixed-race barmaid in figure hugging jeans and a black vest top, with whom he had been gently flirting for the past few months. She smiled warmly at him and mouthed 'one minute' as she fetched a couple of Budweisers out of the fridge for a girl further down the bar. He smiled and nodded back at her.

He felt so tightly wound and irritable; the noise of the bar was making his head throb and people were pushing and shoving behind and either side of him to get space at the bar. Squeezed and constricted, his heart rate increased; he felt ready to snap.

Closing his eyes, he forced himself to breathe and zone out. Control the emotions, he whispered in his mind. Be the water, not the wave.

"Jake… Jake?" The voice felt distant but loomed louder and his eyes snapped open. The roaring of the bar came back and he saw the barmaid standing in front of him.

"Everything OK, honey?" she asked with concern.

He blinked and smiled. "Sorry, Jess, I was a million miles away there. Tough day."

"Anything I can do to make it better?" she asked with a wink, placing a soft hand on top of his.

"If happy hour includes bourbon, then you might just be my hero," he said, laughing.

"I think I can manage that," she said, turning to the optics behind her, before placing two double whiskeys in front of him.

He picked one up and threw it straight down. He exhaled and felt an immediate feeling of relaxation fall over him, right through to his fingertips.

Smiling at Jess again, he said, "Like I said, my hero," as he handed her twenty dollars. "Keep the change."

"How about I don't keep the change and you take me out sometime," she said, trying and failing to look nonchalant.

Now Nikita put his hand on hers, and pushed the twenty-dollar bill into her hand before tenderly closing it. "Trust me when I tell you that taking the money is by far the better choice for you," he said, looking earnestly into her eyes and noticing that his American accent slipped slightly as he said her name.

"Maybe I'm a big girl who can make my own decisions," she said with a mocking smile. "One day you'll give in and go out with me!"

"I hope you're right," he said with a smile, before picking up his remaining whiskey and moving away through the crowds, eventually extricating himself and arriving at the booth where his colleagues were sitting.

"Was beginning to think you weren't coming, man," said Blaine, clapping him on the back, "Matthew, scooch over there," he said to the short black man with baleful eyes next to him, as they moved along to create space for Nikita, and pushed a White Russian in front of him.

"Look who's finally dragged himself away from the barmaid," said Chang archly, sitting directly across from him, next to Rodney.

"Why do you care if he's talking to the barmaid?" said a thin girl with long blond hair.

"Yes, Sarah, as Zara said, why do you care?" Nikita asked with a smile playing at the edge of his lips.

"I don't care a bit," replied Chang. "I just thought he preferred a better class of girl is all."

Zara snorted and said, "Like you, you mean," causing everyone to laugh and Chang to flush. Suddenly, Rodney started choking on an ice cube from his White Russian, providing a timely distraction for Nikita and Chang. Matthew started pounding on his back with all his might and the ice cube was eventually dislodged, shooting across the table and onto the floor.

"Dude, you aren't supposed to try and eat a White Russian," said Matthew as Rodney leant on his arms gasping for breath, White Russian dribbling right down the front of his shirt.

"You saved my life!" he said to Matthew and tried to give him a hug.

"Dude, get off me; you're all wet!"

"Let me give you a hug of gratitude, damn it," the big Rodney said, spreading his arms.

"Show it in words instead, man," said Matthew, pushing him off.

Nikita looked across at Chang as the others were distracted trying to stop Rodney from crushing the diminutive Matthew. She was looking at him, still flushed, and he smiled intently at her as he took a sip of his whiskey, and she relaxed, smiling back. He turned back to the melee next to him, with Rodney now trying to plant a kiss on Matthew, and felt Chang's foot rub against his leg. This caused a slight flutter in his stomach that he hadn't felt since his time with Elysia in Skyros all those months ago, in what felt like a different lifetime, and a different version of himself. He put her from his mind as he knew he must, but it was a constant battle. The job was all that mattered. The job and his family.

After a couple of hours — and multiple White Russians — one by one the CIA's elite team of Soviet counter-intelligence agents began to filter out of the bar. Nikita had been switching between bourbon and the milky vodka cocktails all evening and was enjoying a warm feeling and no thought of the search for the Black Russian. His sides hurt from laughing. He couldn't recall laughing before this assignment; even his childhood had been overshadowed by the hate of outsiders and laughter had rarely escaped his lips once old enough to know that he was hated and hunted. Eventually only he, Chang and Blaine were left.

"We should be heading home," said Blaine. "I could do without another sit down with the chief again tomorrow."

"Yeah, probably a good call," said Chang. "Do you guys want to split a cab? We're going in the same direction, sort of."

"Good plan," said Blaine, and Nikita nodded in agreement. They made their way outside, weaving slightly and hailed a cab.

"Man, oh man, work is going to suck tomorrow," said Blaine, squeezing in beside Nikita and Chang. "Shift over, guys," he said, shuffling over, forcing Chang firmly against Nikita. He could smell the tobacco and perfume in her hair and could think of little else.

"Maybe there's nothing in Sykes' theory and we're golden," said Chang, resting her hand on her leg so that her little finger was nearly touching Nikita's.

Blaine laughed. "He's never wrong is the problem. Made us look like idiots in there today!"

Nikita chuckled, but his thoughts were focused entirely on his little finger which he shifted slowly and as subtly as he could towards Chang's. He felt drunk and reckless.

The taxi drove out of town. As it passed through the crossroads Nikita had stopped at earlier, he saw that another diagonal stripe had been struck across his own on the mailbox. X marks the spot, he thought hazily, and despite his drink-infused brain he found his mind drifting to what his next step was. He was brought suddenly back into the present at the faintest of touches to his little finger as Chang's finger had moved to touching his.

Blaine was talking in almost a monologue about how much better the cocktails were in New York, but now Nikita moved his finger on top of Chang's, and they interlocked. He could almost feel the tension crackling between them, while Blaine talked on, completely unaware.

Ten minutes later the cab pulled up outside Blaine's apartment building and he got out, and threw them ten bucks for the cab before ambling his way up the path. The taxi pulled away and now the tension between them was palpable.

They were now holding hands fully and Nikita chanced a glance at Chang and found that she was already looking at him. Her stern face was softer than he'd seen it before and her eyes wide.

He leant in, but hesitated halfway, a moment of soberness in a night lost in a mist of whiskey and cocktails. But before he could pull back, she had grabbed his head with both hands and pulled his mouth to hers, kissing him deeply and passionately and all other thoughts of consequences drifted away. She tasted of cigarettes and vodka, a heady combination for any Russian, even one such as Nikita.

He didn't remember leaving the cab or the walk up to her house. He remembered kissing her deeply against her front door before she fumbled with keys and they fell inside.

They lay for a moment on the floor, facing each other with their feet still outside the front door. She pulled him to her once more and they continued kissing.

In his drunken state he suddenly became aware that they were there for the world to see. "Let's go inside," he whispered. "You never know who's watching in this town."

She smiled as he helped her up and he kicked the front door shut behind them. He kissed her hungrily once more before picking her up and carrying her into her bedroom.

When Nikita awoke the next morning it was still early, and it took him a minute to adjust his eyes to the gloom, feeling momentarily disorientated. He felt Sarah's arm across his torso and patchy memories of the night began to flow stutteringly back to him. Suddenly he became very aware that he was naked, and by the feel of her body against his, so was she.

Unfortunately, his upbringing in Russia had not helped him to be able to drink like one and his head felt like it had been split down the middle.

He pulled himself silently up and out of the bed, careful not to wake her. She stirred slightly but drifted back off to sleep as he picked up his clothes from the floor and went out into the living room where he dressed as quietly as he could. He ran some cold water from the tap in the kitchen and splashed it on his face before turning to leave.

He was at the front door when a voice behind him said, "You're not quite sprinting out the door but it ain't far off."

Nikita sighed and turned. Sarah was leaning against the door frame across the room, a bedsheet pulled roughly around her. Her hair was ruffled and her eyes squinted in the light. Despite her looking beautiful, Nikita suddenly wished the night before had never happened. She lit a cigarette and the feeling was reinforced.

"No, no, I just need to get home to change before work," he replied. He walked over to her.

"Don't make me regret fucking you, Jake," she said, lifting her head and blowing the smoke to the side.

He fought his instincts and pulled her to him kissing her on the lips. She hesitated then put her arms around him and kissed him back. The sheet fell to the ground and he could feel her firm breasts pressed against his chest and the feelings that had brought him here the night before began to stir slightly. The desire to crawl back into bed with her and rest his aching head grew stronger. But he knew duty called, and he could not miss work at such a crucial time.

He unfurled her arms from around him and admired her slender naked body before him. "I have to go," he whispered. "I'll see you in the office."

"Don't make it weird at work," she said in her semi-confrontational way.

"Of course not," he said, winking at her and leaving.

As the door shut behind him, he groaned to himself. He needed to find a way of relieving tension without being reckless with people's hearts… or his own liver. He couldn't risk compromising his ability to do his job exceptionally. He could feel himself becoming too comfortable with his life as Jacob Marshall. The life of an ordinary guy with ordinary friends, having an office romance.

I am not Jacob Marshall. I am not Nathan Martins. I am not Nikita Allochka. I am the Black Russian, he repeated to himself, and gave himself a firm slap on each cheek, before breaking into a run which he maintained for the seven blocks back to his own place. The sun was just covered up and stung his eyes as it lifted above the horizon. Every moment of the run was painful because of the pounding of his feet which echoed throughout his body and right through his head, but he forced himself to maintain his five-minute mile pace and swiftly covered the distance. By the time he reached his apartment, he was drenched with sweat and after doing a cursory check for bugs and listening devices around the apartment, an exercise he carried out diligently every day, he jumped straight into the shower. He stayed under icy cold water for as long as he could, before switching it to scalding hot and then dropping back to freezing again and jumped out. He felt cleansed and ready.

Walking out of the shower to his bedroom, he stopped suddenly. Something was not right. He fastened the towel firmly around his waist and slipped his hand under the dressing table, pulling out a Beretta M9 pistol from its hiding place. Barefoot, he crouched low and cocked his ear, pulling back the slide to kick the first bullet into place.

He was sure he had heard something in the other room.

He trod gently, his feed not making a sound on the carpeted floor, out of the bedroom and into the hallway. He kept his back to the wall and eased back the safety on the gun, which he held up in front of him, while remaining in a semi-crouch himself, moving sideways slowly and soundlessly.

He sniffed the air. He could smell alcohol and tobacco, and wondered if Sarah had followed him round. He paused, debating whether to lower the weapon in case it was her, but not wanting to be an open target if it was not.

He balanced it in his left hand and lowered it to one side where it was out of sight, but ready to swing up at the slightest sign of something untoward.

He moved forward, with more purpose now, into the gloom of the open plan kitchen/living room.

"You," he gasped.

CHAPTER 17

"Da, menya," replied Colonel Klitchkov, looking absurd to Nikita in civilian clothing. Dressed in a flannel shirt, jeans and trainers and lounging on his sofa, the colonel looked like an old Californian hippy rather than one of the most senior and powerful men in the KGB.

"And I think you mean you, sir."

"Of course, yes, sir. What are you doing here, sir?" Nikita whispered, looking alarmed.

"You left the signal," Klitchkov said simply.

"Yes, sir, but that was for Notrowski and I was going to leave shortly for our neutral meeting place," Nikita replied, emphasising the last part of the sentence. "My cover will be completely blown if you are seen here."

Klitchkov raised his eyebrows.

"Sir," added Nikita.

"Your handler Notrowski understands that I am replacing him, and he knew better than to question me. Believe it or not, agent, this is not my first day as a spy. I am well aware of the risks and of the importance of your anonymity to our national security."

"Of course, sir, this just feels very reckless..."

"Enough!" snapped Klitchkov. "One year in America and you have become insolent. Question my actions again and I will return you to the cold box in Russia. I hear that helped you to learn respect before, but perhaps you are still an impetuous Nigerian child," he said mockingly.

Nikita's face tightened and he looked coldly at the colonel. Suddenly he was aware of the tight skin on his thigh from the gunshot wound way back on the Kamchatka Peninsula.

"I am a Russian... sir," he said, trying to control his voice.

Klitchkov laughed, the demonic, condescending laugh he had first heard in his Kamenka shack years ago. "Of course, you are, my boy."

"I have done everything you have asked of me."

"For love of Russia? Or for your family?"

"They are one and the same to me, sir."

"You always were an exceptional liar," Klitchkov said, smiling brightly.

"You would rather I separate them?"

"There are those in the KGB who would have me be kinder to you. Yerin is concerned you have not been given enough of a reason to love Russia and could too easily be turned," Klitchkov said, folding his hands in his lap and looking at Nikita to see if he would pick up his challenge.

A silence fell between them in which they gazed at each other, weighing up whether to embrace a conflict or avoid one.

Nikita pushed his anger back down, and decided to swallow his pride. "The Soviet Union has always been my home, my country and in my soul. It has fed me and kept its promises to care for my family. The KGB is a tough life because it has to be. Holding grudges is futile and a waste of energy that could be better served in the service of our general secretary's goals."

"In another life you could have been a poet, comrade," Klitchkov said without a hint of humour. "But your point is a good one. We are an agency of business, and that is what I am here for. You have done good work these past few months. Exceptional work in fact." His demeanour was unrecognisable from just moments ago. "Now tell me why you signalled that you required an unscheduled meeting with your handler. But first, I am working on the assumption that you sweep your apartment for listening devices on a daily basis, da?"

"Da... of course, sir," Nikita said, feeling insulted at the hint of a suggestion that he would not have.

"Then proceed on why you broke with the KGB convention of avoiding contact with case officers as much as possible. I have gone many months without meeting a handler in some of my early missions."

Nikita glanced at the clock on the wall. It was seven thirty a.m. He did not have long before he would need to leave for work.

"I fear that the Americans are closing in on us. The missions I have been directed to carry out, they are too numerous and the Americans have taken notice."

"You are questioning your orders?" the colonel asked, looking irritated.

"Of course not, sir, which is why I carried out the missions without hesitation, and with great success. But despite there being no hint of scandal around the... deaths, there is a clear link between all of them. They have asked my team to investigate what they were calling the Black Russian, but are now calling the White Russian."

At this, Klitchkov burst into laughter. "The White Russian! You could not make this up. The American dogs!"

Nikita couldn't help but let a slight smile escape in spite of himself. "The name change was a directive that came straight from the president," he said, smiling more broadly. At this Klitchkov broke into a fresh wave of giggles. Nikita looked at the colonel, holding his sides giggling, with concern. Despite all of his training, this was the most unpredictable and unreadable man he had ever come across. He was either insane or brilliant. Most likely both, he thought to himself.

Klitchkov wiped his eyes. "Apologies for my indiscretion there, agent. Please do continue."

"Sir, as I'm sure you know, I have been charged with analysing the KGB itself, particularly Yerin. But our station chief has now asked me to work with the analyst investigating Soviet adherence to the INF Treaty, and also the analyst looking into the White Russian. He has begun questioning the reasons for the death of the secretary of defense..."

"Has he indeed," said Klitchkov, placing his palms together and balancing his chin on his fingers, lost in thought. "It seems the vultures are beginning to circle around the feast."

Nikita didn't reply, allowing his superior to focus on thoughts. He walked over to the window and peered through a crack in the curtain to check the street for any unusual behaviour. Nothing out of the ordinary could be seen, but he remained in a state of high tension. He would not be allowed to live if his true identity was uncovered. He was no fool; if the Americans captured him but didn't kill him then the Russians would in order to prevent him revealing their secrets.

"Are you throwing them off the scent?" Klitchkov inquired.

"Wherever I can, sir, but the closer they get, the greater the threat to my cover."

"Your cover cannot be blown under any circumstances. Are your nerves holding?"

"Sir?"

"There have been some concerns raised that your edge may have gone too soft."

"On what grounds, Colonel?" Nikita asked, raising his eyebrow.

The colonel sat back and attempted a relaxed position, though his stiff soldiering posture made the act look rigid nonetheless. "I imagine you like it here in America; you are able to fit in better perhaps than in Russia."

"I prefer it in Russia, sir. There I know who the racists are because they tell me to my face. Here they hide it, instead saying what they think is the politically correct thing to say, while they avoid shaking hands or the police find reasons to pull you over."

The colonel smiled. "You have been drinking a lot, da?"

"Have I been away from Russia so long that drinking is now frowned upon?"

"High level assets such as yourself are held to different standards. I do not understand; you always refused vodka throughout your training."

"I am doing what I can to gain the trust of my team. Their guard drops when they drink, sir."

"And what of your guard, agent? Where was that when you went to bed with your colleague last night? A japóška no less — why was I not surprised?" Klitchkov rolled his eyes callously.

"You were spying on me?" Nikita demanded angrily, ignoring the pretext of the colonel's comment.

Klitchkov stopped smiling. "This is the KGB, you arrogant little shit. A spy organisation. You think yourself above everyone else? You let your youth betray you. Nobody escapes our eyes."

"Sorry, sir, I am angrier at myself for not recognising my tail."

"Perhaps if you stopped drinking that brown whiskey shit and drank a Russian man's drink you would have kept a greater hold on your senses.

"Possibly, but if I start drinking neat vodka that might set alarm bells ringing."

"Possibly, agent, possibly."

"I cannot deny spending last night with a woman from my team. But she is an asset I need to keep close, as she is the analyst assigned to investigating the White Russian."

Klitchkov said nothing but studied the young assassin's face. It appeared earnest, but then his training had taught him to appear earnest.

"Very well, I will take your word for the moment. Her name?" he said, withdrawing a small notepad and pen from his pocket.

"Sarah Chang," replied Nikita without hesitation. "Notrowski already has her details, along with everyone else in my unit." He saw Klitchkov writing her name down in Cyrillic characters along with some further notes that he couldn't decipher from his distance.

"At some point every asset must be burned. You will be able?"

Nikita nodded, showing no emotion. "It is what I have been trained for."

"Very well. You are right to gain her trust; if she gets too close you will need to use this to your advantage. What have you given them on Yerin?"

"So far very little. I'm reporting accurately what I've been able to decipher from the outside, which is that his movements appear very normal, and that no unusual KGB activity is visible. I need to give them something else. Something on our possible retreat from Afghanistan perhaps?"

"We never retreat!" said Klitchkov with scorn. "It is a victorious withdrawal. If I ever hear you use the word retreat again you will wish you had stayed in the cold box. It is a word that struck fear into all of us who fought for victory against the German Nazi pigs many years ago. I did not fight to defend Stalingrad through the bleakest of winters in 1942 to raise Soviet agents who talked so carelessly about retreats."

"Yes, sir, your bravery in the war is famous. What I meant was that perhaps the… victory in Afghanistan presents an opportunity to feed the Americans a story to divert their attentions away from the INF Treaty."

"Do whatever you must to turn their attentions away from investigating our nuclear disarmament," he said shortly.

"And what of the White Russian lead? It would not be prudent to eliminate anyone else connected to the Cold War."

"Agreed. There is a plan in place."

"Who do you have in mind?" Nikita asked.

"That is classified, agent."

"I will need to know my assignment, sir."

"Not every assignment is carried out by you, Allochka. You are part of a network, do not forget that. You are far from the only agent we have in the CIA. While you are significant, you are not the only vital asset. Everyone can be replaced."

Nikita looked at him, and he knew that they were both fully aware that he was irreplaceable and an agent it would take years to replicate. It did cause him to think about who else was a CIA mole. Most, he imagined, would be American double agents, but he was curious to know if any others from the Soviet Union had been so deeply embedded.

"Of course, I understand, Colonel. Please forgive my assumption."

"I know you excel at fooling lie detectors, which is what made your entry into the CIA possible. But even the most steadfast and resilient of people can crack when pressure is applied to the right place. What you do not know you cannot divulge. It is standard protocol as you well know. You receive instruction related to your mission alone; anything else is not your concern. What is your concern is maintaining your cover and giving the Americans whatever it is, they need to look elsewhere. There are plans in motion to ensure that US and NATO staff see what they need to see at our mid-range nuclear sites."

"Has there been a change of strategy, sir?"

"Of course not, this is the tip of an iceberg we have been developing for years. Do not fear, comrade, your cover is safe and we will ensure that the Americans get what they need. Now let us talk about how to sow the seeds of doubt into their theory of the White Russian..." said Klitchkov, leaning forwards and chuckling again at the code name.

***

Half an hour later, Nikita was in a cab on the way into town to his car. He noticed that the chalk marks on the mailbox had now disappeared.

His head was whirring from his conversation with Klitchkov. It felt so strange that the colonel would visit him in person; it was what his handler was trained for. It only served to pile pressure on him for what was a mission already pushing him to the edge of his nerves. He could feel the weight of the Soviet empire pushing down on him and it felt crushing. As he got out of the cab and into his own car, he spotted a liquor store already open for business and felt a pull to get himself a drink to prepare him for the day. Removing his hand from the door he slapped himself round the face. "What are you becoming Nikita?" he said to himself, and started up the car, pulling off and making his way to work. He needed his wits to be razor sharp if he was to successfully manufacture another deception of an entire intelligence agency and government.

Chewing his lip, a habit he had developed when deep in thought, his mind was completely preoccupied with his conversation with the man he could not figure out. Sometimes he hated him; sometimes he felt he was just being pushed to become what he must. Sometimes he longed for an easy, normal life. Certainly, he wished for a life of peace. Sleeping was become increasingly elusive to him. During the days, he barely spared a thought for his victims who were now piling up considerably. But at night, that was when they returned to him. Their faces, the light in their eyes fading until extinguished, the souls that would be waiting for him in the afterlife. He considered himself a rational man and gave little credence to such things as an afterlife during his waking hours, but the night brought with it doubts, fears and a desire for there to be something greater than himself that could save his soul.

Recently he had come across Theodore Roosevelt's words which had since become his mantra. 'Nothing in the world is worth having or worth doing unless it means effort, pain, difficulty. I have never in my life envied a human being who leads an easy life. I have envied a great many people who led difficult lives and led them well.'

The irony of using the words of a former US president as a motivation for his current pursuits wasn't lost on him.

After going through the daily security checks, he parked his car and headed into the ugly, largely concrete Central Intelligence Agency offices, enduring further security checks. Then he made his way through the labyrinth of corridors to the dingy rooms of the Soviet Counter-intelligence Branch, all the while running on autopilot.

He hadn't given a moment's thought to Chang until he keyed in his passcode, entered the office and saw her standing over by the coffee machine, talking to a middle-aged woman with hair drawn tightly back who he knew to be a researcher named Julie.

He paused, and she glanced over at him. They made awkward eye contact before he looked quickly away and made his way over to his desk. He couldn't afford distractions, and the words of Klitchkov echoed around his head. 'At some point every asset must be burned.'

Blaine was sitting bleary-eyed at his desk and grunted at Nikita as he sat down. Nikita was in no mood for conversation so set his bag down, and checking that Chang was no longer at the kitchen point, made his way over. He made himself a strong black coffee which he drank there and then, before pouring himself another, and getting himself some water. Arriving back at his desk, he took two aspirin and, despite feeling sick, the caffeine and drugs soon began to course through his veins and he felt an improvement.

He was very aware of Chang glancing at him out of the corner of his eye, but he focused instead on the large list of papers on the tray in front of him that he needed to work through. Field agents were gathering vast tomes of information for him to sift and analyse on a daily basis and it could be gruelling work requiring high levels of concentration.

He could hear Blaine muttering to himself as he was wading through his own pile, circling paragraphs and underlining words.

"You're doing it again, Blaine," Nikita said.

"Sorry, dude, I just find it so much easier to concentrate if I read aloud to myself."

"Most of us grow out of that at around the age of ten."

"At my high school most graduates only had the reading age of ten so just be grateful that I'm able to read at all."

"You're right, what was I thinking? I'm so grateful," said Nikita.

"You're a mean drunk."

"On the contrary, I am a very loveable drunk. It's the hangovers that make me mean."

Blaine laughed and then scrunched his eyes up and rubbed his temples. "Don't make me laugh this morning. Not cool."

"You're right, silence would really be the best thing for both of us this morning," said Nikita, winking.

Blaine scrunched up a piece of paper and threw it at Nikita. "OK, OK, point taken!"

Nikita returned to his papers, many of which were reporting largely insignificant information. He had to go through them in painstaking detail; it was the not the sort of work he had imagined doing when being trained to be a spy. So many of the days working as an analyst for the CIA, particularly in the Soviet Counter-intelligence Branch, were spent poring over reams of paper; pages and pages documenting the movements of KGB officers and political figures in a bid to understand underlying intent, to make connections, identify trends and predict future activity and movements.

However, working as an embedded spy made the process slightly different. For Nikita, he could clearly put faces to many of the names he read about, and had to fight the urge to give up information on those Soviets that had treated him most cruelly. His days were an exercise in swimming against the tide, while doing enough good analysis to keep his job.

He was constantly astounded at the amount of paperwork the CIA produced, and the level of contact CIA agents were required to keep with station chiefs. At the KGB it had been instilled in him to avoid leaving a paper trail at all costs. Cables were rarely sent, and every KGB agent from junior lieutenants up to rezidents was tested regularly on their ability to covertly dispatch pouches of undeveloped microfilm, which would be sent on to Moscow to be developed and printed. A KGB officer was held personally responsible for every single piece of paper that he printed. 'You are expected to be self-sufficient and able to handle your assignments with minimal input. You do not seek support from your superiors unless absolutely necessary.' The words of his trainers echoed around Nikita's head.

Sorting through the papers he came across a document that he knew would be there. The file was a plain pale brown, no different from many of the others, but this one was titled 'Domestic Activity'.

Unusually, it hadn't come across from the Federal Bureau of Investigation, but was a file that had been passed to him from the Soviet-

East (SE) European division of the Department of Operations within the CIA, based within these very headquarters. Nikita knew of the department, with their inevitably being a great deal of overlap between the two, but also a great deal of competition, and the SE division usually tried to avoid handing over information to the counter-intelligence division if they could avoid it.

There was nothing to distinguish the file at all, but upon seeing it Nikita instinctively knew that this was the one he had been looking for. He opened it and placed it down on top of the other files and papers. There were only three pages in the folder. The first was headlined 'Suspected USSR activity on US Soil'.

SUSPECTED USSR ACTIVITY ON US SOIL — OCTOBER 1987

It is well understood that there are spies from the Soviet Union operating on US soil, mainly from the KGB. However, following the signing of the INF Treaty, espionage activity has appeared to slow as relations between both nations show signs of improvement.

Recent reports from the FBI and NSA point to potential increased covert Soviet activity on American soil, with numerous assassinations that would be in direct contravention of the rules of the Cold War to date, and if proven, could be considered an act of war.

In light of General Secretary Petrenko's policy of Glasnost and suggestions that they may be withdrawing from the Afghan-Soviet war which would be in direct contravention of the Brezhnev Doctrine's principle of 'Never Letting Go', it is unlikely that they would seek to undo so much of the progress we have made in cordial relations with the Politburo. However, the SE department is seeing increased activity through the East-European satellite states, particularly in Czechoslovakia, Hungary and Lithuania. We request the aid of the Soviet Counter-intelligence Branch in investigating mercenary activity from hard-line Soviet communists.

One figure, identity unknown, was seen in Odessa, Texas on the day of the death of Secretary of Defense Simon Conlan. Although identity is unknown, it is an individual we know to have links to the KGB and is a suspected rogue KGB agent. It is suspected that he may either be, or at least has links to the assassin, code name The White Russian.

REPORT COMPILED BY SOVIET-EAST DIVISION.
ZB.

Nikita turned the page over and saw that the second page was a grainy A4 photo. It was black and white and the numbers in the corner combined with the low quality of the image suggested that it was a freeze frame from closed circuit television footage. The image was taken on a dark street with which he was unfamiliar, but the figure at the centre of the image was unmistakable — the handsome face with high cheekbones and mouth curled in a perpetual half smile laced with contempt. Agent Taras Brishnov. On the back of the photo had been scrawled, 'Captured in central Odessa, Texas. March 21, 1987.'

He turned to the next page and saw that it was another photo. This one was of better quality and looked to have been taken with a long lens camera. It showed Brishnov, this time much more clearly and several years younger, dressed in the KGB uniform of the long grey coat belted in gold at the waist, and a matching grey ushanka. Long black leather boots disappeared up underneath the long coat, while his hands were hidden under black leather gloves. He was shaking hands with the imposing form of former Soviet General Secretary Leonid Brezhnev with his hunched shoulders and thick, slug-like eyebrows. Alongside them stood Viktor Yerin, looking no younger and no less serious, but somehow less disapproving. Behind them the crimson flag fluttered boldly, the golden star, hammer and sickle clearly visible in what must have been a stiff breeze.

Nikita let out a low hiss, put the photo down and closed the folder. He then opened it and inspected it all once more. He looked at the face of his fellow KGB agent from the dark hair, taking in the scar and the straight nose down to the firm jaw, to the dead eyes. He absorbed everything about the man who he despised but who had saved his life. The man he must now burn.

It was incredible that a man who had been operating within the KGB since the days of Brezhnev (replaced back in 1982 following his death) and had completed countless missions both foreign and domestic, had kept his identity completely unknown until now. For that, Nikita had to admire him. After being a fully-fledged KGB agent for little more than a year, a trail of breadcrumbs already led to his existence as an agent even if his identity remained hidden. Yet Brishnov had remained under the radar of even the CIA agents embedded within both Brishnov and Petrenko's inner circles, a feat for which he commanded respect.

Surveying the report once more, his eyes landed on the letters at the bottom of the document. ZB.

Were they the initials of the other high-level Soviet asset operating within the CIA? If he was going to be liaising with him, why had Klitchkov been so cagey about the identity of other operatives? Perhaps they were not initials, but a departmental acronym unfamiliar to him.

He picked up the file and walked over to Chang, cursing that it was her that had been assigned the role of researcher on the case of the White Russian. She was gazing intently at her screen on which were microfilms of newspaper cuttings that he could not see clearly from where he stood. Behind the computer was a large cork board on which were pinned more newspaper clippings and photos of people that were hauntingly familiar to him. It represented a photo album of his US assassinations and it felt uncomfortable seeing it so brazenly in front of him.

He averted his gaze and threw himself down in the chair next to her.

She looked up and smiled awkwardly.

"How's the head?" he asked, smiling.

She looked around nervously. "Not too bad. Everything OK? You never come over to my desk."

"Well for some reason I thought today maybe the rules had changed a little," he replied coyly.

She frowned at him and whispered angrily, "Why are you talking like this in the office?"

"OK, chill out," he said, holding his hands up defensively, which only seemed to serve to agitate her further. He lifted the file in front of her. "I may have something that could bring us a little closer to the White Russian."

She raised her eyebrows. "Oh really?" she said in a voice dripping with cynicism. She waved a hand at the photos and clippings on the board. "Because if you can see anything in these deaths to link us to a Soviet assassin, you're a far better analyst than me."

I can't take too much credit, but the guys over at SE seem to have a theory."

"The SE are coming to us with a theory?" she said disbelievingly.

"More than a theory actually, there's a solid lead to pursue here. I guess they're pretty swamped with all the activity in the Eastern Bloc at the moment. I hear Hungary is on the verge of another revolution."

She grabbed the file from his hand and skimmed across the report before looking at the two images.

"It's tenuous. Barely a lead," she snapped. "I mean are we sure this is the same guy in both the photos?"

"Come on, it's clearly the same guy. Look at the cheekbones, the shape of the face."

She traced the face of the CCTV shot. "I can't see a scar on his face here."

"Of course you can't, the resolution is terrible. Why are you resisting this?"

She looked at him crossly. "It feels a bit manufactured."

"What do you mean?" he said, confused.

She lowered her voice to a whisper again. "That the day after we sleep together you find a way for us to work a case together."

He looked at her, surprised. "Jesus, Sarah, look we are both professionals and we have a job to do. I have enough on without creating cases to work just to be closer to you for a few hours more a day. Do you hear yourself?"

She said nothing so he continued. "You're investigating the existence of a covert KGB agent carrying out assassinations on US soil, and I'm leading on KGB movements and operations. We have a duty to the American people to pursue it and try to prevent any more deaths. If you don't want to work with me on this then I'm sure I can ask the chief to find me someone else who will. This is the sort of case that analysts die to get their hands on."

She softened slightly and brushed the hair from her eyes. "Sorry, Jake, I'm just a bit tired today for some reason." She smirked at him. "And this case is driving me nuts." She pulled out a cigarette, lit up and breathed out, closing her eyes in thought. "If this White Russian is real…"

"I know," he said, nodding. He coughed as she blew smoke in his direction, but she ignored him.

"Christ, I figured I would be doing low level analysis when I joined, not investigating the existence of a KGB agent that could cause the outbreak of World War Three. Have you ever seen this guy before?" she asked, signalling to the photo of Brishnov which lay open on the desk next to her.

"Never," he said without missing a beat. "Which is incredible if he was senior enough to be close to both Yerin and Brezhnev. Like Yerin, perhaps he was very much Brezhnev's man, which would support the SE's theory that he's potentially now a rogue agent."

"This would be a hell of a lot easier to look into if they hadn't cracked our codes and executed all of our agents on Soviet soil in the past couple of years."

Nikita pulled the report from the file. "Any idea what ZB is?" he asked, pointing at the letters at the bottom of the page.

She peered over at it. "No idea. I guess initials of someone over there."

"You don't know who?"

"Jake, I don't even know where their office is, let alone who those vultures are. What does it matter who put the report together anyway?"

"Hmmm? Oh no, I don't suppose it does; I was just curious. I mean where did they get the idea to look into CCTV footage on this particular street?"

She shrugged. "Head up there and ask if it bothers you so much. Our job isn't to ask questions but to find the answers."

"You're right. I might not survive a trip into the lion's den of the SE office. They're probably all white," he joked in an undertone as he stood up, fighting the curiosity and desire to meet another KGB asset within the CIA.

"We have to take this to Sykes," Chang said. "If nothing else it puts the involvement of the nuclear disarmament process out of the picture. We need to loop in Blaine too."

"You think we should go to Sykes with no proof and just another empty theory? I could do without another dressing down. Let's ask Blaine." He signalled to his desk mate who was looking increasingly worse for wear, and looked relieved to have a reason to step away from his paperwork.

"What's up? If you're going to suggest the bar again tonight, then no way man. I can't keep pace."

Chang laughed. "What happened to your strong Irish blood?"

He looked mournfully at Chang. "You don't look much better."

"Charming," she said, crossing her arms. Blaine spluttered to try and correct himself but Nikita saved him. "Yes, we all look awful. This isn't about drinking though, this is about the case Sykes wants us to work on, and we have a new lead that could save you a lot of grunt work."

"I don't hate the sound of that," said Blaine, brightening slightly. Nikita passed his colleague the file and watched his eyes widen as he looked through. "You guys think this is legit?" he asked.

"Jake does," said Chang archly. "I'm not so sure, but it's the only lead we've got and it would fit with the current political climate in Russia."

"I can't deny that it makes me happy. Trying to predict Russian disarmament is difficult enough without it becoming part of a major conspiracy to crush America. Definitely a line worth pursuing. Look into it before telling the chief though; he doesn't like empty theories. I found that out the hard way when I suggested the Boston Celtics would win the playoffs this year. Big mistake."

"I agree," said Nikita. "Sarah, we need to find answers on this and fast. Lives depend on it."

"OK. First of all, we need to find out who the White Russian is, and where he is," she replied.

"I'll find the who, you find the where," said Nikita. "If he is close to Yerin then I should be able to track down someone who can give me that information."

They each returned to their desks with a renewed energy and sense of purpose. Nikita sat down and smiled inwardly. So far, the plan was working.

CHAPTER 18

Agent Taras Brishnov almost shook with excitement. Being forced to play second fiddle to the black piece of shit, a man he exceeded in rank, experience, kills, and not to mention the fact that he was actually Russian, had started a fire of rage in his gut. Now, finally a mission worth his quality.

From his days growing up in Leningrad he had always felt different to others. Other children shunned him and he viewed them all with a cold detachment. The only time he felt anything was when he was allowed to cause them pain.

Pain.

That was everything. Pain was power. Pain was pleasure.

He snaked the barrel of the gun over the quivering form of the woman below him, enjoying her whimpers. She could not be much older than eighteen and looked half starved, but those big brown eyes drove him wild.

"Pwease, you are hurrding me," the skinny young woman pleaded dully, the leather strap stretching her mouth and drawing blood as she tried to speak. Bruises on her arms showed that she was used to cruelty, but rarely did she feel as afraid as she did now. The leather strap wrapped around the back of her head and looped into a handle which the KGB agent had his hand through and was pulling back.

"Hush, child," he crooned, trailing the barrel of his Desert Eagle down the spine of her pale white back as he stood behind her, with her crouched on all fours on a shabby four-poster bed. Not usually his gun of choice, it felt too showy and he preferred something much subtler. But for an occasion such as this he could not deny it gave an enormous sense of power.

"This is a very special day and we must treat it as such. Do you know why it is so very special?" he asked. The girl said nothing, and he tugged on the strap sharply causing her to groan with pain.

"I asked you a question, my dear," he said flatly.

"Why it speshal?" she said, her head jerked round as he pulled at the leash again. A thin trail of blood was trailing its way down her neck from the corner of her mouth.

Brishnov unbuckled his belt and pulled down the zip of his swollen trousers and his eyes rolled into the back of his head as he forced his way inside the young prostitute. He snaked his finger up the trail of blood, before putting the gun to her temple as his pace quickened.

"Pwease no," she said stutteringly, trying to grimace and get through the ordeal. He laughed cruelly and pushed the gun harder into her temple, so that blood was drawn from there too, and he felt himself become even more aroused. He let the gun drop onto the bed in front of the woman.

"This day is special, my love, because I have been asked to kill the vice president of the United States."

Now she began to cry and the tears made their way down her cheeks, mingling with the blood and sweat around her chapped and gagged mouth. "Pwease, I donn wanna know," she sobbed, knowing what him providing her with that information meant.

She began to squirm against the bonds around her wrists, which only served to drive the man behind her even wilder.

"I am going to strike a fatal blow right to the heart of these capitalist pigs who think to govern the world. Soon America will fall to the might of Communist Russia," he gasped as he pounded faster and pulled back harder on her leash so that her body was contorted painfully. Now the blood fell thickly from her mouth and she was crying in fits.

He broke into a stream of Russian that the girl didn't understand, and she tried to push him backwards with her foot but he was so strong that she had no hope of overpowering him. He pulled her head around to the side so that she could not see him reach for the gun.

He allowed the leash on her head to relax and she prayed to God for the first time in years that he was showing her mercy, but then she felt the cold metal of the gun's barrel press against her skull.

"Please no!" she screamed, in her terror having managed to bite clean through the leather at her mouth. His pace was fast and furious and he was grunting amidst the solid monologue of Russian that he uttered in a fast, low voice.

The screaming only served to spur him on and suddenly he tensed and shouted, "Mat' Rossiya!" As she screamed once more, and her back arched, he pulled the trigger of the Desert Eagle.

She slumped forward and he gasped as drool dripped from his mouth and he shuddered from the intensity of the pleasure.

He wiped his mouth on his sleeve and looked down at the pitiful form in front of him, a mixture of blood, sweat and tears and the shame flooded him, as it always did.

Looking around the room as if taking it in for the first time, Brishnov looked at the crumbling four-poster bed with the well-worn satin sheets and sputtering candles around the walls. How could he have been so careless?

"Bol' do udovol'stviya," he said to himself. *Always pain before the pleasure.*

To become a slave to his own depravity was unforgivable. And with an American girl no less. His father would never forgive him.

But then, he probably would not have forgiven his son for killing him either. Taras Brishnov's father had been a cold man who would warm himself on cold Leningrad nights with strong vodka and even stronger kicks to his young son. Like every beaten dog, one day he turned on his master. It was Brishnov's first kill. He fervently hoped this American hooker was not his last.

He moved over to the window of the room, which had been painted over, and with some effort, forced it open. The seasoned KGB agent looked out at the deserted alleyway below and weighed his chances. Backing himself, he jumped out without a backward glance at his pitiful victim and landed on all fours on the cold concrete a floor below, rolling to absorb the impact.

After brushing himself down, he stalked off, the cold killer once more with no thoughts of the flesh to distract him.

The White Russian was on the move.

As he walked away, an expressionless face with a toothbrush moustache and large thick glasses appeared at the window of a building opposite the brothel and peered after the assassin, focusing the lens of a bulky camera and snapping him silently. He took out a pen and made a note in a small notebook he produced from within his long coat, before snapping it shut. On the front cover were the letters ZB.

***

Viktor Yerin walked purposefully through the ornate gilded halls of the Kremlin. For a man well into his sixties he moved well, the result of a daily regime of calisthenics and a history of military discipline carried with him throughout his adult life.

The chairman of the KGB was dressed in a dark grey suit and black tie, and in his hand carried a briefcase. As a key member of the Politburo, the supreme executive and legislative body of the Communist Party and Soviet Union government, for the past three years he had been able to move with ease through government halls, but it was rare that the leader of the Soviet Union summoned him directly. Or at least it had been, but times were changing.

Walking straight past the secretary, Yerin paused outside the heavy wooden door of the leader's office, then setting his shoulders, raised his head and knocked.

"Da," came the reply, and he pushed open the door.

Yerin remembered the office as it had been under Brezhnev. He even remembered it from a visit once while Nikita Krushchev was general secretary, when he had maintained the look and feel Stalin had enjoyed. Back then there had been a highly decorative, polished wooden floor and walls of deep crimson. All that now remained was the dark oak desk behind which sat the leader of the communist world and the largest nation on the planet, surrounded by grey walls and a largely colourless room.

Mikhail Petrenko pushed himself up from the hard wooden chair. "Viktor, thank you for coming," he said in his firm voice and shook hands with the KGB leader. "You look tired, comrade," he added.

"Work loves fools," said Yerin, reciting the Russian proverb.

Petrenko laughed. "Yes, but no water runs under an idle stone," he replied with a proverb of his own. He gestured towards a chair at his desk. "Please sit," he said and returned to his own seat. He sat looking at Yerin, his hands folded in front of him.

Stirring uncomfortably, Yerin asked, "You summoned me?"

The smile faded slightly from Petrenko who with a grunt pulled open a drawer at his desk and delved into it. Yerin surveyed the man before him. His skin was almost grey, and the size of his belly had crept over the mark from portly to fat.

He produced the bottle of vodka and the two glasses he had been searching for.

"I keep the good stuff for those I know will appreciate it," Petrenko said smiling, and Yerin saw that his nose was a deepveined red as he poured the clear liquid into the two glasses. "Nazdarovje," said Petrenko, raising his glass, which was echoed by Yerin.

"To the matter of business then," said the Soviet leader. "I want an update on the situation in America; I feel devoid of information."

"You are not receiving my missives, sir?" asked Yerin, knowing full well that he had been.

"You and I both know that there is a great deal missing from your missives, Viktor, and I would know the full story. I am hearing rumours that they have uncovered the Black Russian. Tell me this is not true."

"It is not true," Viktor replied coldly. He prided himself on the thoroughness of his reports.

"Come now, Viktor, you are very sensitive for a man who leads the world's greatest and toughest security agency. I also know that you are a master of clandestine work and missives can fall into the wrong hands so easily. But now in person I would know all that is too sensitive to be written down."

Yerin nodded, pacified. "The Americans have begun to get dangerously close to the truth, but Colonel Klitchkov is devising a plan to lead them elsewhere."

"You think him cleverer than the CIA, FBI, NSA and US government?"

"Without a doubt, sir," replied Yerin without a trace of humour. "I do not yet know the full details of his plan, but as it stands the Black Russian's identity remains intact, and we are working to ensure that the agent we call Kolokol remains unmasked."

"Is the influence of Kolokol still as great?"

"This year alone he has given us over thirty foreign agents of the CIA operating in Soviet territories. We believe we have now gathered the vast majority of American spies in Moscow thanks to him. He has been the single greatest asset we have ever possessed."

"You did excellent work in turning him, Viktor. But I am concerned about why they are getting so close to our Black Russian."

"The agent has carried out his missions perfectly, and is doing excellent work in undermining the CIA's Soviet counter-intelligence work."

"If he is so perfect then how do they know he exists?"

"At present, sir, they remain unaware of his existence; they merely suspect that a KGB agent is on US soil carrying out assassinations. They have exceeded expectations in putting together a trail of breadcrumbs from the deaths, despite our efforts to ensure all of them looked natural or accidental."

"You have a silver tongue from your years in politics, Viktor!" chuckled Petrenko. "But either you have underestimated our enemy, or you have made a grave mistake with the missions you have sent our agent on. Which is it, I wonder?" the general secretary asked, suddenly serious.

Viktor said nothing.

"We both know that you have far too much experience to underestimate our American adversaries, which means that your orders are where the problem is. Give me the list of all of his missions."

Yerin opened his briefcase and withdrew a sheet of paper. Petrenko's eyes widened and he looked over the top of his glasses. "You are not serious, Viktor."

"Yes, sir, they were all targets identified by our analysts that needed to be eliminated. The research was good."

"Be that as it may, to order the elimination of this many key figures in such a short space of time, is madness! It looks almost as if you wanted them to find out."

"I assure you, sir, that I acted only in the best interests of the country."

The Soviet leader threw a photo down in front of Yerin. "And tell me, comrade, how is this acting in the best interests of the country?"

Yerin wiped his glasses with a handkerchief. Placing them back on, he peered down at the photo. It showed him standing next to a black state security car, seemingly deep in conversation with an ugly, overweight man wearing an ushanka and a long coat. A gap between the fur of the hat and the collar of the coat revealed a tattoo of a three-ray swastika.

His eyes bulged. "You are spying on me?"

"Do not insult me with false naivety, Viktor. Why are you colluding with Lev Veselovsky, the known leader of the neo-Nazi group Pamyat?"

Yerin was clearly working to remain calm, but shifted restlessly on his chair. "It was part of an investigation into the growing far right movement, sir. Strictly routine. Sir, I assure you I am not aligning myself with him. I have served loyally for many years."

"If it was the photo alone, perhaps I would believe you. But the facts are not in your favour, my friend." He read a message from a piece of paper on his desk. "'Lev, together we shall free Russia from the brink of collapse and the shackles of our rudderless leader'. I can go on if you want, Viktor? The letter is quite illuminating and appears to have your signature at the bottom."

The colour had drained completely from Yerin's face, and his knuckles were white as he gripped the chair.

"You have two choices; resign right now, or force me to declare you a traitor and enemy of the state, for which you know better than anyone the penalty."

Yerin's face had turned beetroot red with fury. "You cannot remove me. The KGB are loyal to me."

"The KGB are loyal to the Soviet Union, something that you managed to forget when being blinded by pure ambition, Viktor. To seek to provoke nuclear war with the United States before we are prepared… it would mean the destruction of everything we have built."

"You have built nothing," spat Yerin through clenched teeth. "You only seek to take us apart piece by piece with your perestroika shit."

Petrenko sighed. "Come, Viktor, you are one of the very few even in the Politburo who knows of my grand plan. Perestroika, Glasnost — these are not real; they are words to manipulate the world to the will of the USSR. You disappoint me greatly, Viktor. I thought we could revive the fortunes of our nation side by side. You cleansed the American spies so wonderfully! What did Veselovsky promise you? I will have your honesty."

"Honesty!" Yerin laughed. "You lie to the world with a dagger behind your back and you ask for my honesty! You make Russia a home for Jews, chernozhopiys and gypsies and talk of making us great again. You are contaminating us enough with Turkmen and Armenians. Your nuclear plan will not succeed; our Empire will have collapsed before you can ever bring it to fruition. All relying on Klitchkov's favourite, a Nigerian no less, to save us. We must destroy our enemies now. There is only one way for the Soviet Union; splendid isolation."

"You Hohli fool, Viktor," sighed Petrenko, deliberately antagonising his victim further with talk of his Ukrainian origins. "Pamyat is a cancer that is spreading like Hitler's Germany and enough blood has been spilt by this nation fighting the very thing you choose to promote. You fought at Leningrad to defend us from their evil. Now, it is you that is evil. Pamyat will be stopped, and now so must you be."

"We both know you can't just accept my resignation," said Yerin, sinking into his chair, defeated. "You have a revolver in your desk; please use it, General Secretary. It would be merciful."

"Alas, Viktor, you know that is not the way out for traitors. First, we will need to know everything you know. If you cooperate, perhaps then we will show mercy."

"It is too late to stop what is already in motion."

Petrenko pressed a button under his desk and immediately two armed guards walked in. Behind them sauntered a familiar face.

"You!" said Viktor, fury in his eyes once more as he looked upon the face of one of his key protégés.

"Yes, Viktor," replied Maxim Denisov, dressed in full navy KGB uniform, complete with the hat despite being indoors. "Let us not make this awkward. I am prepared to treat you with more respect than a traitor deserves, but only if you do not make things difficult."

Yerin did not move. "Please kill me," he pleaded.

"Very well," said Denisov and drew the ceremonial revolver from the holster at his belt and pointed it directly at the face of the old man, whose will, immediately dissolved, and he held up his hands, sobbing.

"Lieutenant-Colonel, remember where you are," said Petrenko sharply.

"I am not a politician," the KGB trainer said in his reedy voice, "I am state security, and this man has made our state insecure, sir."

"You also report to me, or have you forgotten the discipline that you preach to your recruits?"

Denisov immediately holstered his weapon, and saluted Petrenko. "No, sir." He whistled to the two guards who picked up Yerin by the armpits and dragged him from the room. Denisov again saluted and walked from the office, drawing the doors closed behind him.

The general secretary of the Soviet Union sat down heavily, and poured himself another glass of vodka. He walked over to a cabinet and opened a small freezer, from which he withdrew some ice cubes, and added them to the glass.

He raised his glass. "To the last of my trusted comrades," he said to himself, and took a sip of the cool alcohol.

Picking up the phone on his desk, he pressed number one. "Anna, get Colonel Klitchkov here as soon as possible."

***

VILLAGE OF SURKHAB, EASTERN AFGHANISTAN.

Colonel Klitchkov climbed down from the helicopter and stepped delicately over the bullet-ridden body of a young Afghan mujahideen soldier lying in the middle of the street, and gazed around him.

The small village was made up of low, square rammed earth wall and mud brick buildings built up into the low hill behind him, with the larger number pooled around him on the main dusty track leading through it. Bodies lay scattered throughout the village, with many buildings destroyed. Most of the corpses were dressed for combat, but women and children could also be seen among the dead.

Ahead in the distance he could see the looming white peaks of the Spīn Ghar mountains, stretching in a spine that separated the Eastern spur of Afghanistan from the north west of Pakistan. They sparkled in the midday sun, a mass of peaks, rocks, canyons and caves.

A trail of people were making their way away from the village towards the mountains. Some were already there and could be seen beginning their ascent.

Colonel Klitchkov squinted in the sun. "What level of opposition have we faced today, Captain?" he asked the strong-jawed soldier standing behind him.

"They have fought strongly despite their inferior numbers, sir. There is a covered approach to the Spīn Ghar range using the Tobagi Plain which many have used. It has made our superior force inconsequential. We are doing our best to flank them. Losses have been great on both sides. Once they get to Tora Bora, we will not be able to reach them. The men are not used to mountain combat; the Afghans will win any battle up there."

Colonel Klitchkov looked round sharply at the captain's words. Tora Bora was a network of limestone caves naturally hollowed out over millennia, and the home of the great mujahideen warlords who had been fighting relentlessly for almost nine years to repel the Soviet invaders.

"So it is the famous Tora Bora caves they seek refuge in? This may well be perfect for what I plan, Captain."

"Sir?"

"It is not your concern, Captain. Your concern is to finish the job here."

"I do not take orders from the KGB," the muscled officer said with a slight sneer. The reputation of Klitchkov was fearsome, but he could crush this old man in his hands if he wanted, he thought to himself.

Colonel Klitchkov looked curiously at the soldier before him. "During the Battle of Stalingrad, we would crucify soldiers who did not show respect to their superiors, and leave them there as a reminder to anybody else who was thinking of doing the same thing. It is a practice I wholeheartedly support. I even carried it out a few times myself," he said clinically, showing no emotion.

"What are your orders, sir?" The captain asked quickly, instantly realising his misjudgement of the man.

"Kill them."

"The mujahideen?" the young captain asked, his tanned skin glowing in the intense sunlight.

"All of them," Klitchkov said with chilling detachment. "Destroy the village and then tell your men to enjoy the women if they wish to contaminate themselves with these Muslim peasants."

At that moment there was a woman's scream from one of the nearby huts and the crack of a gunshot. A Soviet soldier strolled out of the crumbling hut, buckling his trousers and laughing. The sound of a baby crying could be heard from the building.

Klitchkov looked at the captain. "I see my instructions were unnecessary."

The soldier froze as he saw Colonel Klitchkov and his face dropped in horror. He stood to attention and saluted the colonel, leaving his trousers to fall to his ankles. His grey underwear was stained with blood.

"Prostite, Colonel! Prostite!" he said, apologising to the point of grovelling.

The colonel smiled. "You are enjoying the spoils of war, comrade?"

The soldier, whose pale face was flat and quite wide, with spots around his chin and a tattoo of a curvy woman on his arm, relaxed slightly. "Da, sir!" he replied, leering. "I think these bitches actually like it."

Colonel Klitchkov laughed merrily and walked towards the soldier. In a smooth motion he withdrew his revolver and shot the soldier in between the legs.

The man screamed and dropped to the ground, holding the hole at his crotch and trying to stem the bleeding. What remained of his manhood could be seen on the floor next to him. He looked up in horror.

"Now, soldier, spoils of war are for the victors. Not for a job half done," Klitchkov said and emptied the remainder of his bullets into the man on the floor.

Klitchkov turned and walked casually back towards the captain, whose face had gone white with fear, matching the grey of the colonel's hair.

"Now, Captain, I expect you to better discipline your men... and yourself," he said. "Otherwise, I will be forced to treat you the same way as your subordinate back there," he added, waving the gun over his shoulder in the direction of the dead soldier, and giggled a shrill, manic laugh.

"Yes, sir, of course, sir," the captain replied, standing to attention and saluting the colonel.

"Very good," said Klitchkov, tucking the gun back into his belt, still chuckling. "It is important that you destroy all of these citizens and soldiers; is that understood? Scorched Earth tactics, raze it all to the ground. It needs to be complete by the end of today, with nobody remaining other than the warlords in those caves. You are now under KGB jurisdiction for this offensive."

"Understood, sir," replied the captain, the colour beginning to slowly return to his face.

"I can get you any resources you need. Succeed in this and there is a promotion in it for you, provided you can keep it in your pants for the next twenty-four hours."

A young man in KGB uniform stepped down from the helicopter. "Colonel? We have just received a message from the Kremlin asking you to contact them as a matter of urgency, sir."

"Very well," replied Colonel Klitchkov, and started walking back towards the helicopter. As he passed the captain he added, "Radio through to HQ when the mission is complete. If you fail, do not bother coming back at all." He climbed back into the helicopter; the rotors began spinning immediately as the engine fired up and clouds of dust blew in all directions.

The captain covered his eyes from the dust before squinting upwards at the chopper moving off over the foothills, quickly just a black speck against a field of blue.

Only then did he allow himself to exhale, gasping on the dusty air. It was one of those rare occasions where the myth paled in comparison to the reality.

Inside the helicopter, Klitchkov watched as the mountains passed far below him and wondered how effective the region would be for his plans. The principles were perfect, but he knew too well how rarely perfect principles translated into perfect execution.

He closed his eyes wearily. "What is the time in Moscow?" he asked the KGB soldier across from him.

"It would be just after twelve hundred hours, sir."

"I have lost track of time in these recent days with much travel. How long until we land at the base in Tashkent?"

"It will take just over two hours, sir, conditions permitting."

"Was there any mention of the nature of the Kremlin's request in their transmission? Our work here is too important to be abandoned at this key moment. The future of the Soviet Union depends on it."

"I understand, sir. But they gave no indication, only of its urgency."

Klitchkov's smooth granite jaw rippled as he clenched his teeth and counted the minutes until he reached the capital of the Uzbek Soviet Socialist Republic.

Two hours later, the helicopter began its descent towards the large square of grass behind what had historically been the government offices of Russian Turkestan. The sprawling city was stretched out for miles ahead of them, the largest city in central Asia.

The city was a testament to durability, being reborn from the ashes of Genghis Khan's destruction and rebuilt again following the earthquakes of 1966. Now little of its Silk Road history could still be seen and despite its southern location there was a chill in the air which suggested winter was on its way.

Colonel Klitchkov, however, cared little for the aesthetics of the city, or indeed its weather, but more about its strategic location. Rooted in the south of the USSR, it had the great territorial advantage of bordering China and the Turkestan states, and beyond that Afghanistan, Pakistan and India.

The helicopter had barely landed before he was striding his way across the well-kept lawns to where the Tashkent commissar stood waiting.

The commissar held out his hand in greeting but Klitchkov strode straight past him and into the building beyond, his dusty black boots clicking on the tiled corridors, his KGB assistant hurrying to keep up.

They entered the communications room, which was a hive of activity of humming monitors, ringing phones and reams of post being sorted into boxes. All of the staff stopped and looked up as the doors slammed open.

"Everybody out," barked Klitchkov's assistant while the colonel leant nonchalantly against the wall, inspecting his fingernails.

Nobody moved, so the young KGB soldier drew his weapon and fired it at the ceiling. There was a deafening silence followed by the scraping of chairs and steps as everybody in the room hurried to get out.

As they filed out of the room, Klitchkov put his arm in front of the last person to leave, an elderly woman who was shuffling towards the door. "You, stay," he commanded.

The woman stopped her shuffling and tutted. She turned and walked back to her radio desk where she sat down heavily, her white permed hair wobbling as she brushed away dust that had fallen from the bullet hole in the ceiling. "What do you want of me?"

"Get me the Kremlin; I understand they are urgently trying to contact me," said Klitchkov sharply, walking to stand beside the woman who began expertly negotiating the system in front of her with her veined, knotted fingers.

"Not via radio, you old crone, that will be too easily intercepted. Dial them for me," he snapped.

She tutted again, and picked up the phone next to her desk, patiently putting in the numbers she was clearly familiar with on the rotary dial.

"Da? This is the commissar's office for Tashkent; I have Colonel Klitchkov of the KGB waiting for an urgent message," she croaked.

She put her hand over the receiver and said to the colonel, "They are patching you through, dear," before handing him the telephone.

He raised an eyebrow at her tone but clearly decided against commenting on it, instead taking the phone from her grasp and putting it to his ear.

"Colonel?" said a wheezy voice at the end.

"Denisov?" Klitchkov replied, surprised. "What are you doing at the Kremlin?"

"I have been reassigned back to Moscow, sir. Is the line secure from your end?"

"Da, they have full encoding equipment for the commissar's communications here."

"Good. Yerin is gone; they need you back in Moscow immediately."

"Gone? What do you mean?"

"All will be explained to you upon your return here, sir; even a secure line can be tapped."

"I am overseeing a vital mission in Afghanistan at present; I cannot return to the Kremlin until that is complete. It is a matter of national security."

There was silence at the other end and he could hear voices faintly discussing it.

"OK, Colonel Klitchkov. Our esteemed leader has decided that Yerin is a Nazi traitor and has removed him from his position with immediate effect. You are now Chairman of the KGB."

"What are you saying, Maxim? Livenko was Yerin's deputy. I am several steps down from leading the KGB," said Klitchkov, fearing he was part of a hoax.

"Petrenko fears others in Viktor's circle may be entwined in his treachery. You are now the head of the KGB. You will be required in Moscow as soon as your Afghan operation is completed." There was a moment's pause before he added, "Congratulations," and hung up the phone. The line went dead with a hum, and Klitchkov replaced his receiver, a look of ecstasy on his face.

***

More than eleven thousand kilometres away in Washington DC, Vice President Gerald T. Phillips stood in the traditional home of the vice president, Number One Observatory Circle in quiet contemplation, a state he was best known for. He had not tried to use the vice presidency as a place to press his own agendas, but instead had patiently and quietly done whatever was asked of him by President Callahan for seven long years.

He had stepped away from his bickering campaign team in the other room to clear his head, and gazed out at the grounds of the United States Naval Observatory. Secret Service agents could be seen patrolling the grounds. He couldn't stand them, and not for the first time he wondered if he was making the right decision but the wheels were too far in motion now. Too many people would be let down, and he knew the burning ambition in the pit of his stomach would never go out; he owed it to himself to try.

The vice president saw his glazed reflection in the window, smoothed down his pale brown side parting and allowed himself a small smile. Who would have thought that the boy raised in Connecticut would be so close to becoming the leader of the free world?

Phillips walked over to a drinks cabinet and poured himself a scotch whisky, taking a small sip and releasing a sigh. He left the room, waving his new bodyguard away; the implacable man seemed to take his duty too seriously and was never more than a couple of feet away, even inside his own home. "Take the afternoon off, John, I'm perfectly safe in my own home," Phillips said to the wiry but solid man of an indistinguishable age due to a perfectly smooth face devoid of any blemishes. An unusual look in a bodyguard.

"I believe that is what the secretary of defense thought too, sir," the serious man said stiffly.

Phillips sighed, too resigned to the reality to try arguing back despite his position of superiority. With the tumbler of whisky still in hand, he returned to the large office he kept at the home, and the din from the carefully selected members of his team subsided. He leant against the doorframe and took another sip of whisky.

"So where have we gotten to?" he asked, surveying them through his wire-rimmed glasses.

His campaign manager Ed Sheen, a young man with dark blond hair and a weak chin, sat back with an arrogant confidence, and pulling the cigarette out of his mouth, blew out smoke and smiled at him. "We are good to go, boss," he said in a voice tinged with Georgian drawl. He handed over a sheet of paper that had been scribbled all over. Peering over his glasses, Gerald Phillips was able to discern the makings of his speech, the speech that would announce his intention to seek the Republican nomination for the presidency.

"Your handwriting is horseshit, Ed, but you guys have put together a good-looking speech," he said with a wry smile and looked at each of the four-strong team one by one.

"Lisa, type this thing up for me and let's get this show on the road," he said, looking at his assistant, a prim young woman with dark hair who clearly had eyes for Ed. "I want to run through it a few times before the press conference tomorrow."

"Yes, sir," she said, taking the paper back from him.

"What time have you booked the press for, Terry?" he asked Terry O'Connor, his press secretary.

"At sixteen hundred hours, Mr Vice President. The president can't be seen to endorse you so it's best that we don't hold it at the White House. As it stands, we're set up to do it on the steps of the Capitol, but I could get them here if you would prefer. It's already the worst kept secret in Washington that you're going to run, so no reporter is going to miss it. You will have the headlines tomorrow night, sir." Little did Terry know how prophetic his words would be.

"If there is one thing politics has taught me, Terry, it is that nothing is ever certain. It would be just our luck that the Berlin Wall falls over this afternoon," he said and his team laughed uncertainly. It was rare that Gerald Phillips made a joke, and rarer still that he would deal in hypotheticals. A serious man with a serious face and a serious history covering everything from US naval aviator to director of the CIA and on to the vice presidency, he dealt only in fact. Humour was for those with something to hide.

"I advise we keep it at the Capitol," said Ed. "It will be a good reminder of the great work you've done as vice president in these last two terms of office. You should be able to ride the goodwill people have for Callahan all the way to the Oval Office."

"That's President Callahan, Ed. He deserves our respect, as does the office." He reprimanded his campaign manager, but he knew that Ed Sheen had not enjoyed the rapid rise he had by being respectful or nice. He was a master of the dark arts, and the vice president knew he would need all of those tricks if he was to secure the Republican nomination, let alone the presidency. He was not so naïve as to think he could get there on good faith and honesty; politics was a dirty world, and he had no qualms about playing dirty to meet his ambitions.

"Ah yes, of course, Mr Vice President. No offence intended," said Ed with thinly disguised impatience.

"None taken, young man. I agree, the Capitol reminds people that I am their vice president, a man they can trust to lead. We will only irritate reporters if we move the goalposts now, and we don't want to start off the campaign with irritating the very people we need on our side." He

207

glanced at his watch. "Let's keep going; there's a lot more we need to plan and prepare still."

Ed clapped his hands. "You heard the VP, let's crack on. Terry, I need to know your recommended press campaign schedule by the end of today," he barked. "What have you got so far?"

There was a lot of scrambling around for papers and cursing, and Gerald Phillips stepped out of the room once more. He hoped the Oval Office was quiet.

***

Across town, KGB Agent Taras Brishnov was ready. Nothing had been left to chance; it would be so easy. Tingles of excitement were running through his body as he looked out over Capitol Hill. This would be his pièce de résistance; after years lurking in the shadows, he would be thrust into the spotlight and be the most celebrated KGB agent the USSR had ever known. Finally, he would get the adulation his years of service deserved; finally, there would be true fear in the heart of the capitalist west.

***

Nikita twiddled his thumbs before leaning forwards on his desk and resting his head in his hands. He wasn't used to being caught in indecision, a state that he had been trained to avoid, a state that got spies killed.

This was a turn of events that he had not foreseen.

On the desk in front of him sat the telegram that had just been delivered from one of his few remaining legitimate US spies in the USSR.

YERIN REMOVED. COL KLITCHKOV NEW KGB HEAD. HIS CURRENT LOCATION UNKNOWN.

Not for the first time, Nikita wondered who the CIA agent in the Soviet Union was. Despite Yerin's systematic removal of almost every single

208

agent they had behind the iron curtain, a few still remained, providing valuable intelligence. Not being trusted with the identity of those remaining agents was something Nikita was grateful for as it meant he was supplied solid intelligence without being questioned on how he had obtained it, and meant that he would have no further blood on his hands.

Since Yerin's dismantling of the CIA spy network, the identity of any remaining had been kept highly classified and a closely guarded secret known only to the very highest echelons of the agency. So far, the CIA continued to believe their spies had been caught due to intercepted communications and it had barely been floated as an idea that there might be a mole in their ranks. Whoever ZB was, he had done astonishing work.

With Yerin gone, he considered what it might mean for the agency and his own position. His greatest fear was that his own identity would be revealed by a Russian defector, and with Yerin ousted he might be tempted to leak state secrets.

Then he thought of Chairman Klitchkov and realised that he would never allow Yerin or his cronies to live. The Kremlin had no room for an opposition.

He picked up the telegram and walked over to Sykes' office. Knocking on the door, he heard the chief's voice say, "Enter."

Sykes was sitting at his desk on the phone, a cigarette hanging out of his mouth and his eyes looking more bloodshot than ever. He looked up and waved Nikita into the chair opposite him.

"… Still looking into it. Yes, Mr Secretary, as soon as there is any more information, you'll be the first to know," he said and rolled his eyes at Nikita. "Of course, sir, you have my word," he said again before putting the phone down heavily. "The secretary of state is all over my ass since the FBI told him about the White Russian — blames us for letting him go to the president with it without any facts."

"Never mind that, sir, this is bigger, and this is fact," said Nikita and thrust the telegram onto the desk in front of his boss.

The chief took a drag on his cigarette, picked up the telegram and immediately began coughing and spluttering fitfully. He put a tissue to his mouth and after some time the coughing abated.

"Jesus, Marshall, give me some warning before you give me news like that. Yerin gone? I thought he was infallible. God knows he did a good enough job killing all of our agents. Do you know any more?"

"Nothing yet, sir — this just came in from one of our agents in Moscow. I expect it will be on the news tomorrow but it doesn't lessen the shock of his replacement being Chairman Klitchkov."

Sykes grunted. "Nothing surprises me any more about the communists. What do we know about Klitchkov?"

"A fair amount, sir; I built up a file on him."

"Give me the highlights."

"Sure thing. Andrei Klitchkov was born in the city of Volgograd, then called Stalingrad - a little shout out to Stalin's arrogance - in 1927 and his mother died at birth. For this his father blamed him, drinking heavily and beating him regularly. He grew up on the fringes at school, always poorly dressed and bullied and shunned by his peers for being different. It's then I believe he developed his cruel streak, by retreating into his own vicious fantasies and dreamt of being a ruler himself, which was all he had known in a world that had shown him little kindness—"

"Jacob, I want the career highlights, not his therapy session analysis," interrupted Sykes.

"Of course, sir. KGB psychological profiling is very thorough; you'd be amazed at how—"

"Marshall!"

"Sorry, sir. When the USSR entered World War Two in 1941, his father was conscripted into the Red Army, but died in one of the first battles of Operation Barbarossa; I'm not clear exactly how or where. I wonder did he shed a tear for his departed old man?"

"This is your last warning," snapped Sykes.

"By this point Andrei, only fourteen, showed early signs of his cold determination and found a way into the army despite being significantly underage. There he fought valiantly, gaining great fame for his exploits during the Battle of Stalingrad. He won the medal for the defense of the city, as well as the Medal of Courage. Due to the incredibly high death toll, he, quite incredibly, became a captain by the age of fifteen and was awarded the Order of Suvorov for his leadership against a numerically superior force. However, he became better known for his cold ruthlessness and detachment from the atrocities he was both surrounded by, and more often than not committing. He would personally shoot anyone in his company who turned away from the field of battle, and famously never allowed his men to retreat even in the face of certain failure.

"From there, his career is easier to follow. He stayed with the Soviet Army for another decade after the war before being recruited by the KGB in 1956 and led the more clandestine charge against the leaders of the Hungarian Revolution. Since then, he has been a key player within the KGB, but has never got close to a position of clear leadership due to his coldness, even by Soviet standards, and a tendency to go off-piste a little too often."

"You have done your research on him," said Sykes. "How worried should we be?"

"He's an interesting character," acknowledged Nikita. "But he has never been under consideration for the KGB secretariat, nowhere near. He was second chief directorate of the KGB for counter-intelligence, but there were several other candidates well ahead of him, and it was generally accepted that Oleg Livenko was next in line."

"His deputy?"

"Yes, sir. Like Yerin he was a Brezhnev fan and a hard liner, but Klitchkov is far more unpredictable. If the general secretary doesn't keep him on a tight leash, it's not unreasonable to say he could light the touch paper on the Cold War. He's a lifelong servant to the USSR; the one thing we know is that patriotism runs to his core. But it's the equivalent of jumping from colonel to general, which he probably will get now too. It's a real curve ball of an appointment and smacks of a scandal involving Yerin, as they're obviously wanting someone not too affiliated with him. I suspect Yerin's days are numbered."

The phone on Sykes' desk began to ring, startling them both. "Find out more about why he was removed; we need more intelligence. I want to know what game Petrenko is playing here, and what sort of leader of the KGB Klitchkov is going to be," he said before picking up the phone and waving Nikita away.

Nikita picked up the telegram and stalked back to his desk. His head was spinning; had Klitchkov known when he saw him only days ago that he was in line for a promotion? He couldn't imagine that to be the case; the chairman of the KGB did not, and could not, visit assets on foreign soil.

As he got to his desk, he saw a large envelope. He sat down and opened it and inside found a number of photographs.

The first showed the unmistakable figure of Agent Brishnov walking away from the photographer down a dingy alleyway.

The next showed a gory image of a woman lying on blood-drenched sheets, still tied up and naked; little was left of the back of her head.

Nikita noticed there was a slight bulge at the bottom of the envelope and in it he found a cartridge casing of a .50 AE Magnum bullet, one of the largest cartridges you could get in a handgun. Nikita only knew of one gun that could hold the bullets — the new Israeli-manufactured Desert Eagle.

Not many places in Washington DC would sell such cartridges. And the KGB definitely did not provide its agents with Desert Eagles.

"Hey, Lahart, did you see who brought this envelope in?"

"Yeah, some guy, about twenty minutes ago," replied Blaine distractedly, not looking up from his work.

"Can you be more specific?"

"I wasn't paying attention; I'm right in the middle of something. I think he had a moustache."

"A moustache? That's it?"

"Yeah, a toothbrush moustache."

"Like Hitler?" replied Nikita incredulously.

"I was thinking like Charlie Chaplin, but I guess I'm not as judgy as you," said Blaine, now looking up and smiling.

"Forget it," said Nikita, turning back to the documents in front of him. He turned over the photos. On the back it said, *'Taken at Oldham St, Baltimore MD. ZB'*.

Those initials again. He walked over to Chang and showed her the pictures. "Looks like I have a lead to go on. You going to come with me?"

"We're analysts, not field agents, Jake," she replied sternly.

"Today I think we're both. Come on, we're not taking him down, just trying to find him," he said in response to her look of incredulity. "That's what analysts do, the research."

"Fine," she said, grabbing her coat. "But a visit to Baltimore was not what I had planned for my day."

It was a sixty-minute drive from the CIA headquarters on McLean to their destination in East Baltimore and Nikita fought the urge to accelerate. Sarah sat chain-smoking with the window down and saying little, both of them aware of how much was not being said.

He slowed to a stop as they pulled into Oldham Street outside a Greek Orthodox church. It was a visibly run-down street with flat roofed buildings, many of which had once been warehouses, lining either side. He pulled out the photograph from the envelope on the back seat and they put their heads together to examine it. He could smell her perfume and tobacco blend and found it distracting.

He had to resist the temptation to kiss her. She must have sensed it as she looked at him sharply. "Come on man, we're on the job; focus."

He was taken aback but didn't know why; this was Sarah's way. At least you always knew where you stood. Except, he thought, he actually had no idea where he stood with her.

"Sure. Now where is this alleyway? It isn't a long street; it shouldn't be hard to find. We might find a clue," said Nikita, although privately he couldn't picture a world in which Brishnov would leave any trace behind. But then, he had already been more careless than he could have imagined, like he was a man with nothing to lose. "Don't forget your gun," he said to Sarah, handing her the High Standard HDM pistol that had fallen onto the floor of the car by her feet. Inwardly he squirmed at the thought of being so careless with a government-issue firearm. Denisov would have put him in the cold box for such an offence. His own was firmly clipped into the holster at his waist.

"You take this side of the road, and I'll take that one," said Sarah, and they dispersed. Within a minute, Nikita had found the spot. A narrow alleyway at the side of a low concrete building, casting it in gloom despite it being the middle of the day. He could see the window that his comrade had clearly jumped out of following his crime.

He walked along it, eyes everywhere. The alleyway was bare, with the only signs of life the occasional cigarette butt.

He walked back and called Chang over, but she also was unable to see any sign of Brishnov's presence.

"I didn't expect any trace. This guy has gone under our radar for years. I'm just astounded he blew the brains out of a prostitute; it's like he wanted us to find him," said Nikita.

"Unless this is a different guy. I mean all we can see is the back of his head in this photo," Sarah replied.

"It's the only lead we have," Nikita replied flatly, getting irritated with her constant negativity. "What gun stores are there around here?"

"Damned if I know," she shrugged.

He bit his lip. "OK, well let's scatter and find out."

"You mean separate?" she said, looking suddenly nervous.

"Well… yeah," he responded. "How did you get into the CIA?" he asked sarcastically.

"Say that again and I won't let you in when you come round after drinking too much at the bar tonight," she said with a straight face.

"Now who's being unprofessional?" Nikita replied acerbically. "Do your job." He turned and walked up the street. He didn't fear for Sarah; they had all done basic field training, she could take care of herself.

He glanced over his shoulder and saw that she had crossed to the other side of the street and was making her way in the opposite direction.

He absorbed it all as he had been trained to do. So much of his training had to lie dormant for long stretches of time, ready and waiting for the day he would need to call upon the skill he had spent years finessing. Within seconds he knew the location of every car, where every potential enemy hiding place was and every camera, though there were not many.

After ten minutes of walking through largely residential streets, he came across a short high street, with a Greek bakery, greengrocers, hairdressers and a smattering of cafes and restaurants. It felt like an old-fashioned street from a different era. Shop signs were painted on the brickwork and people of all ages sat outside the cafes chatting. As he passed them, he arrived at a quiet crossroads, and looking down to his left he saw what he was looking for.

A gun shop stood out, newer and shinier than the faded old shops of the high street. Mellor's Firearms was printed in block white on a black background, and an A-board outside boasted that ammo could be bought by the bucket.

Nikita walked confidently over to it and entered the door without hesitating. Inside was like walking into a KGB armoury, with guns of every description glaring down at him from racks on the walls.

The young man behind the counter was on the phone as he entered but immediately stopped talking as he saw Nikita walk in. "I'm gonna have to call you back, dude," he said and put down the receiver. He cocked his head and surveyed Nikita. He was muscled but with a beer belly and was wearing a t-shirt two sizes too small that didn't quite stretch over his bloated waist. "Can I help you?" he asked, looking oddly furtive.

"I reckon so… Larry," said Nikita, reading the name badge on the shopkeeper's chest. He withdrew his CIA badge and flashed it at the shopkeeper. "I'm from the CIA and I need to know if you sell a certain kind of ammo," he added.

"You sure you're from the CIA? You don't seem like the CIA type," the young man said with undisguised cynicism.

Ignoring him, Nikita persevered. "It's cartridges for a Desert Eagle. I need to know if you sell them, and if you sold any recently."

Larry laughed. "A Desert Eagle? Man, the Israelis keep them all for themselves, you won't find them here," he said, but Nikita noticed he'd started rubbing his fingers together nervously.

"Well of course, you do need a special licence to sell them and I know you wouldn't want to break the law like that," said Nikita, "but obviously we have to do our due diligence and somebody got their hands on one round here."

"Wish I could help you, man," Larry shrugged, throwing a nervous glance over his shoulder.

"You wouldn't mind if I just took a look in the back, would you, Larry? CIA, we have to cover all the bases you see; I can't go back to my boss saying I didn't look properly."

"You gonna need a warrant for that," Larry said with wavering defiance.

215

Nikita brought the heel of his hand up and drove it up into Larry's nose. He passed out immediately as blood spurted from his crushed nose.

Stepping behind the counter and over Larry, nudging him onto his side to avoid him choking on his blood, he walked into the back where he was sure he would find what he was looking for. Civilians had so many tells.

Sure enough, there on the floor, with no security whatsoever, was a box with Magnum .50 AE on the side. They'd barely tried to hide it. But then nobody ever challenged gun shops in the US, for which Nikita right now was intensely grateful. There was no sign of any Desert Eagles so either they had quickly sold out, or Brishnov had acquired the only one that Larry had managed to get his hands on. It didn't matter either way.

He spotted a bottle of Jim Beam on a kitchen surface at the rear of the room, and walked over to it. He unscrewed the cap and took a swig straight from the bottle. The pressure in his head eased immediately and he felt its warmth ooze through his body. Opening the cupboards, he saw a thermos flask, into which he emptied the whiskey before pocketing it. A groan from behind him said that Larry had come to.

Nikita walked back towards him, and Larry's eyes widened in fear as he saw him approaching. He tried to push himself back up.

Nikita did it for him. Grabbing him by the collar, he lifted him up with ease and pushed him against the wall.

"Now, Larry, I don't like it when I'm made to do things the hard way. I don't care if you're selling Desert Eagles. How about you tell me what I need to know."

Larry crumpled immediately. "Fibe, what d'you want?" he sputtered.

Nikita let him go and stepped back. "Excellent, I'm glad we can work together nicely. Did you sell an unregistered Desert Eagle and some of those .50 cartridges to this man?" he asked, showing a photo of Brishnov to him.

"Yeah, I thig so," Larry sputtered through his bloody nose. "Didn't like him much to tell you the truth."

"But enough to sell him one of the most powerful handguns ever made," Nikita said, lifting an eyebrow.

"What's the big deal, who is he?"

"That's classified," said Nikita. "But he ain't a goodie."

Larry hung his head pathetically. Nikita almost felt sorry for him.

"I'm gonna need some of those cartridges as evidence, and I need to see any CCTV tapes you have from when he came in."

"Sure thig" said Larry miserably, and fetched a handful of the cartridges which he emptied into Nikita's cupped hands. He then walked to the door and flipped the sign to say closed, locking the door behind him and waved Nikita to follow him as he walked into the back.

The shopkeeper unlocked a door next to the kitchen counter to reveal a small, cluttered office within. A television screen glowed in the darkness, until Larry flicked on the light, a fading naked bulb giving the windowless room a dull yellow cast. He grabbed a cloth and wiped down his bloody face, wincing as he touched his broken nose.

He began rifling through the video strewn across the desk. "I think it was about three days ago he came in," he said, selecting one of the tapes from the desk and jamming it into the large boxy Betamax player.

An image of the shop flickered onto the screen. He began to fast forward, showing the speeded-up movement of a small trickle of customers entering and leaving the shop.

After a few minutes, the unmistakable figure of Brishnov appeared. He expertly managed to avoid his face ever being captured on the camera, but there was no doubt in Nikita's mind about who it was. The lithe figure walked with confidence, but managed to be somehow quite forgettable. Forgettable to anyone who didn't know the things of which he was capable.

"That's the guy," said Larry. "He was pretty excited when I mentioned the Desert Eagle."

"I don't doubt it," Nikita muttered. He popped the tape out. "I need to keep this. Do you have any footage from outside the shop?"

"No problem, officer," Larry said, still jumpy every time he looked at the CIA agent before him. Nikita rolled his eyes. "We have a camera, we have to by law, but it's a bit temperamental." An older and more battered Betamax player was on the floor next to the desk, humming slightly. He picked up a box of the tapes on top of it and handed it to Nikita. "I never bother to label them; don't even watch them, not much to see out there. The day you're looking for will be in there somewhere."

217

Nikita said nothing, only pocketing the tape and bullets and taking the box of tapes from Larry before walking out of the shop. It would be days before Larry relaxed from the visit, and weeks before his nose stopped hurting.

As Nikita walked out of the shop, a man bumped heavily into him. "Hey, guy, look where you're going," the man exclaimed angrily.

Nikita threw his arm up angrily, but once he was around the corner pulled the piece of paper out of his pocket that the man had deposited there.

For information: Petr Chrastek, Apartment six, Ridgeon Court, 14th Street.

Nikita memorised the name and address before chewing the paper bit by bit and swallowing it. The KGB taking such bold action must mean that Brishnov's move was close on the horizon. He didn't have much time to gather the evidence to lead the CIA to the Soviet assassin.

He began walking back towards the car, deciding how to proceed. As he walked past the Greek church, he heard voices talking loudly in Greek and a group of women came out through the doors of the building. He carried on walking back towards the car to wait for Sarah to return.

Suddenly a voice tentatively called, "Nathan?"

He froze. That voice was tattooed into his memory, but he could scarcely believe it.

CHAPTER 19

Nikita turned around and saw her. Her golden eyes were wide with surprise, but her eyebrows quickly dived into an angry frown as her suspicions were confirmed.

"Elysia," he whispered.

She was about thirty yards away, standing with a group of women aged from around fifty upwards. They were all staring curiously at him, wondering how Elysia knew this haughty black man.

"Elysia, páme," said one of the women, a stern-looking lady with light brown skin and a steely grey perm.

"Tha se piso," Elysia said distractedly, waving them away. *I will catch you up.*

The woman clucked disapprovingly but walked off with her fellow churchgoers, throwing looks over her shoulder the whole while.

Nikita looked nervously over his own shoulder at the car. He couldn't let Chang know he was anyone other than Jacob.

He walked swiftly towards Elysia, whose face was settling into one of serious anger.

"Elysia..." he said, putting his hands on her arms. She shrugged them off. "Hi," he finished lamely with a smile.

"Hi?" she responded caustically.

"This is so... I mean... what are you doing here?" He asked, reverting to his Floridian drawl with a stutter.

"I don't see how that's any of your business."

"No, you're right. It's good to see you though," he said earnestly. "I just didn't expect..."

"I told you I was thinking of coming back to Greek Town. But then I don't know why I would imagine that you would remember any of our time together as it was clearly so meaningless."

"Meaningless? Elysia, it meant more to me than you could know. I'm sorry I left—"

"Without so much as a note," she interrupted. "Just as my uncle had died."

"I'm so sorry—" he began.

"Sorry you used me?" she said, her dark eyes burning into him. She had never looked more beautiful to him.

"Elysia, I wish I could explain," he said, desperately trying to think of the words, still stunned at bumping into her so far from the place in which he knew her. "You... you are the most amazing woman I've ever met. Our time together was so perfect I was afraid I would only ruin it by staying."

"Oh please," she said rolling her eyes.

"Elysia, I'm bad news," he said, gazing intently at her. He again put his hands to her arms, "Men like me can only hurt women like you."

"Men are so stupid."

He laughed. "I'm not arguing with you there," he said, noticing that her expression had softened just a little. "I don't tell the truth enough, but believe me when I say that what we shared was the most real experience I've ever had."

"You talk as if I'm some weak little flower that will break. I was perfectly fine with you and perfectly fine without you; I can make my own mind up if you're bad news or not," she said, lifting her chin. "You hurt me; you really hurt me," she added, softly, her eyes liquid.

"I'm so sorry," he sighed. "And I'm sorry that I underestimated you." He couldn't help himself and asked, "Did it mean something to you too?"

She let her arms fall to her sides, and cocked her head to one side. "What it meant to me isn't something you deserve to know right now. Why are you here?" she asked. "We're a long way from Florida." Surveying him properly, her eyes noticed the gun at his hip for the first time with alarm.

He heard a door shut behind him and closed his eyes briefly, knowing he had another argument ahead of him. He glanced behind him and saw Sarah sitting in the car, staring coldly in his direction.

"I have to go, Elysia," he said.

"Well, this is more of a goodbye than last time," she said, colour returning to her face as her temper rose once more. "Does your girlfriend know about us?"

"Not my girlfriend," he said, "my partner," and tapped the gun at his waist.

"Am I likely to see you loitering outside my church again?" said asked directly.

"I… don't think that would be a good idea," he said, hating himself.

She laughed cruelly. "Why am I not surprised? Another man who wants only one thing and then runs away."

"It's not like that, Elysia… I can explain. Meet me at that bar around the corner tomorrow at eight?"

"Maybe," she said, throwing her long hair over her shoulder and marching away without looking back.

He turned and swiftly marched back to the car, bracing himself.

"Hey, Sarah, I have a couple of leads," he said, throwing the video tapes onto the back seat, trying to get ahead of any caustic comments she might make. It didn't work.

"Is that your other girlfriend?" she demanded. "Is that why you wanted to come here? And right in front of me?"

"Come on, who do you think I am, Sarah? I was asking if she'd seen anything the other night," he said, trying to pacify her.

"She seemed pretty upset for someone you were just asking questions."

"She didn't like cops," he said, sighing. "She said we cause as many problems as we solve around here."

"Stupid bitch," Sarah said caustically, and he felt a desire to defend Elysia rise in his chest, but he managed to suppress it. "Doesn't she know we're here to help?" She tutted.

"I can't believe how jealous you got," Nikita said playfully. She shoved him in the arm, but a slight smile played across her lips.

"Tell me about these leads," she said.

"I found the gun shop. I've got the CCTV footage of our guy. Definitely the same one as in the picture of the guy with Yerin. We may be able to trace his vehicle from the external footage."

"Now we just need to find out who he is. You said leads, as in the plural..." she said.

"I did. So after I left the shop I was walking down the street and walked past an alley, and this guy with a cap pulled down over his head and sunglasses on whistled me over. He was wearing this thick heavy coat so I couldn't even say if he was fat or thin, but he said 'if you're looking for answers look for Chrastek on 14th Street'. Then he just walked off. I pursued him but he wouldn't say anything else, just 'Ridgeon Court'."

"Some field agent you are," she huffed sarcastically. "Who the hell was the guy?"

"I know, I know. We're both in unfamiliar territory here so cut me a break."

"Come on, leads don't just appear like that though, Jake, you know that."

"I know. It stinks but I don't see what choice we have."

"We don't, but it feels wrong. What's a Chrastek anyway? Sounds Russian, hardly bodes well."

"I believe it's a Czech name, although I don't know if that bodes any better. I guess we'd better go and find out."

Sarah sighed. "And there was me hoping we would get to clock off early and amuse ourselves today," she said, stroking his arm coyly.

"If we work hard now, we can play hard later," Nikita said, trying to flirt but his mind still on Elysia.

"Deal," she said. "Now where the hell is 14th Street?"

***

They pulled up outside Ridgeon Court on 14th Street fifteen minutes later and looked up at the giant concrete slab that was the block of apartments. It ruined the otherwise picturesque street, right in the heart of Greek Town and the brutalist fifties architecture would have fitted comfortably back in Kamenka, Nikita thought. Along the residential street, men could be seen sitting outside the front of their houses drinking wine and eating olives. For one blissful moment, Nikita was transported back to the

Skyros bar of Elysia's grandfather, with the sunshine, good wine and her perfume.

"Dude, wake up, I don't want to hang around all day," chirped Sarah, snapping him out of his reverie.

"Of course, let's go; don't forget your firearm."

She rolled her eyes and climbed out of the car. They approached the building cautiously; Nikita kept his hand firmly on the handle of the weapon at his waist. The entrance to the building was propped open, and walking inside they saw a list of the apartment names. Next to the number six read P Chrastek.

He pointed to it. "That's our guy."

"Or girl," she commented.

"Or girl," he agreed.

The elevator doors had an old-looking 'out of order' sign stuck to them, so they headed for the stairs which were gloomy, damp and scattered with cigarette ends and the occasional hypodermic needle.

"Lovely place to live," Sarah said. Nikita didn't reply; instead, his senses were on high alert. He wished he hadn't had to bring Sarah with him, but it was vital to the credibility of his information.

Nikita hated situations like this — going in blind, with no reconnaissance, no preparation. Always know more than the target, Denisov had said constantly. Now he didn't know if it was a target, an asset, an informer or an assassin.

If the KGB were prepared to burn Brishnov, perhaps they were prepared to burn him also. But then Brishnov was Yerin's favourite. Everything about this went deeper than his paygrade.

They climbed the stairs and reached the landing. Nikita drew his weapon and signalled Sarah to stand behind him.

"Oh, come on, man," she said, pushing his arm aside and marching up to the glossy black door with a golden number six gleaming on it, at odds with the surroundings.

Nikita pocketed his gun but kept one hand loose and ready to fire, nudging Sarah to one side. He could hear Debussy's *Clair De Lune* drifting gently from the other side of the door and the sound of footsteps.

The door opened a crack and he could see a bespectacled brown eye of a middle-aged man peer out. As he saw Nikita, he smiled and opened the door. "Ah, our esteemed—" he paused as he spotted Sarah next to him and saw the warning in Nikita's eyes. "Intelligence services," he finished, smiling at both and welcoming them in. He'd done it poorly and Sarah looked curiously at them both before walking on into the apartment.

He was of medium height, with the look of a once handsome man ageing badly, with a rounded belly and thinning hair which had been brushed so as to give it the appearance of volume.

They followed him further into the apartment. On the walls hung Goya and Rembrandt prints, with bookcases showcasing delicate leather-bound original prints of classics.

"Can I furnish you two with a beverage?" asked Chrastek, in delicately accented English, as he walked over to a drinks' cabinet standing against the wall.

"Nothing for us," said Nikita, eager to get the meeting over with as quickly as possible.

"You knew we were coming?" Sarah asked sharply.

The man chuckled. "You won't mind if I do?" he said, ignoring Nikita's question. "Please, sit," he said, beckoning to the ornate furniture in the middle of the room. Nikita selected a crimson chaise longue to perch on, while Sarah sank into a deep armchair. Petr Chrastek remained standing. "You are here for information?"

"Who are you?" Sarah asked directly.

Petr gave a thin smile. "I'm many different things to many different people. I like to, as the Americans say, keep my fingers in many different pies. But to you, I am a man who can point you in the right direction."

"How do we know you aren't a Soviet spy?" she asked.

His eyes flickered to Nikita in a smirk. "You don't. I will give you information, my dear; you can decide what to do with it. My employment is none of your concern," he said as he took a sip from the small sherry glass held gently in his hand.

"Petr, tell us what you know," said Nikita impatiently.

"Very well," said the Czech man. "You are looking for a KGB assassin," he said as a statement, not as a question.

Neither of the CIA agents responded, waiting for him to continue.

"I know who he is. But first I will need something from you."

Sarah laughed. "I knew it. You're a fraud."

"Sarah, he already knows more than he should." Nikita looked at Petr. "What do you want?"

"Immunity," whispered Petr.

"Immunity from what?" demanded Sarah.

"From any indiscretions that may surface against me," he said dismissively.

"You know full well we can't give you blanket immunity when we don't even know what the charges are," said Nikita.

"Then, I will keep my information to myself and the vice president will die," the reluctant informant replied.

There was a taut silence, in which the two CIA agents stared at each other.

"What bullshit is this?" Sarah said, standing up. "Come on, Jake, this joker is clearly wasting our time."

"If you leave, then you are consigning the vice president of the United States, and most likely the next president judging by the polls, to death. And very soon too," Petr said coyly.

Sarah froze in place, clearly torn. "Come on Chrastek, spit it out," said Nikita, his eyes boring into him. Why was he making it so hard to get the information he had been placed by the KGB to provide?

"Not without my immunity," the paunchy man said, inspecting his nails and polishing them on his shirt.

"Fine, but if you have the knowledge you claim to have, immunity or not you will be forever known by the American intelligence services. You've come this far, and you brought us to you, so why play this game?" said Nikita.

"Just give me my immunity. I know your department has the authority."

"Incorrect. Immunity comes from way above our pay grade I'm afraid, buddy."

The Czech man's face tightened and he ground his teeth in obvious frustration. He turned his back, gazed out of the window and hummed along to the classical music emanating from his record player.

Suddenly his face was pressed against the glass as Sarah had pounced and twisted his arm behind his back. He yelled out in pain.

"We tried to do this the easy way, but you will tell us what we need to know. Forget immunity, your life will be made total hell; I will see to it personally," she said with strength belying her slight frame.

"Sarah, come on," Nikita said, "you can't strong-arm a civilian."

"Nobody knows we're here, Jake, nobody at HQ knows who Petr Chrastek is, if that's even his real name. I'm not leaving here without the information locked in this crumbly head of his," she said, tightening her grip on his arm and causing him to cry out again. "Now help me out," she said as she twisted the informant round and slammed him into the floor, digging her knee into his back.

Nikita squatted down in front of him and looked into his eyes. "Dude, it's really worth your while to just tell her what she needs to know; she isn't pissing around here."

The man's face had turned beet red with anger and pain, but he glanced at Nikita, a look of knowing passing between them. He had played it very well, thought Nikita. "Very well, very well! Let me go and I'll tell you," he spat out.

"Too late, old man, give me information and I'll let you go," she said viciously, digging her knee into his spine.

He wailed in pain. "Brishnov! His name is Brishnov, Taras Brishnov!" he cried, his East European accent strengthening as he lost control amidst the pain. "Now let me go, you monster," he said, and she relented slightly as he slumped forward, his face buried in the shagpile rug she had pressed him into.

She dusted herself off and sat primly back on the armchair.

"Ok, now the rest, Chrastek," said Nikita calmly, throwing an angry look at Sarah.

The man turned over, walked to the window and poured himself another sherry, sipping it and taking a deep breath. "You are animals who deserve no information and everything that happens to you."

Sarah stood up and threw a painting from the wall onto the floor, preparing to stamp on it.

"OK, OK! You have made your point, you, brute," he said, fussing over the painting. He sat down with a sigh. "Taras Brishnov is the KGB's most secret weapon. The one you call The White Russian, or is it the Black Russian?" he said to Nikita.

"How could you possibly know that?" said Sarah sternly. "That's classified."

"I've forgotten more things than your tiny Korean mind could ever hope to comprehend," he said poisonously to Sarah.

Her eyes hardened in fury, and Nikita laid a hand on her knee to calm her. He looked at Petr. "Stop poking the bear, Petr," he said, "unless you also have something to say about the size of Nigerian brains?" His own eyes were now intense with anger. Petr said nothing. "I didn't think so," said Nikita. He withdrew his gun from his belt and laid it on his lap. "Now my patience is being severely tested, so I suggest you start talking. You have my word we will ensure your safety," he said earnestly.

Petr looked nervously from one to the other, and seemed to cave in on himself somewhat. He looked down at the floor. "Tomorrow Brishnov will assassinate Vice President Gerald Phillips when he announces his intention to run for president on Capitol Hill," he said in a monotone that sounded a little recited. "He has gone rogue in the face of what he sees as weak Soviet leadership and intends to strike a deadly blow at the heart of America." He gazed out of the window and added, "I do not imagine it would be his last strike either." He looked at Nikita benignly. "I cannot deny that it is a relief to have shared this information; now do what you want with me," he said and held his wrists out in supplication for arrest.

But the arrest would never be made, for at that moment the side of his head burst in a shower of blood and he slumped sideways.

CHAPTER 20

Sarah screamed and Nikita threw himself towards her and dragged her behind the chair, expecting further shots.

Peering from behind the chair, he could see the single clean hole in the window where the sniper shot had entered.

He crept out from behind the chair and moved swiftly to the side of the room and out of sight of the window. With his back to the wall, he tentatively peered through the angle of the window. He ducked and moved to the other side of the window and did the same thing, looking for possible sniper locations. The assassin was clearly a pro, with no sign of them visible anywhere. But they must be close; the destruction to the entire right side of what had recently been Petr's face was a testament to that. The white shag rug that he had been groaning into only minutes before was now thickly matted with the blood of its owner.

Nikita walked back over to Sarah and as he did, he heard the whistle of a bullet fly past his head and lodge itself in the wall in front of him. He flung himself down to the ground and commando crawled back to where Sarah was.

Her face was white with shock and she was cradling her ankle which was visibly swollen.

"We need to get out of here," he said to her. "Now." She nodded silently. "Can you walk?" he asked her.

"I think so; I think it's only a sprain from the fall," she said stutteringly.

He helped her up tenderly, but moved her swiftly out of sight of the window. He looked at the other hole in the window and the placement of the bullet in the wall. The shooter had to be on the roof of the building opposite. If he didn't have Sarah with him, he would back himself to be able to track them down in minutes.

With her arm over his shoulder, Nikita helped her from the crime scene and deposited her in the car, scanning the rooftops as he went for any sign of the sniper. "Wait here," he said to her, and with his gun held low to the ground made his way back to the apartment. There could be nothing to implicate him for the Americans to find.

Covering his hands with socks from Petr's bedroom drawer to avoid leaving any prints, he expertly swept the apartment. The apartment was all style but little substance, with nothing of much note.

However, as he did a final sweep of the lounge, he spotted a scrap of paper on the floor under the sherry decanter which had narrowly avoided being destroyed by the first bullet.

He snatched it up and his blood ran cold when he saw it. Hearing sirens in the distance, he stuffed it into his pocket, and hurried from the apartment. The second shot had not been meant to kill him. It was a warning; he had never been more sure, of anything in his life.

***

They were silent as they drove back to Washington. Sarah was shaking and going into shock. He rubbed her leg and stroked her as he drove, hoping that warmth and some human contact would help her to relax. For all her tough exterior, she was a tender soul, and that, he thought, was probably what attracted him to her the most. He smiled at her warmly, and tried to push Elysia from his mind.

They got to HQ and, with Sarah limping badly, made their way as quickly as they could to the offices of the Soviet Counter-intelligence Branch. They walked straight into the office of Sykes without knocking.

"What the hell!" Sykes remonstrated, before seeing the look on the faces of the two agents. He immediately fell silent.

"Boss, you need to hear this," Nikita said urgently as he helped the still shocked Sarah into one of the chairs. He didn't take a seat himself; instead, he began striding back and forth, the adrenaline still coursing through him. He could feel Larry's hipflask against his chest and longed to take a long drink from it. Not now, not yet, he thought to himself.

"For Chrissake stop pacing and tell me what's happened," demanded the chief.

Nikita stopped pacing and looked at Sykes. "The White Russian is real and he's going to kill Phillips," he said with as much sincerity as he could muster.

"Phillips as in the vice president?" he replied, with a smirk. "Is this some kind of a joke, Marshall?"

"No, sir. The White Russian is a rogue KGB agent who intends to hit us right where it hurts. What's more, we know who he is."

He threw the photo of Brishnov down on the table. "Taras Brishnov, the KGB's greatest prize, and the jewel of Brezhnev's crown. With Yerin gone, he's lost his last remaining mentor."

"Jesus Christ, you better have some proof for this."

"Our proof is lying on a white shag carpet in Baltimore with the side of his head blown off," said Nikita, who began pacing again.

The vein in Sykes' temple looked ready to burst. He gave Sarah a cigarette and lit it for her. As she exhaled the smoke, she relaxed slightly and her hands trembled less.

"You two had better start at the beginning," Sykes said, lighting a cigarette for himself.

"There's no time, Sykes," said Nikita angrily. "We need to secure the VP."

"You're upset, so I'll allow your insubordination this once," said Sykes. "Now sit your ass down and tell me everything. And talk quickly," he said with a coldness that left no room for argument.

"OK, but before I do can I get these video tapes over to an analyst to see if he can trace the car registration?"

"Come on, Jake, you know the chances of that car being registered to a KGB spy are pretty slim. Now start talking."

Nikita relayed everything from receiving the tip off from the SE division through to his and Chang's visit to Baltimore and what they had uncovered.

As he finished recounting the murder of Chrastek he sat back, but Sykes was leaning forwards, looking calmer than Nikita had ever seen him. "OK, you're both dismissed. Go home and get some rest; tomorrow could be an intense day."

Nikita was stunned. "But, boss, you need us to help track Brishnov down!" He noticed with alarm a hint of the Russian slip into his American accent. Mercifully Sykes did not.

"You're analysts, not field agents. You've done great work, and stay close to your phones as we may need you. Let the experts track him down," he said in his best attempt at kindness.

Nikita stood up and left the room without saying anything. He knew he'd pay for his disrespect, but the mission was too vital to his own identity remaining a secret for him to sit back and watch from the sidelines.

Sarah followed him out, limping slightly, still shell-shocked but with some colour returning to her cheeks.

He turned to her and swallowed his anger at her. "Let's get you home," he said, putting his arm around her and helping her walk out, not caring how it might look to the rest of the office.

"Can I stay with you tonight?" Sarah asked him, looking almost childlike up at him.

He paused. "Sure, of course you can."

"You're sure?" she asked dubiously.

"Of course," he said again, but only to keep his cover. Inside he was a maelstrom of feelings.

They didn't speak on the drive home, but Nikita tenderly helped the still shaking Sarah out of the car and into his apartment.

Sitting her on the sofa, he went to make tea for her. While the kettle was boiling, he took a long slug from Larry's thermos flask and exhaled heavily.

When he returned to the living room Nikita found Sarah crying softly, and felt a momentary pang of irritation. On the scale of the things, he had seen and done in the past year, the death of Petr Chrastek ranked fairly low.

He collected himself and sat down beside her. He put his arm around her once more, feeling awkward.

"It's my own fault," she whispered.

"Of course, it isn't," Nikita replied. "You had no way of knowing what was going to happen to Chrastek."

"Not that! But that I was there at all. I'm an analyst, Jake. I'm good at research, at numbers, at puzzles, but this? I only learned how to fire a gun at the team field training we did," she sobbed. "I'm not cut out for it."

"You're a fantastic analyst, Sarah; we aren't designed for field work," Nikita said kindly.

"You are!" she exclaimed. "You were so comfortable, and so quick to jump and protect me."

"That was because I care for you, nothing more," he said. "Anybody would have done the same."

She shook her head, looking more like her old self. "No, they wouldn't, Jake. I thought you were just an analyst, but there's more to you."

"What do you mean?" he asked cautiously, noticing his shoulders tense.

"You're heroic."

Nikita laughed bitterly. "Trust me when I say that I am no hero."

"Just my hero then," she said, smiling and kissing him gently on the cheek before snuggling up to him.

Nikita smiled at her but felt cold inside. There was ice in his veins and all he could think of was Brishnov. While Brishnov was alive, he knew that nobody was safe. Not him, not Sarah or Blaine, not even Elysia. Brishnov would have seen him with her earlier. Nobody was safe.

After some time, he felt the steady breathing of Sarah against his arm and lifted her gently, carrying her to bed and covering her.

Returning to the sofa, he opened a bottle of *Old Forester*, something he had developed a taste for since his visit to Simon Conlan's ranch. It sat easier with his government salary than the *Very Old Fitzgerald*.

Pouring the bourbon into a scratched tumbler, he picked it up and gazed into the golden spirit, getting lost in the deep colour of it and the warped view of the room through it. He threw the glass down in one and filled it once more, sitting back and allowing his dark thoughts to envelop him.

***

Across the world in Afghanistan the air was thick with blood. Blood, dust and death. It sat heavily on the plains and mountains of Spīn Ghar, along with the corpses of hundreds of Afghan men, women and children. And no small number of Soviet soldiers.

The young Soviet captain looked out across the Tobagi plain where many of the civilians had hoped to find safe passage, and his jaw bunched as his teeth grated. Suddenly he couldn't fight the bile at the back of his throat and vomited onto the dry ground in front of him. He was not the first to have a weak stomach that day, and certainly wouldn't be the last.

Gazing back across the plain to the village, he was cast in shadow by the mountain behind him. The echoes of gunfire and screams from the caves rang around him.

The mujahideen had fought ferociously, employing guerrilla tactics. They nestled among the crags and bushes of the Spīn Ghar mountains, firing mortars at the slopes as the Soviet forces climbed towards the Tora Bora caves. The young captain's thoughts were disturbed by the sound of raised voices behind him. He turned and walked into the cave which was angled so as to be invisible until you were right upon it.

As he entered, he saw two Afghan mujahideen on their knees in front of Sergeant Pogrevniak and one of his privates, both of them aiming their AK47s directly at the prisoners.

Both of the prisoners held their backs straight, full of dignity, their otherwise pristine white robes becoming dirty on the mossy cave floor.

The captain walked to them and the two Afghan soldiers raised their eyes to him from under the heavy cloth wrapped around their heads. One was older, roughly late fifties with a thick grey beard and clean shaven over the lip, his face carrying a dignified wisdom. The other could be no older than twenty-five, with a round face and sharp nose.

Sergeant Pogrevniak pushed the barrel of his weapon against the forehead of the elder prisoner. "Can I decorate the walls with the blood of this scum now, Captain?" He laughed, his lips pulled back tightly over crooked teeth.

The captain pushed the gun down. "We treat our prisoners with respect, Sergeant."

"These aren't prisoners, they are raghead scum."

The captain struck the sergeant around the face with the back of his hand. "Speak that way about me or our prisoners again and I will have you court-martialled, Sergeant."

Fury filled the face of Pogrevniak, who in turn struck the young private standing next to him who had let out an involuntary chuckle at the reprimanding of his commanding officer. The smile quickly left his face. Both retreated to the far side of the cave, watching with a mixture of curiosity and anger.

"Do you speak Russian or English?" The captain asked them falteringly, in the one phrase he had memorised.

"We speak both Russian and English, but our English is better," replied the older mujahideen in a cultured accent.

"Why do your people continue to fight?"

"It is a Jihad. We will fight to the death against the enemies of Islam," the young Afghan soldier said angrily.

"This is why religion is poison," said the soldier. "You would allow your women and children to die in the name of God."

"Religion may be poison," acknowledged the elder soldier passively, "but God is real. Faith is real. With a faith in a higher power, we can accept death gladly, knowing that paradise awaits."

"That is a good way to avoid ever living," the soldier said, rolling his shoulders to try and relieve them of the tension.

"To the contrary, my friend, it means that we all have the opportunity to find peace with our mistakes, remedy our wrongs and live with no regret. Can you say that you will live with no regrets over the massacre of an entire village of innocent people? Why do white men feel the need to invade, demean and wield power over those who are different?"

"I am following orders; this is not personal," the captain said stiffly to the gentle old man.

The old man looked benignly up at him and lowered his hands from his head. The captain said nothing. "Put aside the violence, Captain, and look for love," he said gently.

The captain laughed — a loud, humourless bark. "There is no love to be found in these caves, only death."

"It does not matter where you are, God can find you," the old man replied before adding in Russian, "S milym rai i v shalashe budet."

"If you love somebody, you will have heaven even in a tent," repeated the captain. "You know Russian proverbs."

"The beauty of that one always stayed with me, Captain. Now, it is time to do what you must. Go with God, for Allah is merciful," he said and kissed his comrade on the cheek. They both closed their eyes.

"Allahu akbar," they both whispered. The gunshots echoed throughout the mountain, but it was their words that rang longer in the mind of the young captain, who would be forever changed.

***

"You have done well, Captain," said Chairman Klitchkov waspishly. "You are certain no civilians escaped? It is vital for national security that the events of the Spīn Ghar Mountains remain unknown."

"Yes, sir," replied the captain into the radio receiver, fighting to keep the tremble from his voice, as the racking regret began to course through his veins. "We are still clearing some of the deeper caves; it is a labyrinth that runs deeper and farther than we could ever have imagined, but I have the perimeter sealed and the surrounding area has been scorched of all life," he said, closing his eyes.

"Excellent. Now I need you to stay in your current location and secure the caves. It is to become a base for an important operation."

"What operation is that, sir?" enquired the captain.

"That is above your rank, Captain, but perhaps not for long. Instructions will be forthcoming shortly," he said enigmatically and put down the receiver. He quickly picked it up again and dialled another number.

"Da?" said the high-pitched voice of Maxim Denisov when he came to the phone.

"It's Klitchkov—" he began.

"Ah yes, our esteemed new leader," he interrupted drily.

"If that is your attempt at brown-nosing, it needs some work," said Klitchkov mockingly. Denisov said nothing. "How would you like to serve our homeland, comrade?" asked Klitchkov.

"I have spent my life serving her," said Denisov caustically.

"Calm down, lieutenant-colonel. This would not only be serving the Soviet Union, but ensuring her greatness for generations."

There was a pause. "I'm listening," said the cold voice.

"Very good… I think you have earned your wings. I have a highly classified operation that I need you to oversee. Report to my office within the hour," Klitchkov said and hung up the phone.

Less than twenty minutes later Denisov stood at attention before the new chairman of the KGB.

"You are ready to serve as you have never before, Maxim?" Klitchkov asked carefully.

"Without question, sir."

"It will be dangerous. You could lose your life in the service of your country."

"There is no more honourable way to go," Denisov said, knowing what his superior wanted to hear.

Klitchkov stood and walked around to the young officer and pinned to his chest a badge of gold and red stripes. "I do not suffer failure, Colonel."

"Colonel?" gasped Denisov, showing more excitement than any had ever seen him display.

"Do not cause me to regret it."

"No, sir. I will follow you wherever you command," said Denisov, with no sign of his former air of cold indifference.

"Yes, I think you will do perfectly," said Klitchkov. "Now sit; the details of this operation are the highest level of classified and any mistakes will have repercussions on a global scale. There is a great deal to orchestrate, and I must now place it in your hands."

Klitchkov put his feet up on the desk in front of him and smiled. Everything was coming together perfectly. He then began to unfold the complex plan he had been working on right under the nose of Yerin.

***

Nikita awoke with a jolt, momentarily confused by his surroundings. As his eyes accustomed to the gloom, he realised that he was on the sofa. If his eyes had not revealed it to him, the stiffness in his neck would have. As he pushed himself upright, the splitting down the centre of his forehead forced him back down and he tasted bile in the back of his throat.

The empty bottle on the table in front of him revealed the source of his pain and he shut his eyes, wishing it away. That did nothing to rid him of the hangover and with a groan he forced himself up and made his way into the kitchen. He made himself a strong black coffee and washed down a couple of paracetamol, with the hot bitter liquid and another groan.

As the coffee hit his stomach and the caffeine entered his veins, it all came rushing back to him. Brishnov, the plot, Chrastek's head exploding, Sykes' hesitation, Sarah's emotional collapse and Elysia's return. Elysia. He could not get her from his mind, but knew he must. Everything depended on the resilience of Jacob Marshall. Nathan Martins did not and could not exist in Washington, and nor could Nikita Allochka.

He rubbed his eyes and thought again of Brishnov and the vice president. Making his mind up, he crept into his bedroom, moving soundlessly. He could see the gentle rise and fall of Sarah's body under the bedsheets as he grabbed some clothes and left the room, dressing silently in the living room after dousing himself with cold water.

Twenty minutes later he arrived at the CIA headquarters. Hurrying through security, he marched quick time through the labyrinthine corridors and into the office of the Soviet Counter-intelligence Branch.

Blaine was already at his desk, his eyes bloodshot. "Jesus, you look horrible," he said to Nikita as he dropped heavily into his chair.

"You're no oil painting yourself, buddy," Nikita replied drily, rubbing his own eyes and trying to ignore the sick feeling burning in his stomach.

"I've been here all night; what's your excuse, wise guy?" retorted his colleague.

"Why have you been here all night? What have you found?" Nikita asked sharply.

"I've been pulled onto your investigation. I've managed to trace the registration of the White Russian's car—"

"What did it show? Tell me everything," interrupted Nikita.

"Nothing doing, man, it was hired under a false name of some guy from Delaware who kicked the bucket years ago."

"That took you all night?" Nikita said with a raised eyebrow.

"Of course not. There's some strange movement happening in the USSR since Yerin was removed. Some guy named Denisov seems to have been dropping in on their nuclear sites and disappearing with a load of staff."

"Did you just say Denisov?" Nikita said sharply, stunned.

"That's right. Maxim Denisov. You know him? I'm not familiar with the name."

***

EAST SIBERIAN TAIGA, USSR, OCTOBER 1986

Nikita looked ahead of him at his fellow KGB recruits. Of the hundred and fifty he had started with almost five years ago, only fifteen now remained. They were marching in single file through the largest forest on earth, along a rough game track that had been flattened out by many boots. The East Siberian Taiga stretched for hundreds of miles in every direction, a thick, dense forest of larch, spruce, pine and fir. The days were still uncomfortably hot, with the air thick with mosquitos. But at night the subarctic frigidness of the long Siberian winter was beginning to creep back in, with temperatures plummeting. It had been an uncomfortable night on the forest floor. The other recruits had huddled together for warmth, but Nikita knew better than to try and get so close to them. Instead, he had spent the night with his eyes open, sitting propped against the tree, ears alert to the wolves, bears, reindeer and other deer, but nothing had dared approach the coiled springs that were the young KGB agents.

The hardened trainees all wore the long thick grey coats of their order. No one displayed anything that would suggest their discomfort, although several of the recruits had removed their ushankas, the ear flaps all currently pinned up.

Nikita liked to always bring up the rear when marching in this formation; it allowed him to keep his eyes firmly on his comrades, who had spent that past four years doing all they could to sabotage him.

Currently nothing could be heard other than the firm footsteps of their knee-high black leather boots. The forest was eerily subdued. Not even the wolves had risen yet.

The track began to incline before falling away sharply, zig-zagging down the slope, forcing the men to use the thick pine trunks to stop them from losing their footing. The track pulled away sharply to the left at the foot of the slope and suddenly opened into a clearing that stretched for over a thousand yards.

On the floor at the edge of the clearing was a wooden wall, with guns held in place by wooden pegs serving as racks. As they got nearer, Nikita could see there were three different types of firearms: Dragunov sniper rifles, Kalashnikov automatic rifles and Makarov PM pistols. There were also a series of knives, the like of which Nikita had never seen. They had fierce double-sided blades and thick round steel handles with rough circular grips, and a curious outcropping of metal at the foot of the blade.

Standing next to the wall of weaponry was their tutor, Maxim Denisov. He was deep in conversation with two men, one whom he recognised even from behind as the man who had changed the course of his life, Colonel Klitchkov. The other was a new face to Nikita — a solid looking man around sixty, with thick wire-rimmed glasses and a stern grey suit. The way the other two men looked to him, Nikita could immediately tell that he was their superior.

"I think that is Viktor Yerin," Yuri Popov, the recruit directly in front of him, whispered to Neski in front of him.

Neski looked briefly over his shoulder. "Of course it is Yerin. He dines often with my father," he sneered, before throwing his standard look of disgust at Nikita and turning back to face the front and continuing to swagger.

As they got to the men, they moved out of single file, instead lining up opposite the wall and the three men, waiting for them to finish their conversation.

The three stopped talking abruptly and turned to face the recruits who all stood to attention and saluted their superiors.

"These are the best we have produced, sir," Denisov said laconically to Yerin. Even by Denisov's standards, Nikita was surprised with the indifference he showed to those superior to him, merely just adhering to the most basic of formalities.

Yerin surveyed him with disapproval before looking back to the men. He walked along the line, looking at them closely.

As he came to Neski, the young man stepped out and offered his hand. "Excellent to see you, Viktor — my father sends his regards," he said pompously.

Yerin stopped and stared at the arrogant trainee. Denisov and Klitchkov looked mutinous.

Looking back at his two colleagues, Yerin ignored Neski's proffered hand. "Are you training our agents to be insolent and to break ranks now?" he asked.

Neski's eyes widened in horror before he dropped his hand and stepped back into line. "Sir! Sorry, sir."

"You would shame your father?" Yerin asked Neski, whose face had whitened and all trace of arrogance gone.

Klitchkov stepped in. "Agent Neski will of course embrace his punishment for his impudence, which will give him ample time to reflect on his errors, won't you soldier?" he said, looking at the young man.

Neski nodded frantically.

"Sobchak, Maklako, help this sinner discover the meaning of penitence," Denisov said slickly to two of the other trainees.

The two recruits stepped out of ranks and without a word grabbed Neski and began dragging him into the woods.

"If he screams, do not bring him back," said Yerin coldly. Klitchkov chuckled, turned back to the recruits and nodded to Denisov who was now facing Nikita, studying him. Denisov turned behind him and picked up one of the curious-looking knives from the rack, around four metres away from Nikita. He weighed the knife in his hands, holding it out perpendicular to his body, his palm holding the weight and his fingers wrapped around the top. His thumb gently rested on the metal notch protruding from the top of the hilt where it met the blade.

There was silence as all the young KGB recruits stood resolutely at attention, almost quivering with vigilance. Their years under the tutelage of Denisov had led them never to be restful, and to always expect the unexpected. The cold, clinical teacher had a flair for the dramatic, and many of them bore scars to remind them. Yerin and Klitchkov, however, while more relaxed, were nonetheless staring at Denisov with cautious interest.

"Allochka, down!" screamed Denisov suddenly. As he said it his thumb pushed down in the crook of the metal notch on the knife handle.

The blade shot out from the handle, directly at Nikita's heart.

The second's notice that Denisov had given him would have left almost anyone else in the world impaled like a stuck pig. But it was not for no reason that Nikita was the best recruit in the KGB programme. Already he was on the balls of his feet, too aware of Denisov's cruelty to be unsuspecting. His training had taught him that to fall backwards was quicker than to fall forwards and it was this training that saved him. Had he dived forwards he would have thrown his head into the path of the blade, but as he fell backwards the blade whistled past his ear, almost slicing the skin.

He landed heavily on his back, knocking the breath from his lungs, but instantly leapt back onto his feet with ease, and stepped back into line. Barely four seconds had passed.

Denisov stood with the handle of the knife in his hand and a spring hanging from the end. There was silence all around, before Yerin began applauding.

Nikita felt cold inside, but his heart was beating overtime. Surviving by a split second produced a massive amount of adrenaline and he controlled his breathing to stop his hands from shaking.

Klitchkov smiled knowingly.

"What is this amazing contraption?" asked Yerin, showing more emotion than his face was used to displaying.

"The Spetsnaz ballistic knife, sir," answered Denisov. "It travels at speeds of over sixty miles per hour and is capable of piercing body armour... or slow KGB soldiers," he added with a wry smile.

Yerin smiled again. "He knew it was coming, I presume?" he said, twitching his head in Nikita's direction.

"No, sir," said Denisov.

The smile immediately faded from Klitchkov's face.

Yerin turned and looked at Nikita. "You did not know of the knife attack?"

"Niet, ser!" barked Nikita.

Silence descended on the clearing once more as Yerin continued to inspect him, now smiling. In the distance they heard a scream and the smile faded instantly from Yerin's face.

He stepped back and surveyed the men. "Well at least we know you have managed to train one of them well. How many more would have managed to avoid your attempts to kill them, I wonder?" he mused.

Denisov's expression was flat. He walked past the men to retrieve the blade.

"The intention is that our men will be behind the blade rather than in front of it, sir," said Klitchkov. "Let us see them in action for firearms training," he added to Denisov, who nodded and began walking down the line, handing guns to the soldiers.

When he got to Nikita, he thrust a Kalashnikov into his arms, his eyes burning with hatred. It was a sentiment Nikita was used to being on the receiving end of, but he gazed coldly back, still thinking about how Denisov had done his best to kill him so brazenly.

As they lined up, aiming at targets of various distances across the clearing depending on their weapon, Nikita allowed himself a glance at the woods behind him from where Neski's scream had echoed — but there was no trace of him.

None of the young KGB soldiers ever saw Neski again.

***

"Yes, I know of him," said Nikita, working to collect himself and clear his head of his memories from the Taiga. "But he heads up their KGB training programme; he has nothing to do with their nuclear activity."

"It seems your sources are a little out of date if these nuclear site visits are anything to go by."

"You said he is disappearing with lots of staff?" said Nikita.

"Yes, but I doubt he's recruiting the—"

"And warheads too?" interrupted Nikita.

"That's the strangest thing; it's like he's just leaving them there with a skeleton staff," Blaine said patiently. "It doesn't fit with how they've always operated. Reports on the ground are that their troops are flooding out of Afghanistan as well. It's like they're just suddenly throwing in the towel on the Cold War."

"It does sort of fit with what Petrenko has been saying, I guess," said Nikita with his best attempt at sincerity. Blaine nodded dubiously. "Where have they got to on the White Russian now?" Nikita asked, working to keep the urgency out of his voice. "If what our informant said is true then the clock's ticking fast."

"That's Chang's remit, not mine, pal. I'm surprised she's not here."

"I think she was a bit shook up from some shit that happened yesterday. I'm sure she'll be here later."

"You'd know…" said Blaine with a wink.

Nikita's face flushed.

"This is the problem with working in an office of spies, kinda hard to keep anything from us." Blaine laughed. "Don't worry, your secret is safe with me, and probably everyone else in the office," he added, clapping a hand on Nikita's arm. "Jeez, how hard are your arms! I didn't know you work out."

"I do what I can," said Nikita, smiling, before standing up and heading to Sykes' office. He knocked and entered without waiting for a reply. A cloud of smoke billowed out to him. As it cleared and he approached the desk, he saw his boss sitting rubbing his temples, a cigarette burned down to the filter glowing in between his fingers. If Blaine had looked bad, it was nothing on Sykes, whose face was grey and screwed into a frown, eyes bloodshot and hangdog.

"Marshall, what do you want?" he said.

"Have you found him yet, boss? Have you found Brishnov?"

"No, we've had people on it all night but we're no closer to apprehending him. But that's the least of my problems. The vice president is refusing to reschedule his press conference today, even refusing to wear a Kevlar vest."

"What! Why?"

"Says it would send the wrong message and it would be letting the terrorist win."

"Does he have any idea how dangerous Brishnov is? He's not some two-bit terrorist with a homemade bomb, he's one of, if not *the,* world's most highly trained and deadly assassin."

"I know that and you know that, but politicians care only about perception."

"Well, his stupidity could work to our advantage at least, sir."

"How the hell do you figure?"

"Taras Brishnov is clearly on a different level to any spy we've encountered before. We know now that he has been a key KGB asset for many years, yet we didn't even know of his existence until the other day. That's despite having all of our Soviet agents reporting to us throughout Brezhnev and Petrenko's reign, up until Yerin's recent dismantling of our spy network over there. Never once did this guy get mentioned. Yet we know he was close to General Secretary Brezhnev and Yerin, until his recent decision to go rogue, for which we just don't know what his motivations are."

"I hope there's a point coming in this somewhere," said Sykes sarcastically.

"Yes, sir. The point is that we're never going to track this guy; he's too good at staying under the radar. The advantage of the VP's pig-headedness is that we know exactly where Brishnov is going to be and when. He's coming to us so we don't need to go find him."

"You're suggesting using the vice president as bait," Sykes spouted sternly.

"Absolutely," Nikita replied flatly. "If Phillips insists on putting himself unnecessarily in harm's way, let's leverage that in our favour."

"I'm not sure that will hold up in front of a congressional hearing," said Sykes with a wry grin, "but it does appear that it's our best option. However," he said holding up his hand before Nikita could interrupt, "we also have to continue the search for him. The honey trap should be the last resort. Otherwise, the shit storm that will explode if we fail will destroy us both."

"Yes, sir."

"Now go and put a plan together, sharpish," Sykes said, waving him away. "And for Chrissake get the VP into a Kevlar vest."

"I'll do my best, sir."

"You'll do more than that if you want to have a job to come into tomorrow."

Nikita nodded and left the smoke-filled room, inhaling deeply as he stepped into the recycled air of the windowless office.

An hour later he was standing on the sloping driveway of Number One Observatory Circle, having come through a series of rigorous Secret Service security checks. He looked up at the wood-trimmed Victorian building, a gleaming white masterpiece of symmetrical turrets and verandas, and braced himself for a meeting with Vice President Gerald Phillips, a man who had become an essential part of the political fabric.

As he climbed the steps into the porch, which was framed on four corners by thick white pillars, and approached the front door, it opened before he was able to knock.

"Ah you're our man from the CIA?" asked a man in his early thirties, his dark blond hair brushed over his ears in a look that belonged more to the fifties than the late eighties.

"Yes, sir, Jacob Marshall," Nikita said, holding out his hand. "But I'm afraid you have me at a disadvantage."

The young man clasped his hand firmly. "Ed Sheen. Now follow me; I could only get you a coupla minutes with the VP," he said with a confident swagger.

He led Nikita through several interconnected rooms. "You gotta get the VP to wear a vest," he said over the shoulder of his tan brown suit. "Don't get me wrong, him getting shot would put us up ten points over any other candidates, but that's no good to us if he's dead," he said with an insincere chuckle.

"I'll do my best, Mr Sheen…"

"Please, call me Ed," he said with a wave of his hand. "He can be a pretty stubborn old shmuck so don't let him dig his heels in too hard. Don't be fooled by the bland exterior; he's sharp as a tack."

"Duly noted," said Nikita as they came to an ornate wooden door with a gleaming brass handle. Outside it stood an ageless, slender man with hazel eyes in a suit that left you in no doubt of his strength. He surveyed Nikita with fleeting distaste before arranging his face into a look of impassiveness. Nikita thought he looked like a child's head had been placed on the body of a granite warrior.

"Hey, John, the CIA are here to try and talk some sense into Gerald."

"It's Mr Vice President to you, Mr Sheen; show some respect to the office," replied the stiff man guarding the door.

Ed turned to Nikita and rolled his eyes. "The vice president," he said sarcastically, and with a thinly veiled flicker of exasperation, "recently hired a new bodyguard who takes his work awfully seriously, despite the fact we're surrounded by Secret Service."

John stepped forward and for a moment Nikita thought he was going to punch Ed, but he instead spoke to Nikita. "Please raise your arms," and then proceeded to give Nikita a very thorough patting down, before stepping aside.

As Nikita went to enter the study, John leant in and said, "One thing I agree on with Mr Sheen is that you must convince the vice president to wear a vest."

"It sounds like it may be a thankless task but I'll do my best," Nikita said earnestly to the curious-looking man who nodded and opened the door for him.

The room was a jarring fusion of pastels and turquoise insisted upon by Audrey Phillips, combined with the traditional colonial cornices and baroque wooden finishing.

Vice President Gerald Phillips was sitting at the desk, his chin perched upon his hands, seemingly lost in thought. A gilded crystal decanter filled with whiskey stood upon the polished walnut desk, alongside a boxy Amstrad and a huge Motorola DynaTAC mobile phone. As the door closed, Phillips snapped from his reverie and looked over to Nikita placidly.

"CIA here for you, sir," said Ed from over Nikita's shoulder.

Nikita stepped towards the vice president who stood from his chair. "Agent Jacob Marshall, an honour to meet you, Mr Vice President," he said brightly, offering his hand.

Gerald Phillips shook the hand across the desk and waved at him to take a seat. "So I suppose you're here to tell me not to speak at Capitol Hill today, Agent Marshall?"

"No, sir, I quite understand the importance of giving a show of strength in the face of terrorism."

Phillips's face gave no sign of surprise, but his voice took on a lighter tone. "I'm pleased to hear you say so, son. I will not wear a vest."

"However…"

"How did I know there would be a however?" the vice president said drily.

"You misunderstand, sir, we have absolutely no intention of getting in the way of your press conference; it's an important speech for our nation."

"Which is exactly why I can't stand up there, the man who will ask our troops to go to war, and be too afraid to stand on the steps of our own Capitol without a Kevlar vest. I would look pathetic."

"I wholeheartedly understand, Mr Vice President."

"But?"

"But we can't ignore the fact that the 'White Russian', a man we believe to be one of the most lethal assassins — probably the most talented spy the world has ever seen — is on a one-man mission to murder you. You won't be able to continue your great work for the country if you're lying dead and riddled with bullets, because I'm sure you know that KGB always empties an entire magazine into its victims."

Nikita slowed his pace now that he had reeled Phillips in. "You're too vital, not just as our vice president but also as our future president. Imagine the symbolism and the threat to national security if you were mowed down on the steps of the Capitol! So we just ask that you throw on a Kevlar vest — standing there and speaking is the show of strength, not what you're wearing."

The vice president leant back in his chair and pushed the tips of his fingers together, the hint of a smirk playing upon his lips.

"You sure you're not a politician? That kind of spin is straight from the playbook of Ed here," he said, winking at Ed who grinned back.

"I'm sure I could find a position for such an eloquent guy," Ed added jovially.

"I think I'll stick to national security if it's OK with you," Nikita said awkwardly.

Gerald Phillips released a low snicker, the closest he ever got to laughing. It sounded like dry grass rustling in a strong breeze.

"Fine, you've got me, spin doctor. I'll wear a vest. Now get outta here before I change my mind," he said, his face taciturn one more.

"Thank you, Mr Vice President, you've made a very wise choice," Nikita said as he stood and drew a sheet of paper from his inside pocket. "I've taken the liberty of making a couple of suggestions for how to minimise the risk of being shot during your speech, sir; I hope you'll cast your eye over them," said Nikita, looking intently at Phillips and offering his hand. The vice president raised his eyebrows but gave a small nod, shaking Nikita's hand before allowing him to be led out of the room by Ed and past the lurking bodyguard outside the door.

"That was inspired!" Ed exclaimed. "You played him like a fiddle, massaging his ego then going in for the kill."

"I think he knew full well what I was doing," Nikita replied candidly, "but the point is it worked, so I'll take it." He breathed a sigh of relief; thank god for his Neuro-Linguistic Programming training under the KGB's psychological warfare expert Roman Gryaznov. Reading people, quickly identifying their weaknesses and using them to bend them to your will. The CIA had afforded him no such training. He was, after all, only meant to be an analyst.

They reached the front door and as he stepped outside Ed said, "Whatever you call it, good job in there, agent." Ed shook his hand, his eyes widening at the strength in Nikita's grip.

Leaving the house without a backward glance, Nikita stepped into his car and headed not for the office, but straight to Capitol Hill.

When he arrived on the steps of the Capitol Building, he gazed up at the gleaming white structure, the seat of legislative power in the United States. Decisions made by the congress within rippled across the world. If he was successful in his ultimate mission, he wondered what would become of this historic site.

Currently it appeared more of a tourist thoroughfare than a political behemoth, with groups being led this way and that by guides, and heavy cameras being lugged around by starry-eyed visitors from across the globe.

He turned and gazed down the long stretch of lawns towards the towering Washington Monument a mile and a half away and the Lincoln Memorial beyond it. His eyes scanned everything and missed nothing, a constant stream of information flooding into his brain; nothing escaped even his periphery. The twitchy gardener tending the roses; the people in the tourist groups who didn't look like typical tourists and the ones that did; the suited politicians milling around the entrance to the Capitol Building who were sweating excessively or looking nervous. He saw them all.

Nikita strolled up the steps and leant against the wall in the shadow of one of the pillars, from where he continued to survey the scene before him. Looking around, he tried to identify possible sniper locations. There was plenty of tree cover lining the lawns but setting up and taking a sniper shot from there without being spotted would be close to impossible. Buildings lined the lawn, with the various Smithsonian museums all representing ideal locations from which to aim at the steps of the United States Capitol. Even with tightened security, Nikita doubted it would prevent an agent such as Brishnov from gaining entry and clearing a room with a view of the Capitol.

Already he could see Secret Service agents setting up along the roofs of many of the buildings, and several milling across the lawns, putting up barriers and keeping a close eye on any possibly furtive lurkers.

After absorbing the area for thirty minutes, Nikita walked down to a payphone and made two phone calls. The first was to the office.

"Yes?"

"Sir, it's Jake—"

"Where the hell are you?" Sykes interjected.

"I'm at the Capitol; I wanted to get here early for some reconnaissance."

"You're not a field agent! Get back here now, Marshall, I swear to God."

"Sir, as the department's KGB expert I think it's important I be on site for this one. I have some understanding of how they think and operate."

"So much so that you didn't even know that this guy existed until yesterday," Sykes said caustically.

"The VP is going to wear a vest now," Nikita said, changing the subject rapidly.

"How did you manage that?" Sykes murmured, softening a little.

"I just highlighted how it was in the best interests of the country; he's a sucker for a bit of patriotism."

"Good work. He's not an easy man to persuade," Sykes responded before pausing. "Very well, stay on site and do what you can to help. But don't get in the way of the Secret Service. Unlike you, they're actually extensively trained for this sort of thing."

"Sure thing," said Nikita. Already he had identified at least five easy ways to murder the vice president on the steps of the Capitol Building and get away before anyone even realised what had happened.

But he could be sure that if he had thought of five in just half an hour, Brishnov would have reams of angles that he had been plotting, possibly for weeks.

After he put the receiver down, he slotted a few more coins in and made the second call.

After ringing for some time, a woman's voice answered timidly. "Hello?"

"Sarah, it's me," he said, "How are you doing?"

He heard her breathe a sigh of relief. "I'm glad you called. Where are you?"

"I'm at the Capitol; this is where Brishnov's going to try and take out, Phillips."

"Isn't that the Secret Service's job?" she said quickly, almost snapping. "We've done more than enough! Why would you put yourself back in the field?"

"Don't worry, the only one in any danger today is the vice president. He should be here soon and then we can put this whole thing behind us."

She sighed again. "I wish we could turn the clock back to yesterday morning, to being in bed together."

"Instead let's look forward to the clocks rolling forward and being in bed together again tonight. Are you going into work today?"

"How can you even ask that after what we saw yesterday?" she demanded.

"I'm sorry, of course you aren't. Let me know if you need anything."

"Just you to come back in one piece. Maybe we can get takeout."

"Perfect, take it easy and I'll catch you later."

He hung up and rubbed his eyes. His chest felt constricted and it was hard to breathe. There was no place for a girlfriend in the world in which he was operating. When I get home, I'll end things with her, he thought to himself. It's the only way, before it's too late.

He set his shoulders and went back to the Capitol steps where a small platform was being erected for the vice president to stand on. Secret Service agents, garbed in black suits with mirrored sunglasses, were clearing the front of the building and shepherding people to a safe distance. Deciding against introducing himself to the man in charge, he lurked in the shadows of the trees and continued to consider all of the angles. If it was him, a sniper shot was the obvious option. Near impossible to spot or to defend against, the difficulty in pinpointing where the shot came from until later made escape much easier. But somehow it just didn't feel like that would be Brishnov's style. The way he had killed the prostitute, allowing himself to be photographed, the murder of Chrastek, the blowing up of the Texas bar; this was a man who had tired of hiding in the shadows and taking no credit for his successes.

To the inexperienced eye, it would appear that Brishnov had become reckless. To Nikita it spoke of a series of deliberate moves on a chess board that were set up to deceive.

He cleared his mind and focused again on the task at hand. The old stone steps had now been cleared, and glancing at his watch Nikita could see that the time of the press conference was nearly upon him. Across the lawn, the press corps had gathered, a roiling mass of reporters and photographers, notepads, pens, long lens cameras and scuffed shoes. The sky above was stormy grey but it looked as if the rain would hold off until after the vice president's speech, which he didn't imagine would be too long.

He didn't have to wait long, as it was barely minutes later when the motorcade appeared, travelling fast along Independence Avenue South West. The black saloon was almost hidden by the rotating, flashing ensemble of police motorbikes and oversized security vehicles.

Nikita sank further back into the shadows, draping his CIA lanyard around his neck in plain sight to ward off any suspicious Secret Service snipers, and set himself up with a clear view of both the politician and the crowd in front of the platform.

Vice President Gerald Phillips approached the platform with his security guard John running point ahead of him, his smooth skin and long nose dulled in the sunlight. Anyone in the way quickly evaporated under the glare of the wiry bodyguard. Secret Service personnel, all in black suits and sunglasses, flanked the vice president and followed from the rear.

They stopped to one side of the platform as Ed Sheen passed them and took up his place at the microphone.

"Good afternoon, ladies and gentlemen," he said heartily, enjoying his moment in the spotlight. "Thank you all for coming. The vice president will be making a short statement and no questions. Without any further delay, I give you Vice President of the United States, Gerald Phillips," he finished flamboyantly, with a hand out in his boss's direction.

The vice president smiled broadly and began walking with short steps towards the platform, suddenly looking very much his age. He stumbled slightly as he climbed the steps, but John was on hand to steady him. He fruitlessly tried to smooth down his charcoal grey suit, bulky over the Kevlar vest, swept a hand over his severe side parting and laughed as he got to the microphone. "What I'm about to say will hopefully offer more stability to the country than my footwork on these steps!" The press corps indulged him with a smattering of laughter which died down immediately as the vice president raised his hand and the smile faded from his face.

"I want to thank you all for coming; I can see some friendly faces in there, yes even in the press corps," he said to another ripple of smiles.

"You may be asking why I chose this spot for what I'm about to say. This may not be where I earned my stripes — I have Texas to thank for that — but without a doubt it's where I earned my stars serving the American people, here at the Capitol Building, an emblem of what this country stands for — liberty, freedom and an iron will.

"And it is for that reason that I've chosen a place that is not about me, but is about the history and the future of this country, to announce my candidacy for president of the United States."

At that moment a banner unfurled down the wall behind him, reading 'Gerald Phillips for President' on a deep blue background, with a red stripe through the centre.

There was some polite applause from the journalists, but a more enthusiastic reaction from the gathered crowd which had been drawn by the media circus, with two media helicopters now circling overhead.

He signalled to his wife Audrey and she bustled over, John stepping back out of the way, his eyes watchful. Her white perm was set perfectly in place, impervious to the gentle breeze down the National Mall. He put his arm around her and they both fixed their faces into smiles and waved. He then released her and she stepped to the side.

Nikita's eyes were furiously searching the landscape, scanning the buildings with his keen eyes for any window ajar and gleaming gun barrel, anyone in the crowd looking even vaguely suspect. He identified some possible candidates in the crowd, but no one of Brishnov's stature and nobody who on closer inspection met the requirements he was looking for as a would-be assassin. He had suspicions, but nothing was certain and his heart was racing with suspense. Yet all seemed calm, which only served to increase his anxiety.

"For the past seven years, the president has done great work, and I've worked tirelessly as his vice president to support that great work. But now I want to make this country even greater. Normal protocol would have me fill a hall full of supporters in a state that loves me, to announce a run for president, with champagne and streamers. But running for this great office is not a party, it's not about being surrounded by yes men, it's about doing what is right for the United States of America!" he exclaimed with his fist held triumphantly aloft.

"Seven years ago, the world was beset by a cold front, but through tireless work we have pushed it back while ensuring that things never became too hot, and that our relations with the Soviet Union are stronger than they have been for decades. I don't want to see the blood of American soldiers spilt on foreign soil, or any soil for that matter. I want us to enter a future without fear, a future of—" he coughed slightly and wiped a sheen of sweat from his brow.

"A future of pe—" he coughed again, and put a hand on the microphone to steady himself.

He smiled a crooked smile, and went to continue speaking. As he did, his eyes rolled back into his head and his legs folded under him. He fell backwards onto the steps as Audrey rushed to his side, just failing to catch him as he landed heavily. The steps were lit up by the strobe light effect of thirty camera flashes furiously flickering as the press throng closed in and Nikita ran from his hiding place towards the vice president.

The Secret Service quickly pushed the horde back, but there was one person missing. The one person who should have been right by the vice president's side throughout the speech. John the bodyguard.

Nikita was already on the hunt and pulled his handgun from the holster, holding it low while beginning to spring after the dark shape ghosting towards the very trees Nikita had loitered in earlier. Sirens were wailing as blue lights flashed in the distance, closing in on Capitol Hill. Whether they were ambulances or the police, Nikita couldn't tell. There was no time to wait and find out; he must find John. John would lead him to Brishnov and he could end this whole sorry saga.

Brishnov.

If John was running, did that mean that Brishnov was still near, surveying the whole scene, perhaps with a sniper now that the perfect misdirection had been performed? "Follow the lead you've got," Nikita muttered to himself.

He began running hard towards the trees, John no longer visible. Covering the ground in seconds, Nikita paused under the canopy of the spruce trees. They weren't densely packed but provided enough shade for a dark suit to fade into in the overcast afternoon.

Searching the area, Nikita absorbed all the information in front of him, and saw the lithe figure of the bodyguard who was across the road nearing the Rayburn House Office Building. He began his pursuit once more, crossing the grass and hurtling across the street, dimly aware of the blaring of car horns and screeching of brakes as he did so. He cared little, his focus entirely on the man he was pursuing, some hundred yards ahead of him.

John was fast, almost seeming to glide across the ground, so unlike a typical bulky bodyguard. But Nikita was faster.

Even in hard shoes, Nikita was making up ground quickly, but as John passed the Rayburn Building, he threw a glance over his shoulder and saw Nikita gaining on him. He turned a hard left and charged directly into the congressional office building.

Nikita groaned. This could complicate matters considerably.

He then heard multiple gunshots and his chest tightened, knowing exactly what he could look forward to once he entered.

Slowing as he reached the doorway, situated beneath grey stone columns, he held his HDM pistol in both hands and stood with his back to the wall next to the doorway, listening intently. There were no screams or shouts, only silence, which was the worst thing Nikita could have hoped for. He could almost smell the blood.

He nudged the door open with the barrel of his gun and stepped silently into the building, keeping the wall behind him and searching the entry hall with the pistol. Blood was already pooling on the floor, but it was the bodies that Nikita focused on more.

Three security men lay dead on the ground, two behind the concierge desk inside the building, slumped back in their chairs with double taps between their eyes. Another lay next to the metal detector at the entryway, staring blindly up at the ceiling. He couldn't have been older than twenty-two but a wedding ring gleamed on his lifeless left hand.

Three others also lay dead, one Nikita recognised as a congressman, while a man with wispy grey hair lay slumped over a woman in her thirties who even in death was still holding the stack of papers she must have been carrying.

All of the deceased had been killed in identical ways, and Nikita felt the hairs on the back of his neck quiver with suspicion.

He set his shoulders grimly and moved down the corridor, fiercely determined. His breath was heavy from the sprint and he paused to regain control, remembering Denisov's words: 'if you act on adrenaline, you act without control. There is no such thing as a KGB agent with no control, because they will be dead either by their own failings or by the enemy's hand.'

The corridor was deserted, and Nikita was grateful that it was a weekend and most people were not in work. Nonetheless, a building such as this should never be this quiet. Perhaps the gun shots encouraged people to hide, he thought to himself hopefully.

At the end of the corridor, a staircase opened up to the right, and double doors led outside on the left. He quickly spotted the hint of a bloody handprint on the bannister of the stairs.

He immediately moved towards the doors. No KGB agent, double agent or otherwise, would be careless enough to leave a handprint when being pursued. There was also the fact that the victims had all been shot. "No reason to have blood on your hands unless you chose to," Nikita muttered as he saw that the fire alarm connected to the door had been disconnected, deactivating it. He pushed the doors open.

A bullet missed Nikita by a fraction of an inch, ringing as it ricocheted off the metal doors. He threw himself back behind one of the doors. He chanced a glance around and saw John moving swiftly over the street towards the Spirit of Justice Park, now only about forty yards ahead of him. Leaping out from behind the door, Nikita hurtled across the street and into the park, closing the gap rapidly.

When he had closed the distance to around fifteen yards, he raised his gun. "It's over, John. Don't make me shoot you," he shouted.

The bodyguard slowed to a stop in front of the fountain in the centre of the small, deserted park which was merely a green topping for an underground car park. He turned and raised his arms and grinned at Nikita.

"Drop your weapon," Nikita said, moving closer.

John withdrew it and tossed it towards Nikita, who nudged it away with his foot. The temptation to just pull the trigger was huge and he fought to keep control.

"What did you do to the vice president?"

"Some good old fashioned novichok agent, comrade; he will not survive. He was dead before he even took to the stage. Dead before he even got into the car," John said with a chuckle.

Nikita laughed. "Is that right? Then give me a reason not to shoot you."

"Control, not adrenaline," whispered John from underneath his long, curved nose, his accent slipping to reveal a thick Soviet accent.

Nikita cocked his head to one side and fired.

CHAPTER 21

Far from looking surprised, John merely smirked as the shot deflected off the stone statue in the middle of the fountain directly behind him.

"I am not here to talk with you, whoever you are; I am only here to take you in for the murder of the vice president," said Nikita.

"Then he is dead? I have fulfilled my mission?" John said desperately, a look of ecstasy crossing his face.

"Like I said, I am not here to talk. The next shot will not miss; I give you my word on that."

"You don't behave like a CIA analyst..." John began, falling silent as Nikita walked towards him, but the smirk didn't leave his face.

Nikita pulled John's arms behind him and prepared to put handcuffs on him. As he did, John pushed backwards, hard, driving Nikita into the low wall around the fountain. He lost his balance and fell into the water, but managed to hold onto the bodyguard, pulling him with him.

Before he was able to spring to his feet, John was on him, holding him under the water. Looking up at the face from underwater, Nikita thought John looked strangely distorted and multi-hued. Almost automatically he swivelled and swept John's leg. It barely moved but did enough to loosen the pressure on him momentarily to get out of the hold by placing his wrists between John's hands and forcing them upwards and outwards.

Nikita propelled himself backwards, cracking his head on the stone wall. He stood up dizzy as John launched a fresh attack at him. Nikita ducked the assault, noticing that it hadn't been a trick of the water, and John's face really had become blotchy. He came up from his low position with an uppercut which John attempted to dodge, but Nikita caught the end of his nose, which came away from the face and flung up into the air, coming to land in the water behind him.

Nikita looked at the face in front of him with no hint of surprise. The long, curved nose had been replaced by a short, horribly familiar, straight one. The sallow, smooth skin tone had now been largely washed away by the water, leaving a pinched, pale face with broad, high cheekbones. And an angry scar running from the corner of one eye out to the ear.

"Hello comrade," Taras Brishnov sneered in Russian. As he spoke, his facial muscles seemed to relax and unbunch from the position he'd been holding them in to become John. The rounded face became thinner and gaunter.

"You do not seem surprised," he said curiously.

Nikita did not reply, instead throwing himself at him, but Brishnov stepped calmly to one side, leaving Nikita swiping at thin air and stumbling forwards. Brishnov kicked him ferociously in the lower back, causing Nikita to wail out loud despite himself and fall forward onto the wall again.

Both men were soaked to the bone, and Brishnov was laughing now. "So much fuss made over the Black Russian," he spat. "So much energy wasted on so pathetic a man, a dirty little African posing as a Russian. Hell will freeze over the day any Russian breeds with a black," he said, all trace of the smirk now gone.

Nikita sat in the water and looked desperately for a way up. He felt for the knife in his boot but Brishnov kicked his hand away contemptuously.

"Every trick, you think you know, I have been doing for a decade longer. They call you the greatest Russian agent? You are nothing more than Klitchkov's pet."

Nikita laughed bitterly. "Perhaps, but rather his pet than his sacrificial lamb, sent to the slaughter and betrayed by his own country." The smile fell from Brishnov's face.

"You lie!" he said, thrusting a fist at Nikita, who ducked and threw a counter punch at Brishnov's side. Brishnov spun and launched a rear kick at Nikita's knee; Nikita jumped above it and launched the side of his hand at Brishnov's neck.

To onlookers it was hard to keep pace with the two elite KGB agents, both trained in the same skills, but both with very different approaches. The rapid thrusts moved like lightning as they danced and splashed their way around the fountain.

Brishnov's style was one of rapier-like flicks and movements, but from a clearly stiff military background. Nikita moved more slowly, but with more fluidity and more strength. He attacked less but made more connections with his opponent. However, Brishnov's connections were more damaging and began to take their toll. Both were looking for a weakness in the other to exploit, and both struggling to find one.

They broke apart, both gasping for breath, both struggling to maintain a firm foothold on the mossy bottom of the pool. With a jolt, Nikita realised he could not beat Brishnov. Not with his fists.

"Why do you think I came here today? Why do you think I was with Chrastek that day you shot him?" asked Nikita.

Brishnov said nothing, just eyed Nikita again with his cold smirk.

"My order to pursue a threat to the vice president did not come from the CIA. It came from home. Klitchkov passed on orders from Yerin himself. Yerin ordered you to be killed," lied Nikita.

"This is why you can't trust blacks," sneered Brishnov. "I know Yerin better than you could possibly know; he would never betray me."

"He betrayed you, and so has your country. You are lost with no hope, Taras," whispered Nikita, reverting back to English as he became aware of a crowd of people drawing near. He caught sight of flashing blue lights in his periphery just before he heard a familiar voice say, "Jake!"

In his peripheral he saw Sarah Chang standing there, her eyes wide with horror. It was then he realised it wasn't water trickling down his face, but blood. It distracted him for just a millisecond too long as he felt Brishnov's fist power into his belly, driving the wind out of him. He tried to draw breath but couldn't and looked desperately up at Brishnov.

"A girlfriend, Nikita?" he continued in Russian, shaking his head and tutting gleefully.

Sensing the danger, Nikita fixed his face into a look of ambivalence. "Just a pleasant distraction, although unlike you I don't play with my food quite so violently," he said, choking through shallow, rasping breaths. He tried to block the look of intense sorrow that fell across Sarah's face.

Brishnov laughed harshly, then launched himself suddenly at Nikita once more. Unable to stand, Nikita did the only thing he was able to do and fell backwards, grabbing Brishnov on his way and performing a tomoe-nage by pushing his foot into Brishnov's chest and using Brishnov's own momentum to thrust him outwards and out onto the concrete beside the fountain.

Standing as quickly as he was able, he drew a sharp breath, his lungs gratefully drawing it in despite the pain still in his chest. Before he could turn, he heard a scream and closed his eyes in pain before looking to the skies.

Turning around, he saw that Brishnov had his arm around Sarah's throat and a gun to her temple.

There were further screams as the smattering of people around fled, trying to escape the crazed gunman. The police, now on the scene, held back at the edge of the park, unsure what to do.

Nikita stepped out of the fountain, a stream of water flowing off him, his wet clothes weighing him down heavily. "Let her go, Brishnov, she has nothing to do with this," he said calmly.

"Rule number one, comrade, never get attached; you know that," Brishnov said blandly.

"There is no leverage here, Taras, she means nothing to me."

Brishnov said nothing, only smiling as he began to drag Sarah to the end of the park.

"Jacob… please," she pleaded to him. Her already puffy and red eyes were full of pain, tears streaming down her face as she looked with such hurt at Nikita. The sight tore at his heart and he felt utterly helpless. This was all his fault.

Brishnov and Sarah reached the edge of the park, people clearing a path as he waved the gun in their direction. He heard a police sergeant barking, "Hold your fire! Hold your fire!"

As Brishnov dragged Sarah across the road, Nikita took a deep breath and began to furiously weigh the odds. He picked up his gun from the ground and began to chase after them, still trying to formulate a plan, immune to the cries of the people around him and the shouts from the police. A police helicopter was overhead now and he knew it wouldn't be long before the TV helicopters appeared too. This needed to be ended quickly.

Brishnov let off a shot in Nikita's direction before smashing the window of a red Ford Escort parked next to him and throwing Sarah inside. Nikita was only yards away when Brishnov got the engine running and pulled away in a screech of tyres.

Nikita ran into the road and waved his arms frantically in front of the oncoming traffic. Two cars back he saw a motorbike, and running to it, flashed his CIA badge and shoved the man off it, his cries muffled through the black helmet.

Nikita caught the bike before it fell to the floor, threw his leg over the seat and was on the move without a second glance. The bike roared beneath him as he worked the throttle and he was nearly thrown backwards by the power of the forward thrust. He held on tightly and moved quickly through the gears, weaving between cars with his eyes fixed firmly on the red Ford two hundred yards ahead. It turned onto South Capitol Street SW and Nikita swung onto the highway in pursuit, narrowly avoiding a bus which beeped its horn loudly as he powered past. Brishnov's driving was masterful, selecting the narrowest of gaps to power through, causing confusion and leaving dense traffic for Nikita to make his way around. Nikita, head low over the handlebars, wound his way through the traffic, finding slim holes between cars to snake through. The superior mobility of the bike had him closing on Brishnov fast.

Glancing at the speedometer, Nikita saw he was passing a hundred and ten miles per hour and the bike was beginning to shake, protesting against the speeds it was being pushed to maintain.

Suddenly Brishnov veered into the opposite lane of traffic, escaping the onrushing cars by a hair's breadth before careering down a slip road in the wrong direction. Nikita had no choice but to follow, the bike leaping over the tarmac and forcing the on comers to slam on the brakes, one clipping Nikitaalmost sending him from the seat. He skidded, put a foot down and pushed himself off once more. Seeing Brishnov putting more distance between them and fully opening the throttle, Nikita aimed the bike up the slip road and followed Brishnov down a side street which was lined by metal fencing on one side and a building site on the other. Beyond it he could just see the glistening waters of a river. The tarmac was cracked and buckled, sending bone shaking tremors through Nikita's body as he was forced to slow to keep control of the bike. Taking advantage of a brief smooth patch of road, he drew his gun and aimed a shot at the car's wheels. He hit his target first time, the rear left tyre exploding.

The car was sent into a wild skid as Brishnov worked to regain control of it. Sliding sideways, Nikita briefly saw Sarah's terrified face looking pleadingly at him before it spun, and with sparks flying from the bare rear wheel, gained some purchase and pulled off again.

Realising that he could no longer outrun Nikita, Brishnov accelerated across the road and into the building site. Nikita roared after him as the car disappeared behind some stacked shipping containers next to a tall orange crane.

Slowing as he approached the containers, Nikita cautiously edged around the corner but a bullet pinged off the metal crate next to him and he threw himself off the bike and back around the corner.

Peering around, he saw Brishnov forcing Sarah up the crane at gunpoint as he followed on. She was begging him to let her go.

"Use your training, Sarah," Nikita said to himself, hoping that her limited field training would kick in and give her a fighting chance. But even as he said it he knew it would be fruitless for her to try and take on someone with Brishnov's skill and experience.

What didn't make sense was Brishnov's decision to climb the crane; it was backing himself up an alley and Nikita knew he had been trained better than that. He also knew that Brishnov never did anything without thinking.

Nikita looked to take a shot at Brishnov but he'd positioned himself cleverly, making a clear shot difficult without risking hitting Sarah too.

He realised that Brishnov couldn't get a shot at him either while climbing and Nikita dashed from his hiding place and leapt onto the crane, climbing after them as quickly as he could. Brishnov and Sarah were working their way along the arm of the crane now, and past the driver's cabin, which was hanging over the cold blue waters of the Washington Channel. Looking along the channel, Nikita could see its meeting point with the much larger Anacostia and Potomac Rivers, all three waterways diverging into one single, vast, muddy brown river.

The arm of another crane was positioned close to the end of the one Brishnov and Sarah were currently edging their way along. As they reached the end, Brishnov began shouting at Sarah, who was paralysed with fear at the hundred foot drop below them to nothing but the concrete waters of the Channel. He was urging her to make the jump to the second crane and she was shaking her head frantically.

Eventually Brishnov made the decision for her, giving her an almighty shove, propelling her off the end of the crane. She screamed and for one horrible moment Nikita didn't think she would make it, his breath catching in his throat.

But then her hands closed on the wrought iron metalwork just half a metre away and she scrambled on, lying flat against the crane and hugging it tightly, beyond tears now. Brishnov jumped lightly across, seemingly unconcerned by the huge drop below them.

Nikita moved along the arm of the crane as swiftly as he could, the metal cold and rough under his hands. The crane felt like it was swaying in the wind, giving him moments of vertigo, and he clung on tight, his knuckles white. Firing a shot felt impossible when he could barely even look at anything other than the metal. How had Brishnov known that heights were his one remaining weakness? The answer came to him like a thunderbolt. Yerin.

He heard another scream and opened his eyes to see Brishnov treading on one of Sarah's hands. Despite the increasing wind, the KGB agent stood with perfect balance, knees slightly bent, in total control as he pushed harder on the hand, while staring at Nikita with that same one-sided smirk he seemed to save just for him.

With an extra push of downward force Sarah screamed again as she was forced to let go, and losing her balance, slipped to one side. She was hugging the side of the arm of the crane with her arms, and although she looked after herself well, spending a lot of time in the gym, even her strong arms would not be able to hold that position for long.

Nikita cursed and let one arm go from the crane and with great caution drew his gun once more and aimed it at Brishnov.

"Sarah, hold on for me!"

"Jacob, please, don't let me die," she sobbed.

"Jacob?" Brishnov sneered, "Is that what he told you his name was?"

Nikita let off a shot, and his heart leapt into his mouth as he nearly lost his balance, his shot widely missing the mark.

"Come now, comrade, do you not think she deserves to die knowing the truth about her lover being a KGB agent?"

Nikita laughed. "You don't know the truth even when it is staring you in the face. I've beaten you, Taras."

He avoided Sarah's gaze, knowing the look of confusion and betrayal that would be spread across her face.

Brishnov's smile faltered. "There is no world in which you could beat me, Allochka. I am the best. I have undermined your identity, I have killed the vice president of the United States despite your efforts to prevent it, and now I have drawn you to a height, your greatest fear, where you will watch your girlfriend die. My homeland does not need sub-saharans to make it greater than ever before."

Nikita laughed once more, adamantly not looking down but aware his legs seemed to have frozen into position. "Your arrogance has made you blind. You think you killed the vice president? It was all so obvious. Novichok powder in his whiskey? Come now, I've read your files; it's the same old routine you've pulled three times before. You think I didn't know that was how you would play it?"

Brishnov's smile had now taken on a fixed position as Nikita continued.

"You have no imagination, comrade. Right under your nose I advised the vice president not to consume any food or drink given to him as I knew there was a plan to poison him. I even knew which nerve agent you'd use, which is why he agreed to that impressive display of acting on the steps of the Capitol there. It would get him great air time and he could claim to have worked towards bringing down the White Russian. I have to admit though, your disguise did fool me. I thought maybe you'd turned Ed Sheen."

Now any trace of the smile was gone.

"I heard your entire conversation with Phillips; you gave him no such instruction."

"I gave him a piece of paper outlining my plan. I was perhaps eighty per cent confident you had no intention of trying to take him down at the Capitol, so I gambled that you would have no interest in reading my suggestions for how to avoid being shot there. Of course, there was every chance I was wrong, and even more chance he would not go along with it, but I thank you for being so predictable."

"Then why chase me?"

"Some of us still follow orders; some of us have not become traitors."

Brishnov spat. "You would lecture me on Soviet loyalty?" He jumped, shaking the arm of the crane as he landed, causing Sarah to slip further. "We were great, and the likes of you and that fat oaf Petrenko are destroying sixty years of Soviet dominance. I only ever served my country faithfully," he said, his face falling into sorrow before hardening once more and looking at Nikita with eyes full of hate. "What is more important to you, I wonder? Your kill order on me, or saving this Asian mongrel?" He shrugged and without blinking, swung his boot and kicked Sarah hard in the side. She whimpered but clung on as tightly as she could. Nikita fired another shot, but he felt dizzy from the height and it clipped off the crane behind Brishnov. He began sidling along as hastily as possible, trying to shift his leaden legs and block out the swaying of the crane and the rushing of water below. The noise of it felt like it was inside his head. Brishnov kicked her again and this time she screamed and slipped off.

She was hanging by one arm now and Nikita's heart was pounding in his chest as Brishnov scampered lightly along the frame towards the crane's cabin.

Nikita looked at him longingly, caught between two imperatives. The mission. His training. His nemesis. Or Sarah.

He reached the edge of the crane as Sarah's screams became a wail, her strength beginning to fail. She was trying to reach with her other hand to even the burden on her arms but couldn't lift herself enough to get a purchase.

Suddenly they were all distracted by the sound of a muted explosion in the distance, and despite his training to never look away from his target, Nikita couldn't help but gaze into the distance as a plume of black smoke rose into the air, obscuring the Capitol Building. Or possibly what had once been the Capitol Building.

Brishnov was smiling. "Look how the American empire crumbles! I could not have done it without you, comrade," he said, laughing openly. "The vice president was an order I was happy to carry out, but there is so much more happening than you know."

Nikita's vision swirled as he made the mistake of looking down at the gap between the two crane arms, and he nearly blacked out. His fingernails were drawing blood, so tightly were his broad hands fixed around the boxed end of the crane.

"Jake! Please help me!" cried Sarah as she looked with horror at him frozen in place, snapping his attention back to her. "If you let me die, I'll kill you," she said, coming back to herself for one brief moment, which brought him back to himself. Her eyes screwed up in pain. "I can't hold on any longer." She wept. "Please Jake, jump. Jump. JUMP!" she shouted as he roared and flung himself forward. But the impact of his landing shook the frame violently and with a scream Sarah lost her grip and fell.

Nikita's hand caught nothing more than her fingers which immediately began to slide through his grip. He flattened his body against the crane and swung his other arm down, flailing blindly with his face buried in the lattice metalwork of the crane, only able to see patches of Sarah's body. He felt his hand close on her wrist and with a sigh of relief began to pull her up.

As he felt her take some of her own weight, he pushed himself up. Sitting now, he hooked a hand under her armpit and helped pull her up.

They both lay panting on the arm of the crane, both holding on tight.

"Thank you for saving my life," Sarah spluttered, pushing herself up while clinging on grimly to the crane. "But who the hell are you?" she asked, colour returning to her face and anger flitting across it.

At that moment the world seemed to grind into slow motion for Nikita as he heard the crack of the gun shot. Sarah's face froze into a look of shock as blood immediately began to spread from her left breast. Her eyes closed, and she fell backwards onto the crane.

Nikita's head snapped up and he saw Brishnov hanging from the doorway of the cabin, one arm and leg holding him in place while his right arm was extended from the fatal shot he had just aimed at Sarah.

Nikita cupped her face in his hands. "Sarah!" he cried.

Her eyes opened in terror. "Jake, please," she gasped. "I'm afraid to die; please don't let me die," she sobbed, her slim body trembling. "Don't let me die!"

Nikita didn't need to check the wound to know that it was fatal and he felt a cold pain clutch his heart. "Sarah, I'm so sorry; this is all my fault," he said, choking on the words and working to keep hold of his American accent, living a lie right to the end.

She shook her head and with great effort put a hand gently to his cheek. "You have a good heart; I've seen it," she said. They were the last words Sarah Chang ever said to him. The spark suddenly faded from her eyes and her hand fell down, as with a sigh the air left her lungs.

Nikita roared with agony as the pain split him down the middle, and with no longer any care for himself or his fears, leapt to his feet and began to charge towards the cabin. Brishnov swung back inside it and Nikita could see him manning the controls. The whole contraption began to hum and vibrate, sending pangs of vertigo shooting through Nikita's head.

"Denisov would be disappointed in you, getting attached," spat Brishnov.

"You had no need to kill her," shouted Nikita. "She was an innocent."

"There are no innocent Americans," Brishnov shouted back, smiling broadly again at the sight of the dense black smoke climbing up to the sky from the heart of the American political landscape.

Before Nikita knew it the arm of the crane began to rise rapidly as Brishnov flung the joystick upwards. Nikita fell onto his back and began to slide down the arm of the crane, the metal scraping the skin from his back as he fell. Immune to the pain, he drew his gun and began to fire at the window of the cabin, which cracked but didn't break. In the corner of his eye, he saw Sarah's body falling towards the waters below. Brishnov ducked down and swung out of the cabin, making his escape.

The dead end of the cabin was rushing towards Nikita and he knew it was the end.

With one bullet left in the chamber he took one last shot at the departing Brishnov, who had nearly disappeared from view, just one arm left swinging him down onto the ladder.

The bullet carved straight through the bicep of the assassin. No sound escaped his lips as his arm went slack and he tumbled sideways, struggling to reach for a grip with his other flailing arm, before his body began to follow the limp form of Sarah towards the crushing blue of the Washington Channel below.

Nikita was unable to stop his own trajectory and smashed straight into the Plexiglass of the cabin windows which had been weakened by the gunshots. He smashed straight through it, slamming into the far side of the small cabin.

The small metal box lurched and he felt the crane sway slightly, as it lurched to a stop, pointing upwards like an arm desperately reaching for the sun. For a moment Nikita thought the cabin itself would rip off the framework and began scrambling for the exit hatch. Mercifully, after a moment, the whining of the metal ceased and all was still, leaving Nikita alone, staring into the azure waters below which had claimed the bodies of Sarah and Brishnov. The height bothered him less now he was in the relative security of the cabin, alone only with his heartbreak.

His eyes scanning across the rippling water, he looked for any trace of either of them but could see none. His sombre thoughts were suddenly intruded upon by an amplified voice. "Come out with your hands up; you are surrounded."

Peering through the shattered window, he saw that the building site was packed with police, and a SWAT team was carefully scaling both cranes, guns poised at the ready.

He groaned, with pain at his loss and with the thought of what would await him if his cover, now flimsy at best, was penetrated. So many years of work — would they be wasted now? As so often happened, the faces of his family floated before his eyes, and as so often happened, it steeled his heart and set his shoulders.

He poked his head out of the window and immediately saw around twenty paramilitary officers snap their assault rifles to focus on him. He immediately ducked back in. Seconds later he raised his hands and led with them, his body following after.

"Relinquish your weapon and lie face down on the crane with your hands behind your head." The police captain's voice echoed through the megaphone two hundred feet below. Nikita held up his gun by the nozzle and made a show of tossing it back inside the cabin before lowering himself slowly onto the crane arm, which was at a sixty-degree angle, leaving him still largely upright.

His phobia came rushing back to him as he pressed his face against the rough metal frame and the distance to the ground loomed before him. There was no way he could put his hands behind his head without losing his balance and toppling off.

He heard the SWAT officer clambering through the hole in the cabin behind him. To many it would probably be scarcely discernible above the swirling wind at altitude, but to a highly trained KGB agent it might as well have been an elephant climbing the ladder.

Bracing himself, his muscles were set when hands grabbed him roughly from behind and pushed his face heavily into the crane.

"Don't move," a gruff male voice grunted behind him, the voice muffled by his combat mask. "Do I have to make you climb down in handcuffs?"

"Don't worry, I'm on your side," Nikita replied with as much assurance as he could muster, his face drawn and tight. Climbing down a crane in handcuffs wasn't how he wanted to go.

"Sure, you are," grunted the officer. "Now take the lead and climb down slowly. No sudden movements or I have full authorisation to shoot."

Nikita said nothing, but turned slowly, and cautiously entered the tiny cabin. Following a nod from the SWAT officer, he lowered himself gently through the hatch underneath. His feet struggled to find the ladder for a moment and his stomach lurched as he was forced to glance down. The gun pointed at his face didn't help his frayed nerves, but as his foot found a solid metal rung. He looked skywards, for reasons he couldn't explain, and began the long descent.

Now looking outwards, he gazed across the water for some sign of Brishnov. A fall from this height would surely have killed him, especially with a bicep torn by a bullet.

He allowed himself to get lost in his musings as a distraction from the precarious height he was at, his body going onto autopilot as the heavy footsteps of his captor moved steadily above him. He didn't need to look down to know that there would be numerous weapons focused on him throughout his descent.

As he neared the bottom, with the ground close enough that his vision didn't swim he could see police cars, police officers, SWAT vans, and standing directly beneath him, Sykes. Further back, pressed against a line of police tape were the press. They were being held back by a line of police officers, but long lens cameras with large flash attachments were working furiously, despite the remonstrations of the officers attempting to contain them.

He climbed off the ladder and was immediately thrown to the ground, a knee in his back from the SWAT officer who had descended with him. His arms were pulled behind his back and handcuffs clicked roughly into place, before he was hauled to his feet.

Facing him was Sykes, a grim expression on his face. How much did he know? How much had he surmised? Sykes nodded to the officer holding Nikita and walked away, his face unreadable. He climbed into a black limousine which drove off as soon as he closed the door, forcing some of the press to squeeze out of the way.

Nikita was bundled into a police car, his head pushed down and in, the locks on the door clicking into position as it closed behind him.

***

Nikita had been waiting in the interrogation room for what felt like hours, although it was hard to gauge in the windowless room, lit only by a dim fluorescent strip glowing above him. His hands were cuffed to a bar on the table, but he had seen no one since being deposited in the room and the door locked behind him.

While he had seen no one, he knew it didn't mean that nobody had seen him. Aside from the camera pointed straight at him in the corner of the room, he was facing a large mirror. He had no doubt he was being watched through it by a room full of people on the other side.

His mouth was dry and sticky; a mere drop of water would provide instant relief. No matter, he had endured far worse than thirst. A classic interrogation technique — make him uncomfortable, make him desperate. He focused his mind back on the predicament at hand. What had happened to the Capitol? Suddenly Brishnov's methods made a little more sense. Ever since he had run from the scene under the guise of John, Nikita had been struck by the oddity of it. At that point Brishnov's disguise was still intact; running away only drew attention to him. "And drew eyes away from the Capitol," Nikita muttered to himself, realisation kicking in.

At that moment, the door opened and in walked a man with short dark hair brushed across his forehead, thick glasses and a faintly grey and jowly face. Tightly clipped under his nose was a salt-and-pepper moustache. It perched above a small, expressionless mouth that looked like it had been compressed. The small, watery eyes were magnified through the thick wire-rimmed glasses, more akin to goggles. They gazed placidly at Nikita as he sat down in the chair opposite him with his back to the mirror and undid the cuffs binding Nikita to the table. He pulled out a pack of Lucky Strikes, offering them to Nikita who shook his head, before putting one into his own mouth, showing yellow nicotine-stained teeth. He lit the cigarette, blowing the smoke unapologetically into Nikita's face before pressing the record button on the tape recorder next to him on the table.

"Mr Marshall, I'm Zach Burn of the CIA," he said in a dry voice. Nikita's head immediately snapped up. ZB.

"You won't have heard of me," he said, widening his eyes discreetly, "but suffice it to say I have heard of you. After your antics today, I daresay there are few who have not heard of you." He tossed his black and white lighter onto the table and glared at him angrily.

"Can someone please tell me why I'm being held here? I just brought down the White Russian and did my job," Nikita said angrily.

"Oh, we know that. The problem is, so does the world. Your job is to operate in the shadows, but now the world has seen you kill a Russian agent on American soil. When things like this happen, it makes it very hard to keep the Cold War cold. We need you to tell us everything you know. Like why was a desk analyst the one who took down the White Russian?"

"You need me to justify apprehending a terrorist?"

"You call him a terrorist?" Burn replied quizzically.

"And I suppose you call him a freedom fighter?" Nikita replied flatly.

"Whatever we call him, I wouldn't call what you did apprehending."

"Oh? And what would you call it?"

Burn opened his mouth and said nothing, smiling subtly. He pulled out a small notebook and began writing in it, the smoke from the cigarette between his fingers snaking upwards towards the ceiling.

Nikita said nothing, sitting in silence, keeping in full control and trying to look for any hint or clue from Burn.

Burn closed his book and looked up at Nikita. "You're being sent to Russia," he said, eyeing Nikita closely to see any trace of his reaction. Nikita gave him none, saying nothing, offering only a small nod. "You have made yourself too visible here, but some feel that you have demonstrated hitherto unrealised abilities as a field agent."

"But I'm an analyst," Nikita protested gently.

Burn arched an eyebrow and smirked. "Indeed. Nonetheless it is believed you represent an ideal target for the KGB to turn you as an apparent double agent."

Nikita nodded, as if weighing up the suggestion. "I see," he said non-committedly before changing the subject. "What was the smoke from the Capitol? It sounded like a bomb."

Burn's face darkened momentarily. There was a haunted look on his face that put Nikita's senses on edge. "That's part of a separate investigation that you don't need to concern yourself with." He put a hand into his pocket and for a moment Nikita thought he was reaching for a gun, but he withdrew a small hipflask.

"I hear you're a whiskey man, but I'm afraid I prefer vodka," he said with the faintest hint of a wink, offering the flask to Nikita. Nikita didn't move and Burn chuckled. "From what I hear it's not like you to turn down a drink these days! Fear not, agent, it's not poisoned," he said, taking a sip himself before offering it once more to Nikita.

Nikita snatched it from his hand and took a long sip, feeling the cool liquid running down his dry throat. His body craved water but the vodka satisfied some other need. He felt calmer.

"You think the Russians will accept a black man into their ranks?" he asked softly, breaking the silence.

"Did you think the Americans would?"

"I'm not interested in getting into a conversation about who is the most racist; I'm interested in what results I'm expected to deliver in a country known to be the most hostile to my race. Right after I've very publicly killed their most prized asset."

"You need to pay more attention, agent. You're not being sent as an undercover agent, you're being sent with the express instruction to let the Russians turn you into a double agent. We don't imagine you'll be long in Russia; they'll want you to return to the US pretty quickly."

"You think the Russians won't consider this or be the least bit suspicious?"

Burn pushed his chair back and stood up. "That will all be part of your briefing, agent. Far be it from me to say whether I think there is any merit in the whole plan, but you have a difficult road ahead of you."

"It can't be any harder than the road behind me," retorted Nikita.

"Indeed." Burn held out his hand. "For tonight, you are free to go home. Get some sleep; tomorrow will be an even bigger day."

"Have they found the bodies?" Nikita asked, trying to keep his voice even.

Burn looked him in the eye. "Nothing so far, agent, but those waters run fast and a dead body can get carried a long way. Don't worry, we'll find them."

Nikita waited until Burn had left the room, this time leaving the door ajar, before collapsing back into his chair.

He felt numb, but not nearly numb enough. Sarah's death kept playing over and over in his head. Her delicate face, the moments of warmth and vulnerability she would reveal underneath the tough and prickly exterior, the kisses they had shared. She just couldn't be gone, it didn't seem real. Guilt flooded through his entire body. He had thought killing Brishnov would alleviate the hatred, but somehow it had only exacerbated it. It ran cold like ice through his veins.

Finally, he thought of Elysia. It must be nearly time for them to meet in that Baltimore bar. He wanted nothing more than to hold her and get lost in her tenderness and kindness, to tell her all the things he longed to say.

But he knew he never could. Sarah was dead. She was dead and it was his fault. If he hadn't got involved with her, she would never have been there today. She would still be alive.

He thought back to the KGB training camps. Every single tutor had warned them of the dangers of getting involved with people, not only when on assignment but at all. "You have given your love to Mother Russia, and cannot afford to share that love with another woman," Denisov had told them all. "A woman will get you killed. Spare them and yourself."

Killing machines, that is all they are, he thought to himself. Follow orders, kill, murder, spy and betray, and repeat until we are discovered or discarded. No matter how good he was, Nikita allowed himself to realise for the first time that he might never reach thirty, and if he did, he would have defied uncountable odds. There was no room for Elysia.

I'm *lonely*, Nikita thought to himself, with some surprise. But he was only able to observe it, not feel it. He stood and walked out of the interrogation room, and made his way through the building. It felt surreal after all he had just been through to walk out unchallenged. From outside it looked plain, with no indication of the CIA facility that lay inside. He recognised the area, and as there was no offer of a ride from his CIA colleagues and he wasn't about to ask, he began walking into town, following his feet and trying not to think.

His feet led him back to his favourite bar and as he walked in, memories of the night Sarah and he had finally got together consumed him. Making his way to the bar, he could see Jess serving another customer. She glanced up at him, trying to finish with the customer, but he purposefully walked to the other end of the bar to where a scruffy-looking young barman was standing.

"Whiskey," he croaked at the barman, who didn't ask what kind, but pulled a bottle of Jim Beam from behind the bar. "Will this do?" he asked. Nikita nodded and the barman put a tumbler on the side. "Ice?" he asked, putting the bottle down as he reached quizzically for the ice bucket.

"No," Nikita grunted, grabbing the bottle and glass in one hand and throwing down a handful of crumpled notes. "Keep the change," he said as he made his way back to the booth he'd happily sat in so recently, and allowed himself to descend into bitter reminiscence and let the alcohol take him.

At one point, Jess came over to speak to him, but he responded coldly to her questions and poured himself another whiskey as she stalked away looking offended.

He caught sight of his reflection in a mirror near his table and gazed at the craggy face looking back. Was he twenty-two? Twenty-three? Twenty-four? He couldn't recall, but the face looking back had deep puffy bags under the eyes and a hint of grey in the dark stubble lining his jawline. He took another sip of whiskey. At least his body was still in reasonable condition. Aside from the long scar on his thigh, still paining him in cold weather, his young body had recovered well from the many hardships it had been put through.

As he gazed wearily at his reflection, he began to see Elysia's face. He shook his groggy head to put her from his mind, but the image remained. As it cleared, he realised it wasn't Elysia, but Jess gazing at him from the end of the bar. He smiled uncertainly at her.

***

It was the toilet flushing that caused Nikita to wake. His head felt heavy and his mouth thick and fuzzy but he was instantly alert and reached cautiously under his bedside table for the revolver he kept there.

He held it under the cover, pointed in the direction of his en-suite bathroom door. He heard movement behind it and his body was coiled and tensed, ready to move.

The handle slowly pushed down and out stepped Jess, wearing nothing but a black bra. She looked at him and grinned. "Easy boy, I have to go," she said, raising her eyebrows at the raised bump in the covers.

He exhaled and smiled back, turning onto his side and sliding the gun under his pillow. "Oh, come on, baby," he said, his throat dry and raspy.

Nikita's aching mind quickly began to piece the night together, cogs turning painfully. Much of it was a blur.

He pulled her down and kissed her as she giggled. Her dark brown body was young and firm under his hands; she felt warm and smelled of jasmine. He held her close and closed his eyes, enjoying the closeness before she pushed him away. "No seriously, I was due in for my shift at the bar ten minutes ago."

"Call in sick," he murmured, kissing her again.

"I can't, I can't," she said, forcing herself off him and standing up. The moment the contact was broken he felt revulsion in himself. She looked so beautiful standing there, her hair all tousled, as she pulled on her t-shirt. But it did absolutely nothing for him; he just wanted her gone.

"No, I understand," he said, pushing himself into a sitting position before a wave of nausea forced him back into a horizontal position.

Nikita closed his eyes and tried to transport himself away, but the faces of his family swam behind his eyelids, followed by Sarah before settling on Elysia. "Right, I'm outta here," Jess said pointedly. When he failed to open his eyes, she spoke more loudly. "I'm going, Jake." He opened his eyes reluctantly. She was standing next to him. With a groan, he swung his feet down and stood up, swaying slightly.

She caught him. "Show me to the door?"

He nodded silently, hating her, but hating himself more. Every part of him felt horrible.

Following her to the door, he held it open as she stepped outside and looked at him. "Are you not gonna say anything?" she said.

"What do you want me to say?" he asked, confused.

"If you don't know then maybe last night was a mistake," she replied crossly.

He sighed. "Maybe you're right, Jess."

Her eyes instantly welled up. "Great to know where I stand," she said angrily, turning away and marching down the path to the road.

Nikita knew he should call after her but he didn't have the heart. He'd make it up to her next time he was at the bar. Either that or find a new bar, he thought to himself as he closed the door.

He walked to the bathroom and splashed cold water on his face, to feel more awake, before making his way to the kitchen to make some strong coffee. He still could barely remember anything from the night before.

Opening the cupboard, he realised there was no coffee there, or anything else. Nothing in the fridge either, other than some old mouldering ropa vieja — his failed attempt to recreate his favourite Cuban dish. With a groan, he threw on some clothes and headed out to the shop.

Half an hour later, he was placing the paper bag full of groceries onto the passenger seat of his car when he looked up and saw the face that had dominated his thoughts for two days.

CHAPTER 22

Elysia stood a few yards away, her eyes burning into him. She was wearing blue jeans and a loose-fitting white shirt that her long curls tumbled across. This time there was no sadness, only fury.

"Ely—" he began but she quickly held up her hand and interrupted.

"I knew you wouldn't show, but for some reason I convinced myself that you might not be a coward after all and would face me like a man."

This time Nikita didn't bother to try and contradict her. "You were right on both counts. I was a no show and I am a coward."

He braced himself for the barrage that was to come in his direction. But it didn't come.

She stood staring at him, her hands on her hips caught between defiance and something else that Nikita could not place.

"How did you find me?" he asked tentatively.

"Get in the car," she snapped, striding towards the car, grabbing the shopping out of his hands and putting it on the back seat, before flouncing into the passenger seat with no small amount of dramatic flair.

Nikita rolled his shoulders and stretched his neck. His head still hurt and whatever was coming would not be enjoyable. He climbed into the driver's seat and reached into the back, plucking a bottle of Pepto Bismol from the shopping and taking a long drink, before wiping his mouth and screwing the cap back on. Then he turned to face Elysia, whose beauty knocked him for six. He rubbed his eyes and took another swig in an effort to cure his hangover.

"What do you want, Elysia?" he said slowly, working hard not to let his Russian accent reveal itself. "Why are you here?"

"Just drive," she replied sharply.

He said nothing and started the engine. They drove in silence, the tension fraught between them. Nikita sat stiffly, keeping his eyes fixed firmly on the road. The motion of the car was unpleasant for his fuzzy head.

Eventually, after several minutes, keeping her facing forwards Elysia said simply, "I know, Nathan."

Nikita kept his hands straight out on the wheel and didn't falter. Her statement left him considering the implications.

"Ti?" he asked, switching to Greek to keep the 'what' from sounding too accusatory.

She smirked briefly. "I know who you are. Who you really are," she stated flatly.

"Is that right?" he said as he took a right turn. "Do tell."

"You want to know how I found you?"

"That is another question I would be very interested to hear the answer to," Nikita replied as he pulled up to his house.

"Where are we?" she asked swiftly.

"This is my home. Do you see what I did there — I answered a question," he replied drily. "Let's talk more inside."

She was striding up the path before Nikita had even opened his door. He had to reach past her to open the front door and caught what felt like a fatal waft of her perfume. He forced himself to be impervious and followed her inside.

"Sit down," he said sharply as he closed the door.

"Excuse me?" she replied.

"Sit down and start answering my questions."

Elysia laughed. "I think you're forgetting who you're talking to. I'll sit when I damn well want to," she replied defiantly.

Nikita looked skywards, and upon entering the kitchen, pulled a bottle of wine from his shopping bag and poured them both a glass. Carrying them over to the living room, he sat down in the armchair and placed both glasses on the low coffee table in front of him.

"Isn't it a little early for wine?" she asked sharply, lowering herself onto the sofa, eyeing him strongly to see if he would comment.

"I'm all out of coffee," he grunted, taking a sip of the dark red Nemea.

She took a tentative sip from her own glass and raised her eyebrows. "Greek wine?"

He shrugged. "What can I say, you gave me a taste for it."

Elysia looked pleased, but Nikita swiftly followed up. "Come on, Elysia, enough with the cryptic statements. You have no idea what I've gone through since I saw you two days ago."

"I think I might have a hunch," she responded. Nikita opened his mouth to start talking but she stopped him with a look. "When you didn't show up again yesterday, I was furious and wanted to let you know it. But you're like a ghost, flitting around from Skyros to Baltimore, giving nothing of yourself away. I can't explain it, but I just felt compelled to try and find you; I had to know…" her voice wobbled and left the sentence hanging tautly.

"Go on," Nikita whispered.

"As I sat waiting in that shitty bar, I was watching the TV which was showing a live high-speed pursuit. Even from distance, I knew you immediately. You aren't in the police, are you?"

Nikita said and did nothing, but gazed sadly into her eyes, his skin prickling with sorrow. He took a sip of wine, just to do something other than get trapped in her eyes. It was helping to settle his stomach if nothing else.

"You don't have to answer, I know the truth. You're CIA. I doubt Nathan is even your real name, is it?"

Nikita shook his head; there was no harm in her knowing that much at this stage.

She slumped. "Then nothing you said or did when we were together was true." There was a silence in which silent tears fell down Elysia's face. The pain he was causing her was unbearable for Nikita.

He leant forward and took her hand gently in his. "Elysia, there is so much I would tell you and so little that I can. But please know this — you meant more to me than anyone ever has done and since we parted you have occupied my every thought."

She laughed disdainfully. "Sure. Like I could believe you even if it was true."

"Can you believe this?" Nikita said, as he pulled her up and kissed her deeply on the lips. She kissed him back and he pulled her close.

"Get off me!" she suddenly exclaimed, pushing him away. She put her hand to her mouth and looked up at him.

"The feeling in that kiss is something reserved only for you, Elysia, always for you," Nikita said hesitantly in his deep, slow voice.

"I don't know what I can believe any more."

"How did you find me?" Nikita asked again. "I need to know."

Elysia slumped back onto the sofa. "I didn't find you," she sighed. "I did come to Langley to find you but had no idea where to look. I thought maybe I'd head to the CIA building and see if they would tell me anything. I stopped to get something to eat, and there you were in the car park."

"Come on, Elysia, you can't expect me to believe that."

She shrugged. "It's up to you what you choose to believe. The gods must have wanted us to see each other again."

Incredulity was plastered across Nikita's face. "There is no such thing as a coincidence in my line of work."

"It wasn't really a coincidence. I came to find you; it just happened a lot easier than I anticipated. If you are CIA then you aren't very good at it."

"If I was CIA, which I'm not saying I am, then there would be no point in trying to hide in Langley," he responded, with a small smile. His words fell into the silent hole between them. They looked awkwardly at each other, both unsure what to say, what to do. It felt like the gap was growing between them.

"Is there a version of you that could ever be vulnerable?" she asked softly after several minutes' silence.

He looked at her sadly, his eyes feeling like they were hanging low into his face. He wished there were tears he could call upon. He began to speak but Elysia interrupted. "Maybe just don't answer," she said abruptly.

"I would give my heart to tell you everything, Elysia, but it would cost me my soul," Nikita said hesitantly, the words almost catching in his throat. Every time he looked at her, he could feel guilt, feel Giorgos's death. His burden was to carry that secret to his grave, to spare Elysia the hurt it would cause.

"I think that is the most real thing you have ever said to me," she replied, laying a hand gently on his knee. "What's your real name?" she asked tentatively but almost challengingly.

"I don't want to lie to you, Elysia."

"Then don't," she said crossly.

"Right now, I'm Jake, Jacob Marshall," he said, wishing he could be himself just for a moment. "There's so much you don't understand. If I give you the answers you seek, I would put us both in very great danger. How can you expect me to knowingly do that? If you've seen the footage on TV today, you've seen what happens to the people close to me."

"That was the woman I saw you with in Baltimore?"

He nodded silently, the sorrow flowing up in him again. He emptied his wine glass in one swallow and refilled it.

"The answer isn't at the bottom of the glass, you know, especially this early in the day" Elysia said pointedly.

Nikita's face tensed. "How can I know that if I don't try?" She said nothing, looking down at her lap. "You're probably right, but I don't know what rules I should believe in anymore," he said with a sigh. "You have no idea where my answers lie, Elysia," he added flatly.

Elysia stood. "You're right, I don't," she said, her eyes flashing. "But I'm on your side, if you would only let me be."

Nikita stood up. "I'm getting pretty tired of you telling me what to do, Elysia," he said crossly.

"I'm getting pretty tired of watching you sit silently drinking your thoughts away," she retorted. "Was that what you were doing in Skyros? Drinking to forget?"

"Why do you ask so many questions?" he replied, his voice rising quickly.

"Why do you always do that? Throw everything back onto me," Elysia shouted, shoving him in the chest. "You act so strong and silent, all brooding and tough, but you know what I think? I think you're just a coward."

"That's the second time this morning that you've called me a coward," he said, irritated.

"Well, you are, just a scared little coward," she said, her voice rising.

"Elysia…" Nikita tried to stop her, feeling his blood rising in a way he could never remember it doing before.

"Taking the easier way out always, just running away, aren't you?"

"You have no idea what I've endu—"

"Go on; run away again, I can see you want to!" Elysia screamed at him.

"SHUT UP!" shouted Nikita, his hands shaking with fury, his eyes ablaze. "Please stop. PLEASE!" he begged. Control was slipping from his grasp with terrifying pace.

"WHAT ARE YOU SO AFRAID OF?"

"THAT I MIGHT LOVE YOU," roared Nikita.

His eyes immediately widened in horror. It felt like a dagger of ice was driving its way through his body.

Elysia froze. Her hand, which had been raised, dropped to her side. She glared at him, breathing heavily, their faces only inches apart. Nikita was trembling. The silence was horrible.

"Look Elysi—" he began, but was cut off as she threw her arms around him and pulled him to her ferociously and passionately. He hesitated only a moment before wrapping his arms around her and kissing her deeply, allowing himself to get lost in her body.

It was some hours later when he awoke and saw her lying next to him, her body rising and falling slowly, her face looking so peaceful and perfect. He felt so many things and could immediately feel the rising anxiety in his chest.

Elysia's long eyelashes fluttered open slowly and she smiled at him. Seeing the worried expression on his face, she stroked his cheek and then rested her hand on his heavily scarred chest. "Get out of your head. There are a million things for us to worry about, but for now let's just enjoy a few moments without worrying about the past or future; just get lost in this moment right now."

Nikita exhaled heavily and lay back, relaxing. He rolled onto his side and wrapped Elysia in his arms, their bodies fitting together perfectly. He breathed deeply on her hair and felt an unfamiliar feeling spread around his body from his heart. He felt, in just that moment, completely happy.

***

Taras Brishnov floated cautiously towards the shore, awkwardly trying to pull the body of Sarah Chang with him. Every single part of him hurt.

He had fallen into the foaming waters where the deep Potomac River met the Washington Channel and Anacostia River, and it was those bubbles which lowered the density of the water that had saved his life. Nonetheless, he felt like he had fallen into wet concrete and he hurt right down to his bones.

Crawling up the cold, grey shale bank of the Potomac River, blood was flowing freely from his upper arm, dripping heavily onto the face of Chang as he squatted and pulled her up onto the short beach. Behind him was a concrete bank and he moved the pair of them up against it and allowed himself a moment of rest against the wall, out of sight from all, as the stormy grey sky darkened. He ripped a strip of cloth from Chang's shirt and tied it as a tourniquet to stem some of the bleeding and plotted his next move. To believe that he was dead it was vital that the US authorities found neither body, thinking they were both flushed far out towards the Atlantic by the current.

Tentatively, Brishnov lifted his head above the concrete wall, ignoring the swell of blood that squeezed out of the deep gash on his arm. Before him lay the runway of Washington National Airport.

He grinned and his eyes burned with the fury of revenge.

***

The phone in the Oval Office was ringing. It had been ringing steadily for the past minute but President Ernest Callahan couldn't face answering it.

His attention was on the television next to his desk with the news cycle showing one homeland security fiasco after another. None of it made the slightest bit of sense.

It looped back to the clip of the vice president collapsing on the steps before cutting to images of the shootout on the building site. The images were then replaced by the face of the opposition, explaining in excruciating detail how badly it boded for national security if the president couldn't even manage to keep his own vice president safe. It was hard to argue back, even though he was fully aware that Gerald Phillips was sitting quite comfortably at home, basking in the massive surge in public favour he was already enjoying, just in time for his run to be president. "None of that helps me though," muttered the president, picking up the phone and slamming it back down. Within seconds it began to ring again. Once again, he ignored it. Minutes later there was a knock on the door.

With a sigh the president grunted, "Yes?"

His receptionist poked her head around the door. "Mr President, I have Gordon Sykes of the CIA's Soviet Counter-intelligence Branch here; he says it's urgent."

"Why is everything everyone wants me for always urgent?" he asked forlornly.

She shrugged with a smile. "I'll show him in, sir," she replied gently, as he waved his arm to bring him in.

"Mr President," Sykes said respectfully as he entered. He had done his best to tidy himself up, with a tie and jacket, but his efforts hadn't stretched as far as fastening the top button of his shirt, or flattening his rough and ready hair which looked as if it hadn't changed since he climbed out of bed.

The president shook his hand and waved him to the sofa opposite his own as he sat down and crossed his legs.

"What's so urgent, Gordon?" the president asked wearily.

"We've run the tests on the powder used to try and poison the vice president and there is no longer any doubt as to the culprits."

"Go on," Callahan said reluctantly.

"The vice president has been targeted by a nerve agent which is part of a group of nerve agents known as novichok."

"That sounds…"

"Yes, sir, Russian. It is made uniquely in the Soviet Union. It's a powder so fine that it can be absorbed through your very skin and is incredibly hard to detect. It is the deadliest nerve agent ever made."

The president paused, rubbing his jawline with one hand and gazing to the heavens for a moment. "But we already knew he was a rogue Soviet agent; this isn't anything new."

"Agreed, Mr President, but until we track down the body, this is the only undisputable evidence we have of Russian involvement."

"Sure, but what the hell are you doing about it, Sykes?" The president demanded, his voice rising. "This was too close, I'm taking a hammering on homeland security issues out there," he said, waving his arm in the vague direction of the windows.

"Yes, the papers haven't been too kind this morning." Sykes chuckled before stopping abruptly under the president's cold gaze. "There... there is a plan in motion, sir." He faltered. "I'm working with the Soviet East Department on using the public nature of the whole operation to our advantage."

He paused, but the president said nothing so he pressed on.

"It was actually one of my analysts here in the Soviet Counterintelligence Branch that took down the White Russian—"

"Did you say an analyst? This wasn't in my goddam briefing!" spluttered the president.

"Yessir, Agent Marshall, he's a fine asset to our department, so much so that he's now been promoted to special agent status following his exploits today. It seems he's been wasted behind a desk."

"What use is he now that the world has seen him?"

"As I was saying, sir, it's that very fact that we are hoping to turn to our advantage. We are hoping to position him so that the Russians attempt to turn him as a double agent."

"This needs to start making sense very quickly, Sykes," Callahan said ominously.

"My apologies, Mr President, it's a complex plan. Agent Marshall is going to be sent to the Soviet Union, with the explicit orders to make himself just conspicuous enough to be picked up by the KGB. They will easily recognise him from his exploits in the news, assassinating one of their finest. He will then lead them to attempting to turn him. It would appear a major coup for the Russians to turn a national hero."

"Only if they don't kill him first," the president commented flatly.

Sykes shrugged. "No spying mission is ever without risk. He's an orphan with no strong ties, but is a patriot and the single most effective analyst I've ever known. Perfect for a mission such as this one. If he succeeds, we'll be able to re-establish our clandestine operations in the east now that Yerin has been ousted."

"What do we know about his replacement? This Klitchkov fella?"

Sykes smiled. "This is the best part, sir. Agent Marshall is our national expert on the KGB and is particularly familiar with Klitchkov, so will be perfectly placed to navigate their murky hierarchy. As we understand it, Klitchkov is no less cunning than Yerin but ill-prepared for the politics of his position. He's very much a military man."

"Are you saying that those who have served cannot then take office?" The president asked with an arched brow.

"Of course not, Mr President, but Klitchkov's military career has led him down a very different path to the one you so successfully navigated. Chairman Klitchkov is made to follow orders, not build creative political strategies. Or at least so our sources suggest at this stage," he added cautiously.

The president nodded his head, absorbing the information and attempting to process the new strategy. He grunted. "It's unusual for a man of your position to come directly to the president with this," he said, watching Sykes' reaction closely.

"Permission to speak freely, sir?" Sykes asked nervously. The president waved his hand in permission. Sykes cleared his throat and his hand moved to his breast pocket where his pack of cigarettes resided, out of habit, before remembering where he was. "Well, Mr President, to be frank, we suspect there's a mole in the White House. We are still trying to investigate what started the fire in the Capitol while Agent Marshall was bringing down the White Russian, but we suspect foul play."

"You mean to tell me that not only did a renegade Soviet spy manage to position himself, almost overnight, as the personal bodyguard to the vice president of the United States, but that they have also managed to get someone right into the home of the US Congress? What the hell are we giving you all these taxpayers' dollars for, Sykes?"

"Precisely so that we're able to identify when there's a mole somewhere in the system. It's really more of a job for the FBI…" Sykes tailed off under the glare of the president. After only a few seconds of silence, he crumbled under Callahan's gaze. "We'll find the mole, sir."

"I thought you might get to that conclusion," the president said sternly.

"Until we do, I would advise you to keep the circle around you small; no one can be trusted until we get to the bottom of it."

"Very well, Sykes. But I want our guy into Moscow ASAP. I like Petrenko, but I don't trust him just yet. I need to know what the hell is going on over there. I can't tell if we're at the end of a long war or at the start of a new battle."

"Yes, sir," said Sykes, standing and shaking the president's hand before turning to leave.

"Oh, and, Sykes?"

"Yes, Mr President?"

"Is there a code name for Agent Marshall yet?"

"I don't believe we've got that far yet."

"The Black Russian feels a little more appropriate this time around, wouldn't you say?" he said with a wink.

Sykes smiled weakly, holding his eye roll until he was on the other side of the door.

***

Colonel Andrei Klitchkov sat in his office of brushed steel and mahogany, a combination of old and new that he felt reflected him quite nicely. He sat with his feet up on his desk and leant back in his chair, playing with his favourite revolver.

The Russian M1870 Galand was perhaps his most prized possession. His grandfather had kept it when retiring from the Russian navy in the early part of the century and it had been passed on to his good-for-nothing father. He had mainly used it to try and pistol whip Andrei and his mother when rolling in from a night of overindulgence, which turned out to be most nights. Fortunately, the vodka made him slow, and Andrei and his mother grew adept at getting out of the way. Most of the time.

His father had asked to be buried with the weapon, but there was no way Klitchkov was going to allow such a fine weapon to rot underground. Instead, he had thrown in an old Smith and Wesson in front of the unsuspecting crowd. He massaged his left knee. His whole career he had been forced to disguise the natural limp carried from a childhood injury given to him by the boot of his father. He refused to show any weakness, but it never stopped hurting.

He played with the catch of the Galand that released a lever to pull the barrel and cylinder forwards, unlike any other weapon he knew of. The well-oiled catch made a satisfying click as he released and reattached the lever, lost in thought. His thumb played over the extra thick rims of the four and a half line cartridges buried in the cylinder. Embossed across the top of the barrel were the characters 'A Liege 1887'. A classic weapon, a rare weapon. A weapon he might yet reserve for the man who had failed him in Washington, he thought to himself.

The room was dark in the early hours of the morning. He cherished this time just before the sun came up where all was utterly silent, even here in Moscow. The deep reflection time was the closest thing he was able to get to sleep beyond two a.m. A long sleep was a luxury he had unwillingly forsaken long ago.

He looked at the FBI report in front of him, headlined 'No Smoke Without Fire'. At the back of the report a grainy photocopy of a photograph had been pinned, showing a plume of smoke rising up above the Capitol Building. So much of the operation had been a success, but all he could see was failure.

Brishnov had been eliminated. He had been a brilliant spy, but had become unpredictable. There was no room for unpredictability in Klitchkov's KGB, and the order to take down the vice president was the perfect trap to eliminate him. Whether or not the vice president survived was incidental. Now, Nikita was an agent who followed orders, he thought with a smile, thinking back to the news footage of him sending Brishnov plunging to the waters below.

But this smoke. This bomb. This was something else altogether. So much was so carefully poised.

He picked up the phone and dialled. It rang for some time before a sleepy voice answered. "Da?"

"Nam nuzhno pogovorit," growled Klitchkov. *We need to talk.*

"Sechaz?" moaned the reedy voice.

"Yes, now!" snapped the colonel, putting down the phone. He stood and walked to his window, overlooking the Moskva River, hazy in the softly falling snow, and watched the bobbing lights of the boats moored there. On the opposite side of the river a kiosk was setting up with a large Pepsi logo painted across its awning. "The wheels of change will come off if we do not regain control," he muttered to himself, his head disappearing in thick smoke as he lit a huge cigar. It had been a gift from Fidel himself. But nothing could last forever.

PERESLAVL-ZALESSKY, ONE HUNDRED- AND FORTY-KILOMETRES NORTH OF MOSCOW

The snow lay in droves around the picturesque town of Pereslavl-Zalessky, which sat upon the banks of Lake Pleshcheyevo. The white walls of the many monasteries glistened in the early morning light, illuminating the winding streets of the town, which lay in the hushed silence that comes with the first snowfall.

The snow covered all manner of sins in the once stunning Pereslavl-Zalessky, the town beyond the woods.

Shortly before the Moscow Olympics in 1980, the government had carried out a mass arrest of people they considered 'undesirables' and moved them to Pereslavl, in a bid to improve Moscow's image when the eyes of the world landed upon it. While Moscow's reputation soared, so did crime in the once sleepy Pereslavl.

At the heart of the plunge in Pereslavl's reputation was Lev Veselovsky, who had put the town on the map for a completely different reason. Neo-Nazism.

During the Brezhnev years of economic stagnation, many people in the Soviet Union had begun to look for an alternative, for another extreme. So came the birth of Pamyat, a three-ray-swastika-bearing, white supremacy group intent on an ethnic cleansing that Hitler himself would have been impressed by. When they encountered their own idea of an undesirable, they acted quickly, extremely violently, and with no mercy for their victims.

But this morning Lev Veselovsky refused to contemplate anything but staying in bed for as long as possible. It was cold outside but warm under the covers, thanks to Tatiana. She wasn't cheap but was worth every penny.

She tried to cuddle up to him, but he pushed her off. He didn't pay her the big roubles for cuddles.

"Zebis'," he grunted at her. *Fuck off.*

Tatiana's lightly tanned face, clad in fake eyelashes and thick makeup to cover a pimply complexion, pouted.

Veselovsky ignored her completely, and with a sigh swung his short, white legs over the edge of the bed. Standing, he stretched, forcing his grubby white vest up over his huge, bloated stomach. He licked his hands and tried to smooth his comb-over flat to his head before attempting to comb the thin grey moustache perched above his small, red mouth. He hastily pulled on a shirt to combat the cold, fastening it up beneath his several jowly chins.

"Levyyy," called Tatiana, draping her luscious figure across the bed seductively, her long black hair fanned across her back.

He again ignored her and waddling to the door, opened it and said once more, "Zebis'," before walking out to face the day with a smile.

As he entered his grubby kitchen, he froze, the smile dropping from his face as quickly as it had arrived.

"You," he gasped.

"Da, menya," sneered Taras Brishnov.

CHAPTER 23

It was not by accident that Veselovsky had risen to the top of the Eastern neo-Nazism movement. He took a moment and lit a cigarette. Blowing out a cloud of smoke, he said, "You are not dead, Taras."

"Not yet, Lev," croaked Brishnov in reply.

They were silent for a moment, eyeing each other cautiously, before Veselovsky grinned broadly and laughed. "I knew you could never be killed by a chernozhopiy!" he exclaimed, kissing Brishnov firmly on each cheek and embracing him like a brother. Pulling back from the embrace, he surveyed the fallen spy, who had dark circles beneath his eyes and a bloody bandage around his left bicep. "You look terrible."

"Coming from you, that is damning indeed," Brishnov said with a smile.

"Come, come, sit with me; I want to hear everything," Veselovsky said, hefting his huge frame into an unfortunate wooden chair.

"There will be time to tell stories later, but our plans are on a knife edge. They will torture Yerin and he will speak."

"Viktor would not betray us," Veselovsky said flatly. "He is a patriot."

"Yes, but he is still a man. Everybody gives in to torture eventually."

"Then he will die a dog."

"Perhaps," replied Brishnov. "But you should prepare to go underground."

Veselovsky spat. "I will not hide. Trying to hide is what has brought our homeland to its knees. Hiding and giving refuge to Jews and chernozhopiys, while displacing true Russians to places like this," he said, raising his arms around him.

Brishnov sat back and grinned, stretching his scar so it went taut and pink, a distraction from the dark circles under his eyes. Fury and madness burned within them. "You lead me to my next point, comrade. We have a unique opportunity to strike a blow to the very heart of the Politburo, and to give us a global voice that will have the people calling for us to lead. It is the perfect time to strike. First we strike against the party, and then we destroy the capitalist dogs in the west."

"And where will our fist fall to launch this strike?"

"There is only one thing that motivates the one they are calling the Black Russian." He spat the words as if chewing on something bitter. "He serves only to protect his family. It is a secret that Klitchkov has held close."

"So what do I care about the motivations of that scum?" replied Veselovsky indifferently.

"Yerin knows where his family are. We must reach him in jail, and the information he can provide will draw Allochka to us like a moth to a flame. His crucified body will be a rallying call to the people of the Soviet empire."

Veselovsky was pensive for a moment, before he stuck his bottom lip out and began nodding with increasing encouragement. "I like this plan, Taras. Let us seal it with a drink," he said as he walked to the kitchen cupboard and withdrew a clear bottle of vodka. He poured it into two shot glasses and raised his glass. "To a new Russia," he proposed.

"To revenge," replied Brishnov coldly. A flicker of concern crossed Veselovsky's face but he quickly hid it, drinking down his shot.

"I don't know how you made it back, Taras. Shit, I don't know how you are even alive. Through the door over there you will find some entertainment that is well deserved. Rest now, because we have much to do."

Brishnov did not smile, but his eyes flashed with a look too terrible even for Veselovsky to hold. "Do you need her for anything more?" Brishnov asked.

"Niet," Veselovsky said, his mouth taut. She had been his favourite whore, but if anyone frightened him in this world, it was Taras Brishnov.

"You can come out of hiding now, Boris," called Brishnov as he disappeared into Veselovsky's quarters.

Looking brutish but guilty, Veselovsky's right hand man emerged from the shadows. Boris was a tall, thin man in his sixties with a heavily tattooed neck, proudly displaying various fascist symbols, many of them conflicting. He had a heavily ridged brow with enough brains to be second in command, but not enough to challenge for the leadership, thought Veselovsky. In his hand he clutched the straw hat he had taken to wearing.

"Boss," he said reverently, handing him a steaming mug of coffee. "Four sugars, just as you like."

Veselovsky took it without a word, just gazing into the dark brown liquid.

"I think we should discuss Taras," said Boris.

"Can it wait until after breakfast?" Veselovsky replied, his small watery eyes glowing with displeasure.

"I don't think so," said Boris. "His motives do not sound so pure any longer. Revenge burns inside him."

"We cannot imagine what he has gone through to be here. Do not delay my breakfast because you have a weak stomach."

"Lev," said Boris, using a rare level of familiarity and sincerity with his old comrade in arms. "We must be careful."

"We will. But whatever the motives, the plan is a good one," he replied, nodding. "Either way, we get to do a bit of cleansing which is always fun," he added with a weedy smile.

CHAPTER 24

"I don't suppose you're gonna tell me where you're going?" Elysia queried, her arms folded.

"Elysia..."

"OK, don't tell me. But one of these days Jacob Marshall or Nathan Martins or whatever your name is, you're going to give me some answers!"

"Is that so?" he said, spotting the slightest hint of a playful tone in her voice as he put his bag down and pulled her to him.

She tried to hold the cross look but it quickly faded as he kissed her.

"Don't think you can kiss your way out of this one," she said between kisses.

"I wouldn't dream of it," he replied, kissing her more deeply. She threw her arms around him and he was deeply tempted to pull her back to the bedroom but dragged himself away with great effort. "I have to go. I wish to God I didn't, but I have to go."

"When will you be back?" she asked, her eyes wide.

"I don't know," he replied honestly. "Maybe a week, maybe a month, maybe years."

"Don't say years," she whispered.

"Elysia..."

"I know, I know. Don't wait for you, you know how I feel about you et cetera et cetera," she said, rolling her eyes. "I understand more than you think I do; it doesn't take a genius to figure some of this out. You come back as soon as you can and we'll figure things out then. Just... just..." her lip wobbled as she tried to say the words.

"Elysia..." he protested, trying to stop her.

"Just stay alive," she said and his heart almost broke as he looked on her face, for maybe the last time. She pressed something wrapped in brown packing paper into his hand. It was small, the size of his palm. "Don't open it now, but take it with you, to remind you of me."

In the taxi as it pulled away, Nikita unwrapped the gift, and froze. Staring back at him was pocket-sized Black Russian Terrier, perfectly carved, from Cyclades ebony.

***

Thirteen hours later, Nikita strode out of Sheremetyevo International Airport in Moscow. The FBI had bestowed a new identity upon him, intent on trying to make his visit look as genuine as possible. He was now Wilmer Jambo from the Communist People's Republic of Angola, coming to Moscow to take advantage of trade agreements between their two communist nations.

He had tried to tell them that in the Soviet Union he was going to draw attention wherever his passport was from, and that the need to go to such lengths for subterfuge was pointless, but it had fallen on deaf ears.

After three over-zealous strip searches upon presenting himself at customs, the airport security staff had reluctantly let him through.

He stepped outside and breathed in the bitingly cold Moscow air. "Ludshe doma mesta," he muttered quietly under his breath, enjoying the feel of his native tongue in his throat once more. *"No better place than home"* He pulled the hefty dossier about Angola that the FBI had thrust upon him to strengthen his cover from his bag and tossed it negligently into a bin as he passed.

He was surprised, almost cross, that there was nobody to collect him, and with some belligerence headed to the taxi rank. Three taxi drivers refused to take him, the last not even attempting to hide his disgust, saying only "No black arses," before pulling away. Finally, the fourth taxi took him with some reluctance, and he ordered it to take him to the Kremlin. After months in the US with only sidelong glances and whispered words, it was almost a pleasure to know how people really felt.

He was around fifteen minutes from the Kremlin, passing through the Begovoy District when a black ZIS-115 pulled suddenly in front of the taxi, forcing the driver to slam on the brakes.

"Sadnitsa!" cursed the taxi driver, but swiftly fell silent as men in black suits carrying weapons leapt from the car and pulled the back seat door open.

Nikita was unsurprised by the turn of events, and ignoring the ferocious honking of horns, climbed from the cab and stepped into the back seat of the KGB vehicle.

"Subtlety was never your strong suit, sir," he said as he sidled in to the plush leather interior of the classic armoured car, next to his former trainer.

"Shut up," replied Denisov placidly as the two men climbed back into the front of the car. He ordered them to take them to a location with which Nikita was unfamiliar.

Nikita didn't bother to ask where they were going as he knew Denisov would not tell him, but he kept his eyes on the road outside, mentally mapping their journey. He could not help doing it everywhere he went; it had been trained into him by the man at his side. KGB operatives were drilled to within an inch of their lives on memory and concentration tests, getting them as close to an eidetic memory as possible. It had been another area in which Nikita had excelled.

They passed the turn for the Kremlin, instead carrying on over the Bol'shoy Kamennyy Most highway, taking them over the Moskva River and taking a left towards the Repinskiy Skver square. They slowed and turned down a narrow street cast in darkness, that could barely accommodate the long four-tonne vehicle. Nikita looked behind him and saw that upon their entering the street a screen had immediately closed behind them, hiding it from view.

He sat back in his seat. "Ludshe doma mesta net," he muttered to himself once more under his breath with a gentle smile. Suddenly Skyros, Texas, Cuba and Washington all felt like a distant memory, and none of it felt so wrong any more.

They drove under a low stone arch and into a long brick tunnel which curved around to the right and downwards. The tunnel was pitch black, only illuminated by the headlights of the government vehicle. The air smelled heavy and damp, leading Nikita to the conclusion that they were currently under the river.

The tunnel began to rise sharply, before levelling out. The car stopped suddenly.

"Get out," ordered Denisov.

Nikita stepped out into the gloomy tunnel and saw a thick metal door that looked like it had almost been cut out of the old brickwork. Denisov stepped in front of him and opened the door, casting bright light into the tunnel. Nikita followed and the heavy door closed with a dull thud.

The tunnel they entered was in sharp contrast to the one they had left behind. An homage to brushed steel and aluminium, it felt like a long metal tube, lit by overly bright fluorescent strips which were buzzing faintly. Nikita shielded his eyes as he let them adjust before following the clipped footsteps of Denisov who had not hesitated before striding off to the left.

They stepped into a buttonless elevator which stood open as if waiting for them at the end of the corridor. Denisov withdrew a fob from his inner pocket and pressed it against a small black circle next to the door. A green light appeared above it and the doors closed sharply.

When they opened moments later, Nikita and Denisov stepped out into a large office with floor to ceiling windows, giving a view over the river. In the near distance, he could see Dormition Cathedral and beyond it the bulbous, multihued turrets of the Kremlin. Nikita had often felt that the brightly coloured stripes and dots of the towers were at odds with the grey concrete landscape known as Khrushchvovka which had appeared under the direction of Stalin's successor, Nikita Krushchev. The low concrete apartment blocks had been one of the former general secretary's legacies to the USSR. Normally so drab and ugly, but today, with the view Nikita could see before him, he could for the first time appreciate the majesty of the ancient city.

"Beautiful, is it not?" said the familiar voice of Chairman Klitchkov as he entered the room from a side door and followed Nikita's gaze. Denisov had already settled himself in an ornate wooden chair in front of the desk and Klitchkov signalled to Nikita to follow suit.

Nikita walked over to the chair, taking in his surroundings. The wall on his right was covered by a dark wooden bookcase packed full of dry-looking books. The desk in front of him was also of a dark wood; Nikita guessed that both were mahogany. They were at odds with much of the rest of the room, which followed the theme of the corridor below, with steel light fittings, polished marble flooring and a vaguely futuristic design.

Klitchkov took a seat behind the desk and leant on the arm of the chair. "Welcome home, Agent Allochka. You have done well. Would you not agree, Lieutenant Colonel?" he said jovially to Denisov.

"Adequate," Denisov said shortly, ejecting the word with great reluctance.

Klitchkov laughed. "Come now, Maxim, enjoy the proof of your excellence at the academy."

Denisov said nothing. "Ignore Maxim, Nikita. That is as close as he comes to praise, so take it as such," said Klitchkov, almost gently.

"Thank you, Chairman, Lieutenant Colonel," Nikita said, nodding to both. "But I have only done my job, nothing more."

"Spoken like a true agent," responded Klitchkov. "Now to business. What instruction have the CIA given you for your journey home?"

"I am to make myself visible to the KGB so as to encourage them to turn me into a double agent."

Denisov let out a wheezy sound. Nikita realised it was his attempt at laughter. "The Yankee dogs!" he cried in his high-pitched, reedy voice. "They are so blind to what is right in front of them," he said euphorically.

"This is a fortunate turn of events; we find ourselves in a rare position," said Klitchkov, nodding, seemingly more to himself than either of his colleagues. "You have played the game exceedingly well," he added to Nikita. "Despite being forced to carry out some of Yerin's more questionable assignments out there. Tell me, what do they know of our nuclear disarmament?"

"I don't have much to update beyond what I told you recently in Washington. My former section chief suspects things may differ from the version of events we are feeding them. However, of the three analysts assigned to investigate any links between the disarmament, the Afghan... victorious withdrawal, and the White Russian, only one remains in the department."

"It was your lover that Brishnov killed, yes? The Chinese mongrel?" Klitchkov asked brightly.

"Korean," Nikita corrected. "He saved me having to burn her," Nikita said, with a shrug, though his fist clenched tightly in his lap.

Denisov was staring at him, his eyes giving nothing away but his wide, pursed mouth had the hint of a smirk at the edges.

"Brishnov's last act was a kindness to us; with both you and her out of the team it will hamstring their investigations. Who is the remaining agent?" Denisov asked.

"Blaine Lahart, a very capable analyst. His key area of focus is our adherence to the INF Treaty, but he had been looped in on some of my KGB investigations and Sarah Chang's interest in the White Russian."

"Who they now believe to be dead," Klitchkov commented.

"Who they now believe to be dead, as was your intention," Nikita agreed. "Do we know if the vice president survived or not?" he added.

"We have been unable to glean that information yet; they are keeping their cards very close to their chest with that one. It is of no consequence either way, as long as they continue to believe Brishnov was acting alone and not under the orders of the Soviet government," said Klitchkov.

"And was he?" Nikita asked.

"I've warned you before about insolence, agent," Klitchkov said shortly, in the tone change typical of the man. "I will not warn you again," he said and laid an unusual looking revolver on the desk.

"Of course, sir. Not my concern," Nikita said, holding his gaze.

"Will this section chief revive the investigation?" asked Denisov calmly, bringing the discussion back to business.

"He is like a dog with a bone once he gets an idea and will chase it into the ground if he has to. However, the death of the man they believe to be the one who had been carrying out all of the assassinations may force him to wrap up the investigation; he has very limited resources. I suspect the investigation will end, but he will not forget it and it will only take the slightest hint of foul play for it to be reopened." Nikita paused. "There is one more thing," he added. "During the battle with Brishnov, there was smoke coming from the Capitol. Was this also the work of Brishnov?"

The air suddenly became heavy and tense as the muscles around Klitchkov's mouth tightened. Denisov continued to look unconcerned.

"What do you know of it?" Klitchkov asked coldly.

"Nothing beyond what I just asked, sir," Nikita replied. "But I asked a fellow CIA agent who I thought may have information on it and he told me to mind my own business," Nikita said. Then he added, hoping it appeared as an afterthought, "His name was Zach Burn, by the way," and closely watched the faces of his two superiors.

Both were highly trained KGB agents and to the casual eye gave no indication that name meant anything to them. Nikita's eye was far from casual, however. Denisov either knew nothing or if he did, he hid it unbelievably well. Klitchkov, however, had never been a KGB field agent, and his fingers flexed involuntarily. A tiny tell, but significant to one such as Nikita.

"You know the name," Nikita said. It was not a question.

Klitchkov stood, and turning his back, stared back across the river and was silent for several minutes. The muscles in Denisov's jaw were rippling, showing his teeth were gritted.

"We know the name," said Klitchkov slowly.

"He provided me with the evidence I needed to pursue Brishnov," said Nikita. "He has embedded himself into the CIA well; he is clearly a significant player in the Soviet East Department, for him to be the one informing me of my mission. It was most irregular; I do not know how he managed it."

Silence fell upon the room once more. This time Nikita decided to sit quietly with it.

Eventually Klitchkov shared a meaningful look with Denisov and sighed.

"You are an observant little shit," said Klitchkov ruefully, turning back to face them. "Ah, but there is no sense in keeping you in the dark any longer! The man you speak of is a KGB agent, but he is not a Soviet. He is an American who is working for us. He has been providing us with exceptionally high-quality information for three years now. The intelligence he has furnished us with led to Yerin being able to systematically dismantle the US spy network in the USSR."

"That is a lot of blood on his hands," commented Nikita.

"It is a bloody business we are in," responded Denisov.

"Indeed." Klitchkov laughed. "Yet of late his behaviour has been more erratic and he appears to be spending on a lifestyle that outstrips the significant sums that we are already paying him."

"You can never trust an American pig," spat Denisov. "We should kill him and be done with it."

Klitchkov ignored him. "This fire at the Capitol; it was not a part of our operation." He threw a photo down on the desk which Nikita picked up. It was a poor photo — grainy and pixelated — but just clear enough to make out the face of Zach Burn entering the US Capitol with a briefcase. "This was taken moments after the vice president collapsed and you pursued Brishnov. The security detail at the front desk had left their post to try and protect the vice president, meaning—"

"That whatever is in that briefcase never got checked." Nikita finished the sentence.

"Exactly," Confirmed Denisov.

"Of course, it could be a coincidence. Perhaps Burn had business in the Capitol Building that day, although it did not appear in his report back to us. We are in the business of connecting dots; we are in the business where there are no coincidences. Brishnov had been turned by these neo-Nazi scum, and it appears that Burn has been bought by them," said Klitchkov.

"You need me to terminate him?" Nikita asked dispassionately.

"I think not," Klitchkov replied. "Not yet anyway. My gut tells me it was a failed attempt to destroy the Capitol. Pamyat, led by Lev Veselovsky, are intent on only two things; to ethnically cleanse the Soviet Union, and to make Russia the only superpower in the world, by destroying the United States of America."

"I do not imagine they have had too much trouble gaining support for elements of that in Russia," Nikita commented, then paused. "My handler in Skyros believes there was a Pamyat agent on the island. I did not know what Pamyat was until now so it had made little sense," he added.

"It would have been useful had one of you mentioned that to someone back then," Denisov snapped. "We would have known the depth of their treachery and the reach of their arm." He breathed deeply, and waved a hand. "No matter. But to your point, no, they have not had difficulty recruiting people," replied Denisov, letting his face settle back into its naturally smug expression.

"They are an irritating thorn which has been allowed too much freedom to grow. Petrenko was so preoccupied with keeping our nuclear missiles from the grips of NATO and the US that he did not see that Yerin was plotting with Pamyat to overthrow him until it was too late," said Klitchkov.

"Yerin did this?" Nikita blinked, shocked. "That is why he was deposed?"

"Yerin is a traitor," said Denisov, the smugness evaporating from his face. "One thing is clear, Colonel, he leaked the details of our operation to one of Brishnov, Pamyat or Burn, possibly all three. He has committed treason."

Klitchkov's face turned Nikita's blood cold, as he saw a hatred that even he had never encountered. "We find ourselves in a web of traitors. Who remains that I can trust?"

"My loyalty cannot be questioned," answered Denisov, affronted.

"Nor can mine," said Nikita softly, aware of the disbelief of both of his comrades.

Klitchkov nodded silently. "Perhaps," he muttered. "Brishnov has been eliminated. Yerin, Burn and Lev Veselovsky must all be dealt with. If it is strength they need to see, then let us give it to them." He poured out three more vodkas and raised his glass as if to toast before thinking better of it and drinking it. The other two followed suit.

CHAPTER 25

A dark stain under the armpit was the only indication that the navy-blue uniform was not being worn by its original owner. That man was tied up and dying in a broom cupboard from the stab wound inflicted by the shiv Brishnov carried. He could have brought a proper knife, but the idea of a shiv appealed to his sense of theatre.

The prison guard's hat, with its broad, flat top, was pulled down tightly onto his head and the collar of the white shirt buttoned right to the top button. He tried to ignore the wet, sticky spot at his side and made his way down the gloomy corridor deep in the bowels of Matrosskaya Tishina prison.

The Moscow federal state penitentiary was infamous for its brutal conditions, high death rate and rampant corruption throughout the staff. Built by the general secretary himself, Josef Stalin, in 1945 on the site of an old asylum, the madness inherent in the site had persevered. It appeared a crumbling stone building from the outside, but inside it seemed nothing less than an homage to a Siberian gulag.

Brishnov shuddered. Why would the inmates not simply escape? It had been so easy to break in. The limitations of the mediocre mind baffled him. But then, he thought to himself with a smile, not everyone could be as exceptional as me. And soon there would be no doubt about who was the greatest Soviet agent there had ever been. He unconsciously massaged his bicep; the arm now pained him every time he tried to do anything that was weight-bearing. I will recover, he thought to himself, and I will destroy him.

As he moved further down the corridor, the smell grew steadily worse, and he could hear moans and cries from some of the doors he passed. Reaching the solid iron door, he was looking for, he covered his nose with a handkerchief taken from the pocket of his jacket and opened the slat.

Even through the handkerchief the stench still permeated his nostrils and he couldn't prevent his eyes from watering.

Through the slat he could see Yerin standing upright in a 'Kishka' or gut prison cell, named for its likeness to an intestine. The tall narrow room prevented Yerin from sitting or kneeling down; he could only stand in the years of excrement that had been deliberately allowed to remain, uncleaned, to torment its victims.

"Tut tut, Viktor, you have been a bad boy. How the mighty have fallen," Brishnov said cruelly to his mentor.

Viktor Yerin looked a wasted man. A patchy silver beard had grown over his pallid cheeks. He stood leaning forwards against the smooth concrete wall, a dirty grey vest clinging to his wasted body.

"Taras!" he croaked. "I knew you would come." Relief covered his face and a tear snaked a path down his dirty chin.

"I see our old friend Klitchkov does not take kindly to traitors," Brishnov said disapprovingly.

A scowl crossed the tear-stained face of the old man. "Me a traitor! I will have my revenge on the tyrant."

"That you will, Viktor. But first I need some information."

"Of course, but release me first, Taras, there will be time for talk later," said Viktor eagerly, his face close to the slat.

"Of course," Brishnov replied and Yerin began to sob with relief. "It's OK, sir," Brishnov said gently, "I just need to pick the lock." He began idly poking the keyhole with his shiv, seeming to concentrate. "Tell me, Viktor, where are they keeping Allochka's family?" he asked conversationally.

Yerin sniffed, his usually perfectly combed silver hair lying lank and dishevelled across his forehead. "Why do you need that information?" he asked sternly, a vague shadow of his former authority upon him.

"It is all a part of the plan to strike at the heart of Petrenko's leadership and to overthrow Klitchkov, sir. Allochka must be eliminated, and the only way to reach him is through his family."

"He is our best agent, our best hope for high level intelligence from the CIA," said Yerin sternly. "It would be folly to anger him, let alone to... remove him."

Brishnov bristled at the praise for Allochka. "Perhaps he is not as good as you believe. He has been compromised and is back in Russia," he said, still tapping away at the lock with mock concentration.

"He is?" Yerin said, surprised.

"He is; he has fallen off his American perch. Come now, Viktor, a black could never align with our goal to return the Soviet empire to greatness," he said softly.

"Perhaps you are correct, Taras." Yerin sighed. "Did the bomb destroy the Capitol?" he asked eagerly.

"Your man failed. You should have entrusted someone with more skill. Was he Pamyat?" Brishnov asked, stopping playing with the lock to look at Yerin curiously.

"Of a sort. That is bad news that it did not go well; it was such a good plan." He grunted. "Hurry up with that lock," he added, peering nervously through the slat.

"It is an old lock; it is stubborn." Brishnov puffed, controlling his irritation at the old man's questions. "Where did you hide the family? Dagestan? Tajikistan?" he asked, looking up at Yerin. "Surely not Tatarstan?" he said with alarm. "They will be dead already!"

"Do not be a fool; they murder anyone with so much as a tan in Tatarstan. They had to be more isolated."

Brishnov began to laugh. "Surely you didn't send them to Siberia?" he asked incredulously.

Yerin began to laugh too. It was hoarse and dry from dehydration and turned into a racking cough. "No honest Russian wants a black for a neighbour; where else could I put them?" he asked innocently, with his hands out. "I kept my word; nobody will bother them there."

"Where did you put them?"

"Oh, far north," Yerin said dismissively, waving a hand.

Brishnov stopped pretending to fiddle with the lock. "Where, Viktor?" he asked, his eyes flashing.

Yerin looked into Brishnov's eyes. "Near Talnakh."

"I need specifics if you want me to get you out of here."

"About twenty clicks east of Talnakh, in the foothills of the Putoron Mountains. There is a road that takes you out of the town. After about ten clicks, a track leads off to the left and leads you behind a low mountain. In the valley you will find them."

"Excellent, thank you, Viktor."

"Taras... they have a child," Viktor said hesitantly. "The child is an innocent."

Brishnov looked coldly at his former mentor. "Innocence is entirely subjective. You have become weak, Viktor."

"Remember with whom you are speaking, Agent Brishnov," Yerin replied, drawing his dishevelled body up to its full height. "Now release me."

Brishnov smirked. "I think perhaps you need more time to think on your sins, sir."

Horror crossed the face of Yerin. "Taras, no! We have been comrades for over fifteen years. Think of Leonid! Think of what we achieved together!"

"That was a better time, led by better men, Viktor. I gave everything I had to them, and a ruined Soviet empire is how they repaid me. Goodbye," he said.

"They will hang me!"

"You will get the firing squad, Viktor; it is an honourable way to go." Then as an afterthought, he pushed the shiv through the slot in the door, hearing it land with a plop in the excrement and detritus slathered across the floor of Yerin's Kishka. "If you can find it, you should fall on it; there is more honour in that," he said cruelly.

"Taras, please! I will kill them for you, just name it," he cried. "Please, I beg you!" he sobbed. Brishnov smiled and closed the slat in the door, dulling the sound of his former superior's voice and walked back along the corridor without a backwards glance.

***

Four photographs sat on Chairman Klitchkov's desk. On one was drawn a red cross, cutting the ugly scar on Brishnov's face in half. The others glared up at them: Lev Veselovsky, Zach Burn and Viktor Yerin. All three looked completely different, but there was a similar puffy element to their complexions, the look that comes from too long indoors, plotting the deaths of better men.

"Lieutenant Colonel, I want you to take control of the Burn situation. He is a dog and will receive everything a traitor to the state deserves, but not yet. There can still be value in him and you must handle him with care until such time as we need to dispose of him."

"Of course, sir. I can be of some assistance with Yerin also, perhaps?"

Klitchkov laughed. "You cannot trick a trickster, Maxim; you are too close to this one to behave dispassionately."

Clearly disappointed, Denisov nodded. "Yes, sir."

Klitchkov slid the photo of the moustached Burn slightly towards his lieutenant colonel with the tip of his index finger.

Nikita stood impatiently, his hands clasped behind his back, fingers firmly crossed for his chance to take on the neo-Nazi.

Klitchkov paused. "I know what you would have me do, Agent Allochka. And I would give it to you, were it not for the caution that stays my hand. I shall make arrangements for Veselovsky myself. He is a base traitor who rides upon the coat-tails of phrases like 'take our country back' and 'patriotism' that inflame the hearts of simple minds, and preys on those same people to push an agenda that would bring our nation to its knees. No, this one is mine," he said, a flush upon his cheeks and his eyes flashing.

He moved the photo of Veselovsky delicately towards himself, taking several breaths to calm himself. Nikita gave no indication of his disappointment to Klitchkov, only balling one hand into a fist and massaging it with the other hand behind his back.

"And you, agent," said Klitchkov, looking up, the colour now gone from his face. "That leaves you with Viktor Yerin."

"Yes, sir."

"He is currently being held in Matrosskaya Tishina Prison, here in Moscow. This must be kept a secret; the last thing we need is Amnesty International breathing down our necks. I suspect he will be in no condition to defend himself."

"Sir?"

Klitchkov smiled wildly. "I have had him moved to a Kishka for the past three days," he said, chuckling.

Denisov laughed. "The depths of your cruelty continue to surprise me, sir."

The smile fell instantly from Klitchkov's face. "You think the man deserves kindness?"

"Of course not, sir," stuttered Denisov. "I could not have thought of a more apt punishment myself."

Klitchkov said nothing. He sat down and started making notes in a pad before him. The other two men stood patiently at ease. After several minutes, Klitchkov looked up, irritated. "What are you waiting for? Go! Speak to my secretary for any further arrangements you require. Allochka, report back to me as soon as your mission is complete. You have twenty-four hours," he added, before going back to his notetaking.

Nikita exhaled. Twenty-four hours to plan and execute a break-in to a federal penitentiary and assassinate a maximum-security political prisoner. This had never been on the KGB syllabus.

***

As darkness fell, so did Nikita. Parachuting in silently from the hastily arranged light aircraft high above, the black parachute ghosted him down gently, cutting through the heavily falling snowflakes. Nothing more than a shadow floating through the night skies.

As he descended towards the penitentiary, he quickly gauged his bearings, locating his intended point of entry.

Landing silently on the roof of the vast complex, he was grateful for once for the heavy snowfall that descended with the Russian winters. Dragging the parachute behind him, he brushed out his footsteps as he approached an old stone chimney. Shining his torch down, he could see the metal grating that had been fixed into place to prevent any prisoners from getting any ideas of escape. From a black backpack he withdrew a compact hacksaw and some rope. Standing astride the brickwork of the chimney, he bunched up the parachute and stuffed it roughly into the backpack before lashing the rope around the chimney several times and dropping the remainder down the chimney. Flashing the torch down, he could see it had reached close to the bottom. Clipping the saw to his belt, without hesitating he grabbed the rope, wrapped it around his foot, and swiftly lowered himself down. His feet hit the metal grating heavily, and with a grinding of metal that felt painfully loud in the silence, it gave way and he continued rapidly towards the floor.

So much for maximum security, he whispered quietly to himself, unclipping the hacksaw and storing it out of sight at the side of the fireplace from which he cautiously emerged.

Running silently on rubber-soled shoes, he moved rapidly from the layout drawings he had earlier memorised, again reluctantly thanking his trainers for those draining hours he had been forced to spend training his memory.

Confidently he navigated his way through the kitchens which lay dark and empty. Reaching the exit, he paused and opening the door a crack, peered out. He was on the ground floor. Two guards were patrolling the common area, with cells lining the floors above, which judging by the torchlight, were also being patrolled. He needed to reach the left-hand side of the common area, approximately twenty yards away, which would be impossible with both of the ground floor guards having eyes on all areas of the space between them. He let the door close as one of the guards circled close to him, and considered his options.

He cursed the limited planning time he had been afforded. There were too many variables to guarantee success in a mission such as this, but Nikita knew himself well enough to admit that there was little to compare to the thrill of having to improvise on a mission. Doing so in a prison break-in gave him a shot of adrenaline it would be hard to recreate.

Looking around him, he could see pots, pans and all of the things you would expect to see in a prison, albeit with an absence of sharp objects. His eyes fell on the gas stoves and he moved over to them swiftly. Lighting one of the hobs, he dropped a large pile of dirty rags on top of the flame and swiftly moved back towards the door, carefully propping it slightly open with a one rouble coin. He then hid himself behind a large cupboard door adjacent to the kitchen door.

The flames quickly grew and greasy black smoke began to rise. Within a minute, he heard a cry of alarm from one of the guards and the door burst open. Watching through a crack in the cupboard hinges, Nikita was relieved to see both guards come charging in and over to the flames billowing from the top of the industrial stove. He silently slipped out, and keeping to the limited shadows along the wall, he darted quickly over to the doorway on the left. It was not a moment too soon, as other guards then descended the metal stairwells and ran to see what the commotion was all about.

The noises quickly fell into the distance and Nikita moved with haste down a surgically white corridor. When he reached the end, he climbed down another metal gridded staircase, before finding himself in a crumbling old corridor that could only be described as the dungeons of the prison.

Gas lights were lit along the walls, flickering dimly, and the scattering footsteps of rats could be heard as he made his way along, long tails briefly glimpsed at the edge of the gloom. A terrible odour grew steadily worse the further Nikita got along what felt more like a tunnel than a corridor. He covered his nose but could still taste the stink. What manner of hell was this place?

As he rounded a corner, he saw a guard sitting on a chair next to tap and basin, reading a newspaper. The guard looked up and his eyes widened in horror. He reached for the whistle around his neck, but in three leaping strides Nikita was upon him. With his right hand balled into a fist but with the joint of his middle finger extended forwards he punched the guard hard on the temple. He crumpled instantly. Nikita checked his pulse. He was still alive, but would not be awake for several hours, possibly longer.

He continued forwards. When he reached the end of the corridor, he found the cell that Yerin was inhabiting and silently slid the metal slat in the door open.

He jumped as a pair of fearsome eyes was pressed firmly to the gap. They were gripped by the first tinges of madness.

They widened upon comprehending Nikita. "You!" Yerin gasped, falling backwards against the wall directly behind him in the tiny box that was his lodgings. His eyes were puffy, his lips dry and bleeding.

Nikita was appalled by what he saw, a level of squalor reserved for the middle ages.

"How long have you been in here?" he asked, gasping between putrid breaths.

"I do not know the meaning of time. I think, perhaps three days. No man can endure more. Are you here to kill me?" he asked simply, only seeming to be semi-aware, on the brink of unconsciousness.

"That would be merciful," Nikita replied.

"Then Klitchkov has some other plan for me? I will do anything to be free of this tomb," Yerin said.

"Then tell me everything, and do not lie. You made sure I was trained to detect a lie."

"What do I get in return?"

"I promise you nothing in return. But perhaps you can regain some honour."

Yerin forced his swollen eyelids open to look at Nikita. "I beg you to open the door and let me sit. Do this and I will tell you everything. As you can see, I am in no condition to escape."

Nikita knew he would have to open the cell regardless, and so, nodding silently, he swiftly picked the lock, hearing the tell-tale click of the internal bolt mechanism sliding across. He pulled the door open, stepping aside to avoid the expected flood of Yerin's own filth pouring out. Instead, the door revealed a low wall inside the cell itself to keep the detritus contained.

Yerin tumbled out, his legs giving way and fell over the wall onto the floor. Nikita bent over to help him up to a sitting position.

"AAAHHHHH!" cried Yerin as he rolled over and sliced at Nikita, aiming for his heart with a short sharp object. Nikita fended it off but it managed to draw blood from his forearm, and his eyes blazed.

He disarmed the feeble Yerin and punched him hard in the face, forcing him back to the floor. He looked at the weapon; it was perhaps eight inches long from the tip of the blade to the foot of the handle. At first, he thought it was plastic, but on closer inspection it looked to be carved from bone, with hessian sacking material wrapped around the handle. The blade was around four inches long. Long enough to be lethal.

Yerin rubbed his cheek where Nikita had struck him. It was already inflamed and red, as well as filthy from where he was rubbing with his dirt-caked hands. Never had Nikita seen a more pitiable creature. The filthy grey vest hung down to his thighs, and the once blue trousers he wore were now caked in faeces and wet with urine. Whether his own or not, Nikita could not tell, and did not wish to dwell on it.

Looking up at Nikita with the shiv in his hand, Yerin began to sob — racking sobs that took hold of his entire body — and he curled up against the wall.

Nikita walked some way up the corridor to where he had seen an old faucet and bucket by the wall. The guard still lay crumpled and unconscious. Nikita hauled him back into the chair and propped him up. Best to cover tracks where possible.

Filling the bucket from the creaky tap, he walked back and tossed it over the balled up Yerin, who wailed before sitting bolt upright. Nikita passed him the bucket to drink what was left inside.

Gulping heavily, he drank too much and immediately vomited on the stone floor, before drinking some more.

He wiped his mouth and looked up at Nikita in wonder. "Spasibo," he said simply. *Thank you.* He looked down at the floor, and Nikita could see shame. When Yerin looked up, there were tears in his eyes. "I fear I have done you great harm."

"You barely grazed me," replied Nikita gently, pitying Yerin more and more.

"I am, I think, ready to die," the old man said.

"Not until you tell me all you know of Pamyat's plans."

"At the moment, agent, their main plan... is you."

CHAPTER 26

"What... what do you mean?" Nikita asked sharply.

Yerin sighed. "I lived my life in the service of the Soviet Republic, blindly dedicated to a succession of power-hungry men. I think perhaps I became one of them myself. The country is on its knees; it is only a matter of time before the vultures descend and pick our empire apart piece by piece. Together with Brishnov we sought to unite with Pamyat to take our country back. But from who? From you and your kind? From the Jews? I think now, at the end of it all, the people who it needed taking back from were those very same that had been claiming it was lost. Namely me."

"That is very good, but what do you mean that Pamyat's plan is me?"

"Of course, yes. Some hours ago, I was visited by your good friend Agent Brishnov—"

"Impossible," said Nikita. "Brishnov is dead; I killed him myself. Spout another lie, and I will plant a bullet in your brain."

"Come now, Allochka. We both know you have been sent here to kill me. With some patience I may yet be able to save you. I do not know what happened between you, but I can assure you that Taras Brishnov is very much alive. Perhaps now the last of his sanity has deserted him, however."

"Impossible," whispered Nikita, but a dreadful coldness crept across his heart. It was what he had feared, with no evidence of his body ever found.

"But that fall... no one could have survived it," he said to himself.

"If there is one thing, I can tell you about Brishnov, it is that you should always expect the impossible. Normal laws do not seem to apply to the man."

Nikita was replaying the moment atop the crane in his head; the drop must have been eighty feet, while dealing with a gunshot wound through a bicep. The odds of survival were... small. Tiny in fact.

"I was angry. So angry. Perhaps my judgement was clouded." Nikita accepted it dubiously, not able to shake the image of Brishnov falling from such a height. He shook his head. "Why was he here?" he demanded.

"At first, I had believed, or perhaps just blindly hoped, that he was here to rescue me. What a foolish old man I am. But of course, once he got the information he required, he no longer had need for a man who has lost all of his influence."

"What was the information? Must I drag everything out of you?"

"Patience, agent, patience," Yerin said, holding up his dripping wet hand. The decrepit old man had begun to shake. Nikita pulled his parachute from the bag and wrapped it around him. Yerin smiled benignly in return. "Kindness can be as disarming as violence, I see now. Perhaps it should be added to the KGB syllabus," he said with a rasping chuckle. Seeing Nikita's angry face, the chuckle died. "Yes, yes, OK. I can see I can avoid this no longer." He looked forlornly at Nikita. "He wanted to know the location of your family."

Nikita's eyes were wide with fright. "And what did you tell him?"

Yerin looked sadly up at him. Quick as a flash, Nikita spun, and with the shiv in hand sliced Yerin's throat deeply. His body trembled as he stared in horror at the once great leader of the KGB.

The old man began to choke, but instead of trying to stem the bleeding, he spat and gurgled the words that were only faintly discernible. "I am sorry."

"This is an act of mercy you do not deserve, Yerin," Nikita said, and plunged the shiv into the old man's heart, leaving it planted in his chest. Without a glance back at him he was already running faster than he ever had back up the corridor, fear and fury gripping every fibre of his being.

He ran through the common area, willing guards to attempt to stop him, daring them to stand in his way. But whether by luck or design he was able to get through to the kitchen without being seen. The air was thick with smoke and he could hear voices but didn't ee anybody. The flames seemed to have extended beyond the stove to a doorway next to it and guards were working to get them under control with extinguishers. Hardly believing his luck, Nikita slipped like a shadow through the haze and clambered up the chimney swiftly, covering it in giant thrusts, driven by an overpowering adrenaline. When he looked back, Nikita would never be able to recall how he escaped from the prison.

He untied the rope from the chimney stack and sprinted to the other end of the roof. Looking over the edge, he could see that he had the right spot; the wall ran straight down to the street, with only a spiked, barbed wire fence running around the perimeter at the bottom.

He tied the rope around a robust metal pipe running along the inside of the low wall that stood around the edge of the roof. Then, without looking, he jumped backward off the building and abseiled down, not even looping in his foot as he raced against time. Only one thought was in his mind. My family, save my family.

As he lowered himself down, impervious to the rope burns tearing at his hands, he approached the fence. Brutal looking spikes topped it, along with vast loops of barbed wire. It was around four metres to the ground. He squatted his leg into the wall and forced himself off and out, releasing the rope just as he cleared the fence. He landed with a roll, ignoring the jarring pain that shot through his shoulder and hip, and leapt up before charging down the street.

Around the corner a polished Land Rover awaited him. Feeling under the wheel arch, his hand landed upon the keys, snatching them out. He scrambled behind the wheel.

The handbrake was off and the car moving before the engine even kicked in. He accelerated away, weaving through traffic, ignoring the blaring of horns, his chest constricted and breath short.

"Brishnov is alive and knows where my family is," he muttered, disbelieving. "How could I have been so foolish?" he admonished himself.

As he passed a phone box, he slammed on the brakes and screeched over to the kerb. Leaving the engine running, he jumped out and dialled Klitchkov.

"Allo, ofis Predsedatelya," said a lyrical female voice.

"Dymnav'ya dzen," Nikita replied, quietly uttering the codeword.

"Da, what is it, agent?" replied Klitchkov's secretary coolly.

"Katalina, I need the Chairman NOW. It is very urgent."

"One moment please."

"Da? What is it, agent, this is not protocol?" came Klitchkov's voice.

"Brishnov is alive and knows where my family is."

"Is this line secure?" Klitchkov said sharply.

"I don't give a damn, sir. Did you hear what I said?"

"Understood. Was your evening rendezvous successful?"

"Yes, sir," Nikita replied, exasperated. "But my family—"

He was cut off by a click on the line and the sound of Katalina's voice returned. "Please go to Vnukovo Airport, agent." Then the line went dead.

After running back to the car, Nikita jumped in and made a screeching turn before speeding to the former military airport, now the most popular for private usage.

The journey from Matrosskaya Tishina Prison to Vnukovo Airport should have taken an hour, journeying across the heart of Moscow. Nikita cleared it in thirty minutes, breaking every Soviet driving law going. Miraculously, he encountered no issues with police.

He pulled up outside the airport, parking the car illegally and leaving it there. He was on his way hurriedly into the airport, when an arm grabbed him and pulled him back.

He looked into the familiar cold blue eyes of Chairman Klitchkov, peering out from under his furry ushanka, and wearing a long charcoal coat.

"Allochka, come," he said, gesturing to the same black ZIS-115 in which he had been earlier.

They climbed in, and drove up to a high fence with a gate manned by Soviet Army privates. As the car approached, the gate opened and the soldiers stood to attention and saluted the chairman as they passed. He rolled down the window and saluted in return.

"Chairman—" began Nikita, but was cut off by a raised hand from the leader of the KGB.

"He lives?" Klitchkov asked, eyes staring straight ahead.

"He visited Yerin today."

"You have proof?"

"None. But I am confident Yerin did not lie. He found his remorse at the end."

"Yerin never did anything if he did not stand to gain from it."

"Perhaps. But, Chairman, I must go to my family. If there is even a chance of him being alive, his desire for revenge will know no limits. Please, sir," Nikita implored, on the verge of tears.

Klitchkov looked at him distastefully. "Remember your training, agent. Emotions are for the weak, and they will betray you."

Nikita cleared his throat and set his shoulders. "Of course, you are right," he said with an even voice, though his heart continued to race.

The chauffeur taxied them around the two runways to a private hangar on the far side of the airport. As they entered, Nikita could see the Antonov An-32, the Soviet's answer to the Learjet. The slender, twin-engine aircraft looked like a hawk desperate to take to the skies.

"Will this make it to Siberia?" Nikita asked dubiously.

"Under the circumstances it is our best hope for making it before Brishnov. It can land us safely in Norilsk."

"Our?" Nikita replied curiously.

"You have failed with Brishnov once. Fail again and I will kill you myself," he said icily, patting his side so Nikita could hear the dull sound of a concealed weapon. "Shall we?" said Klitchkov, gesturing towards the waiting plane.

Nikita said nothing. He saw their faces swimming before his eyes in a way he had been able to block for many months. In his pocket his hand clutched the carving Elysia had given him, which he now carried everywhere with him. Holding it helped to calm him slightly. His skin prickled and he moved swiftly into the plane.

Nikita and Klitchkov settled into seats opposite each other in the compact but luxurious KGB transporter.

"Brishnov had many hours' head start; we must fly swiftly. As we know he can be very resourceful. I would very much like to know how he was able to return from the United States with a gunshot wound," said Klitchkov. "I have scrambled for backup, but no troops are based anywhere near Norilsk, so we may be some way ahead of them."

Nikita was silent, not interested in bandying words with his unpredictable superior. He longed for a drink, picturing a whiskey on the rocks, but was determined to keep his mind fully clear. A slight sweat broke above his upper lip. He thought of Elysia, focusing all of his attention upon her. He felt himself calm as the engines fired up and the craft taxied to the nearest runway.

He could see through the window a queue of other aeroplanes which had been forced to pause to allow their take-off. As the Antonov An-32 boomed along the asphalt and forced its way into the Moscow skies, still heavily powdered with snowfall, Nikita sat back in his chair. The military craft sliced through the white night and climbed above the clouds to reveal an inky black, star-studded sky. Nikita forced himself to close his eyes.

"I am coming for you, Taras," he whispered to himself.

It was only four hours later that the plane scudded down on the cracked, icy runway of Alykel Airport in Norilsk, one of the world's northernmost cities, sitting deep inside the Arctic Circle. Thick snow drifts lay at either side of the runway from where they had been cleared. In this part of the world, it was easier to count the days on which it didn't snow that those when it did.

A gentle glow sat on the horizon, signifying dawn. The sun would not rise much higher in this polar winter.

The plane had barely ground to a halt when Nikita was up and waiting impatiently by the door. 'What if I am too late?' kept looping around his mind. Brishnov would show no mercy, and it would be even worse if he had taken the Pamyat thugs with him. Nikita shook himself to rid his mind of the thoughts. Brishnov would not likely have access to a high-speed aircraft able to land in Norilsk. Even with his head start of many hours… it would be very close.

As he crossed the tarmac to the waiting four by four, for the first time in his life Nikita looked up to the inky blue skies and prayed.

He waited for Klitchkov to descend the steps, his body humming with nervous adrenaline. The moment Klitchkov entered the car and sat beside him, he hit the accelerator before the door was even closed.

"Patience, Allochka," Klitchkov snapped. "These roads cannot be traversed in a hurry."

Never had a truer word been said, as even with Nikita's prodigious skill behind the wheel, the roads were caked in hard packed snow and ice, forcing the chain-clad wheels of the UAZ-469 Soviet military off-road vehicle into a throaty roar as he had to rev hard in low gears to avoid spinning off the road. Regular inclines of the pure white Arctic tundra surrounded them for miles, with only the occasional truck coming the other way as a sign of any life. The heater on the dash was turned up full, but still their breath rose in front of them, steaming the windows. After forty minutes of driving in silence, they passed Norilsk itself, but Nikita ploughed straight past, skirting the city's edges.

The few people they passed looked tough and hardened, collars up against the harsh winter. In this unforgiving corner of the world temperatures rarely rose above minus seventeen degrees Celsius at this time of year.

As they left the city behind, signs of life became fewer and further between, with only the occasional stone house set back from the road, candlelight glowing behind the windows and smoke billowing from chimneys, and scrubby, ill-looking trees dusting the white expanse.

Thirty minutes later, they passed the town of Talnakh, an expanse of low concrete buildings spread across a flat plain, surrounded by distant hills. A misty, green glow seemed to hover across the town in the twilight-like haze, inhabited by only the hardiest of people, driven there by the deep nickel mines.

Again, Nikita drove on, the location etched in his memory, despite his only previous visit being well over a year ago.

"What is your plan, agent?" asked Chairman Klitchkov, as they took the narrow winding road beyond the town towards the mountains.

"To secure the safety of my family and eliminate any threats to them or to the state," Nikita said shortly.

"Excellent to see you have thought through every detail of this potentially explosive scenario," Klitchkov said with mock joviality.

Nikita tightened his mouth. "The path to the izba cuts across the top of a low hill before curving down to the building. We will have a good vantage point from the hill top, and any foreign bodies should be easily identifiable in the surroundings."

"And if the enemy is already there?" Klitchkov asked.

Nikita's knuckles whitened on the steering wheel. "They must not be," he replied.

Klitchkov laughed coldly.

"Whose side are you on, sir?" Nikita exploded, before he was able to stop himself.

Klitchkov turned to look at him, his pale blue eyes unreadable. "What did you say to me, agent?" he asked in a horribly controlled tone, eyes looking almost psychopathic.

"You say you will look after my family, but maroon them in outer Siberia. You shoot me in Kamchatka — yes, I know it was you — and then you treat me, you look at me like something on the bottom of your shoe, but then accompany me on a rescue mission. What the hell sort of game are you playing?" he shouted, the words pouring from his mouth like champagne from a corked bottle, his shoulders shaking with the release.

"ENOUGH!" shouted Klitchkov. "Who do you think you are, Allochka? I should kill you now for talking to a superior this way, you insubordinate little shit. Perhaps Brishnov is right and your tiny African mind is incapable of comprehending the greater workings and the grander plan, of considering the complex vastness of the USSR."

Nikita drew his gun and pointed it at Klitchkov, not taking his eyes from the road. "Give me a reason, Chairman."

Chairman Klitchkov did not so much as blink at the weapon only inches from his face. "Threatening to kill the leader of the KGB? That is gross misconduct and treason. Whatever happens today you will face court martial and you will hang. So, OK, agent, I will give you answers, if that is what you seek. Who am I to deny a dying man's request?" he said, grinning.

"Yes, we put your family as far from civilisation as possible, although I must confess it was Yerin's idea. If you can tell me anywhere else within the Soviet Union that they would have been welcomed, I'd be interested to hear. I gave them the only thing I could, a life away from physical and emotional abuse. Believe me, I know the meaning of abuse," he added, his eyes sliding to the side momentarily as he ruminated on some long past hurt. "Shoot you in Kamchatka?" He said, snapping back to his retort. "I do not deny it! My only regret is that I did not wound you further. I knew that we would require you to endure more than any other KGB agent and I had to be sure you were strong enough. You walked miles with a gunshot wound to the leg and high-level blood loss. I challenge you to look me in the eye and tell me it didn't reveal in you a strength and endurance you had never previously known."

Nikita said nothing. The road had narrowed, carved out of banks of snow higher than the vehicle itself. The chain-clad wheels were furiously working for grip on the powdery road. There was not, and would not be, any sign of habitation now until they reached the Allochka home.

"I knew that you had found out that it was me," Klitchkov continued. "The fact you were able to identify that in those circumstances shows that you are made to be an extraordinary spy. Do you know how many others I have done the same thing to, and not one of them has ever known that.

"You think I hate you? That I despise you? Tell me, who was it that recruited you for the KGB?"

"Do not pretend that you had my own interests at heart," said Nikita drily.

"I do not. But I am not in the habit of taking children from their families, yet I have never felt any guilt. Imagine your life in Kamenka now if I had not given you an opportunity that a million young Russian men would dream of. You would not have survived, and neither would your family. I gave you a life, a skill set. You will never go hungry."

"Assuming I survive," Nikita retorted.

"Assuming you survive," agreed Klitchkov. "I cared little for you. Come on, nobody in Russia likes anyone who is not a Russian!" He laughed. "But I admit to finding you now worthy of the title of Russian, more so than many white men I have known. I live in a nasty, cruel world, and make no apologies for being a nasty, cruel man. I must confess that I often rather enjoy it!" He laughed maniacally. "The begging, the pleading of lesser souls gives me quite a thrill. Not to the level of depravity of Brishnov, you understand, but I enjoy the power. I always have. Murder never bothered me. But I am also a man of my word. You may not like my decisions but I have always kept my promises to you. I promised to keep your family safe. That much I will do," he said, before adding, "and I also really want to make that Veselovsky dog suffer."

Nikita looked at Klitchkov and smiled, lowering his gun. "That is something I can help you with," he said, before adding, "sir," respectfully.

Moments later, the walls of snow around them dipped and a track led off to the left. It was not traversable by car, leading up the mountain at a sharp angle. Nikita pulled the car to the side and killed the engine. "We must go by foot from here," he said, as they both climbed out of the vehicle.

Nikita walked around to the boot and threw it open, revealing an array of weapons bound in a heavy cloth. He unfurled the bundle and selected a VSS Special Sniper rifle, weighing it in his hands. It had a highly polished, squared off wooden handle, and a short magazine stock. Wrapped around the barrel was an integral silencer. An accessible and mobile sniper, perfect for a clandestine operation if he needed to take Brishnov out from distance, or while on the move. Slinging it across his shoulder by the strap, he reached down for a Makarov pistol, putting it into his belt, to add to the one in a holster at his right hip. He grabbed then for a weighty Sig Sauer P226, putting it into the shoulder holster.

Klitchkov tutted at Nikita's choice of the Sig Sauer. "A German fascist gun, Allochka? You should be ashamed," he said before picking a pair of AK-47s with obvious delight, also strapping a VSS across his back. They both armed themselves with a variety of cruel looking knives. Nikita's eyes fell upon a Spetsnaz ballistic knife, and he slid it into a concealed sheath between his shoulder blades with a cold expression, remembering again the training in the East Siberian Taiga.

A pair of thick white ski coats and trousers were there also, and Nikita and Klitchkov both climbed into them, before shovelling ammunition into the deep pockets. There was nowhere to hide the truck, despite the fact it was a beacon to any who might be following on from them, but they shovelled snow over the roof and bonnet as much as they could.

Finally, they pulled on fur-covered snow boots, which were hideously ugly but highly effective, and then began warily trudging up the track.

CHAPTER 27

"If Veselovsky is there, we must try to take him alive," Klitchkov said curtly.

"I will try," Nikita responded, checking the stock of his Sig Sauer, before keeping it in his gloved hands, pointing low. "But if he puts any of my family in danger, I will take him down without hesitation."

Klitchkov inclined his head in the shortest of nods, holding the Kalashnikovs in both hands. "I do not know when the backup will be able to reach us. We could be alone for this operation, agent."

Nikita nodded silently.

The track took them up to the top of a low hill which looked down upon a broad, flat expanse, only just recognisable as a lake under the snow dusted across the thick ice, before curving around the summit. As they rounded the far side of the hill, the track veered downwards in a gentle zigzag and there at the foot of the valley lay the stone izba, just as he remembered it. Picturesque in its colourless surroundings, smoke furling from the chimney, a warm glow emanating from behind the curtained windows in the perpetual twilight of the Arctic Circle.

They were both breathing heavily from the difficulty of the climb through thick snow in their multiple layers. Nikita could feel a bead of sweat snaking its way down the small of his back. He breathed a sigh of relief. If Brishnov had already been here, he was certain the scene he was looking upon would be one of massacre and devastation.

Nonetheless, he knew now to take nothing for granted when it came to Brishnov. Lev Veselovsky may have had his own ideas for how to get to them.

Nikita paused, then going down on one knee, peered through the scope of his sniper. Footsteps could be seen in the snow around the cottage but none were visible on the track going down.

He walked off the track and beckoned to Klitchkov to go with him. They sat and leant with their backs to the hill, concealed from the track by a rocky outcrop. Klitchkov roughly dusted their footprints behind him with the sleeve of his coat as he followed Nikita.

"What is it, Allochka?" asked Klitchkov in the hushed voice that always descends on people when surrounded by snow.

"We need to assess the situation."

"The situation seems clear; we have beaten them here and if we hurry, we can help them escape before the enemy arrives."

"We know nothing for certain at this point, Chairman. One thing is definite, and that is that they are going after my family to draw me out. Brishnov will care little if my family live or die; it is me he wants."

"You cannot give yourself up, Allochka," said Klitchkov sternly.

"Because you want to have me hang for treason yourself?" said Nikita, with a cocked eyebrow.

"Perhaps I could suspend your sentence, if you manage to capture Brishnov and Veselovsky," Klitchkov said, grinning.

"You will be pleased to know I have no intention of giving myself up to Brishnov. But my priority here is the safety of my family."

"Of course."

"From this vantage point, the scene looks secure. But the curtains are drawn and we do not know if a trap lies in wait for us. The one advantage we have on our side is that they will assume that I have been left to come on my own," he said, looking at Klitchkov.

"A fair assumption," agreed Klitchkov.

"It is an advantage we must keep in our hands. But first I must scope out the rear of the premises; wait here," whispered Nikita, disappearing off across the hillside without waiting for an answer. With his white hood pulled up, he quickly disappeared into the landscape.

He stepped lightly, careful not to make any clouds of snow or sending any clumps tumbling down the hillside. He longed to just enter the house and embrace the family he had not seen for so long, but he knew he could be wasting precious time and couldn't afford to take any chances.

Working in a wide arc, hugging the rocky hillside, and taking advantage of any crags that would hide him from view, he made it round to the rear of the homestead. As he had expected, there was no sign of anything untoward. Just a squared-off area for a garden. Nikita chuckled;

it was so typical of his mother to demand that they created a garden, when the vast white expanse stretching for hundreds of miles to the Kara Sea was theirs to do whatever they wished with. The entire tundra was their back garden, and none of the animals that survived out there would be stopped by a low wooden fence. Only a rifle would stop the likes of a polar bear or charging musk ox should any of them venture closer to the izba.

Satisfied, Nikita made his way carefully back to Klitchkov's hiding place. He found the chairman sat stiffly, looking at him crossly.

"Do not do that without conferring with me first. Do not forget I am your commanding officer."

"Yes, sir."

"Well…?"

"It appears to be clear, sir. As for our advantage, I suggest I approach the house myself, and you cover me. I will use field signals to communicate from range. I will then secure the premises and gather my family at the rear of the property. It cannot be long until Brishnov and Veselovsky descend upon our position so we must make haste and I do not think we should return to the vehicle via the track. I suggest we go across the terrain, approaching the road further down from the left side of the hill. Do you concur?" Nikita asked.

"I concur," agreed Klitchkov. "If you are inside and I see them approach, I will fire a warning shot through one of the upstairs windows."

Nikita nodded, and without hesitation moved quickly back to the track and ran as fast as he was able in the giant fur snow boots down to the property. His heart was hammering in his chest; the anticipation of seeing his parents and little Milena combined with the fear that all might not be as it seemed was almost too much to bear.

As he reached the foot of the hill, he slowed and padded softly to the corner of the home and holstered the Sig Sauer, instead reaching for the Makarov, a weapon he preferred for close quarter action. He crouched and moved to beneath the first ground floor window. Raising his head, he peered through a crack in the curtains. His heart leapt into his mouth as he saw his mother with her back to him, sitting reading in a rocking chair next to the fire.

He felt nervous and uncomfortable arriving with so much weaponry. It could not be avoided.

He balled his fist and gave the thumbs up to Klitchkov who was invisible on the hillside, indicating the all clear.

Nikita stood and walked to the front door, more confident now but aware of how quickly he needed to convince his family to move out.

With a nervous glance over his shoulder, he scanned the snowy landscape, looking for any sign of life but could see nothing. His hairs were standing on end, adrenaline pumping through his veins once more.

He raised a fist and knocked on the door.

The scraping of a chair could be heard, followed by heavy footsteps coming steadily towards the door.

Just as he had a year earlier, the concerned face of Gabriel Allochka threw open the door, blocking all light with his broad shoulders, casting his face into shadow.

"Father," said Nikita, eyes wide, suddenly feeling childlike.

"Niki!" boomed his father, grabbing him into a bear hug, before pulling away with alarm as his hand landed on one of the weapons Nikita was carrying. "What is the meaning of this?" he asked, confused.

"This is not a social call, father; we are in grave danger," Nikita said, his face serious. He pushed past and into the warmth of the izba, closing the door swiftly behind him.

In seconds, his mother and Milena were upon him, hugging him tightly. His mother pushed back his hood, covered his head with kisses and sobbed with happiness. "My son! Oh, praise God, it is good to see you." She pulled back and inspected him, a huge smile across her warm face. "What a handsome man you have become," she said, beaming, before pulling him to her again. She smelt of summer meadows, warm and fresh; it transported Nikita to a different time and he longed to stay in the embrace.

Gathering his wits, he pushed both off him. His father still stood with his back to the door, and Nikita, pulling Milena into another hug, signalled to Gabriel and his mother with his eyes.

"Milena, how have you become even taller! You are catching me up!" he said with forced cheerfulness.

Mercifully, Sophie had grasped that something was awry. "Milena, you have dirt on your t-shirt; go and change it so you don't get it all over Niki's lovely white clothes," she said gently.

Milena pouted, but clearly knew better than to argue, and dashed off upstairs.

Nikita wasted no time. "I am desperate to spend time with you all, but right now you must listen to me. You are all in grave danger; I do not have time to explain, but some terrible men are coming for you all. I need you both to put on your outdoor clothes, Milena too, and come with me."

Sophie looked shocked, and Gabriel's eyes flashed. "We can't just leave," said his mother. "All of our things…"

"If all goes to plan, you will be able to return at some point," Nikita said. "But we must go, NOW."

Gabriel looked concerned. "Are you OK, son?" he asked softly.

"I will be once I know the three of you are safe," he responded. Then when neither of them moved, dreadful concern and panic welled inside him. "Please," he pleaded, wide-eyed, "we have to go."

Gabriel nodded. "Milena!" he called. "Come here, we are going for an adventure with Niki," he said, as he pulled on his thick black overcoat and pulled a woollen hat down low over his head. He picked up Sophie's coat and offered her a sleeve in which she duly placed her arm with a smile. He tenderly pulled the coat to her other arm and wrapped his arms around her, placing a soft kiss on her head.

Milena's footsteps could be heard pounding down the stairs. "An adventure?" she asked curiously. Her hair had been put into long braids that were bunched on top of her head.

"Yes, I think you are due an adventure with your big brother, aren't you?" Nikita said, his insides churning. "Come on now; put your jacket on as quickly as you can."

"All right, what's the hurry?" she said, flouncing awkwardly somewhere between child and teen.

"Come now, Milena; off we go," said Sophie Allochka, throwing her coat over to her pouting daughter and then putting on her own snow boots. Gabriel went to put out the fire burning in the hearth, and Sophie, still beaming and looking at Nikita with eyes full of love, went to help Milena into her boots, much as she squirmed and resisted.

Nikita cautiously turned the latch on the door and opened it a crack. "I am just going to check… the conditions," he added lamely, but Milena was too distracted by Sophie's fussing and didn't notice.

Gabriel turned his head and nodded, mouthing, "Be careful."

Discreetly withdrawing his Makarov, Nikita stepped outside, closing the door quickly behind him. He held up three fingers followed by a chopping motion to the spot where he knew Klitchkov was watchfully waiting. He then carried out a quick reconnaissance of the property's perimeter. Using the scope on his sniper he scanned the surrounding area but there was no sign of life and all was deathly quiet. Almost too quiet.

He returned to the front door and entered discreetly. His family were all ready and waiting. Their outfits were a range of colours, all of which would stand out like sore thumbs on the glistening white tundra, but it couldn't be helped on such short notice.

"Is everybody ready?" he asked, and they cheered, Milena's eyes looking full of excitement. He reminded himself that he was the only person other than his parents that she would have seen for many years, aside from whoever delivered them their food.

"OK. Part of the adventure is that we have to go as quickly and as quietly as we can round the left of the hill. It will not be easy going away from the track."

"Daddy says we should never leave the track."

"Normally Daddy is completely right, but today is a very special day for a very special adventure!" Nikita said. "Now I need you to all follow me in single file once we leave the izba, understood?"

They all nodded. Gabriel's eyes were an unreadable combination of fire and sadness, while Sophie's face was set with a determination that could not disguise the intense fear. "We are right behind you, Niki," she said encouragingly.

Nikita threw open the door and stepped outside. As he did, he heard the sound of broken glass in an upstairs window.

CHAPTER 28

As he heard the gunshot to the upstairs window, Nikita turned to see his mother coming out behind him and screamed, "MOTHER, TURN BACK!"

She looked down at him with alarm just as he heard the terrible crack of a rifle echo across the valley and he dived at her, as Gabriel grabbed her with a giant hand, and together they propelled her back into the cottage.

Nikita had barely landed before he had slammed the door shut with his foot and leapt onto his feet.

He had dropped the Makarov in the fall and bent over to pick it up. That was when he saw the blood on the cream carpet and his heart froze. He looked up to his mother, just as his father released a heart-wrenching wail that came from the depths of his soul.

Sophie Allochka was lying in her husband's arms, a benign smile forever fixed on her face. That gentle, kind face was blemished in death by a bullet wound just above her left eye.

Gabriel Allochka was covered in blood and rocking with his wife in his vast arms, his eyes closed, a gentle giant.

Milena, pale and wide-eyed ran to her mother and started shaking her. "Mama! MAMA!" she cried, her small fists beating on the now silent chest of her mother.

Nikita ran over, everything seeming a blur. He pulled Milena up and hugged her tightly, and felt the tears coming. The tears he had buried for so many years. He had failed.

Another gunshot through an upstairs window brought him back to his senses. They were coming.

Suddenly his sadness was replaced by a burning, red hot, destructive rage. Then his training reasserted itself. His eyes were ablaze, his own mother's blood spattered across his face.

He released Milena and went to his father.

"Papa," he said, a strong hand on his father's shoulder. "Papa, are you hurt?" he asked, running his hands over the blood-and-brain-spattered face and chest of his father. Gabriel looked up at him with so much pain that Nikita's legs buckled beneath him, falling to his knees, his forehead against his father's.

He pushed himself off, and tried to pry his father's arms from around his mother. He would not release.

"Father, we have to go; they are coming," he said slowly.

His father only shook his head, a fresh wave of sobs racking through him. "Father, please," he pleaded, before adding softly, "for Milena."

At that, Gabriel's shaking ceased and he nodded. He released Sophie with a tenderness that belied his size, and wrenched himself to his feet. He then picked his wife up gently and laid her on the sofa near the fire before turning with fury written through the lines of his face.

Milena had curled up in the corner of the room, her head between her legs. She wasn't crying, but her entire body shook as Nikita lifted her easily into his arms and carried her over to their waiting father.

"We do not have long; they will be through the door any moment. Chairman Klitchkov is trying to cover us, but we do not know how many there are."

"Chairman Klitchkov?" Gabriel said sharply. "I will not go anywhere near that man; look how much he has taken from us."

"He is our only hope now, Father," Nikita snapped. "Follow me upstairs, and do not walk in front of any windows," he ordered, leading them upstairs, focusing only on the situation at hand. He walked into his parents' bedroom which faced out onto the front of the house.

His back to the wall next to the window, he waved Gabriel and Milena down onto the floor and behind the bed, and peered sideways through the window. He pulled back the curtain a fraction, as he removed the sniper from his back, holding it in both hands. The room was cold due to the broken glass from the gunshots and his breath rose before him. He closed his mouth and controlled his breathing. He couldn't afford to give any indication of his location. All was quiet, a blanket of white.

Unscrewing the scope from the sniper, Nikita gazed through it, taking in as much as he could from the tight angle, before squatting below the windows and moving to the other side. From this angle he could see

Klitchkov lying flat on the floor, only the barrel of his gun giving any indication of his whereabouts. He followed the line of the gun and saw two men approaching from the left. They were also clad in white, but were armed also with AK-47s, the staple weapon of every mercenary.

That accounted for the approach team, but neither of them carried a sniper. Where was the man who had taken down his mother?

For a moment, Nikita's thoughts flashed to Klitchkov, but quickly dismissed them. There would be no point in his warning them if he was the shooter.

Scanning around as best as he could without revealing himself, he located the sniper, about forty feet further up the hill, almost directly above Klitchkov. The shooter was squatting, hood down, peering intently through the scope upon a rocky outcrop. Nikita saw that it wasn't a man, but a woman with a sheet of white-blond hair falling down one side of her face, the other side shaven. Even from here, Nikita could see the tattoo on her neck just above the grey puff jacket she wore. He couldn't make it out, but didn't need to see it to know it was a swastika. He ground his teeth, desperate to take her down.

Not yet, he thought to himself grimly as he shuffled back across the room. As he passed Milena and his father, he put his finger to his lips and signalled to them to stay where they were. He padded into Milena's room at the rear of the house and followed the same procedure to check for anybody approaching from the back. He identified three of Pamyat's henchmen making their way towards them before making his way back to the main bedroom where he squatted down beside Milena and his father.

Fear was plastered across Milena's tear-stained face and Gabriel was holding her tightly, whispering that it would be all right. He covered her ears as Nikita began whispering to him.

"We need to hide her, Father. Is there anywhere you can think of?"

"There is an attic which is probably the best option," his father responded. Nikita nodded and picked up Milena who squirmed in his arms, her face pale and her nose running.

"Come, Milena, we are going to play hide and seek."

"I am not an idiot, Nikita," she said angrily. Gabriel led the way down a corridor to where there was an enclave in the ceiling. Standing on a chair he had carried down the corridor with him, he pushed open the wooden slat covering the square. Nikita passed him Milena, to whom he gave a big kiss before lifting her with ease into the attic.

"Milena, you must be absolutely silent no matter what you hear, OK?"

She nodded, looking younger than her years. "Papa, I want to stay with you," she said, sobbing.

"Do not fear, my child, I will be back to pick you up very soon!" he said as cheerfully as he could manage. "Hold onto those tears and we can let them all out together later on, OK?"

She wiped her small face and nodded as Gabriel lifted the wooden slat back into place.

He and Nikita turned to face each other.

"Tell me," said Gabriel.

"Yes, Father. As far as I can tell we have five of the enemy approaching. There is one I expect to be here whom I cannot see, so I would say there are at least six, in addition to a sniper further up the hill. We have Chairman Klitchkov on the mountainside who can give us covering fire, but as soon as he takes out one of the intruders, he will reveal his location will be a sitting duck and we will lose our only advantage. He will not know where the sniper is as she is above and behind him."

"What is your plan, son?"

"First of all, we need to get rid of the sniper, and fast. The approaching teams are all within two hundred yards, but we have no chance of escape with a sniper able to take us out at any point. I will go now and eliminate that threat."

"What will I do?"

"I do not want to give you blood on your hands, Father."

Gabriel said nothing but stepped back into his bedroom and reappeared carrying a pair of old shotguns. "You forget I endured the Biafran War. Nobody escaped that without blood on their hands. I will have my revenge for what these people have taken from us."

Nikita nodded. "I do not have time to argue with you. Cover the rear. If you can take any of those approaching out, all the better. Do what you can to at least keep them at some distance until I am able to tackle them head on." He looked at his father's weapon. "Do those rust buckets still work?"

"You want to be the one to find out?" his father asked with the hint of a smile.

Nikita smiled grimly in return, before setting his jaw and clasping his father's arm momentarily.

Returning to the bedroom, he looked around the room and scoped his angles. He discovered that if he lay on the bed, he would be almost impossible for the woman to spot, but could see her by just widening the crack between the curtains by an inch or two. Dropping to the floor, he began easing the curtain apart, expecting to hear the crack of a weapon firing again, but to his relief none came.

He climbed back onto the bed and lay flat at an angle, gazing through the scope to find the shooter again. He saw her once more. Her crouched position made it a small target, but one he knew he must hit first time.

The gun felt cold and clinical in his hands. Such a small thing that could cause so much hurt. For a moment he despised the sight of it, before shaking himself slightly and refocusing.

She was gazing intently, sweeping her gun slowly back and forth across the house, ready to fire on the slightest hint of movement. Her lip was curled back in what looked like a permanent sneer. The woman who had murdered his mother, the gentlest soul of them all.

Nikita closed his eyes and took a deep breath, focusing his mind, clearing it of all emotion and thought. Just him and the target.

He nudged the telescopic sighting to have her chest front and centre. She was approximately three hundred yards away, and the cold air was still with very little breeze.

He breathed in, and on the exhale squeezed the trigger.

The compressor on the barrel of the VSS dampened the noise of the gunshot, reducing it to a quiet phut-phut sound, though the kickback was still hard into the crook of Nikita's shoulder.

But it was nothing compared to the discomfort of the target, whose cry echoed across the valley as red spread across her grey coat. She fell forwards off the rocky outcrop and tumbled directly down the hill, coming to a stop right next to the prostrate Klitchkov, who could not help but release a short cry of alarm, amplified by the silent snowy surroundings.

Nikita could see that the woman wasn't dead and upon landing had begun grappling with Klitchkov, who leapt to his feet and with a swift motion stabbed her in the throat.

It was a fatal mistake as all eyes turned upon his previously hidden location and the valley was set alight by the crackle of gunfire, just as Nikita heard the boom of a gunshot echo from the room behind him.

There was no longer any point in staying hidden, and Nikita leapt up and closer to the window. There were more men than he had bargained for, and now he could also see the one he had been searching for.

Brishnov was ambling down the track nonchalantly, the huge Desert Eagle clutched in his hand with little in the way of stealth.

Nikita's blood ran cold. Vengeance had been his with the sniper who had taken down his mother, but he would not fail to avenge the death of Sarah Chang this time. He squatted and leant the sniper on the windowsill to take aim at Brishnov, but suddenly the window next to him exploded following a gunshot, and another chipped the stonework just to his left and he was forced back inside, cursing.

"Father! What is the situation back there?" he shouted over his shoulder. He'd been so focused on Brishnov it was only now he was aware of the booming of the shotgun from Milena's bedroom.

"One is down; I think I injured him, and the other two cowards are hiding behind a snowdrift," he called. "They will begin a fresh attack any moment I think." He sounded almost invigorated.

"Ok, try to keep them at bay as long as possible. The sniper is down but I have another four approaching. Klitchkov is under heavy fire."

Nikita moved into the adjacent room, an empty guest room, and approached the window to try a fresh angle. There was blood on Chairman Klitchkov, but Nikita was unable to tell if it was his own or that of the sniper. Either way he was taking heavy fire. Nikita again looked through the curtain and spotted two men on the left, both of whom were showering Klitchkov with bullets, rendering him unable to return fire. As carefully as he could, he turned the latch and eased the window open slightly.

Nikita raised the sniper and got the target in his sight. He didn't have anything to lean the weapon on, but took his time to steady his hand. He breathed deeply and released the trigger. This time his aim was true and the man crumpled instantly. Nikita locked and loaded and took another shot at the other man, who had admirably not stopped firing at Klitchkov despite the fall of his comrade.

The shot buried itself in the snow just in front of the shooter and Nikita cursed. It did, however, do enough to force the shooter to take cover and give Klitchkov a moment's respite.

Nikita didn't pause, swinging around to see where the other gunmen were. More importantly, to see where Brishnov was.

He heard a crash of broken glass from behind him and a yell from his father. "Father!" Nikita cried.

"I'm OK. They are coming though."

Nikita cursed again, and as he turned back to the window it exploded in a shower of glass. Shards covered him, with several cutting tiny slices into his face, one ripping the eyelid on his right eye.

He dropped to the floor and shook the glass off himself. He reached up and pulled some snow from the windowsill, rubbing it over his face and grimacing as some of the deeper cuts protested. His eyelid was flapping over his eye, blood dripping down into it. Nothing he could do about it right now.

Three down in total. Five to go. Their odds of survival were improving.

Nikita returned to his parents' bedroom to try and get a proper view of the situation. Klitchkov had taken down the shooter that Nikita had missed. Four to go. But one of them was Brishnov. Nikita saw him now, crouched behind some low scrubs, talking to the remaining soldier on that side of the house. An impossible shot from this angle. He looked across at Klitchkov, a visible red beacon now. He signalled that he had eyes on the enemy but no clean shot. Nikita returned the same signal.

At that moment he heard a call from his father. "I am almost out of ammunition, Nikita. They are upon us."

Nikita signalled to Klitchkov that he was going to check the rear and dashed to his father. Peering at the window he saw two men clad in black combat gear. They had spread out and were approaching from opposite sides, darting behind low scrubby bushes and snowdrifts.

"Father, you are hurt," said Nikita, noticing Gabriel's hands were covered in blood.

"It's nothing," his father murmured, brushing Nikita's hands away, his eyes focused on the men. Then he noticed Nikita's bloody face. "You're hurt too; what has happened to your eye?"

"It's nothing," said Nikita with a half-smile. "Here, take this," he said, handing his father the VSS Sniper and a handful of the brass bullets.

"Why, where are you going?" his father demanded, taking the gun.

"To give those two something else to think about."

"What about the front?"

"There are two remaining; we must trust in the Chairman for the moment," he said, walking away before his father could argue. "Keep your eyes open for me; please give some cover," Nikita added as he ran downstairs, drawing his two Makarov pistols and going through the kitchen to the side door, staying low. He needed to draw the men away from the house, away from his injured father.

His back to the door, he looked around the kitchen and saw what he was looking for on the counter. A bottle of methylated spirit stood next to the small stove. He grabbed it, along with a rag from the cupboard beneath the sink. Holstering one of the pistols, he also grabbed a mason jar full of rice and emptied it out, then filled it with the methylated spirits. He soaked the rag before pulling it taut over the top of the jar and screwing it into place. Snatching a lighter from the kitchen counter, he moved out.

He opened the door at the side of the house and looked out. He led with the Makarov in his right hand, the Molotov cocktail clutched in his other. All was clear, but one thing was certain; these men were thugs and not trained soldiers. To leave an exit without cover in a hostage situation was unforgivable in the KGB playbook.

Nikita dropped to the ground and commando crawled to the rear of the house, keeping his face low and his hood up to stay as camouflaged as possible. Upon reaching the corner of the house he allowed himself an upwards glance. He could see the thug approaching from the right-hand side straight ahead of him. He was staying low and out of sight from Gabriel's vantage point, his eyes fixed on the windows.

Nikita put his head back down and began to commando crawl again, this time at a right angle directly outwards from the house and away from the approaching attacker, before looping around behind him. Shots began to ring out from the window in the direction of the man approaching from the left, providing good cover and distraction for Nikita. It averted his target's eyes and Nikita saw his opportunity. Jumping to his feet, he sprinted rapidly and silently over the powdery snow and was upon the man before he knew he was coming. The man let out a yelp and tried to throw a punch at Nikita, who sidestepped him and threw a punch to his temple. The man fell down, dazed. Nikita landed on him and with a swift motion from behind, twisted his head rapidly, feeling the neck break under his hands. He dropped the man to the ground before dropping back down himself to keep his cover. The whole attack had lasted no more than twenty seconds.

Three to go.

He paused to consider his options, wiping the blood from his face. He could barely see out of his ragged right eye, but in the distance, he could hear gunfire from the front of the house. Trust in the chairman, he thought to himself with some trepidation. He needed to eliminate this final threat from the rear to secure his fathers' safety, at least for the time being. It would not take much for Brishnov and Veselovsky to break past the bloodied Klitchkov and enter the izba, and there was no clear shot at the remaining shooter. Time to take some risks, Nikita decided. Pulling the hood down low over his face, he rolled over the top of the snowdrift into the open space. If the other shooter saw him, he was a sitting duck.

Nikita glanced up at the window and saw his father look at him wide-eyed. Nikita firmly signalled to him to look away but it was too late. A bullet missed Nikita by inches and he rolled to the side, leaping to his feet and zigzagging away from the shooter. Seeing the threat, Gabriel began firing the sniper at the shooter, forcing him back down as Nikita turned and sprinted as fast as he could towards him. Thirty yards from the man, Nikita dropped to one knee and lit the rag of the cocktail and threw it in the direction of the neo-Nazi, just as a tell-tale click of an empty chamber echoed across the tundra from the direction of the window. The shooter swung back out to shoot at Nikita, but had spun right into the path of the petrol bomb which hit him directly in the face.

A bloodcurdling scream echoed from his mouth as the man, who Nikita could see was barely more than a teenager, snatched at his face trying to put the flames out as his skin melted. He thrust his head into the snow but it was too late, his screaming dying as his voice box burst. Nikita walked over and shot him in the head, looking down with great pity. The young man had probably been brainwashed, falling in with the wrong crowd. As so often was the case, he was too young for war, but old enough to die. Nikita searched the body for any form of identification or anything that may prove useful, but there was nothing to glean.

Nikita looked up at the window but Gabriel was no longer there, presumably having gone to find more ammunition or an alternative weapon. He was relieved. No father should see his son do what Nikita had just done.

He covered the ground cautiously back to the house, thawing snow dripping uncomfortably down every crack in his clothing. As he sidled along the house, he heard a commotion from the front.

When he reached the corner, he peered around the front of the izba to gauge the situation, and his heart leapt into his mouth.

It was over.

CHAPTER 29

In front of the house, forty yards away, Brishnov and Veselovsky stood over their two captives. Chairman Klitchkov and Gabriel Allochka were both on their knees in front of them, heads bowed, faces bloody.

Brishnov and Veselovsky had guns pointed at them — Brishnov at Klitchkov and Veselovsky at Gabriel, and they were laughing.

Klitchkov looked heavily wounded, blood dripping from several places, clearly visible in his white overalls.

Gabriel's clothes were torn, his face bloody from what looked like a pistol whipping, his eyes unfocused and concussed.

Nikita threw himself back behind the wall, the breath driven out of him. If he took out one of the enemy, then either his father or Klitchkov would surely die. He cursed himself for dealing with the rear, his attention should always have been on Brishnov.

"I shall enjoy this, Chairman," he heard Brishnov say.

"Then get on with it. I do not want to waste my time bandying words with a traitorous dog," Klitchkov snarled.

"Me, a traitor!" said Brishnov, flaring. "You betrayed me. I have been a faithful servant to the state my whole life. You forsook me, and so did this Soviet Union. I put duty above everything, above a life," and for a moment there was a look of almost longing that crossed his usually cold face "I will take it all back," he cried, spittle bubbling on his lips. "Pamyat will bring my homeland back from its knees."

Klitchkov said nothing, which only served to infuriate his captor all the more. Brishnov paced back and forth, rolling his shoulders.

"Come, come, Nikita, time is against us," Brishnov called out impatiently.

"Save your sister!" shouted Gabriel, in his native Igbo language, spitting blood out of his broken mouth.

A broken mouth, a broken giant.

Veselovsky hit him across the face with his pistol once more and Gabriel fell onto his side.

"We know you are there, Allochka. It is over," called Brishnov. "You can save your father and sister. All we want is you."

"What?" said Veselovsky sharply. "I will leave no blacks alive. You promised I could crucify them."

"Quiet," ordered Brishnov.

Nikita didn't hesitate and stepped out from behind the wall. "NO!" shouted his father.

The world had gone into slow motion. Nikita stumbled forwards, throwing his Makarov pistols to the floor, unstrapping the Sig Sauer from its holster and casting it aside. He could hear music, and see the faces of Sarah and his mother. He would join them now. It started snowing, and Nikita pushed back his hood, the snowflakes snaking like tears down his face.

"Upon us all, Allochka," said Brishnov softly. "We all must die. There is no place for the Black Russian in the new world."

Nikita looked at his father. "I love you," he whispered and closed his eyes as Brishnov raised his Desert Eagle and fired.

There was a roar and the bullet pinged off the wall of the house to Nikita's right. His eyes snapped open and saw that Klitchkov had driven himself at Brishnov, tackling him to the ground, where they grappled.

Veselovsky looked caught in two minds, whether to intervene or not, but it was near impossible to get a clean shot.

Klitchkov tried to force the weapon in Brishnov's hands back upon him, but the old and wounded leader of the KGB was no match for the lithe and younger agent who quickly began to gain control.

Seeing his opportunity, Nikita began to run towards the pair. Veselovsky opened fire, peppering bullets from his AK-47 haphazardly in his direction. Nikita was grateful that Brishnov had brought a man with no military experience along with him. He was grateful right up until a bullet hit him in the shoulder. The very same shoulder he had wounded in Texas and pain flashed through his whole body.

He didn't stop running however, and without breaking stride kicked Brishnov hard in the face, forcing him onto his back so that Klitchkov could regain control. Another bullet lanced through him, this time grazing the side of his head, filling his skull with a deep burning. Gabriel, also seeing his opportunity, rose like a bear from hibernation and threw a giant fist at Veselovsky, who dodged it just as Nikita was upon him and began to wrestle with him to gain control of the Kalashnikov automatic rifle, blood splashing down from his head and shoulder.

A boom of a gunshot behind him averted Nikita's eyes for a moment and he looked around to see Klitchkov lying on the floor. Brishnov, also on the ground, had shot him through the side.

"NO!" shouted Nikita, seeing Brishnov grinning and climbing to his feet, as the AK-47 was wrenched from his hands by a gleeful Veselovsky. His glee was short lived, as this time Gabriel's knuckles connected with his temple and he fell to his knees, where Gabriel began pummelling his face.

As soon as he saw that his father had dominance of Veselovsky, Nikita grabbed the AK-47 from the fallen neo-Nazi and began firing shots at Brishnov, running towards him. But ever-agile, Brishnov rolled down a snow bank and leapt to his feet. At that moment the magazine gave the fatal click of an empty chamber. Another click, followed by another. Brishnov cackled. "I have to admit you are a determined man, Allochka. But you must accept your fate," he said, raising the Desert Eagle and giggling.

Nikita dropped to the floor, and quickly darting a hand to the back of his neck, he pulled out the hidden ballistic knife. Without looking to aim, he rolled and pushed the clasp, throwing his hand out in Brishnov's direction.

The giggle died upon Brishnov's lips. The blade protruded from his belly, and he stared down at it with shock.

"NO!" he cried in anguish.

"Upon us all, Taras," Nikita said, standing over him and kicking away the Desert Eagle which had fallen from his hand. "We all must die. There is no place for the White Russian in the new world." Then, before turning away he added, "I think the new world will be a better world."

Brishnov's face contracted with pain and fury as he fell forwards into the snow drift.

He turned and saw that his father was standing over Veselovsky, whose face was a bloody pulp on the ground.

Nikita exhaled, feeling his muscles relax, and then the pain seared through his body from his wounds and he fell to one knee.

His father walked over to him and helped him up. "On your feet, my son." His eyes crinkled and filled with tears. "My child, I am so sorry that this is the life you have had to lead," he said and pulled him into a hug.

Nikita let himself get lost in his father's arms and felt tears of overwhelming grief flood from his eyes. His body shook; he felt like a child in an old man's body.

"I am sorry, Father, I promised to protect us all. They have taken Mother," he said as a fresh wave of tears broke through him. "They have killed the Chairman," he said with fresh grief, one that he could not understand.

"Your mother was so proud of you, Nikita. We are all so proud. I have no love for the Chairman, but look what he was prepared to give for you. You a black man, earning the love and respect of white Russians. Despite everything you have endured, you have the most beautiful of souls." Then he moaned loudly, his huge shoulder heaving as the sobs wracked through him. "My Sophie is gone. I cannot believe she's gone. She cannot have gone, she is the love of my life," he cried, as huge tears rolled down his gentle face.

Nikita attempted to close his eyes, but his torn eyelid rendered that impossible. He teetered, his consciousness beginning to slip. He could hear the sound of engines in the distance. Too little, too late.

Suddenly he heard movement behind them and saw that Veselovsky had regained consciousness and was running as fast as he was able up the path, his face puffy and mangled, but apparently still functioning.

Gabriel roared and went to give chase but Nikita grabbed his hand and pulled him back. "Let him go, Father; I can hear the backup coming. He will not get far and we do not have the strength to chase."

His father nodded reluctantly. "A life spent trying to be a hero is a lonely life; it is time to look after yourself now. You have saved Milena. Let me help you inside. You are bleeding too much," he said and lifted Nikita with ease, carrying him back towards the house. Nikita could feel unconsciousness falling upon him. His father put him on his feet at the front door. As Nikita landed unsteadily, the valley rippled with the crack of a distant gunshot.

He snapped around to see his father wide eyed and mouth open.

"FATHER!" Nikita cried, trying to stay upright as the world swayed.

Gabriel held out his hand. "My boy..." he whispered before his eyes closed and he fell backwards.

"No, please, no, no, no," Nikita cried, tears leaking through his torn eyelid and mingling with the blood smeared across his face.

The last thing he saw before the blood loss overcame him was Lev Veselovsky, the leader of the Soviet neo-Nazis, standing on the hilltop, holding the same sniper that had killed his mother, looking down on him with hatred burning through his face. Then all went black.

CHAPTER 30

The regular bleeps coming from a machine, were the first thing Nikita was aware of, and the hum of distant activity. He tried to ignore it, enjoying the sleepy comfort. He had been having a good dream, one of gentle summer breezes and wholesome food on Skyros, one with Elysia's gentle kisses of Elysia.

He heard the sound of someone clearing their throat nearby and reluctantly his eyes fluttered open. Or one eye. The other didn't seem to be allowed to move. The open eye was immediately stung by bright strip lighting above him, and gloomy daylight streaming in through the open curtains to his left.

The bleeping came from a machine connected to him through various wires and tubes, and the clearing of the throat came from his old tutor, Maxim Denisov.

Denisov was sitting cross-legged, with his hair carefully combed into a side parting, his flat mouth nestled into its resting position of faint contempt.

"Welcome back, Agent Allochka. You are at a top-secret military facility on Bolshevik Island in the Kara Sea. The day is December 25, 1987. Merry Christmas."

Suddenly the pain caught up with Nikita and racked through his body. His head burned, and his shoulder was completely numb. Then the rest came back to him.

"My father!" he croaked, trying to push himself up.

Denisov pushed him back down. "You must rest, Agent Allochka. Your father is in surgery."

"He is alive?" Nikita gasped hoarsely.

"For the moment, yes," Denisov said calmly. "He is fighting hard to survive."

"And will he?"

"I am not a doctor. They do not give him good odds. But take solace in the fact that as it stands, he still draws breath."

Nikita breathed a huge sigh. "And Milena?"

"She is waiting to see you. First we must speak."

"Sir, Chairman Klitchkov is…"

"He is dead."

"He died saving me," Nikita said, choked up.

"Then he died the hero's death that he deserved," Denisov said nodding. "I am glad of this."

"Veselovsky? He shot my father. I want my revenge," said Nikita before descending into a cacophony of coughs that pulled at the stitches he could now feel in his shoulder. He became aware of bandages wrapped tightly around his head. A nurse came in and gently fed him some water, which soothed his throat, which felt like a mass of brittle sandpaper. She tutted disapprovingly at Denisov, who smiled blandly at her as she left.

"Careful, agent. Your body has endured much," said Denisov. "To answer your question, Veselovsky eludes us. But not, I think, for long. We shall both have our revenge on the traitor."

"My father severely wounded him. His face is ravaged."

"Good," said Denisov. "Then he will, I think, seek revenge on you also, which is perfect."

"Sir?"

"Seeking him will put you in great danger."

"What's that like?" Nikita said with a smile, before coughs tore at him once more.

Denisov indulged him with a smile. "Then we have much to discuss. I will give you seven days; I cannot afford to provide you with any more, and then I will need you in Moscow."

"I need only five, sir," said Nikita defiantly. "I will have my revenge, and only then will I mourn."

"Then you have become everything we dreamed you would," Denisov said approvingly. "You have done very well, Nikita," he added with the closest thing to kindness that Nikita imagined he was capable of.

Thirty minutes later, Denisov left the room and let in Milena. She approached Nikita cautiously. Nikita could see in her serious eyes that she had aged since his arrival home; she had seen too much.

"Milena," he grunted, his voice beginning to fail him.

"You are OK?" she asked, formally.

"Nothing that a hug will not fix," he said, smiling.

She did not move.

"Everything was OK until you came home," she said coldly.

"I know, Milena. I am so sorry."

"Sorry will not bring back Mama!" she shouted angrily.

"I know," he croaked.

"I miss Mama!" she shouted again, tears streaming down her face. "I miss Mama and Papa and it's all your fault."

Nikita nodded numbly. "I do not deny it, little sister. I tried so hard to protect you all but I failed."

"Yes, you did fail! I wish you had never come back!"

"Please, Milena," he pleaded, feeling like an old man in the battered body of a twenty-two-year-old. "I love you." he said.

"I hate you!" she said, crying full body tears now. "Our mama is dead," she sobbed. "We will never see her again."

He pushed himself up, tears streaming from even his broken eye, and the monitor began bleeping faster. The weight of his failure after everything almost pushed him back down. With a lot of grunting, he sat up, and such was the shock of it that Milena stopped crying instantly. Nikita grabbed her arm and pulled her to him. She tried to resist but even in his weakened condition he was too strong.

"I am sorry, Milena. We are in it together now, and Papa will need you more than ever."

"If he even lives!" she cried. "They said he might not," she said, sobbing, and allowing herself to fall into his arms.

"Then we will need each other very much, Milena. I promise I will not let anything hurt you." Then, forcing a smile, he added, "And have you ever heard of anything beating Father? He will wrap the sickness up in his big arms and squish it, like this," he said, squeezing her gently in his arms.

She giggled slightly and squeezed him back. It made his shoulder scream but he didn't show it. Elysia's words echoed around his mind. 'Get out of your head. There are a million things for us to worry about, but for now let's just enjoy a few moments without worrying about the past or future, just get lost in this moment right now.' He suddenly was aware of how much he missed her, and wondered if he would ever see her again.

He felt tiredness overcome him. "You will go to sleep now," Milena ordered him.

Nikita smiled and felt the overwhelming fatigue take hold of him. "You will stay?" he whispered.

"I will be right here," she replied in a small voice, squeezing his hand, then added "I love you too," in a barely audible whisper as the darkness took Nikita once more.

It was late at night, five days later, that Nikita stood at his father's bedside. Two days and his father hadn't woken from the coma. The doctors said that he might never wake up. Nikita clenched his fist, feeling the stitches in his shoulder pull and relishing the feeling, the pain and sensation. Gabriel Allochka looked so peaceful, his long eyelashes fluttering softly in the air conditioning. It looked like he was merely sleeping and Nikita longed to rouse him, to get back all the years he had missed.

"Veselovsky, I am coming," he said to himself through gritted teeth, before leaving the room and hobbling through the large complex, built largely under the glacier of the formidable island at the top of the world. The more he walked, the looser his muscles felt, but the bandage around his head remained tightly in place, as did the patch over his right eye. He walked through the building until he reached a room midway down a lengthy corridor. Silently turning the handle, he entered and saw Milena asleep in the dark room that they had made every effort to make feel comfortable for a child of her age. Books and games littered the floor and the walls were painted with clouds and rainbows.

He brushed her braids tenderly back from her face and kissed her brow. She opened her eyes sleepily. "Niki," she said softly.

"I have to go away for a few days, Milena; I will be back soon, just in time for Father to wake up."

"You are leaving?" she said, her eyes wide now.

"It breaks my heart to leave you Milena, but sometimes you have to leave in order to get the joy of a return," he said with forced smile. "Sleep now, and be kind to the nurses."

"The nurses scare me," she said. "There are so many people here, Niki."

"How wonderful to have so many different people to talk to" he said with a smile. "I hear you have made friends with another child here."

"Yes... there is one boy who is nice to me."

"Enjoy getting to know your friend as much as you can. Now close those sleepy eyes and return to your dreams, little sister," he whispered, brushing her brow.

Milena's eyes drooped and with a small smile she drifted back off, not stirring as Nikita slipped quietly out of the door.

Outside two men in uniform waited, and saluted him. "You do not need to salute," he said, waving a hand. He often forgot that as a KGB field agent he held the military rank of captain.

"You are a captain of the Soviet Army, and the Black Russian, sir, a title that alone commands respect," one of them said earnestly, a young man with blond hair and a dimpled chin.

Stunned, Nikita said nothing and saluted back, before following them both out to the helipad, a circle kept clear of ice and snow on the roof of the low concrete building.

Waiting was a helicopter which would transfer him to the mainland before the journey back to Moscow. As the helicopter set off into the swirling winds and snow, Nikita peeled off the bandages around his head, and the padding over his eye. He moved his eyelid tentatively. It felt fragile but mended. He turned his eyes to the waiting steel grey seas, peaking and foaming beneath them, unreadable as he drifted into thoughts of loss.

***

It was the next day that he arrived back in Moscow. With no apartment and no Denisov there to greet him, he pulled up the collar of his long black coat, and undid the flaps on the fur-lined ushanka perched on his head so that his ears were covered and warm. It rubbed uncomfortably on his head wound, but was better than the alternative.

It was snowing again, and the cold was bitter as he walked the streets of the old town with purpose. The cobbles were dusted with snow and his black boots clicked on them as he strode through the city that held so many shadows of memories for him.

He passed a bar with large Cyrillic lettering reading Ladya Beer Bar, above the red flag of the hammer and sickle. After pausing, he decided to enter. The bar was grimy and dingy, but busy, with many patrons escaping the bitter winter chill to celebrate the turn of a new year. Grateful to the crowd and heavy smoke for granting some anonymity, he approached the bar and slowly removed the hat.

"Da?" asked the barmaid, eyeing him with the suspicion and disdain he could always rely on in Russia.

He looked longingly at the bottles hanging under optics at the bar. Multiple different vodkas sat there, along with beer taps, but none of the range he had become used to back in Virginia. Nikita rolled his shoulders and flexed his neck, noticing that the lack of choice did not remove the temptation.

"Odin Baikal pozhaluysta," he said coolly, attracting only further disdain from the barmaid.

She pulled up a dusty glass bottle of *Baikal*, the Soviets' answer to Coca Cola and placed it heavily down in front of her. Throwing down some roubles, Nikita said, "Happy New Year," before turning his back on the bar. Bars open to the public were still fairly new in the USSR, and budgets hadn't yet stretched to chairs. Instead, the crowds gathered around standing tables. Tonight though, the bar was so full there was barely any standing area left. Nikita navigated his way to a small empty space by the far wall and sipped the sickly soft drink, trying to convince himself it was whiskey, while glancing idly around the room. In one hand he held the bullet he had always saved for Klitchkov from way back in Kamchatka and stared down at it. Just a piece of metal that he had spent too long thinking about. Under the fold of his coat, he pushed the bullet into the chamber of his Colt 1911. Time to let go, he thought to himself with a sigh.

Appearing to gaze down at his drink, he could see in his periphery a group of men eyeing him angrily. One of them walked to the bar, and after speaking to the barmaid, walked behind the bar and walked down a short corridor. Moments later he reappeared, looking anywhere but at Nikita. When he returned to his crew, they all immediately stopped looking at him, other than snatching the occasional covert glance.

The hairs on the back of Nikita's neck tingled with anticipation. Somehow his KGB training had instilled a sixth sense in him for when trouble was upon him. He slowly finished his drink then with a sigh, braced himself for the freezing streets once more, wishing he could be back in Cuba, being looked after by the kindly Mrs Shapova and enjoying sunsets from his luxury suite.

When he opened the doors, he was hit hard in the face by a blast of freezing air and snowflakes but set his shoulders and moved back out into the dark streets, alert and aware.

He was only thirty yards from the bar when he heard the tell-tale increase in noise rise and fade as the door opened and was swiftly closed, and he quickened his pace. He turned from the main street, lined by the imperious examples of Russian Revival architecture that had blossomed during the nineteenth century. The buildings, icons of an era which Lenin's Bolsheviks had worked hard to bury, now had a faded grandeur. He moved down a street where all grandeur had long since passed. Formidable Soviet concrete buildings were crumbling, along with gloomy red brick warehouses, many boarded up, rising in the shadows cast from the failing gas lamps. The street was utterly deserted, the sounds of the celebrating city dampened in the distance.

A quick scan of the street told him there was nowhere to hide. He could hear the sound of voices and multiple footsteps turning the corner behind him.

The Nazis were coming.

Nikita gave in to temptation and chanced a look over his shoulder and his eyes immediately landed on the face of a murderer.

Lev Veselovsky turned into the street, his face swollen and scarred but unmistakable above a heavy grey coat, a half chewed, uncapped cigarette perched between his broken lips. There were four of them, including the man he had seen make the call in the bar. He was no longer averting his eyes; instead, he snarled at Nikita hungrily, like a rabid dog faced with a wounded bird.

A shot pinged off the cobbles some distance from Nikita and he began to run, his eyes wildly searching for a way out. He heard Veselovsky reprimand the shooter. "On moy," he spat from behind his cigarette. *He is mine.*

Nikita didn't need to look again to know they were in pursuit. He forced his body into a sprint, ignoring the pain searing through him from his head and shoulder, his boots slipping on the greasy cobbles. They were laughing and catcalling behind him, making monkey noises and firing shots off the walls either side of him, taunting him.

The road swung around to the left, giving him a moment of respite from gunfire and he frantically looked for an exit. There was none; he had entered a funnel.

Far ahead he could see a junction in the road and electric street lights glowed, giving him hope. He quickened his pace, knowing he could now only rely on the poor aim of the Pamyat shooters to have any chance of reaching the distant junction. He remembered his father in the doorway, struck by Veselovsky's sniper, and all hope faded.

The rise in volume from the pursuers told him they had turned the corner. The junction was still fifty yards away and Nikita pushed his body harder still. There was nowhere to hide, only a heavily graffitied phone box which would provide precious little cover. He noticed dimly that the footsteps had stopped when gunfire cracked, the noise bouncing off the solid walls of the street as the bullet exploded down the street.

Nikita was thrown forwards by the impact, a short cry escaping his lips as pain exploded through his back and his heart began to slow. As his face hit the freezing, wet cobbles, his eyes closed with a sigh as he thought only of Elysia and her warm scent.

He was aware of being flipped onto his back, and smoke being below into his face. Sirens sounded in the distance and he heard footsteps moving away, but Nikita no longer even thinking of the pain in his broken body as the darkness closed in. "Černyy Russkiy mertv," he distantly heard Veselovsky's triumphant voice say. *The Black Russian is dead.*

CHAPTER 31

Then the light returned.

Nikita rolled onto his front and pushed himself up, his back screaming at him as he withdrew two Sig Sauer pistols from inside his coat, the buttons ripping off and revealing the Kevlar vest beneath.

"Veselovsky! Nikita roared. "Black Russia will never die!" And the world exploded in light.

Veselovsky turned from the phone box he stood beside to see Nikita rise like a monster from the deep and his step faltered as gunfire erupted all around him. He was thrown back by the velocity of the bullet as it hit him in the chest, staggering backwards.

Screams were all around him as black-clad KGB shooters had appeared on the rooftops, peppering gunfire down upon the Pamyat gang. The hunters had become the hunted, trapped on the street with no escape.

Veselovsky stared down at his chest, where blood blossomed from his wound, and back up to Nikita. His face contorted in an ugly fury. "You dare…" he spat.

"Perhaps you are not so much better than me, Lev," Nikita said, holding up a hand to stop his fellow KGB officers from finishing Veselovsky off, walking towards the man who had wanted to crucify him and his family.

Blood was dribbling from Veselovsky's mouth as he furiously worked his face, trying to find the words. He tried to throw a punch at Nikita as he got within touching distance, but Nikita easily dodged it before punching him hard in the side.

Veselovsky fell to one knee, wheezing. The bullet had punctured a lung.

Nikita raised the gun. "Tell me who you called and I will make it a quick death, which is more than you deserve."

Veselovsky spat blood at Nikita's feet.

Nikita kicked him in the bullet wound and Veselovsky howled.

"You will tell me, for better or worse, Veselovsky."

Veselovsky began to laugh, which led to coughs. "You dirty-skinned shit. You think yourself so good, but you know so little."

Nikita shot Veselovsky in the knee, blowing off the kneecap at close range. He screamed and fell to the floor, clutching what was left of his left leg.

Nikita leant down close to his face. "You organised the attack that killed my mother. You tried, and may yet have succeeded in killing my father. You have hunted me just for the colour of my skin, when I have given my life to keep this nation secure from attack. Now stop talking in riddles, because I will have the truth and do not wish to prolong your pain."

Veselovsky said nothing. Blood was smeared across the swastika on his neck, making it appear almost ablaze. Nikita trod on his knee.

"OK, OK!" he cried out, his breathing ragged. "You have not even scratched the surface. He will show no mercy. He has power, and he is closing in on a new Russia. We have people everywhere."

"Who is he? Who is we?" Nikita demanded.

Veselovsky opened his mouth, and a fountain of blood gushed forth, drenching Nikita. He wiped his eyes, and when he opened them Veselovsky lay dead before him.

Nikita cursed loudly. He had his vengeance, but it had given no satisfaction.

***

"It is done," said Denisov as Nikita walked into his office. It wasn't a question.

"It is," replied Nikita, taking a seat in front of him. He looked around the office. "Klitchkov's leadership was a brief one."

"You object to my being the new leader, agent?" Denisov asked, danger in his voice.

"Not at all, sir, I think you are the right choice. I was just reflecting on what has been," Nikita replied without hesitation.

"There is no time for nostalgia in our business," said Denisov. "Have you contacted the Americans to update them since your arrival?"

"No, sir, with everything that has happened there has been no opportunity."

"Then you must do so swiftly."

Nikita nodded, and for a fleeting moment confronted the challenge he would face explaining to the CIA what he had been doing, but quickly dismissed it. The advantage of Yerin's removal of US spies meant he could create a robust story. "Who can I trust now, sir?"

"A KGB agent is asking me about trust?"

"Even KGB agents must trust their employers."

"Why do you ask?"

"Veselovsky... right after he shot me, he made a phone call," said Nikita, watching Denisov's face for any hint of a reaction. He gave none.

"Go on, agent," Denisov said.

Nikita made a decision to trust him, realising he had no other choice and no one else to confide in.

"He informed the person on the phone that the Black Russian was dead. As he lay dying, I pressed him for information and he said that he had been sent by someone else, someone who was closing in on us and a new Russia."

"Did he indeed? And what else did he say?" Denisov asked curiously.

"Only that the man had power, and that they had people everywhere."

"Lying?"

"Maybe. But I think not," said Nikita.

Denisov balanced his chin on the point of his fingers and looked thoughtful. "You have told no one of this?"

"No one yet, sir. You understand why I raised the issue of trust."

"I do," Denisov said. Then he rubbed his chin and added, "They think you are dead."

"Maybe I am," Nikita sighed.

"It presents an opportunity," Denisov replied, ignoring his tone.

They sat in silence for several minutes as Denisov ruminated on the situation, before looking up at Nikita. "We need to get you out of the Soviet Union. You stand out too much to take good advantage of our hidden enemy believing you are dead."

Nikita's heart skipped a beat as he thought briefly of Elysia.

"Back to the US?"

Denisov gave him a knowing smile. "Niet." He stood up and walked to one side of the room where a slide projector sat, facing a cold, white wall next to the door. He pushed the power button and it flickered into life, humming and whirring. He then switched off the overhead lights, casting his face into shadow and the room into darkness.

"What you are about to see, Agent Allochka, is as classified as it gets. Any leak or sharing of this information will be considered treason, punishable by death. Do I make myself clear?"

Nikita nodded.

"I said do I make myself clear?" Denisov said coldly.

"Yes, sir," Nikita responded. Denisov nodded and clicked the first slide into place.

A blank page swam into focus, with just the words 'OPERATION ILLUSION', stamped across a white background.

On the next slide, Nikita saw a map he was familiar with, showing the entire USSR and the surrounding satellite nations. There were pins on a number of locations across the screen.

"You recognise this no doubt, from your time with the CIA," Denisov said.

"Yes, sir. All of the locations of our intermediate range nuclear missiles."

Denisov nodded, satisfied. There was a click and a map of Afghanistan appeared on the screen. A square was over a small area in the east of the country, close to the border with Pakistan. Another click, and the grainy image zoomed in to that section. At the top of the image was stamped SPĪN GHAR. Clearly taken by a reconnaissance aircraft, it showed dry and dusty mountains surrounded by an arid landscape.

"Have you heard of the Spīn Ghar mountains, agent?"

"Only from the legends of the network of Afghan caves, sir."

"They are much more than legend, Allochka," replied Denisov, clicking the next slide into place which showed a partially hidden cave on the side of a dusty mountain. Even in black and white, Nikita could recognise the pool of blood on the pale floor.

"You found them," he said.

"It was Chairman Klitchkov who eventually tracked them down after years of searching."

"And he took them?"

"He did. It was not pretty," he added with a curled lip as the next image slid into place showing a litter of Afghan bodies stretching into the distance. Nikita's stomach churned and his heart turned cold.

His mind began to race, and Blaine Lahart's voice was echoing around his head: 'There's some strange movement happening in the USSR since Yerin was removed. Some guy named Denisov seems to have been dropping in on their nuclear sites and disappearing with a load of staff.' Klitchkov's voice followed on: 'Do whatever you must to turn their attentions away from investigating our nuclear disarmament. Things are never what they appear… '

He looked up at Denisov, unable to disguise the horror in his face as comprehension began to dawn. "The bombs…"

"Yes, they have been successfully moved to the caves. The operation has been in the planning for longer than you can imagine. The great forces of the world are moving, and we must ride the crest of the wave or else face utter destruction. It is our final roll of the dice."

"So the treaty Petrenko signed…"

Denisov laughed. "A piece of paper we manoeuvred the Americans into signing. A masterful display of political fencing from our much-maligned general secretary. Yerin knew of the plan but lost faith; he lost patience. Fortunately, his ill-conceived bombing of the Capitol ended up being more smoke than fire; Burn failed him. While the US disarms, we will build our nuclear strength to unprecedented levels. Soon, comrade, we will strike, and the world will tremble at the Soviet might."

Nikita sat in silence, the enormity of the global deception settling upon him. Only one thing ran through his mind; Elysia would be right in the eye of the storm.

"You will go to Afghanistan and oversee the nuclear armament operation."

"But what of the neo-Nazis? What of the hidden power?"

"That is no longer your concern."

"They murdered my mother! And probably my father! For nothing more than the crime of having a different colour skin!"

"Actually, I have received word that your father is awake."

"What? You only tell me this now!" Nikita exploded, leaping to his feet, no longer controlling his emotions.

"Remember to whom you are speaking, agent," Denisov replied, a warning in his voice.

Nikita slumped into his chair, his head in his hands. He looked up at Denisov. "Is he well?"

"No, but it seems he will survive."

Nikita released an enormous sigh and a low chuckle born of relief and exasperation.

"Very well, sir. I will go to Afghanistan."

"Excell—"

"But I do have one condition," interrupted Nikita.

Denisov raised his eyebrows. "KGB agents do not set conditions, they follow orders. I thought I had trained you better than that."

"I know my training all too well, sir. But I think you will agree that we find ourselves in a unique situation. The KGB failed me. The reason I joined was solely to protect my family. You did not do this. My request is not a great one, but will mean there are no distractions from my role in the Afghan mountains."

"Spit it out," Denisov said flatly.

"I want my family moved somewhere they can better fit in. Where Milena can enjoy a normal life, surrounded by other children. Somewhere they will not be targeted by Pamyat, or whatever other racist movement our beloved country spawns next."

"You could use some further training in diplomacy, I think, Agent Allochka," said Denisov.

Nikita said nothing.

"Very well. Perhaps Kazan? They may feel more at home there?"

"I was thinking rather further afield, sir."

"Go on," replied Denisov, rolling his eyes.

"Perhaps the United Kingdom?"

"The UK? You must be mad!" laughed Denisov.

"Nigeria?"

"Ah, there was the real request," Denisov replied knowingly. "They cannot go to a non-communist nation, Allochka, you know better than that."

"OK then, Cuba?"

"Cuba?" said Denisov raising his eyebrows. He looked as if he were chewing on his cheeks as he ruminated on all the pros and cons.

"They will be able to blend in, and they are our greatest ally in the west. You will give them a good home in a good neighbourhood, nowhere remote," Nikita said assertively. "This is non-negotiable. Do this and I will of course continue to fulfil my duty."

"Yes, yes, OK. I will make the arrangements," Denisov responded with a great deal of obvious restraint.

Nikita laughed. "I'm going to need that in writing, sir."

"Very well, now let us return to the mission at hand," said Denisov, waving a hand in irritation and returning to the slide projector.

Nikita settled into the seat, and tried not to think about the devastation planned for the place he had called home for the past year.

***

The wind whipped and whirled around the three heavily-clad figures, silhouetted against the perpetual twilight of Bolshevik Island, a spit of rock and ice in the lost north of the world.

The Kara Sea rocked and churned far below them as they stood near the cliff edge and looked upon the peaceful face of Sophie Allochka, surrounded in brightly coloured traditional Nigerian garments, before two Soviet soldiers rested the lid of the coffin into place and began to lower it into the frozen ground.

Nikita had his arm around Milena, whose arms were wrapped around his side. Gabriel Allochka leant heavily on his other shoulder, his face grey and pale. They had advised against his attendance, but all had relented when they saw the look in his eyes.

"This is not where I would have picked for her to be laid to rest; it is not Nigeria, and there is no colour or singing. But it is as wild, beautiful and unique as she was," Gabriel said softly.

Tears fell freely from the eyes of Nikita, and a shiver ran through his soul. "I am sorry I failed you, Mother. You were the very best of us all," he muttered.

"There was no failure, Niki. She was so proud of you. She loved you both so very much," said Gabriel.

The two soldiers stepped back, and Denisov stepped forward. "You lived with honour and integrity. May you find the peace in death that we were not able to give you in life. May you rest in peace, Sophie Allochka."

Nikita leant in and whispered to him. "Of course. Rest in peace, Sophie Wadike."

The soldiers raised their guns and fired two shots into the air, the cracks echoing over the icy ground before being lost in the swirling winds and slate-grey seas.

Milena sobbed heavily, and the three Wadikes embraced each other. Denisov signalled to the soldiers and they withdrew.

"When will we see you again, Niki?" asked Gabriel.

"I do not know. Sooner than has become the norm I hope, Father. It hurts me to leave you more than ever before," Nikita said, blinking to fight back further tears.

"When will it end? Let your mother's death not be in vain. Nothing is more important than family. Remember your promise to leave once you returned from the US?"

Nikita gazed out into the freezing mists. "I do what I do for us, Father. One way or another, I think the end is in sight."

They turned and walked towards Denisov who led them down a track back towards the compound.

"Your helicopter is ready, Agent Allochka."

"Do not go, Niki! I want you to stay with us!" cried Milena, gripping him tightly.

He peeled her off. "Just think, Milena, next time I see you, it will be in the warm sunshine, with beaches and trees. We can swim in the sea together and chase the fish!"

"But I cannot swim," she said, looking down, embarrassed.

"Then it will be the perfect place for me to teach you!" he said.

"Promise?"

"I promise," he said gently and kissed her on the forehead. "Now take Father inside before he collapses. He is going to need you to look after him now."

Nikita and his father pressed their foreheads together, but there were no words.

Without a look back, Milena took her father's hand and led him slowly back to the waiting medics.

Nikita watched them go and turned to Denisov. "If you break your promises, if they are mistreated..."

"Do not worry, agent. On this, we have learned our lessons. Now, are you ready?"

Nikita turned to face the sea and cleared his mind. "Afghanistan."

"Afghanistan," agreed the leader of the KGB, "and the saviour of the USSR."

THE BOOK MAY HAVE ENDED, BUT NIKITA'S STORY WILL CONTINUE.